PEACOCKS ON THE LAWN

Noelene Jenkinson

AUTHOR'S NOTE

The goldfields were not the main period of Australian development as might be thought. Beforehand, nearly all land fit for grazing south of the Murray River was explored and occupied in a remarkable colonisation in a corner of the British Empire. These colonists subdued the wilderness and laid the foundations of national stability with the establishment of flocks in the bush on the first pastoral runs. Property homesteads and mansions in Melbourne emulated the life left behind in the Old World. In the eighteen sixties and seventies Merino studs flourished, and the new immigrants adapted and accepted their new environment.

Many Western District pioneers were lowland Scottish farmers and so Duncan Penross was born. As a background to my fictional story and squatting family, I have used real names, places and events based on historical research and blended into the fabric of my tale.

Among countless other volumes of Australian pastoral history resources that I consulted during my research into **PEACOCKS ON THE LAWN**, I drew heavily on Margaret Kiddle's *"Men Of Yesterday, A social history of the Western District of Victoria 1834-1890"* planned as early as 1949 and first published in 1961. It was the awesome detailed research bible upon which I constantly drew in writing this saga alongside the dual volumes of *Pastures News* first published in 1930 and *Pastoral Pioneers of Port Phillip* first published in 1932, both by R.V. Billis and A.S. Kenyon.

Australia: For uncounted centuries, this enormous continent dreamed in a silence broken only by the elemental sounds of its native creatures. This silence was shattered at last...

- From *"Pioneer Settlement in Australia"* by Robert Ingpen

PROLOGUE

In the beginning, the Earth lay dark and silent. The Father Spirit was saddened because there was no life on it. In a cave beneath the plains slept a beautiful woman, the Sun. The Father Spirit woke her and begged her to bring the earth to life. The Sun opened her eyes and, as her rays spread over the land, the darkness disappeared. In the billabongs, the sand and the water mated to create life.

*

Tens of thousands of years ago, the Spirit Fathers of the native Wada Wurrung people trod the plains and lived within sight of the mountains. The tribe puzzled one day when, without reason or warning, kangaroos, wallabies and birds suddenly took flight.

When the earth trembled and the mountains breathed fire, men seized their spears, lubras bundled piccaninnies onto their backs and fled to safety, watching the alarming fire in the sky from afar.

A black cloud erupted like a clap of thunder and the terrified natives gabbled, wondering if it was the voice of an angry ancestor. At night, the rim of the volcanic cone and the oozing lava flow glowed a fierce red.

Ash was hurled upward and the prevailing westerly winds carried it over trees and grassland. Showers of the suffocating warm dust buried grass and stripped leaves from trees. Lava blocked creeks and waterholes, ruined once-fruitful patches of roots and vegetables, started bush fires and drove the game away.

The silent wasteland lasted for a long time. But slowly the soil once more grew rich, nourished the grasses and attracted game.

*

Leaping flames cast shadows across the dark bodies gathered in a circle around the central communal fire for warmth. A framework of boughs supported the dome shaped hut, covered with bark and plastered mud, a narrow opening pointing toward the northeast.

Outside in the gathering gloom of an autumn afternoon, slanting rain hammered relentlessly on the dense forest, turning the riverbank to mud. Further up the long valley, powerful winds swept across and echoed against the dark cliff walls.

Within days the hunters would prepare for the long trek to their winter home on a distant plain to the north. There, in caves and shelters destined to be covered by the stormy waters of Bass Strait, they pursued a way of life unchanged for generations.

*

The natives spied the great white bird skimming the surface of the sea. It flew slowly away until they saw its wings disappear over the horizon.

The deep ridges in the ground were a mysterious sight, unseen before by the people in their hunting and wandering. The natives crouched down and touched them, chattering about it among themselves. What had made these signs in the earth?

At the first sight of a white man, the people waved green boughs as a token of peace. Could these pale faces be the returning spirits of the dead?

A SQUATTER OF THE OLDEN TIME

I'll sing you a fine new song, made by my blessed mate,
Of a fine Australian squatter, who had a fine estate.
Who swore by right pre-emptive, at a sanguinary rate,
That by his rams, his ewes, his lambs, Victoria was made great.
Like a fine Australian settler, one of the olden time.

(Traditional ballad)

CHAPTER 1

Melbourne 1838

Duncan Penross stood, feet astride, gripping the rail on the deck of the barque now lapping at anchor in Hobson's Bay, impatient to go ashore to Melbourne. His thick brown eyebrows squinted above a pair of perceptive blue eyes assessing this new country. A dozen other vessels anchored in port, lively with lighters and other small craft plying goods, passengers and wool between ships and shore. He scowled. It looked nothing like the Scottish lowlands he'd left four months earlier. He doubted the sluggish brown waters would be rich in trout like the Teviot that flowed through the small valley where he had lived amid the rolling windswept mounds of the Cheviot Hills.

His narrowed gaze settled on the whaleboat drawing alongside. Duncan burst with urgency to plant his boots on dry stable land and investigate the grazing lands to be had for the taking in the Portland Bay district.

Because it would be a long time before he sampled another one, he blocked thoughts of the diverting willing widow who had eased many a long night on the voyage and relieved stormy afternoons in her cabin as they sailed east from the Cape across the turbulent southern ocean.

'Let's away and have a look at Port Phillip, eh Lincoln?'

Duncan hauled a carpetbag over his shoulder and

deliberately nudged the gentleman travelling companion he'd met on the passage because he knew his rough ways irked him.

Lincoln winced but forced a polite smile. 'After you.'

Duncan laughed in his face, barely able to tolerate such banal courtesy. The spineless man couldn't make up his own mind if someone wrote the decision for him on a piece of paper. The man would be a handicap. But he wouldn't lose him yet. He might come in useful.

Eager to disembark and escape the confining ship, Duncan gruffly elbowed others aside, leaving Lincoln to scramble awkwardly after him and fend for himself.

As they were rowed ashore and up the Yarra River, the scrubby ti-tree and shrubs at its grassy banks baked beneath the glaring late summer sun. Duncan noted the contrast with the softer light of home where cloud shadows moved across the heather and the mist would blow in wisps around his father's small stone house.

The tinkling sound of bell birds pierced the stillness. It would be early spring back home and the end of another harsh winter. Port Phillip's seasons were upside down. As Melbourne village emerged into view, an oarsman fastened the boat to a stump and the passengers jumped ashore.

Duncan and Lincoln trudged the mile or so into town, a nucleus of tents and huts of weatherboard or wattle and daub with wooden shingles or bark roofs, grouped in clusters or scattered along the track marked with surveyors' pegs.

At the British Hotel not a hundred yards from the landing place at one end of William Street, Lincoln halted.

'Not here,' Duncan said. 'I've another in mind.'

Scowling but unquestioning of his friend's decision, Lincoln, as always, yielded.

A bank and post office occupied a small brick cottage. Another boxy structure with a ship's bell suspended from a gallows-like frame seemed to fill duty as a church.

Dust rose in stifling clouds from the unpaved streets,

merely cleared tracks without a footpath, but lively with pedestrians, horsemen and bullock drays lumbering past, fouled with animal and vegetable matter. Groups of half naked blacks armed with spears wandered about, shouting out what sounded like *cooee* to one another, followed by half-starved mangy dogs.

Men sported whiskers, beard or moustache and wore large cabbage tree hats against the sun but the roads were devoid of women and old men. Striding out in silence, the newcomers absorbed their surroundings. Lincoln mopped his ruddy sweating face and neck with a large handkerchief, his steps slowing as he wilted in the treeless heat.

Although unaccustomed to it, Duncan embraced the strong sun. Only tough determined men would succeed here and he reckoned to be one of them. He gripped his bag tighter, feeling alive with excitement.

Over a hearty enough dinner of wild fowl and kangaroo meat stew that night at the Lamb Inn, a sprawling one-storey building frequented by squatters, Duncan eavesdropped and struck up advantageous conversations. He plied crusty weather-beaten old chums with colonial beer, prompting them for information about the rich pasture lands Thomas Mitchell had discovered two years before.

'Much of its dense scrub, unfit for anything,' one declared.

Reading the exchanged winks, non-committal glances and shrewd eyes beetling out from a wrinkled face barely visible in a forest of hairy whiskers, Duncan ignored half of what was guardedly divulged. Canny to his boot soles, he was sharp enough to depend on his own judgement, knowing others also coveted the same abundant lands. Fierce jealousy, he gleaned, simmered around new arrivals.

'Lands are being settled against government approval but it will come. It must.' Another sagely nodded with a dour scowl, clenching an unlit pipe between his teeth.

Duncan liked the cheeky philosophy of land for the

taking. He'd never favoured rules. It cheered him to hear Scottish and other accents in the room as they talked and the candles burned low late into the warm summer night.

'You've come at the right time of year. In winter you'd not get through for months.'

When Lincoln dared complain about the summer heat, men chuckled.

'You'll soon get used to it, lad.'

Duncan saw his companion bristle at the label and slur on his smooth boyish looks.

'Only summer for another month then the autumn will be far more pleasant and reliable.'

One man fell into deep thought and stroked his magnificent tobacco-stained whiskers. 'Some are buying up half acre allotments here in town. First ones sold for only a few pounds. If you hold onto 'em, you could make yourself a tidy profit.'

'You'll need to find yourselves a good river first. Crucial for your stock.'

Duncan encouraged their frugal shreds of information by buying them all more beer.

'When you've found your land you put in your application for a licence to depasture. It'll be automatically granted. You can get information from the Surveyor General's office.'

'How much land would that be then?' Duncan faked mild curiosity while his chest burst with excitement.

'Fifty square miles each run. That'd be twenty or thirty miles of river frontage with back country extending maybe twice as far.'

'That's the size of an English county.' Lincoln gaped and, for the first time since their arrival hours before, his eyes sparked with interest.

The well-soaked colonial companions chortled. 'Aye. Twenty thousand acres could run half as many sheep.'

Despite their initial caution, the wary men's eyes flashed

into life as the night deepened. All bitten by the lure of adventure and wealth, the men continued to smoke and drink until Duncan gleaned that most land west of Melbourne and near the port of Geelong was held by only a few men. He planned to be among them. Soon.

'Land for the taking. Sounds too good to be true.' Lincoln quibbled, disbelieving, as doubt crossed his face.

Impatient, Duncan stopped himself from dragging William out into the street and shaking some sense into him.

'It's true enough all right, lad,' the locals assured him, loose tongued now with beer. 'For a ten pound licence each year and a flock of sheep, costs less to get established here than other countries.'

'How do we mark out this run, then?' Lincoln sat forward, elbows on his knees, still unconvinced, drinking little and yawning.

The old men exchanged exasperated glances and shook their heads. 'Blaze the trunks of trees along the perimeter of your boundary.'

'Who else is out there already?' Duncan asked.

'Two or three years ago, John Wedge from Launceston surveyed the district. Dozens of men now. Manifold, Sutherland and Russell have runs along the Moorabool River. Andrew McNaughton's opened The Woolpack and he's trying for a licence.' The speaker puffed on his pipe in thought. 'And there's the Henty men further west at Portland Bay. They've interests in whaling as well.'

'This time of year you'll be able to travel light. All a man needs is a horse, a saddlebag for a change of clothes, a blanket and a packhorse to carry your tucker and gear. Might be weeks out on the track.'

'You could strike the natives,' one man sagely warned. 'Don't always take kindly to us movin' in.'

'If they don't trouble me, I won't trouble them,' Duncan muttered, remembering them in the streets earlier in the day. Seemed harmless enough. Didn't look like they'd give much trouble. Mounted on a horse with a rifle, he doubted they'd be a match for his skills.

'There's few enough of 'em.' One man burped. 'They don't make any use of the land. Just hunt and wander over it. Don't see why they should object.'

Early next morning, Duncan and William set about finding themselves good horseflesh to withstand the tough colonial conditions. For fifty pounds each, they secured three of great muscular strength, sharing the cost of an additional packhorse and supplies.

When it came to outlaying capital, William, apparently a younger son of English gentry, had no limitations. Although Duncan was forced to budget, he had learned thrift from his father who had generously spared some of his meagre savings for his second son to make a start in the new land.

Duncan remained mindful of his lesser resources and the need to watch every pound for buying in stock later. He estimated on making forty or fifty miles each day if they set their sturdy mounts to a steady canter.

At a general emporium in town, the men acquired flour, China tea and salt meat. Together with a gun and ammunition for defence and to kill food if their supplies ran out, they added dungarees and shirts.

Duncan treated himself to a copy of the slim four-page weekly newspaper, The Melbourne Advertiser, to learn as much as possible about the colony. He filled with disappointment to read only of timber and other goods for sale, vital for building the new colony he was sure but no value to him. There were basic advertisements for a bakery, John Batman's store, Fawkner's hotel and others. Movement to and from the colony was covered by news of local shipping between the port and Geelong, or Launceston and Hobarton on the island of Van Diemen's Land to the south. Plus mention of a boat service between Williams Town and the opposite beach across the bay.

But the mention of the Derwent Bank Agency caught his interest and he paid a visit to set up an account.

Manager, Charles Swanston, said, 'I can arrange credit,' and assured Duncan that settlers often asked him for an advance on their wool clip. 'I'll offer one shilling per pound if the wool is good quality and well got up,' he added generously.

Duncan failed to stem his growing excitement, asking questions of everyone he met at every opportunity, particularly businessmen and traders. He wished his enthusiasm was contagious enough to move William to show more anticipation for the significant journey they were about to undertake.

The Englishman had finally yielded to replacing his fine suit for more durable and sensible colonial clothes to ride inland.

Two days later, the men set off west on their fresh horses in the early morning to gain some hours on the track before the heat of the day. Fully kitted out in moleskin trousers, rough bush shirts, boots and spurs, pouches for tobacco and flint matches were clamped to their hide belts. Mandatory hats shielded them from the scorching sun and a handkerchief knotted around their necks.

Duncan's spirits soared as they headed away from civilisation into the bush. Brought up in Scotland where land features were small scale and travellers confined to narrow roads and pathways, here you could leave or follow the track at your pleasure. Unfenced grassy plains, empty and silent, stretched to the horizon.

After two days, a cool breeze swept through, easing the heat on men and horses. The long grasses leaned before the refreshing wind as though a hand brushed over their feathered tips.

As they slowly progressed through the untrodden wilds, Duncan's broad chest expanded with exhilaration at the splendid sight in every direction. Even in late summer, water flowed across the volcanic country, although in places the grasses had browned in seed and the ground was yellow with dandelions.

Duncan retrieved his gun and fired it into the air just to hear the echo above the silence.

He slapped his thigh, the rifle butt resting on his other hip. 'Country's beginning to appeal, eh Lincoln?'

Even William grinned at his exuberance. 'They weren't exaggerating, Duncan. Plenty for all, I should say.'

'And money to be made.'

They rested in the heat of midday and continued later in the afternoon until dusk when they set up camp under a clear and starlit sky. But now, when the breeze dropped, everything rested. Not a murmur of air stirred the dry gum leaves overhead as if the bush listened and waited.

William dozed by the fire and the hobbled horses languidly cropped nearby. Duncan turned over a small stone with his boot, probably never touched before. Backed up against the peeling bark of a eucalypt, he tried to imagine this bountiful Eden invaded with flocks and herds. His ambition swelled. He'd make his fortune here, build a mansion with peacocks on the lawn and return home a man of property and leisure.

His idle thoughts drifted back to Scotland. The rough sheep grazing on the hills that rolled toward a grey horizon. The squat cottage he knew as home that seemed to have grown out of the very ground where it stood, a part of the rocky landscape. An oblong box, smoke curling from its chimney, withstanding wind and weather, the bare hills providing no shelter.

His father, George, and older brother, Alistair, left the house about five. His mother and three sisters set to the milking, cheese making and churning. It was always little Aislin's job to feed the fowls and gather the eggs.

Being still winter now, the menfolk would be tending the

stock, preparing for ploughing and spring. All but the most essential work on their small farm ceased on the Sabbath. His mother even considered letter writing too frivolous for the holy day.

Duncan's loins stirred at the memory of long walks on Sunday afternoons to the neighbour's croft. As a teenage lad, when the husband was away, he'd savoured the wife's delights and acquired a lusty appetite for women. She'd wrapped her legs around him and taken him to the pinnacle of an exciting hill he'd been fortunate many a time thereafter to crest. She'd furrowed her hands through his thick wavy hair and panted out his name, skirts and petticoats hitched to her waist, shirt untucked and loose so he could knead his hands over her breasts and suck them until her nipples grew hard like pebbles in the field.

Duncan squirmed against the tree and adjusted his crotch.

On the third day of their exploration, they stumbled on the primitive shanty of the Golden Fleece Inn at Werribee, halfway between Melbourne and Geelong, built of slabs and roofed with shingles.

Long tree shadows striped the track guiding their approach. Barking dogs unsettled the horses but drew a hostler to the front door who took their mounts and directed them inside.

Duncan ducked as he stepped into the low sitting room. Walls and ceiling were lined with canvass and whitewashed. A deal table in the middle held a large brass bell and a single candle. A few gaudy ornaments were displayed along a mantelpiece.

At the far end, sofas were made up as beds. A man slept in one, his boots and clothes piled on the floor alongside, a pistol butt protruding from his pillow. The smell of ale and bacon reeked the air. From the tap next door came the laughs and oaths of men well into their drinking.

William was appalled by the wretched surrounds but Duncan ordered a meal that turned out to be bacon and eggs, and tea without milk.

Judging by the songs and shouts from the rowdy guests, selling liquor was the inn's main purpose. The revelry lasted until daylight and sleep was impossible. At first light, the men washed in the creek, mounted their horses and left.

Following wagon tracks, they turned south for Geelong, another metropolis in the making, boasting two stores, a customs station and the Woolpack Inn.

According to a teamster last night, the only useful conversation they'd had, the land they sought lay north along the Moorabool River valley. West along the Barwon River also held potential but Duncan's instincts told him to strike north.

Next day they crossed Fyan's Ford several miles upstream. Duncan itched to push the horses harder, excited by abundant creeks and streams running down from a small mountain range. The countryside grew greener and richer with every mile.

Emu and wild turkey abounded. Mobs of great kangaroos half hidden in the grass propped motionless, ears twitching at the vibrations of approaching hooves. Brightly coloured birds screeched and flitted among the branches of white trunked gums. Startled white cockatoos took flight, circling and resettling their snowy plumage, covering the limbs like blossom.

Surprised emus loped off in fright. On a thrilling whim, Duncan took chase leaving William behind but soon realised he had no chance of closing his quarry's growing gap. Duncan conceded and reined his horse, dismounting to step out the length of the animal's running stride.

'Nine or ten feet, Lincoln.' Duncan marvelled when he rejoined William, impressed by its speed. 'No wonder ah'd no chance to catch it.'

Within days, Duncan's hunch proved correct. 'I've found ma run, Lincoln.'

The plains stretched to infinity, dotted with trees. Duncan galloped to higher ground for a view. The land was rich and the site beautiful. A handsome piece of country. Duncan slid from the saddle and planted his feet on what he decided would be Penross soil. He gaped at the pastures waiting for sheep. His sheep. And his road to wealth.

Shrewdly reading the resentment in his companion's squinted eyes, Duncan said, 'Plenty for all, ah'd say. We'll make camp.' He nodded toward the distant river. 'And start exploring boundaries tomorrow.'

Lincoln had been a follower for the entire journey, contributing little, and could find his own run.

As twilight stretched gold beams across the lush untrodden pastures, they pitched a tent by the river, built a fire and unloaded supplies from their packhorse. His senses on alert, Duncan stilled and listened as he filled a billy can with fresh water. Seeing nothing, he shrugged off the intuition.

Conscious of William's dark mood, he said brightly, 'I'm thinking there'll be more grand pastures further east, Lincoln.'

'We'll find out soon enough,' he said with reservation.

As darkness fell, they ate their simple meal in silence and later nursed a pannikin of hot tea laced with colonial whisky. Duncan filled a pipe and stretched his boots toward the glowing coals.

'If we hunt tomorrow, we should have some fine fresh meat for our supper,' he said, amid the echoed sounds of bull frogs, the aggravation of mosquitoes and the distant howling of native dogs.

Getting no response, he unfurled his swag and laid down by the fire for the first sleep on his own land. At daybreak, he rebuilt the fire and set unleavened dough in the ashes to bake. Looking up, he caught movement a short distance away. Two black women were digging in the ground near the water's edge. Catching sight of him, they sprinted away.

Duncan kicked William awake. 'We've got company. Natives. Best keep an out from now on, eh?'

William warily propped his rifle at his side.

All day as they surveyed and marked boundary trees,

taking rough distances for enough description to lodge his claim, Duncan prickled with the canny feeling they were being watched. He thought he saw dark shapes behind a stand of trees but when he looked, they melted into shadow.

Late in the day with a kangaroo slung across the saddle on front of him and nearing camp, three black men rose from the tall grass ahead and blocked their path.

Bare-chested and upright, the brown skinned men glared with wild eyes and gabbled in their own language, making terrifying gestures. One moved forward a few paces, shaking the bunch of spears in his hand.

William reached for his rifle.

'Leave it,' Duncan hissed and slid from his horse.

He smiled as he approached them, arms spread wide. If he seemed friendly, they might not cause trouble. He'd just found his land and intended to keep it. Preferably without bloodshed.

An older man stepped forward and, unflinching, held his gaze. His abundant straight black hair was tinged with red, his nose flat and widespread. The scant animal pelt apron in front and behind was all he wore and hung from a skin belt. He drove the blunt ends of their spears into the soft earth.

To Duncan's amazement, he said in broken English, 'Here, my country. No more come back.'

They must have had contact with other whites. Duncan swept one arm in a wide arc and pointed to his chest. 'Duncan. This my camp.'

The native flung back his head, his eyes sheltered by bushy jutting brows. 'Wantem bacca,' he demanded.

Hiding his surprise, Duncan shared some from the pouch in his belt. Their anger seemed to disappear at the offer of the cheap gift but they lingered.

He untied the kangaroo from his horse and, struggling beneath its weight, offered the animal in goodwill. It meant he and Lincoln would go hungry tonight for the long summer evening was finally drawing in and daylight would soon be lost with no chance for more hunting.

With happy grins, the natives took it and walked away.

William scowled. 'They would have been happy with the tobacco.'

'Maybe,' Duncan said, 'but this is no time to be making enemies. Ah've a mind to keep them friendly.'

The men stayed in the bush long enough to select William's run on thousands more glorious acres east adjoining the Penross boundary. Having chosen their land, Duncan grew anxious to return to Melbourne and lodge their claims. But to help safeguard their rights, they had been advised to build a hut on their properties so, for weeks, the ring of axes echoed through the richly timbered bush. They split logs into thick planks and placed them end to end in a frame. The gaps they plastered with mud. Smaller poles were used for rafters above which they fashioned a thatched roof from the abundant long grasses, leaving it overhang the side walls for protection from rains.

Duncan, sun browned and strong, bore most of the workload from the less physical William. From time to time, the natives appeared, watching from a distance. As the men's rations depleted, they depended on guns and fishing lines, their hunting rewarded with roast duck, grilled fish or kangaroo. With mild nights, they slept on blankets before the fire.

Unshaven and weary, the men finally saddled up their horses and headed east back to Melbourne to lodge their claims, buy their flocks and return to take possession of their runs.

Once back in civilisation again, the sudden activity surprised Duncan. In the past weeks he had grown attuned to the silence and space of the bush finding himself anxious and longing to return.

They secured rooms at the Lamb Inn again and, after a hasty bath, shave and a meal, Duncan trawled the dingy night streets for a woman to ease his needs. Eventually he found a rare if slovenly female living in a tent on the edge of town, a friendless unfortunate who had apparently and not uncommonly fallen on troubled times in the hard young colony.

Next morning, not waiting for Lincoln to appear and with the lease papers safely in his possession, Duncan strode down to the Yarra River. Sheep and cattle were being imported from the south across the waters of the Bass Strait in Van Diemen's Land as fast as vessels could carry them.

After inspection and negotiation, he secured a thousand decent looking ewes plus an equal number of Merino descent, withholding cash reserves for the unforeseen that undoubtedly lay ahead.

He had heard you could double your flock within a year after lambing with each animal yielding maybe two pounds of fleece or better. With luck, the sale of wool would cover his costs and provide enough profit to stay afloat.

Duncan eyed his small pen of stud rams – his *boys* – with their fierce looking curly horns and faces almost lost in great folds of wool. They had cost him five pounds each and were his ticket to wealth. If any of those beauties went missing, the culprit would pay dearly. He dreamed of making something grand of his life and would stand no interference with his plans.

The next few years promised to be hard and lonely but with only poor farming prospects back home and his burning desire to succeed, he doubted he would regret his decision to leave. Alistair would take over the family farm and he was welcome to it. His smitten brother only had eyes for Maggie MacInnes and he wagered it wasn't long before they wed with a brood of bairns crammed into the cottage.

His three younger sisters were all handsome girls and would find husbands. At least, Mary and Lara would. He wasn't so sure about Aislin. She was a wild one, always disappearing across the fells.

Shaking himself free of memories, Duncan focused on hiring workmen. If local gossip ran true, it would be his biggest challenge. He scoured public houses until eventually one publican led him out to a back parlour, a long room with a narrow table down the centre littered with bottles of ale, brandy and champagne, and a collection of tumblers and pewter pots.

Disreputable specimens of eight men sat or lay on benches along the wall, lolling, singing or quarrelling in various stages of inebriation. One played a fiddle, another stared at the floor under his feet, swaying.

'They're mainly thieves, drunks and Irishmen. All broke and needing to work again. Good luck, mate,' the publican grinned.

Standing determinedly astride, Duncan planted his hands on his hips and bellowed, 'Ah've work for three or four good men on the Moorabool. Who's willin' to sign on with me?'

With wages high and their last cheque spent, Duncan expected them to leap at the chance to be solvent again, at least for a few months. Only half the men were coherent enough to raise their heads and show a spark of interest when he spoke.

'A pound a week and rations,' Duncan appealed. 'Name's Duncan Penross. Ye can find me at the Lamb.'

While the men sobered up, Duncan headed to the general emporium for a year's supplies for half a dozen men.

By evening at the Lamb, only two men waited, scowling, smoking and dishevelled. A wiry little Irishman name of Irish and a burly man called big Mick. All workers were only known by nicknames it seemed. Duncan assessed them. Although they were a disastrous looking lot, apparently old hands no matter how drunk were better than new chums any day. They looked strong enough and, once they dried out, he prayed they gave him a decent day's work.

'Me mate's a bullock driver. Looking for work again finishin' wool cartin',' Irish said, his voice thick with accent.

'Send him around then.'

At a table in the Lamb's front room the men signed contracts for six months to cover droving out to his run, setting up the outstations and shearing in spring. No one blinked when he threatened prison or forfeiting wages if they bolted.

With the appearance of Red the bullocky and another lad the next day, Duncan's labour force swelled to four.

They assembled on the Yarra where the sheep were temporarily penned. The early morning sunlight glared off the brown sluggish Yarra waters, the four wheeled dray hitched to eight restless bullocks yoked in pairs. Red had loaded the equipment from the emporium. Besides flour, pork and sugar, Duncan provided tarpaulins for rudimentary shelter for his men. The hut already built was for himself. He'd added pots, pannikins and tin dishes along with clothing, tobacco and tools.

Despite his shrinking finances, Duncan had invested in spare horses and sheep dogs.

Having farewelled William Lincoln the evening before, still buying stock and seeking men, Duncan mounted his horse and shouted, 'Move out.'

The dray groaned its protest. The wagon wheels creaked and Red's beasts bellowed at his roaring curses. Red cracked his whip and the new squatting party inched under way in a cloud of dust, to the sound of barking dogs. The shepherds and smelly bleating sheep brought up the rear. Lumbering from town heading for the bush, Duncan had no idea when next he would return to civilisation.

As the long dreary days drew on, the cavalcade pushed through timber and creek beds, the wagon forging a path ahead.

Duncan sat proudly astride, cantering its perimeter, scanning the straggly procession veiled in a permanent cloud of dust, mindful that it represented the beginnings of a dynasty he would one day leave to his sons.

Late each day, Duncan left the convoy and set off on foot

into the scrub with a pistol and a dog. He had learned that twilight brought out kangaroos to feed. As his skills and aim improved, his efforts usually yielded a kill which he slung over his shoulder and fetched back to camp.

At night, the hobbled horses' bells tinkled in the still twilight as a roaring fire was lit and the party set up camp. Irish proved a capable cook, his first task always to fill a big kettle to simmer over the flames and set damper to bake in the ashes.

The men lit smaller fires around the sheep to prevent them straying. They ate their meal in silence, smoking a last pipe before turning in to sleep on a bed of boughs, a saddle pillow and a blanket against the cool night until their watch. Red slept beneath the dray. As the night advanced and settled in, the bullocks bellowed mournfully, the sheep stirred and bleated, and the dogs rose from the fire to stretch.

Deliberately setting himself apart to establish himself as the boss, Duncan took the measure of his men. He shared a turn as watchman cantering around his flocks before rousing the next man and shaking down for the night. He lay on his back with his hands behind his head and marvelled at the clear sky and the immense dome of stars.

It took almost a week of sunburnt days to reach the run, every day the sky one continuous vault of blue.

On arrival, Duncan set the men to building makeshift huts that could be dismantled and reassembled as necessary elsewhere on the run. His own hut became the home station located on his favoured site on a slight rise above the river. He organised three out stations some miles from his hut and five miles apart with one shepherd and flock on each. To ease the boredom, he set up a rotation system for his men so each in turn spent time at the home station helping Duncan build his most urgent outbuildings – a stable, storeroom for saddles, tools and harness, and the all-important shearing shed ready for spring.

In the first weeks, he kept Mick at the home station to

make headway with cutting timber. The big man's arm muscles bulged like tree stumps every time he swung the axe. Once the heaviest slabs were split, Duncan sent him out on the run with a flock. Although he had a hunch, after seeing the giant man work, he would hate being idle.

Duncan's hut was crude with only a stool and crate, his bed a frame of saplings with sacks and skins stretched over the top. A temporary inconvenience he determined to endure, looking ahead with a stoic patience against his nature, knowing tolerance would one day bring its rewards.

He found no hardship in isolation, conditioned by many a lonely day tending sheep on the slopes of the rocky wild hills of the pastures rising from the Teviot's sinuous valley back home. At times his thoughts drifted to other men doing the same thing; setting up runs, wresting the land while they may. He knew George Read had taken up Cargerie nearby in January with the Mercers recently moving onto Mount Mercer and Smyth settling on his Ballarat run.

Aside from making the daily unleavened damper and dipping into the provisions, mutton became a staple. The kangaroos that fed in large numbers while early dew was still on the grass made a tasty stew in the camp oven outdoors set in a bed of coals. If they came in late from working, the frying pan sufficed for mutton chops with a yard long handle for use on the open fire.

Duncan took pleasure in supper after a day's labours or riding. Light for his evening meal came from a scrap of wool or rag used as a wick in pieces of fat pork or mutton. While he drew on his pipe, he squinted over a daily station journal to keep details of his sheep, expenses and the weather.

Although the wants of himself and his men were few, he had a limited ability to supply them. For the time being, his men seemed content enough. The shepherds were constantly moving flocks around the run as they depleted the lush grasses. Duncan was more concerned at predators to his precious sheep. At night, the sobbing howls of wild dogs raised the hair on a man's scalp. Unafraid but prepared, Duncan kept his pistol handy and warned the men to keep a tight watch.

Waking to the sight of the grassed flats each morning was a wondrous spectacle, the shady trees washed by crisp sunlight as it broke through and rose above them. Birds and songster magpies sent their music across the silent bush, and the raucous laugh of the jackass echoed on the evening air as the sun slowly slid to the horizon.

As summer cooled into autumn, chilly nights followed milder days. Soft showers of rain often swept through drenching the bush and thickening the grass.

Once a week, Duncan rode to the out stations to deliver rations to the men, check sheep numbers and their condition, hunting the wild dogs along the way. Daily at sunrise, each shepherd released his flock from its hurdle yards where they were protected overnight then supervised as they wandered and grazed during the day.

Lunch was a flagon of tea, a piece of damper and slice of cold mutton, a dog as companion. It was easy but lonely work until, at sunset, the shepherd brought the animals back to the out station and into the yards.

As the weeks passed, it became clear that not all of Duncan's sheep would make it through to shearing in spring. As he rode into the first out station, an agitated Irish, still in camp with the flock hurdled, ran up to his horse as he approached.

'Native dogs attacked last night, boss.'

Cursing, Duncan dismounted and walked with him down to where the violence had occurred. Three mangled carcasses and tufts of bloodied wool littered the grassy ground.

'How the hell did ye not see them, man?' he exploded, furious to see his profits decreasing with each assault. Every ewe and ram was precious for breeding and potential money in the bank.

'They were hidden in the shadows, boss, so they were. I

swear I didn't see 'em until the dog started barkin' and I heard the noise.'

'Dog's more valuable than you then, man,' Duncan bellowed out his irritation. 'Keep your bloody eyes peeled in future.' He turned aside and spat on the ground. 'Use what meat you can and bury the rest,' he growled. 'Did you shoot any of the thieving bastards?'

'Hard to see them in the dark, boss.'

Duncan growled his exasperation and personally checked his rams, noting down the new tally for his journal. Disappointed at the loss of good breeding ewes but relieved to see none of his *boys* were among them.

From time to time, ewes mysteriously disappeared. When he questioned the men, a likely explanation was, 'The natives, boss.'

Dusky buggers were as stealthy as the dogs. He would set them straight when they next came to visit. Finding the natives' camp was impossible because they constantly moved so he bided his time until they appeared, as they always did, unexpectedly from the bush.

Fury raged in his gut because on their previous visits, he made sure he stayed friendly giving them flour, tobacco and mutton without the need for stealing. Duncan thought they were on good terms because they even brought their piccaninnies and he always greeted them with a smile and respect. With winter on the horizon and leaner hunting times ahead, the tribes would be tempted again but he couldn't afford to lose the stock.

Before he rode away, Duncan eyed Irish carefully. On some visits he noticed the wiry little man's red bleary eyes and suspected he had a secret supply of grog. If he had been tipsy last night and not doing his job... Duncan balled his hands into fists. Ironically, the old hand had proved to be the most reliable so he let the few losses pass. All he could do was put the fear of God into him and pray any casualties were low.

Settling in for another quiet Saturday evening on the run,

Duncan was surprised to see his old mate and neighbour, William Lincoln, emerge through the lengthening shadows, swaying on his horse.

As William slid from his saddle, surprised the man had found his way, Duncan held the reins and extended a hand in greeting. 'Lincoln, welcome to ma home.'

William winced at his friend's fierce grip. 'Penross.' The man's breath reeked of liquor and he planted his sun browned hands heavily on Duncan's shoulders. 'It's good to see a familiar face again.'

Knowing the man's weak nature, Duncan understood his lapse. Out here, every day was the same. Tedium could fox you if you let it. All the same, he frowned over the refined gentleman's state of disarray, filthy clothes and whiskers.

'Come in, man.' Duncan thumped him on the back. 'This is cause for a celebration.'

He held aside the sheepskin nailed over the door opening and the men went indoors. With no windows, the interior was dim so Duncan lit the fat lamp although it was daylight outside. He set a bottle of brandy on the tea chest that served as a table between them, feeling a sneaky guilt for encouraging the man when he was already maudlin from drink.

The more Lincoln drank, the more he loosened his tongue. Eager for news, Duncan turned a ready ear to William as he unloaded his problems. He had barely collapsed onto the tree stump Duncan had rolled into the hut for an extra chair, than his visitor began hurling accusations and abuse.

'I've come to warn you, Penross,' he said firmly, 'that your sheep are straying across the creek and onto my western boundary. I'll have no trespassing on my run. Your shepherds need to keep a closer watch.'

Duncan bristled at the slurred criticism because he checked his flocks weekly. They had argued over that stream when they were marking out their runs with both claiming it but nothing resolved.

Not wasting an opportunity, Duncan decided to

manipulate the dispute to his advantage while Lincoln's brain was dim, and he chewed over how he might win the disagreement.

He decided to start out by being agreeable. 'I'll go out and check the situation myself, Lincoln.' He had no intention of doing any such thing but he intended making mileage out of the irritating predicament.

'I've sent a man to Geelong after the Police Magistrate, Penross. He should arrive tomorrow. We had an agreement,' he blustered. 'We shook hands on it.' In his confusion, William tried to sound stern but failed.

Duncan sighed heavily and scratched his head. 'I don't say as I remember, Lincoln, but if that's what will satisfy you then the Magistrate will sort it out all right.'

William was more lucid than he thought. He needed that eastern creek come autumn when his flocks increased.

'I trust you're gettin' established on Lakeham,' Duncan said to distract him and poured whisky into two tin cups. He had a fondness for the liquor but never allowed it to cloud his judgement. He pushed one toward William and raised the other. 'To our prosperity, eh Lincoln?'

Duncan swilled his drink and filled his pipe. Now, seeing the advantage of the watercourse, he calculated how to convince Lincoln to share the creek and somehow try to bluff his way out of this.

Swallowing his golden liquid, William scowled, his smooth aristocratic face browned from outdoor life, his eyes glazed over in contemplation.

'Bloody workmen,' he grumbled and followed with a string of muttered oaths.

Duncan's ploy had worked as his neighbour moved on to complain of other trials. 'Never do as they're told. Useless lot of layabouts. I bribe them with extra rations of rum but it only makes them worse.'

'I'm not surprised, Lincoln. You need to be firm with them. Show them who's boss. But I agree, the men can be an unruly lot, for sure,' he sympathised, knowing his own men were always under control, if a mite independent. Ex-convicts relished their freedom. 'But with a shortage of labour and high wages, we're not in a position to complain.'

'I've lost count of my dead and missing sheep. I had trouble early on with the natives and gave them a blast from my carbine. But even warning them off does no good.'

'Have you tried being friendly?' Duncan ventured. If his neighbour turned the blacks hostile, it could mean trouble for all of them.

'To those savages?' William thundered. 'Never.' He shook his head and drained his drink. 'I confess, Duncan, it's harder out here than I imagined. Not sure how long I'll stay.'

Duncan was hardly surprised by Lincoln's confession but they had barely started. 'Tough it out, Lincoln. There's fortunes to be made.'

'I'm considering putting in a manager and going to live in Geelong or Melbourne.'

'Nothing much for you to be doing in town though.' It was clear William's boredom produced sprees to blur his misery. Duncan couldn't see how he could be helped by trading one monotony for another. The man simply wasn't born for farming.

After supper while enjoying a pipe together, Duncan slyly challenged his guest to cards. Lincoln took the bait and, by the early hours of the morning, Duncan had another thirty pounds in his pocket. He greedily calculated how many more rams he would buy before he fell asleep.

He woke at sunrise, as usual, before William had stirred on his pallet next morning. Gripped by a burst of devilment, he coaxed the ashes into life again and fried chops, then fired off a pistol shot and bellowed, 'Breakfast.'

William scrambled from his bed in alarm and stumbled to his feet, blearily reaching for his carbine. He glared mutinously at Duncan as they ate outdoors. His glum mood persisted until the Police Magistrate arrived on a magnificent chestnut horse, leading a convoy of troopers. A bugle sounded as they approached, all of them armed with carbines, pistols and sabres. As the Magistrate dismounted, a trooper took the reins.

William rushed forward. 'Captain Fyans. William Lincoln, sir. Thank you for attending.'

The official accepted his handshake. 'I was in the vicinity, Mr. Lincoln, before heading out west.'

Without enthusiasm, William turned to indicate Duncan. 'My neighbour, Duncan Penross.'

Duncan detected an Irish accent of the new arrival and prayed he was a fair man for, even at this late stage, there was always the chance of a bribe. 'Captain. Welcome to ma run.'

While the troopers watered the horses, Fyans unslung his carbine and removed his buckskin gloves and cloak. To Duncan's annoyance, because it allowed him no time to invent an excuse, William launched into a whining description of his complaint.

Sauntering up and down, Fyans fired questions at both dissenters using military terms like *positions* when enquiring about the location of shepherds' huts.

Seeing the Magistrate to be a firm and upright man, Duncan decided against a quiet pay off and let fate take its course. On edge until the official reached a judgement, he silently cursed Lincoln for being so bloody strait laced and causing trouble. With the law involved now, he'd have to abide by it though, if the decision went against him, his flocks might still be inclined to wander.

Duncan hid his delight when Fyans heard a short statement from each man and announced his verdict. He beckoned to a trooper who moved forward and produced a document both men signed, witnessed by the Magistrate who then promptly, his business done, mustered his troopers and rode away with as much spectacle as his arrival.

'Half the creek each. Can't be fairer than that, eh Lincoln?' Duncan was well pleased.

'The outcome is unfair, Penross,' William sneered. 'It was mine. We agreed.'

'It was your idea to bring in Fyans,' Duncan pointed out firmly, holding William's moody glare. 'We must abide by his decision. Papers are signed.'

'You have crossed me, Penross, and you know it.'

In a rare show of backbone, his hostile accusation stung but Duncan felt no guilt. Out here in this primitive pioneering country filled with so much potential, he refused to be cowed. He would seize every benefit he could get.

Glowering with fury, William saddled his horse and without a farewell, turned his mount east and headed for Lakeham.

CHAPTER 2

After the first winter rains, the ground became boggy and, at times, it was even impossible to ride a horse. Duncan squelched for miles on foot tramping to the out stations carrying the shepherds' rations of flour, tea and sugar on his shoulders, a weight of forty pounds in two bags, wading knee deep in water across flooded flats with his collie dog loyally trotting at his heels.

On each return trip, he brought back a culled sheep for the week's fresh meat. Usually a ewe too old to breed or too poor for sale. He had begun saving the sheepskins, finding the extra trouble worthwhile, for their sale helped cover the men's wages.

Duncan marvelled that, unlike Scotland, where snow lay thick on the ground for months in winter and sheep were housed in barns, here in Port Phillip colony his flocks flourished in the milder winter climate without being pampered.

In late September when the weather mellowed with the return of warmer days that slowly dried up the sodden pastures, Duncan and Mick set up the sheep washing pens in the river. Once the flocks had been brought up to the home station, the men gave the animals a good soapy lathering before sending them down to be washed in the long swim of fenced water. The sheep finally scrambled up a landing place on the bank further down.

Over the next week as their thick fleeces dried, they were channelled into temporary yards on clean grass, gradually moving closer day by day to the substantial woolshed ready for shearing. The most important event so far on Duncan's run. His survival depended on his wool clip and he knew it.

Recalling Charles Swanston's words about credit if necessary being advanced against wool of good quality and well got up, he planned to finish by the end of November before the grass seeds defiled his wool.

Duncan had hired a disreputable but skilled crew of shearers after travelling with Red in the dray on the vague dusty track to Geelong. Only months earlier, the small settlement had been proclaimed a town.

While Duncan had conducted his business of hiring men for the spring shearing, he stayed at the slab house Woolpack, more commonly known as Mack's after its Scottish owner, Andrew McNaughton. Despite the small accommodation boasting only four bedrooms, a bar and a detached kitchen, Duncan considered it far more commodious than his hut on the run. While in town, he took the advantage of a particular lady's company and also seized the opportunity to buy blocks of town land at auction.

As shearing approached, Duncan's hirelings arrived in pairs on foot carrying swags and wearing battered hats. Tough bearded men, one of whom trailed a lad alongside. Against his instinct, Duncan hired the youngster as a general shed hand who he could use as a tarboy for picking up fleeces to be flung up onto the woolshed table for sorting.

Once the shearers were settled into the long hut to be used as their quarters for the duration, Duncan wandered down one evening to deliver what he hoped was a rousing speech. He promised a bonus for the man each day who clipped the tidiest fleece.

But not before he had checked off names on his list and read out their terms of agreement. The men, sitting or standing by their flimsy bunks around the walls, or smoking and playing cards at the rough table down the centre, remained indifferent. A few low murmurs and narrow gazes slid around the room. Duncan shook his head as he walked away.

The day before shearing started, the men spent the day preparing their blades for work. Next morning, a whistle blew and the traditional rum was handed around. With its small windows and dark corners, only tiny bars of sunlight dazzled the wool shed dimness.

For six weeks, a constant click of shears, scrambling of sheep and barking dogs echoed in and around the shed. Duncan's prized *boys* each took thirty minutes to shear and paid double but an average sheep was clipped in five minutes.

Into October, the men worked from six in the morning until six in the evening, sweating in their flannel shirts in air thick with the smell of sheep dung. With time off only for a smoke and meals, the men finished work early each Saturday to swim in the river, read books, play cricket on the grassy flats, fish or gamble.

As they worked, Duncan made a point of closely watching each man and only trusted his rams to one or two shearers who appeared most competent. Apart from occasional rain showers, fate remained on his side and the weather held fine until his last ewe was shorn.

After the shed cut out, the men celebrated with lots of drinking and jigging about to the plaintiff strains of Mick's mouth organ and another man's fiddle.

At varying intervals the next day in assorted states of recuperation, the shearers drifted over to Duncan's hut. Seated at a crate, he wrote out cheques and paid off the men at his front door before they straggled away through the bush. Some asked to be signed on again next season. Duncan readily agreed and shook hands on the deal, pleased to notice the two top shearers among them. Seeing the bonus in their cheques, one nodded in appreciation, the other tipped his tattered hat as he sauntered away. Men of few words like most in the bush. Some were moving on to nearby runs seeking more work while others doubtless had plans to drink their wages at the nearest public house.

As soon as his regular men loaded Red's dray, stacked

high with heavy bales of wool, the bullocks struggled away with Duncan's first clip. Once loaded onto the tall masted ships at Point Henry on the coast, his precious cargo was bound for England. A journey of months and a frustrating wait of many more for news of the price his fleeces fetched.

With the English woollen industry converted to factories and a growing demand, the Yorkshire mill owners hungrily bought up all the raw material they could get. Duncan knew Australian sheep men supplied half their needs.

He was canny enough to envision the dawn of his prosperity ahead. If his clip made sixteen pence the pound, he could expect hundreds of pounds profit. Enough to buy more rams maybe from John Henty down at Portland Bay. He rubbed his hands together at the prospect.

Soon the hot summer days slowed the pace of life. Occasionally, the stealthy natives appeared, soundlessly wading across the shrinking river in single file toward his hut. They kept their distance, waiting until Duncan emerged to approach them, as if afraid of infringing on his camp.

Once when Mick was at the home station, they appeared quietly near the hut at twilight laughing and pointing, fascinated by the sound floating from the big man's mouth organ.

When the blacks saw Duncan light a fire from his tinder box, they jumped back in shock and chattered in alarm, cautiously moving closer in awe to inspect this object producing fire.

Duncan revelled in the searing lazy days, remaining unshaven for weeks, planning his strategy for the year ahead. He would clear and plough land for barley and wheat in autumn. Irish had suggested potatoes so Dan had instructed Red to bring back seeds and supplies when he returned with the dray from the coast. The crops would only be of small consequence. Sheep would always earn him the big money and mattered most.

Duncan cared little for the passing days. According to the

calendar, Christmas came and went. He slept late. With the hut door flap down and no fire lit, crows cawed out their harsh cry. Annoyed to be woken, Duncan stumbled from the bed where he slept uncovered during the warm nights and pointed his gun muzzle toward the sun's glare, discharging two angry shots. His dog rose from where he lay outside the hut in its thin strip of early morning shade, tilted his head and eyed his master strangely.

Toward evening, as the day cooled, Duncan chopped firewood or tramped off shooting ducks for supper, the dog panting close behind.

He kept his daily journal of the weather and the run. On his weekly horseback patrols to the out stations, he found most ewes in lamb. Come April, he anticipated doubling his flocks.

But leading a quiet pastoral life held only so much appeal. Duncan longed for more stimulation and intelligent company than his weekly visits to grunting illiterate shepherds and bleating sheep. His tedious days of inactivity caused him to hate everything and he roamed aimlessly, hunting.

On the hottest days he swam in the Moorabool. Native women and children laughed and bathed further down but he never approached them. The energy-sapping heat was occasionally eased by a cool breeze rushing through for a few days before the next hot spell. Each morning before leaving the hut, Duncan tapped the barometer hanging on a nail inside the door but it remained obstinately fair.

Restless and bored, Duncan decided to visit Lincoln, indifferent to his welcome since the creek boundary dispute. He prepared his horse and trimmed its hooves with a chisel. Retrieved his best coat, necktie and best hat from the box in the hut where it had lain for months. With a final polish of his boots, Duncan headed east for Lakeham.

Later that day, a surprised William seemed bright and welcoming enough, with no mention of their previous conflict. With his neighbour's leathered brown face hidden beneath a bushy beard, Duncan sensed an unpredictable edge to the man that hadn't existed months before.

As they sprawled, coats cast aside and shirt necks open in the paltry shade of a eucalypt, its dry leaves rustled by the thick warm air sluggishly stirring above them, Duncan was disturbed to hear Lincoln had shot at trespassing natives and now slept with a carbine by his side.

'Blasted blackfellas,' William cursed. 'The nerve, and in broad daylight. Sneaked up behind one of my shepherds sitting down having a quiet smoke and tapped him on the shoulder nearly scaring the man half to death. He didn't argue when others crept out of the bush waving their spears and carried off a sheep. I tell you, Duncan, I will not hesitate to kill a single one of them if they're caught stealing again when I'm around.' William growled. 'My men have their orders. Tell your men to keep a close eye out, Duncan.'

'Ah've noticed a few missing from my tally.' Duncan squinted out across the glaring landscape tinged with brown as he'd seen it on his first expedition the previous year. An unfortunate consequence of their vast holdings made it impossible to patrol every corner of the run. Easy enough to pilfer stragglers from their flocks.

In the evening after a meal of cold sliced mutton followed by a pipe and whisky, the men played cards in the wan flicker of a tallow candle. They slept under the stars, long since attuned to the night sounds; veiled bush calls and murmurs, and the haunting howls of native dogs.

Over breakfast of fried bacon and slices of stale damper washed down by pannikins of hot tea relished before the thermometer soared again, Lincoln bemoaned the value of his efforts.

'We need to hold on for a few more years, Lincoln. Be worth our while.'

'Even with two lambings every year and the wool clip doubling, I still have my doubts, Penross.'

'Do you cull?'

'What for?' William scoffed. 'I want more sheep and

fleece, not less.'

Duncan hesitated to argue that, in the long term, it may be better for quality stock. 'This country is not all taken up yet, Lincoln. There'll be more sheep coming in and more competition. We need to breed our animals with an advantage over the rest.'

William uttered a jeering laugh of disagreement and tossed the dregs of his tea onto the fire. The liquid hissed as it hit the coals. With more capital, Lincoln had twice the flocks on Lakeham. Duncan's instinct and dwindling funds, on the other hand, until his first wool cheque arrived, kept him cautious. He couldn't afford to be as cavalier as his neighbour.

Weeks later, as summer intensified into February, Duncan woke from an afternoon doze to the alarming sight of a distant curtain of rising smoke. He scuttled to his feet, saddled his horse and galloped toward the thickening column of grey.

Blacks on the other side of the river on his southern perimeter called out their familiar *Cooee* and beckoned for him to join them. Duncan plunged his mount into the shallow water and urged his horse up the other side.

Horrified to see them setting fire to perfectly good pastures on his land, wasting precious feed, Duncan vaulted to the ground and confronted their male leader.

'This my land.' Duncan thumped his chest and shook his head. 'No fire.' He stamped his boot on the licking flames racing through the straw-dry undergrowth toward the stream.

An ancient emaciated man, a bent wreck of humanity who Duncan had never seen before, shuffled closer. Naked and defiant, his white beard hanging in straggly wisps to his gaunt bony chest, angrily shook his fist shouting and gabbling at Duncan.

Slowly, through a laborious process of hand gestures and halted explanations from a younger man in the tribe, Duncan grasped that burning the grass was good. On closer inspection, he noted the blackened areas were controlled.

'Big fella fire all gone soon,' the native reassured him.

After a pause, he tapped his shiny copper chest. 'Me nunga.'

Thinking it was the blackfella's name, Duncan indicated himself. 'Boss, Duncan.'

'Boss,' the man repeated, grinning.

As his fear subsided, Duncan examined his surroundings. The grassfire had burnt itself out at the water's edge. Maybe the blaze had been planned. At this point, he had no idea why and did not care. He was just glad the flames were out.

More blacks emerged nearby, including females. So far, Duncan had only seen and dealt with men. One young woman standing in the shade in particular captured his attention. His gaze travelled over her dark coarse hair falling in plentiful strands to her shoulders, her dusky body well-formed and graceful in its symmetry. The sight of her uncovered and firm jutting breasts triggered deeper male needs.

The women pointed with their noses to each other, clearly discussing him in their own language. Then the tribe gradually dispersed into the bush.

Riding back across the shallow river to his hut, Duncan reflected that, after today's episode, he would be wise to watch the natives and learn from them. Observe the burnt pastures and see how they recovered.

Beneath the clear blue sky and onslaught of merciless heat, it was hard to imagine the possibility of winter rains. But sudden sharp storms soon arrived, growling across the country, flinging fat drops from thunderclouds onto the quenched pastures below.

Within weeks, the weather turned, enabling Duncan and Mick to begin lopping and burning off trees to clear acreage for crops. At either end of a cross-saw, the men worked through the larger branches, setting the most suitable aside for building and the rest for firewood.

They shovelled the earth away from the roots and burnt out the stumps. At night, while Duncan retired to his hut and daily journal, Mick attended the glowing burn, then dug in the ashes next day. Repeating the process until they had cleared enough acres for planting out and a smaller potato plot near the hut for Irish. The ground only needed turning over afresh before they sowed.

Duncan's expectations peaked when his first lambs dropped. Each safe addition increased his prospects of wealth, his primary concern. Another year closer to his dream of creating a fine estate.

Although he had built his home station hut to one side of the rise above the river, he had deliberately left the central ground slightly further back for a more permanent residence. His gaze narrowed over the setting as he visualised a substantial and impressive home, and the family who might one day occupy it with him. But he needed to establish himself first.

As lambing continued, Duncan left the hut for days at a time, morning till night, camping out. The flocks needed constant attention against predatory crows and eagles that circled menacingly overhead. Relentless in protecting his vulnerable and precious new arrivals, Duncan kept his carbine to hand.

He paid his shepherds a bonus for a high percentage of surviving lambs as incentive to more carefully guard his flocks. Yet still at times, in helpless anger, he was forced to watch an eagle hawk swoop down over his terrified sheep and claw up a lamb, soaring away through the air with it as though its catch was only a mouse.

When lambing finished and new tallies were made, Duncan travelled to Geelong with Red in the dray, returning with extra provisions and shepherds for his expanding flocks. One English lad hailed from a farming family so Duncan set him to work ploughing, and sowing wheat and barley, while Irish planted out his potato patch.

Gradually, Duncan's work changed to more supervision and organisation. He found himself on constant vigil.

In spring, a lone contract mailman on horseback, a leather bag hanging from his saddle, arrived with old newspapers and a large welcome cheque to see him through another year with profit beside. Simply addressed to *Duncan Penross on the Moorabool,* he marvelled that his letter had reached him at all.

As the mailman lit a pipe and gossiped, Duncan covered the crate he used as a table with a towel and sliced the damper. He spooned coarse brown sugar into a pannikin and filled it with tea from the iron kettle simmering on the welcome fire that helped warm him now on colder days.

When the leg of mutton on a skewer over the fire had been turned until it browned, its fat spitting in drips onto the coals, he set it out on a tin dish and the men helped themselves to thick slabs.

Being made aware of his sketchy location from the poor address on his mail, Duncan gave consideration to naming his run. He had heard the natives refer to himself and his hut as what sounded like *kooringal,* liked the sound of it and decided that would do.

With pride a few days later, he wrote home to Scotland by candlelight with his quill on a spare page torn from his journal informing his parents that he had settled on what he considered a fine estate that gratified him, claiming it would ensure his wealth. He mentioned his sheep tally and acreage so his family could compare how vast was the land to be had out here in the Port Phillip colony matched against the limited holdings back home. But he took the greatest pride in enclosing a cheque in part payment of his father's selfless loan, since a bank note carried an exchange fee when cashed.

But it was in the depths of the following wet mid-winter that brought Duncan an unexpected and confronting surprise.

He stood astride in his hut doorway peering into the thick rain sheeting across the landscape, avoiding the trail of drops that periodically ran off the thatched roof edges above. He frowned to see Nunga, barefoot and sodden, draped in a kangaroo skin cloak worn over one shoulder and fastened at his chest, materialise through the haze. Curious to see a young tribeswoman thin and shivering at his side, Duncan recognised her as the girl he had admired last summer on the day of the burn off.

Duncan nodded to acknowledge their arrival, making no comment, certain the visit had a purpose.

'Roos all gone. Jumbuc eat all roots,' Nunga said. 'Boss gib blackfella tucker. Wantem bacca.' He held out an empty pipe to be filled and nudged the young woman forward. 'You like it gin. Stop one little time.'

The girl stood quiet and resolute before him, gathering her own pelt rug more tightly around her, huddling into its rudimentary warmth.

Stunned, Duncan realised Nunga was offering him this young woman in exchange for food. The native, in his childlike simplicity took it for granted Duncan would accept the exchange. He noticed that when offered gifts, the natives' anger usually disappeared. It seemed a matter of honour and permissible for Duncan to use this woman if proper compensation was made. In this case, food, growing scarce now in July with the advent of sheep banishing kangaroos and other game to more distant feeding grounds.

Seeing Duncan's surprise and hesitation, Nunga added frankly, 'Nunga mob back there hungry, boss.'

He gestured behind him and Duncan wondered where they were camped in this bleak season for he had not sighted them in months. The girl stood meekly between them, head bent, accepting the proposed exchange.

Duncan's amazement was overshadowed by the right for such a small price that this man was granting. He knew the woman would be only a temporary gift. He had already decided to accept the offer. His agreement would keep the natives fed and content while satisfying his own raging needs.

Duncan smiled, nodding his approval of the arrangement. As Nunga walked away alone, laden with his requested bounty, an unblinking Ginny steadily held his confounded gaze.

He signalled and she followed him indoors. Two candles

flickered low in the murky semi-darkness and, for a moment, Duncan regarded her standing compliant before him.

'Gin? Ginny?'

She stared at him wide eyed, unmoving, silent. He scratched his head, confounded, but excitement and need soon built to such an ache of anticipation, his body stiffened and he found the resolve to step closer and touch her bare skin. It felt like velvet, her dusky face soft in the dimness.

Suddenly she opened her skin cloak and it dropped onto the bare earth floor. Roused at the sight of her nakedness and firm luxuriant breasts, Duncan swiftly discarded his clothes and drew her toward his flimsy bed, praying it was strong enough to support both their weight else he would be obliged to take her on the floor.

Her placid acquiescent manner only stirred him to a greater urgency knowing she was his for the taking. He saw no need to wait and entered her with such a thrill of power and anticipation to savour this young dark-skinned beauty, his thrusting was only brief before the release of his satisfaction.

Afterwards he fell into a doze. When he woke, Ginny was seated cross legged on the floor, once more wrapped in her rough cloak. Unsure if his privilege extended to multiple favours, he beckoned to her. Offering him a gentle guarded smile, her first shy show of emotion, her teeth flashed white against her brown skin, glowing copper in the half light. She slid the covers from her shoulders and returned to him, a warm willing body, accepting his permission.

This time he enjoyed her more slowly, his first turbulent frenzy of need now spent. By nightfall, Ginny was gone.

From time to time throughout the winter, Nunga and Ginny would silently reappear at his hut, standing mute, their mission understood. The natives' arrival signalled the needs of the tribe, Duncan's ability to help and his compensation for the trade.

At these times, Ginny now readily entered his hut no longer as wary and fearful as her first visit, occasionally even beckoning to him with the palm of her hand down, as was her custom, a compliant partner.

Gradually her clipped English developed so they shared a stilted conversation. Duncan found the woman's cheerful humour lightened his loneliness but shook his head in amusement at her mystical beliefs. From her, he learned that the sun woman lit the day and the moon man made his night journey across the sky.

The last of spring shearing was further delayed into November by cold tempestuous rain. Duncan noticed an improvement in his sheep and growing lambs. Those flocks grazing on the burnt country quickly fattened on the fresh sweetened grass and his carrying capacity doubled. With this knowledge, he determined to continue the practice of burning off, vastly increase his stock numbers and begin selective breeding, keeping his rams from the ewes except for lambing.

By early summer, Ginny's young body was swelling with child. Since early spring and amid the long work of harvesting the crops sown until the men sweated in the heat until the sheaves were gathered, Ginny had loitered, spending more and more time within sight of the hut. Duncan wondered if this new situation was because she carried a white man's child and she was perhaps unwelcome in her own people's camp, or simply her attachment to him.

Sometimes she slept alone down by the river covering herself with sand, against mosquitoes. She continually produced small gifts of food, gathering crayfish with her toes or a yam stick from the shallow waterholes or submerging herself amongst the river reeds to catch a duck.

Ginny proved to be a woman of incredible patience and idleness. Duncan showed her simple tasks but grew exasperated by her casual approach to work. If he scolded her, she merely grinned, unconcerned. He swallowed his intolerance, accepting her loyal and simple obliging ways.

By early autumn, Ginny's stomach bulged. He knew the men gossiped and cast side glances at his native woman companion with envy. Duncan kept watch to protect her but he held his fondness for the girl at bay. Ginny could never be a part of his future plans.

Because of the brisk development of his run, Duncan was kept busy, rarely travelling to Geelong or Melbourne although now a regular steamer every ten days plied between the towns for a one pound fare. Temptation was slight for he possessed all he needed in the bush.

Large parcels of land were progressively being occupied with the Wedge family now on a run of twelve thousand acres near the coast on the other side of the ranges and Henry Gisborne appointed the new Crown Lands Commissioner to police the district.

Accustomed now to Ginny's presence around the hut, Duncan frowned one morning as he emerged to build the fire for breakfast, thinking it unusual she was nowhere to be seen. The natives often suddenly disappeared but he missed her happy nature. Her absence emphasised his reliance on her help if promised the simplest of treats.

Toward evening, as he sat outside by the fire writing the day's events and statistics in his journal before the shortening daylight faded, Duncan looked up to see a lone figure approaching. Even from a distance, he knew it was Ginny by the way she held herself erect and her particular unhurried walk. She carried a wrapped bundle and, as she ambled closer, he realised it was a baby. His bastard child.

'Picaninny here,' she said softly, halting across the fire, wary.

Duncan felt a brief stirring of interest soon replaced by indifference but encouraged by his beckoning and smile, Ginny hesitantly approached and unwrapped the naked infant for his inspection. He had sired a son. With a sharp flash of regret, Duncan wished the child had a white mother. He would value a son to inherit the empire he had begun to build.

Ginny lifted her nose in the direction she had just come. 'Me no more go blackfella camp,' she said moodily. 'All gone long time.'

She was banished from her tribe? He had assumed Ginny would be taken care of by her people. Annoyance boiled inside him that she now appeared to be his responsibility. The native traditions seemed harsh, especially since they had offered her to him in the first place.

Duncan sighed with irritation at the inconvenience as Ginny stood silent and innocent before him. She was quite capable of looking after herself off the land but he would not neglect her welfare. Squatters like himself had seized every corner of this country for their sheep and the natives were forced to retreat but whites like himself were the superior beings here. The natives were an uncivilised nomadic people lacking the intelligence to develop the land upon which they roamed.

'Me plenty tired,' Ginny said at last.

Apparently content to present her offspring, she wandered away toward the river. Duncan marvelled that she was up walking only hours after the birth. White women stayed abed sometimes for days or weeks.

Unsettled by the fruit of his loins dwelling in full view of his hut and Ginny's calm tolerance of this addition to her life and exile from her tribe, Duncan set about preparing his supper, focusing his mind by making plans for the year ahead.

Mid-year, with the allotment of new territorial divisions in the colony, Duncan's Port Phillip district became Portland Bay, embracing all the country west of the Werribee River where the big outfit of Glenmore station had been established to the south. To the north, a more distant neighbour, Andrew Scott, had set up on Buninyong run this side of Yuilles on Ballarat.

Watching Ginny's child grow, Duncan noticed she was a casual but loving mother. In the winter, he provided a tent near his hut away from the rising river waters. She had flashed him a childishly pleased grin at the novelty of her home.

In spring, Duncan was amazed to hear from the shearers returning to the run that two single ladies, Misses Drysdale and Newcomb had taken up Smythe's Station at South Corio on the Barwon River.

But in the following years, just when life seemed full and promising, Duncan's early prosperity, along with everyone else in the district, was seriously curtailed and his ambitions challenged. The very boom that he and the other colonial sheep men had created, threatened his downfall with the onset of a depression.

The labour shortage and their high costs combined with debilitating droughts caused a disastrous slump.

Merchants and bankers had eagerly followed the pastoralists. At first prudent, they grew greedy and excited by the rapid progress and grew reckless in hazardous speculation and thoughtless extravagance.

Government administration was also blamed, putting up land for auction at low prices. Frenzied competition caused them to rise out of all proportion to sensible value. Most paper profits were not properly financed and securities became worthless. So, after the heady boom days of limitless markets, there was now nothing to be done with surplus stock. With no market for the increases supplied to a small population, the economy crumbled.

Worse, with the depreciation of station property, Kooringal and all other runs were now only worth half their value. The Land Fund that had been based on the proceeds of Crown Land and financed the shipping of immigrants for labour had virtually collapsed, plummeting to a fraction of its original funds. There was simply no money in the Government treasury. It was broke.

The colony held its breath.

By visiting Geelong, taking the time and trouble to visit his nearest neighbours and keeping his ears open, Duncan gleaned vital information. Combined with his innate frugality, his gritty determination convinced he could survive the slump.

Some had sold out at the height of the boom and returned to England rich. Duncan wasted no energy on questioning if he should have done the same because he had long term plans.

But, concerned for Lincoln, he rode across to Lakeham. It shocked him to see the deteriorating condition of William's sheep. Lincoln's noble background and lack of farming skills held him unfit for the hardships and difficulties of the pioneering colony.

On his arrival, Lincoln was smoking and pacing hear the hut, moaning and forecasting his own ruin. Crushed with despair, grizzling and negative, he complained about the poor quality of the flocks he had kept intact and never sold, classed or culled. His inbred progeny had pronounced defects. Disease and old age balanced out any lambing so his flocks had not increased.

'I hear men who borrowed heavily and paid high prices for their stock are being worst hit,' William grumbled.

Excited, Duncan shared his knowledge about boiling down sheep for tallow. 'It's a way of keeping out of bankruptcy. At least we'd get a standard minimum for each sheep. Worth considering though, eh Lincoln?'

'I'm not losing any of my flocks. I need every one of them if I'm forced to sell.'

'Surely it won't come to that,' Duncan frowned, concerned that his helpful advice had been ignored.

On his return to Kooringal, Duncan immediately made plans and took steps to safeguard his survival. By burning many a candle low at night he worked out that, based on the figure he'd heard mentioned of five to seven shillings for each animal boiled down, it was better money than shearing for his lesser quality sheep not yet bred to his increasing standards.

Duncan rode into the Geelong boiling down works on Corio quay and covered his nose against the suffocating stench and fumes. Walking around with the owner, he saw the unfortunate beasts slaughtered and stripped of their hides then thrown into a vat. Under high pressure, the meat dissolved into fat. Appalled but resigned, he struck a deal for the worst of his sheep. He would do whatever needed to be done. To last through this catastrophe, he needed to slash his expenses and make money where he could. If boiling down was part of it, he'd start droving his flocks into town. Men had already deserted their runs but he didn't plan on being one of them.

The economic trough must subside. He would ride it out.

While he was in town, he spread the word among ignorant new chums, blind to the economic collapse and the quality of stock they needed to buy, that he was willing to sell some sheep. Back on the run, at every out station Duncan combined flocks, halving the need for shepherds. This cut his costs to pay his debts and cover his living expenses. By drafting out his dry ewes for summer lambing, he increased his flocks, adding to his reserves when the revival came. As he was convinced it must.

The few men who remained on the run toiled harder but with other squatters sacking workers, jobs were scarce and they weathered the situation alongside their boss. Day after dreary day life scraped along. Duncan only allowed his men one pair of boots each year, reducing clothing and other rations.

The relentless and heartbreaking drudgery of daily struggle continued until Duncan lived and felt like a pauper. He pored over his dismal accounts at night and had no time or mood for socialising. He rarely left the run for Melbourne or Geelong and visitors were rare. So it was with interest and the possibility of temporary release from labouring that Duncan looked eastward to watch a rider crouched low over his horse approaching the home station hut at a gallop along the river flats.

As he pulled up sharply, Duncan recognised the red haired man as one of Lincoln's workers, his friend's purebred bay mare snorting and sweating from the punishing ride.

'Mick,' Duncan yelled but his big worker was already striding forward from chopping wood, his interest kindled. 'Take care of the horse.'

With a dark searching glare ignored by his boss, Mick led the exhausted animal away. Out here, horseflesh was as precious as every pound of fleece.

The small man gasped out breathlessly, 'It's Mr. Lincoln, sir. He's dead.'

Duncan clenched his jaw, glaring at the man, processing the shocking news. Still within earshot, Mick's head snapped around as he moved away.

'What happened? Where is he, man?' Duncan boomed.

'We didn't touch him, sir. Weren't nothin' to be done. He was already gone. We just left him hangin'.'

'Hanging!' Duncan hissed and his heart lurched.

From the corner of his eye, he noticed Mick halt mid-stride, his lined brown face a blank mask before he tugged the reins and continued leading the horse toward the stable. Duncan buried guilt that maybe he should have seen it coming. He forced himself to take command of the situation and ignored the shock of what his mate had done.

'What's your name, son?' Duncan snapped at the messenger.

'Rusty, sir.'

'Well, Rusty, there's food in the hut. Help yourself while I saddle us up a couple of fresh horses.'

Numb, he followed Mick to the stable where the big man was dragging the saddle off Lincoln's weary animal. His appreciative eyes dragged keenly over its muscular form, bred for stamina. William had always envied and doted on the beast. It had been his pride and joy.

The two men worked alongside each other in tense silence, the tragic situation not needing words. Duncan threw a swag across the front of his saddle for he would not make it to Lakeham much before dark and he might need to stay some nights.

Down at the hut, Duncan told Mick curtly, 'Keep an eye on things,' then rode east with Rusty.

As the sun lowered and they crossed the creek, Duncan

was reminded of his dispute with Lincoln over their property boundary. They reached Lakeham home station as the last fingers of light stretched across the grass outside the hut. Idle workmen hovered, lost, and one of them took care of the horses.

'Where is he?' Duncan addressed Rusty as they dismounted, the first words he had spoken since leaving Kooringal.

Rusty nodded toward the woolshed and led the way.

'Do you have a knife?' Duncan snarled over his shoulder at the younger man, jogging to keep up with his long stride.

Rusty nodded and fumbled in his pocket, slapping the sheathed blade across Duncan's open palm. Bracing himself for what he would find, he took the high step up into the gloom. It took a moment for his eyes to adjust. When they did, they landed on the looped rope knotted around a thick beam above, a small stool tumbled aside. Lincoln's limp body hung dangling and still like a ghost, his snapped neck tilted to one side.

Duncan sucked in a deep breath of revulsion at the sight, mostly for William's humiliation, exposed for all to see. Himself? He'd crawl through mud to get help or save himself. He'd never give up and never consider suicide.

'Help me man.' Duncan barked at Rusty. 'Hold his legs.'

He reached up to slash the rope with one fierce swipe. Lincoln's lifeless body slumped on top of him and Duncan staggered beneath the weight before settling the load across his shoulders.

'What are you going to do with him?' Rusty asked cautiously.

'Give him a decent burial, boy,' Duncan growled.

He wrapped Lincoln's corpse in a large coarse blanket, then set the aimless men to work digging in lighter soil in a peaceful corner under the thin canopy of a eucalypt a distance from the hut. The same tree where the two squatters had lounged and talked one summer.

Meanwhile, Duncan rummaged in the hut for letters or papers for an address in England so he could write to relatives and inform them of Lincoln's demise. As he searched, Duncan cursed himself for not paying more attention to Lincoln's conversations. Bugger it. He had little respect for the man but he didn't deserve to die in such a shameful way. He didn't even know if William's parents were still alive or if the man had any brothers and sisters.

Whatever had driven him to such a gruesome end? He leafed through his ledgers to find Lakeham was bankrupt, all Lincoln's money gone. He swore. He'd warned the useless man. He was no farmer and had also proved to be a coward.

With a spark of excitement, he greedily pounced on the documents for Lakeham's lease, folded it and stuffed it into his pocket. No sense leaving a choice run go to waste, especially one adjoining his, even if it was stocked with mangy inbred sheep. He would soon remedy that. He had no idea where he'd find the money but he'd think on it.

Using the Bible found among Lincoln's stack of books in the hut, Duncan conducted a brief and simple burial service. After each of the men scattered a handful of dust, Duncan helped the men shovel dirt over Lincoln's canvas-wrapped body. They built a stone cairn at the head of the rough bush grave. Sadly, Duncan knew, the last place William would have wanted to be buried.

After pacifying the men's grumbles about not being paid, Duncan stood firm before them, feet astride, assuring them he would see them right if they stayed. He steadily scanned each bearded whiskery face and threatened any man who quit, vowing to track him down and drag him to the nearest magistrate. Then he left the least dubious man in charge until he could send Mick over to manage the run and keep Lincoln's men in line.

Cantering home alone that afternoon with all of Lincoln's papers safely stuffed in his saddle bag, Duncan mulled over why Lincoln had strung himself up. The memory of his friend's body dangling from the woolshed rafters would haunt him for years. Bush life was tough, verging on desperate. He'd seen how miserable the man had been. He would have felt trapped with no way out. On his last visit, William had sounded pessimistic and talked of giving up.

Duncan wasn't so sure the letter he would write to relatives should be the truth. Assuming his family was of equal breeding, the shame and scandal would only add to their grief. If claiming William's death was accidental, he'd bend reality and leave them with fonder memories.

That night back at Kooringal, Duncan lit his candles in the hut and leafed through Lincoln's paper trail searching for a family name and address. William had kept an impressive leather-bound journal mostly proclaiming his despair. No surprises there.

Duncan scratched his sandy hair, sculled another fiery blast of whisky and closed the journal. Feeling an intruder on Lincoln's privacy, he removed a folded piece of paper addressed to a Mrs. A. Linton, St. Mary's Cottage, Church Lane, Norwich. Maybe a relative. It looked like William intended writing home.

Duncan briskly penned a tactful note of gentle explanation to the woman and bundled it up with all of Lincoln's remaining personal papers into a parcel for the mail man next time he came through.

The Lakeham run lease he kept for himself. Although leasing a second property was a perilous opportunity that would strain the last of his funds, it was still a gamble worth taking.

Duncan made a rare trip to Melbourne. Feeling only the briefest misgiving once he held the new lease document in his hands, his deep instincts tipped any qualms aside. He felt confident knowing he now controlled two large runs of glorious country. Stepping out along the street back to the Lamb Inn, Melbourne town seemed strangely subdued compared to his previous visits.

***

The following December, as if to smite him when wool prices were down and he had exhausted the last of his ready cash, a furious hot wind swirled across the district all day. Outdoors, the weary men were half choked with bloodshot eyes from the stinging dust flung at them. The wind wailed as it streamed through eucalypts and she-oaks, hurling sticks and leaves before it. Wildlife disappeared and, as the sun set, the landscape assumed an eerie red light.

Duncan cursed the foul layer of dust that settled on everything inside the hut. Next morning, exhilarated by a change of weather and light southerly breeze, he set to cleaning up and prayed for better times. This cursed country would break your spirit if you let it.

But the following year when English speculators heard unsettling rumours from the colony, investment stopped and they withheld further capital. Banks crashed, and long lists of insolvencies were printed in flimsy newspapers.

In their bush refuge, far from the ruin of a collapsed economy, life on Kooringal run continued its sluggish predictable course. Ginny worked when she felt inclined, her pale skinned toddler son at her feet. She named the boy Duke and rarely punished or corrected the happy cherished child. At times, the lad set Duncan with a steady unsettling stare from his small dark eyes.

Fewer natives appeared these days. According to Ginny, many had died and others moved on. Some men hung about the run. With more land now but no cash, Duncan gave them work and white man's clothes in exchange for a tomahawk, tobacco or food.

Ginny, always innocently merry, scavenged for wild food. On these forage excursions, she disappeared for many hours with her pointed yam stick and dilly bag of woven grasses, Duke in a sling across her back.

In clement weather, she camped by the river but helped Duncan when persuaded and sometimes warmed his bed. If she cooked a meal at the hut, she ate it without hurry or talking. She shared the wild roots, nuts and vegetables, fish and ducks caught by the river, or a possum smoked out of a dead tree. Grubs and snakes were cooked whole in the coals of an open fire. Duncan learned to appreciate her simple offerings as a change from mutton and wondered at her skill and ingenuity. He still found her appealing, her company undemanding.

Duke's strongest attachment was to his mother and he was never far from her side. The lad was quiet but watchful, wary of Duncan. As his golden-skinned half breed son grew, Duncan found his concentration limited. His native heritage dominated.

Sitting straight-backed astride his horse on the rise above his hut, Duncan clenched his jaw, eyes squinted looking down on all he owned to the Moorabool River and beyond. Deep down, he craved a son and heir of his own kind to inherit but that longing must wait until this wretched depression eased.

It took another long year before the colonial pastoralists caught the sense of revival. Even with his dogged thrift and resolve, Duncan was broke, clinging to his runs by the smell of money alone. No matter how desperate things sank, he would never sell. The value of his Geelong town blocks had plunged like all real estate with the market but he refused to take a loss. He waited. Only half of those holding original pastoral licences remained when a fresh wave of ambitious cashed up sheepmen arrived to threaten the squatters' occupation.

With the economy slowly recovering, a renewed rush of confidence surged through the struggling colony. As the depression lost its grip, sheep were in demand again and wool prices improved. The Yorkshire spinners bought all the Australian colonial wool they could get for as much as sixteen pence a pound. Duncan quietly rubbed his hands together and predicted greater profits ahead. His sheep numbers rose. The increase of one year now fully equalled his first five years of punishing toil.

With an energised spirit and swelling prosperity, Duncan employed more men. The natives proved instinctive natural bushmen and excellent trackers of any strays from among his flocks of prized superior stud sheep. They were equally skilled on horseback.

Rumblings were heard in Port Phillip over separation from New South Wales, not least among the reasons being resentment over the large revenues from Port Phillip spent in Sydney. Representatives petitioned the home government in London detailing reasons for the split.

'To think of some gent in London holding control over our colony and the revenues from it. Master of *our* fortune and liberty,' Duncan muttered to fellow squatters.

Landholders were unhappy with the limited and fragile tenure over the runs in which they had invested so much time and money.

'We've earned the right to own the land,' they chorused.

Unrest and conflict came to a head when Governor Gipps released a proposal for a set of new squatting regulations limiting the area of runs to twenty square miles.

This unsatisfactory proposal was condemned and, two months later, outraged squatters planned a large protest meeting in Melbourne to fight for secure tenure of their land and greater control of their affairs.

Duncan rode among them down to town with his neighbours, bellowing along the way 'Downright tyranny' and 'Interfering with our rights'. He rode high and proud on his horse among the cavalcade of mounted horsemen with their bits and stirrups jingling and horses snorting in the frosty air that marched along the roads leading to the meeting place. The crowd was too large for the indoor Mechanics' Institute so it was held outdoors.

With slogans and banners flying in the breeze and highland pipers in full costume, for once Duncan was deeply stirred with memories of home and impressed with the turnout in support. They must have numbered a thousand angry souls.

On the summit of Batman's Hill, they halted and gave three cheers for the Queen. Gathered under a flag with a white star centred on a crimson background, speeches repeated the squatters' arguments and demanded a clear policy on land tenure.

Duncan sacrificed the grand ball in the evening at the Mechanics' Institute. Like many successful fellow Port Phillip squatters, when in town, he patronised the exclusive Melbourne Club, established to accommodate patrons in a manner fitting their emerging higher social status.

Striding along the still primitive and unpaved streets of Melbourne from his lodgings at Scott's Hotel, frequented by many similarly successful fellow squatters from up country, to the Melbourne Club further east in Collins Street, now the chief seat of business in town, Duncan compared the changes since his arrival seven years before, fresh off the barque that had brought him across the world from Scotland to this rough but promising land.

Now officially a town with an elected council, Melbourne sprawled for three miles along the banks of the Yarra by one mile's breadth with many fine shops and stores, their goods displayed in front, and three flourishing banks. There was even a mail run now to Sydney once a week. A fine wharf, customs house and several docks supported the vessels moving in and out for Van Diemen's Land and other colonies. A few brick and stone houses had replaced timber and wattle and daub, with many inns and hotels, churches and chapels. Street names only served to confuse for they were chalked on blackboard and were often stolen or erased.

When he reached it, Duncan climbed the steps of the Club, the comfortable chosen retreat of the colony's upper tier of the pioneering society. A liveried servant greeted him and he soon clasped firm handshakes with men he knew or had not seen for months.

A chance after-dinner conversation following a hearty meal among a circle of fellow bachelors had turned to the topic of isolation and the rare companionship of women.

'Scarce a man without a mistress, eh Penross,' Mortimer announced from behind clouds of cigar smoke.

As it was slipped to him, Duncan readily accepted the name and address of an apparently cooperative lady by the name of Mrs. Herrington.

'If she's so obliging,' Duncan muttered, voice lowered as he knocked back another whisky, 'I wonder she'll be available.'

'Ah,' he smiled through narrowed eyes and a fog of smoke, 'Mrs. Herrington is a most discerning lady. Few gentlemen gain her favour and pay handsomely for it when they do. You might suit. She seems to prefer a rough edge. Widow. Husband was a sea captain. Stranded in the colony after he died.'

Duncan disliked the man but his recommendation sounded promising. Ginny's brown skin and young body had excited him once but he craved the touch of a white woman again.

That had been some months ago. Now, in town again, Duncan handed an addressed envelope to one of the hovering stewards in the Club's drawing room library to be immediately delivered. While awaiting a reply, he digested the pages of the current newspapers, accompanied with whisky and cigars. He missed the country while in town but it was a necessary sacrifice to engage more men before lambing and winter made the roads impassable.

As time passed and never a patient man, Duncan grew edgy.

When the missive arrive, he leapt from his comfortable chair, drained the last of his drink, butted his cigar and marched from the Club. Dismissing a hansom cab, he paced out with boyish vigour west toward William Street before continuing to his destination at its northern end opposite the recently developed Flagstaff gardens.

His hostess insisted upon dusk, so Duncan stood outside her neat stone residence in the early evening, shuffling and eager. From their one previous assignation, it was clear Mrs. Herrington demanded certain standards. Anxious to please, Duncan clutched a knot of lavender and two or three other blooms in pink snapped up from a girl flower seller in tattered clothes and oversized boots. He patted down his unruly sandy hair, stepped up to the white painted front door and knocked.

When it opened, he nodded slightly, said, 'Evening, Mrs. Herrington,' and thrust his posy forward.

Words escaped him as he ogled the composed female vision standing so poised before him. He remembered every inch of her voluptuous body.

Her thick light brown hair was gathered up as before in an elegant sweep. Her tawny eyes twinkled and her rosy lips spread into the hint of an amused smile as she accepted his gift.

'Mr. Penross.' She dipped her head.

What remained of the early evening light shed a pale golden aura over her lacy light coloured dress. Pinched in tight at the waist and enticingly fitted to her full figure, the neck was encouragingly low again, revealing the deep crease between her breasts. Duncan admired a woman who was proud of her wares. No jewellery blemished her creamy skin.

'Won't you come in,' she murmured, turning in a rustle of skirts and waft of floral scent, leaving him to latch the front door and follow along the now familiar hallway down the centre of the house to a small private sitting room at the rear, overlooking a small courtyard faintly visible through folds of lace curtains.

A decanter of whisky and two glasses sat on a silver tray on the low table before a long deep sofa. Duncan recalled how they had sunk into it last time and lost themselves soon after greetings and pleasantries ended.

Their instant attraction had lit a spark of passion that

surprised them both but neither cared to control. Crushed beneath him, warm and willing, the breathless Mrs. Herrington had halted their feverish groping. With trousers bulging, Duncan was desperate for release and feared eviction. But, instead, the dishevelled and flushed woman had risen from the couch and caught his hand.

'I do believe we would be more comfortable elsewhere, Mr. Penross.'

Duncan soon discovered the true nature of the passionate woman behind the cool façade. A woman of unrestrained nature and experience, he eagerly anticipated a repeat performance tonight.

This time, however, she made him wait. Whether from a teasing sense of humour or admirable self-restraint, Duncan didn't care. He ached with strain to take her again and barely lasted through her polite questions, gracious interest in the activities on his properties, and the politics of the day.

Suddenly, conversation ceased and her gaze settled intently upon him. She rose, cast a knowing glance over her shoulder and disappeared. Duncan read her silent signal and followed.

She was lighting a lamp as he entered her bedroom, all white, feminine and sumptuous with an embroidered counterpane and thick lace drapes across the window. That she managed such a small haven of luxury compliments of her select admirers, he preferred not to contemplate. Feeling jealous and an unjustified sense of ownership after such short acquaintance, Duncan ignored his raging envy at sharing this luscious woman.

His resentment faded when she scooped up her skirts and worked beneath layers of petticoats to remove her drawers. Sharing her eagerness, Duncan sat on the wooden chair and pushed off his boots. Before he could remove his trousers, she moved to stand over him, catching his urgent trembling hands with her own, soft and white. She bent over and deftly unbuttoned him to release his erection.

She sighed and whispered as she raised her skirts and settled astride him. 'I want you every way, Mr. Penross.'

Her hand guided him into place, her wetness revealing her equal readiness. Her eyes closed, her head tilted back and she gasped. With her hands on his shoulders, she began to move, rocking and pushing against him. Lord Almighty, Duncan breathed. He was so ready, it wasn't long before he exploded inside her.

They sat locked together for a moment until Duncan growled, 'I want to see all of you,' and quickly undressed her.

At some point they separated and, with all their clothes finally discarded, knelt together on the bed. Her breasts overflowed in his hands and breathless moans escaped her mouth as she led Duncan's hand between her legs for her pleasure. Then he filled her again and they indulged once more, but slowly this time.

She refused his kisses but Duncan found satisfaction in their coupling and her genteel company. The practised Mrs. Herrington loved to experiment. A woman after his own heart. Duncan privately moaned that his bush home was so far away and vowed to visit her as often as possible.

Had she been his own age and not perhaps ten years older, widow Herrington may even have suited as a wife. But being notorious and almost past bearing children that was impossible. As he dressed again hours later, Duncan's chest wrenched with a deep ache at leaving her warm fulfilling company.

'Until next time, Mrs. Herrington,' he said before opening the front door.

'Portia,' she whispered, a black silky robe loosely draped around her body, hair long since tumbled free over her shoulders.

Duncan smiled. Following her murmured suggestion during his prior visit that he should be as benevolent as he felt she deserved, he had discreetly left a small calico bag filled with gold guinea coins. He expected his generosity to play in his favour and reveal the depth of his interest.

But as he retraced his steps back to the Club in the dark unlit Melbourne streets, Duncan's mind began to focus on the future.

An Imperial Waste Lands Act had been introduced that divided the colony into districts. In the intermediate areas that included the whole of the western district of Port Phillip where Duncan's holdings lay, he had first option on the auction of any land within his runs. The annual licence fee remained the same but was applied to land with a grazing capacity of four thousand sheep and a further fifty shillings charged for every thousand grazed on the leased land.

The squatters had won the power of exclusive purchase, security during their lease and compensation for improvements.

Seeing the prospect of golden years ahead and bolstered by this new security, Duncan replaced his hut with a more permanent home. He set his men and specialist tradesmen to building a substantial bluestone cottage on the lower rise above the Moorabool.

A beautiful setting with a view down the slope to the river flats but he reserved the higher level ground further back for the grander homestead of which he dreamed. The modest cottage was a solid rectangle of blocks two feet thick and hand-adzed beams topped with a shingle roof. A full veranda wrapped right around with a chimney of handmade bricks across one entire kitchen wall.

The cottage would be respectable enough for a wife. He imagined a local and wealthy fellow pastoralist's daughter to strengthen his holdings. But first he needed household servants. Although Ginny still slept down by the river with Duke, he hoped he could entice her to help in the cottage under supervision.

When the furniture was finally hauled up from Geelong and installed in his new home, Duncan planted an English oak tree seedling from a neighbouring squatter. Irish, more aging and bent with every passing year, put his green thumb to good use in tackling the garden of his master's vision.

Since the cottage would only be a temporary residence until he built his masterpiece, Duncan kept his concept and plantings with future vistas and the big house in mind.

CHAPTER 3

Prim Englishwoman, Isabelle Waring, and her companion, Irish lass, Maeve Dempsey, stepped through the busy Melbourne streets in the crisp early autumn morning. Both recent arrivals in the colony, they had met by chance at the Melbourne Weekly Courier newspaper office where they presented themselves in response to a Servant Wanted advertisement. Isabelle had dashed out onto the street earlier that afternoon to secure a copy of the broadsheet as soon as she heard the newsboy cry out, for the paper was only printed once a week on Fridays.

They were told to ask for squatter, Mr. Duncan Penross, and given directions to Scott's Hotel where they were to be interviewed in the parlour. Sensibly, they decided to walk together. The road clattered with buggies and wagons trundling past, a constant stream of horses and riders, and hawkers yelling out as they pushed their carts, advertising their wares.

'Not much, is it?' Maeve said wryly, glancing about at the rough town.

'It *is* only a young colony,' Isabelle pointed out, trying to stay positive. She, too, had been surprised upon first primitive sight of it and questioned her decision to emigrate alone and start a new life here. Blackburn was more settled for sure but a grey haze constantly covered everything and many of its townsfolk were poor. A mood of freedom and possibility stirred the air here, unlike the gloom back home, a light hearted cheekiness among the newcomers from which she had taken heart.

'At least there's food but it looks grim when you first arrive, for sure. Tramping from the bay up that bush track for a mile and a half to the river.'

Isabelle grinned in understanding. 'It was a bit of a walk.'

'Praise be for the punt for I can't swim.'

'Town's nicely laid out in a square, though. Easy enough to find your way around. Have you been here long?'

Maeve shook her head. 'Still gettin' used to the place. Right strange to have winter coming when it's full spring back home. What about you?'

'I arrived a week ago from Lancashire.'

'Why did you come?'

'My mother died long ago and I was living at home with my father until he died last summer. All my older brothers and sisters are married but the spinning mills are closing down and shifting further south. Jobs are scarce and people moving away. I had nothing to keep me so, I thought, why shouldn't I, too?'

'Did you sail on your own?'

'No, with a neighbouring family called Farnworth who were emigrating. I've been staying in a lodging house with them and helping the mother look after their young children. I don't like deserting her but I need a job. As soon as I heard the paper boy on the street this afternoon, I bought a copy. When I saw the housekeeper's job, I knew it would suit me fine if I could get it. Of course, it means moving out into the country and I've heard it's isolated but I rather fancy going out to work on a sheep property. It would be a nice change from living in a town.'

'I love the country, too, but the potato famine broke my family. We were tenants on a small plot of land in Offaly. I've a heap of brothers looking for work. There was just my youngest sister, Biddy, and meself at home with our mam. Biddy stayed with mam so I came out with me two oldest brothers, Liam and Michael. Only on account of the government paid our fares, mind. Wouldn't have the money else.'

'They need workers here. Servants are in demand paying your passage attracts people.'

'I'm all for workin' me fingers off to get ahead,' Maeve announced with conviction. 'Do you know what we might be gettin' paid?' Isabelle shook her head. 'Whatever it is, I'll take it. I weren't earnin' nothin' back home and always hungry.'

Isabelle smiled to herself, amused. She liked this forthright girl a few years younger and could see them working well together in the squatter's house. Providing they acquired the positions of course. With servants and labour in demand, there was strong competition for jobs. It didn't pay to be fussy first up, she guessed. She could always move on to something better when the opportunity arose.

When they reached the hotel, they stopped out front for a moment.

'Good luck to us both, then.' Maeve's lightly freckled cheeks plumped out with an optimistic grin.

The girl's confidence boosted Isabelle's own hopes as they stepped indoors.

Duncan Penross watched the girls approach across the parlour as he sat in a comfortable chair deliberately in view of the door, smoking his pipe. They were the first to reply to his advertisement so he sized them up.

The shorter one had fiery red hair with tight curls around her freckled face springing free from under her bonnet. Her bouncy step suggested lots of energy. She'd need it. He'd expect her to work hard and help keep the cottage up to standard for when he brought home a wife. He intended to marry well and impress, although he didn't yet have an idea of his ideal spouse. He'd know when he set eyes on her.

His gaze slid to the taller one. Her glossy black hair was severely caught back from her pale serene face and disappeared, too, beneath a bonnet. She held herself straight with an air of quiet composure, hands clasped together at her waist as they drew closer. He wondered if her features improved when she smiled. Earthy women tempted his male appetite so he grew annoyed with himself for feeling any interest in this prudish specimen with her thin sour lips when he had only last night savoured the delights of his luscious mistress, more woman than either of these girls would ever be. Still, although he reckoned she would be dreich, she'd keep his house in order.

As he looked between the women, it was easy enough to guess who was applying for each job.

The dark solemn one spoke first, all earnestness and business. 'Mr. Penross?' Her large almond eyes widened and critically assessed him.

'Aye.' The red haired lass bobbed a curtsy. He noticed the serious one didn't bother. 'Names?' He didn't ask them to sit.

'Miss Isabelle Waring and I'm here about the housekeeper's position.'

She flushed and seemed to grow a mite flustered. Nervous, he supposed. He couldn't help that and had no intention of putting them at ease. He needed servants and wanted to know they were capable. They looked decent enough. Their dresses were plain but clean.

'Experience?' he barked.

Her gaze sharpened and she swallowed, darting him an indignant glance. 'I ran my family home for many years. I was responsible for all cooking and cleaning and washing. Also the payment of all accounts. I can read and write and am quick with numbers.'

Hmm, sheltered. Lived at home but at least she had some education with a touch of class lacking in the other one. The fact she appeared to regard him as an equal and not superior in any way gained his amusement. She might be staid but she had backbone. He shuffled uncomfortably under her critical stare and felt himself lacking. She was a wee serious but a woman like that would help raise the tone of his household for his future wife.

He squinted. 'Age?'

'Twenty, sir.'

He turned his attention to the other one. 'What about you?'

'Miss Maeve Dempsey, sir.' She curtsied again.

'Age?'

'Eighteen, sir.'

'Experience.'

'I love to cook. I've helped me mam and I'm a hard worker. I could find me way around any kitchen.'

'Can you make bread?'

Her hesitation over his abrupt question troubled him but she didn't blink when she eventually replied. 'Absolutely, sir. I'm not big but I can knead a batch of dough the same as a woman twice my size.'

Duncan grinned to himself. He liked her spirit. Weak people annoyed him. 'Then, being so strong, you could take charge of the washing?'

'For sure I could, sir,' she assured him, earnestly blind to his teasing.

Duncan analysed the two young women standing expectantly before him. He'd hired plenty of men and lived in the colony long enough to determine a person's character on short contact.

He glanced from one to the other and barked out a warning. 'My run is a hundred miles and two days' travel from here.' He waited for one or both of them to back out but they only stared back at him in silence. 'If you don't suit, I'll not keep you on. Understood?'

Miss Dempsey's green eyes twinkled into life and her voice lilted with excitement. She had just caught on that he was offering her a job.

'Yes, sir.'

If Miss Waring, on the other hand, felt any pleasure or satisfaction in his promising remark she hid all trace of emotion behind a sober expression that bordered on disinterest.

'Certainly, Mr. Penross.'

'All right then. Miss Waring, you have the position of housekeeper at thirty-six pounds a year and full board, and you'll be assisted by Miss Dempsey here when you need it.'

She spared him a half nod of acknowledgement. 'Thank you, Mr. Penross.'

Again, those eyes absorbed him at length before she glanced away, once more as if self-conscious, before she won the struggle and regained her poise. He privately gloated over her lapse, for the first time sensing the upper hand. He had no idea what he had done or how he had achieved it, except for giving the woman a job. It would prove entertaining living under the same roof.

'Miss Dempsey, you'll be cook at thirty pounds a year and full board, and help Miss Waring. I'll be expecting you both to earn every penny.'

'Oh, thank you, sir,' she gushed. 'I'll do me best.' She shifted from one foot to the other.

'The steamer Aphrasia leaves for Geelong in the morning from Raleigh's wharf down on the river at half after seven. I expect ye both to be on time.'

'Thirty pounds a year,' Maeve squealed, gripping Isabelle's arm with delight as they strode light heartedly back along Collins Street. 'Could you help me write to me mam so I can tell her? Else she'll worry.'

'Of course, but you best come back to the boarding house with me so we can write it and you can take it to the post office before we leave town tomorrow.'

As they neared her lodgings, Isabelle frowned, strangely troubled. On the one hand she had experienced a fascination for her new employer. A great hulking Scotsman with a face full of whiskers like most men out here. On the other, she disapproved of his rough manners. He was probably honest enough but his clothes didn't fool her for a moment. He was no better than she and Maeve.

Except for his gruff manner, he could have passed for a half decent gentleman. He was tall but she wasn't sure she'd call him handsome, despite a reasonable looking brown face and good head of light coloured untidy wavy hair. His moleskins were just a fit over his muscled legs and his coat swung carelessly open over a blue serge shirt.

She remembered her foolish blushing when Mr. Penross had spoken to her, mortified to let her composure slip. But the bushman's strong personality and engaging charm caused a flighty reaction in her stomach.

Still, she brimmed with an annoying curiosity about him and being housekeeper on his Kooringal run was a place to start. In time, she'd seek a better position.

Maeve was smitten, too, gabbling on and grinning stupidly up at the man all through the short interview. And that was another thing. He either didn't have many applicants or he was short of time for he had taken them on without much fuss.

'Where's Geelong, then?' Maeve asked.

'Further around the coast I believe.'

'Not sure I'm looking forward to more time on the sea after spendin' months on it already gettin' here.'

Isabelle laughed at her wry comment as she led her around to the side door of a small timber house to access her tiny single room at the back. After introductions to John and Elizabeth Farnworth, Lizzie practically fell on Isabelle with dismay despite learning of her good fortune in securing well paid respectable employment.

'Izzy, what will we do without you, lass?' the saddened mother moaned.

Toddler Isaac, the youngest child of four, all with sandy curls, held out his arms. Isabelle scooped him onto her knee. She had never thought of herself as maternal but the softness and warmth and innocence of these children had brought out her protective instincts.

The family crowded into the room she shared with eight year old Sarah. The parents perched on the bed, the younger children wide-eyed and cross legged on the floor.

'I do feel bad at leaving, Elizabeth, for you've been so generous and kind to me but you understand it's my chance to start making my way on my own.'

'Of course, dear.'

The mother squeezed her hand and herded her brood from the room so Isabelle could write Maeve's letter and pack her few belongings together for the morning. It took time but Maeve's letter home was eventually done, addressed and ready to be taken to the crude bark hut post office where it would be entrusted to the next vessel sailing for England. The women arranged to meet at the wharf the following day.

At first light on the Saturday morning, in her usual methodical fashion, Isabelle dressed in her travelling outfit, tied on her only bonnet and double checked all her possessions were in the portmanteau before hauling it quietly to the door.

She and Elizabeth had agreed not to wake the children and distress them further for they had all grown attached, so they had said their goodbyes last evening. Amid firm hugs and dripping tears from Elizabeth, staunch best wishes and a handshake from John, with promises to write, Isabelle bravely turned and waved one last time. A lump formed in her throat at the sight of them both standing in the doorway still in their nightclothes.

Isabelle usually held herself in check but was deeply touched with emotion at their parting. She had been with the Farnworths over six months now and warmly included as part of their family.

It was barely six o'clock but Isabelle had allowed herself plenty of time for the half mile walk to the river, especially since she was lugging a heavy bag. She stopped once to rest but, on arrival, easily noticed Mr. Penross for he stood head and shoulders above everyone around him. It was hard to miss that crop of wild sandy hair. Flecked with ginger she noticed in the bright clear sunlight. Although his uncouth nature was annoying, her spirits rose to see a familiar face again.

'Isabelle.'

She heard Maeve's clear voice calling out to her. Scanning the small crowd waiting to board, she caught sight of her friend's waving arms, red hair barely controlled beneath her bonnet, face wreathed in smiles.

'Did you post your letter?' Isabelle asked.

She nodded. Preoccupied, Mr. Penross barely acknowledged them as they waited patiently nearby to embark on the voyage to Geelong. Following his lead, they hauled their baggage down the small timber wharf where the steamer waited. It was a long low ship with two masts, a central smoke stack and paddle wheels. The women trailed him aboard to a fore cabin.

A short time later, their ferry moved away from shore and started downriver. After a short stop at Williamstown taking on more passengers and cargo, they headed further down the western side of the bay, their vessel chugging and pushing through a slight swell.

During the six hour sea journey, Isabelle found her thoughts centred on their destination, frequently interrupted by Maeve's chatter, until the vessel entered Corio Bay. Eager to glimpse Geelong, the women moved outside.

A blast of wind hit them and they steadied themselves to view a semi-circle of green undulating cliffs ahead on the distant shore rising above a smooth sandy beach. A terrace of houses sat on the slope above. To their left were thickly wooded hills.

They pulled up alongside a steam packet wharf for coastal vessels. After gathering their bags and disembarking, the women followed Mr. Penross. His long strides quickly carried him further ahead so that the women, flagging from the early start and day's travel, were forced to hurry to keep up with him. As they trudged to nearby Mack's Hotel on Corio Terrace,

Isabelle noticed his face had lightened since their arrival and gaining land.

Geelong was unquestionably a wool town with huge bluestone wool stores and loaded drays, not to mention the forest of bare ship masts sticking up at anchor in the bay, the vessels in various stages of loading and unloading.

Mr. Penross loudly greeted the hotel owner, Abram Atkins, by name. Isabelle and Maeve took their hearty evening meal and welcome cup of tea alone together for Mr. Penross had been invited by the licensee to view his architect's design for a new hotel. Later, they gratefully scrambled into the single beds of their shared room.

'I don't mind what I've seen so far of this new colony, Maeve,' Isabelle yawned before she fell asleep. 'And I can't wait to see Mr. Penross' home.'

'I hope it's not as rough as its owner,' Maeve grumbled with good humour.

Isabelle blew out the candle and frowned in the dark. Rough manners, yes, but she predicted he would be a reasonable boss.

Isabelle stirred while it was yet dark at the sound of pounding on the door.

'We're away in thirty minutes,' Mr. Penross bellowed to them from the other side.

She rubbed her eyes, shook a sleepy Maeve awake and hastily dressed. There would be no chance to explore the town. A breakfast of eggs, ham and big chunks of heavy bread awaited them before departure.

Out in front of the hotel, a stocky man, his sun-browned face buried in a forest of whiskers and streaked with ginger to match his tangled hair, was fleetingly referred to as Red. His chunky muscled arms easily swung baggage and sacks of supplies up onto the wagon.

'It'll take all day to get out to the run,' their boss muttered, pacing, 'Make yourselves comfortable up back.' He indicated the rear.

Directed to clamber aboard, the women heaved themselves up to perch and settle as best they could, their boss and Red up front on a rickety wooden bench seat. The sun smiled down, drenching them with warmth. Isabelle could barely believe this was autumn weather with winter approaching. Back home, even in spring, she would likely be wearing her thickest coat and gloves.

The two massive horses struggled to haul the wagon underway and they rumbled inland, crossing Fyans Ford near what they learned was the junction of two big rivers, the Barwon and Moorabool. Another ford several miles further upstream provided access to the lands to the north.

'Kooringal run's on the Moorabool,' Red said over his shoulder, grinning.

Isabelle suspected he was taken with Maeve but the girl gave no indication of the slightest interest.

It wasn't long before Maeve lay down, rested her head on a lumpy sack and fell asleep. Isabelle looked down on her companion and sighed, wishing she could do the same but, after a reasonably comfortable bed and good night's sleep, her excitement bubbled over everything about this strange country. Her home, at least for a while, and she didn't want to miss a thing.

It surprised her to notice a small vineyard with neatly tended rows, their leaves already turning russet. But mostly, wherever you looked, there was nothing but pastures and sheep. Thousands of them. She'd never seen so many in her life, not even in Lancashire. With its wide open rambling spaces, the countryside was not the picturesque emerald green of England. Nor were there any fences or hedgerows. The land just stretched on forever without stopping for as far as you could see.

Occasionally, Mr. Penross and Red's deep murmured tones floated to her in the back but mostly the day's journey passed in silence. Except for the shrieking sounds of vivid red and green birds and the distant bleating of sheep. Only the rare appearance of a traveller heading in the opposite direction for Geelong relieved the tedious miles. Mostly they waved and exchanged greetings.

Around midday, their party stopped to eat and rest the horses. The women jumped down from the wagon and scrambled into the cover of sparse bushland to relieve themselves. When they returned, Mr. Penross had retrieved the basket of food from the hotel. Cold sliced meat, more slabs of bread, boiled potatoes and eggs.

Meanwhile Red had built a fire and boiled what Isabelle learned was a billy, a blackened tin can of water. When it boiled, he tossed in a handful of tea leaves. Later, moist brown sugar was added and he stirred the pot with a twig of eucalyptus. When she drank it, Isabelle tasted the not unpleasant tang of mint. She had smelt the aroma all through the bush as they slowly jolted along.

Despite leaving at sunrise and travelling all day, it was near dusk by the time they reached their journey's end. But sufficient daylight remained that Isabelle could still distinguish the outline and surrounds of a cottage.

Her attention peaked at the sight of the pretty dwelling on the side of a gently sloping hill that led down to a river. A substantial well finished residence. The rectangular dark grey stone building boasted glass windows and doors, and was surrounded by a wide veranda. Young scarlet and purple creepers had begun to scramble and twine their way around the base of the posts, their tendrils reaching upward for the roofline.

The enchanting setting and respectable modest home banished any concerns Isabelle might have had at rarely sighting any other houses or humans since leaving Geelong.

Beyond, in the shadowed distance of encroaching twilight, she vaguely made out thin clouds of hovering dust that led her gaze toward men and animals moving among outbuildings, stables and fenced yards. Against her will, Isabelle's admiration rose. Mr. Penross had already carved out quite a holding here.

With a light enthusiastic step, as the wagon creaked to a stop at the front, Duncan Penross swung down and spread a cheeky beaming smile between his two new employees.

'Welcome to Kooringal, ladies. But keep your wits about ye. The men rarely see a woman.'

With that cautionary word of advice, he led them around to the back of the house. Isabelle and Maeve exchanged glances as they alighted from the wagon, hauling their bags after them.

As they crossed the large stone flagged square courtyard, Maeve stifled a gasp of pleasure at Isabelle's side and placed and hand on her chest when shown the two-roomed detached kitchen and laundry to one side, a miniature of the main house. Mr. Penross introduced them to a wiry little red faced man called Irish, bustling before the huge open fire that lit the room and gave out welcome warmth in the cool evening. From a quick glance inside, the women caught sight of a large kitchen table, huge cupboard, wide sideboard displayed with china, cutlery and crockery, all manner of cooking pots and utensils, a large clock and a chair.

'Irish has a stew goin' when you're ready and ye'll eat out here but I'll expect you both to find your way about and take over the house from tomorrow. Breakfast at daylight and dinner when it's dark.'

The women nodded, taking in all about them.

'Ginny's gone back to her camp for the night but I've told her to come back in the morning and help ye.'

'Yes, sir.'

As Maeve nodded furiously gathering her wits, Isabelle wondered if Ginny was another maid and why she would be camped out. There looked to be more than enough room in the house.

Mr. Penross strode beneath the veranda and in through the back door. The women hurriedly trotted after him, trying to keep up.

'Ye'll find your rooms along there.' He flung an arm toward two doors to their left at the back of the house off a short narrow passageway. 'Settle yourselves in. Find your way around,' Penross muttered.

'Looks to be near a new house.' Maeve whispered to Isabelle in awe at her impressive surroundings after Mr. Penross left. 'Probably never had none before.'

Isabelle shrugged, inclined to agree, hoping that once they knew Mr. Penross' routine, they could run the household with a free hand. Doubtless he would be gone most of the day working anyway, Isabelle thought, glancing down a wide hall past a quietly ticking casement clock.

Meanwhile, Maeve and Isabelle sought out their accommodation to unpack. A small compact room each with a single bed, table and lamp, cupboard to stow personal belongings, a washstand and a wooden chair. Humble though it was, the rooms were neat and Maeve in particular was entranced.

'It's far more than I've ever lived in to be sure.'

Although now past dusk and shadowed, come the morning, sunlight would stream in through the narrow multi paned window Isabelle was sure.

On the first evening of their new life on the property, Maeve and Isabelle settled in and unpacked. With few possessions, the task did not take long. Later, out in the kitchen, they took a meal with Irish, Maeve's eyes bright with excitement over the huge kitchen, fully stocked larder and well equipped laundry.

'Mr. Penross is not a poor man,' she said in a voice soft with awe.

'The boss has worked hard and smart,' Irish said quietly before outlining the weekly rations of mutton, flour, tea and sugar the workmen received in their huts.

Maeve's gaze widened. 'That's more meat than we ate in a year at home.'

Irish shrugged. 'The men eat it every meal.'

'Three times a day?'

'They work hard. Besides, sheep and cattle are to hand. Grain, flour and potatoes have to be carted in.'

'You don't grow potatoes, then?'

'A few but this ain't Ireland, lass. Sometimes we get 'em up from the Henty's down on Portland Bay but mostly they grow 'em in Van Diemen's Land and bring 'em over.'

'Who's Ginny?' Isabelle asked, curious to know about the other female on the property.

'A native girl.' The women exchanged an intrigued glance. 'Lives in a hut down by the river but helps in the cottage. Comes and goes. Not reliable or regular like. Tends to wander off. She'll help when she's about but you'll need to be tellin' her exactly what she's to do, mind.'

Next morning, Isabelle accompanied an excited Maeve, eager to explore her domain and thoroughly investigate her kitchen. The new young cook ran her hands respectfully along the huge jars of rice and sugar, and China tea in chests.

In the courtyard, Irish pointed out the hand pump worked from a huge underground tank of fresh water then led them down broad stone steps to the cellar door outside the kitchen, only its domed roof visible above ground. He unlocked it and handed the key over to Isabelle.

'Shouldn't Maeve have custody of this?'

Irish shrugged as he lit a candle on a small shelf just inside the door. 'Suit yerself.'

Along the walls, Irish told them the line of metal bins was used against damp for bulk sugar, raisins, tea and flour. Above were shelves filled with biscuit tins and jars of jam preserves, tobacco, matches, salt, pepper and pocket knives. Maeve's mouth often dropped open and soft gasps escaped. Even in the dim underground room, her eyes shone with delight.

When they emerged again up into glaring sunlight, bright even on this winter day, a handsome young black woman stood in the courtyard. An olive skinned boy aged about five dogged her gangly legs and bare feet sticking out like pins below a baggy cotton dress hanging loose on her thin body.

'This is Ginny and her son, Duke.' Irish introduced them with an insignificant wave of his arm.

Ginny gave a shy giggle, flashing white teeth and pointed to her dress. 'White fella clothes, Missus.' She looked at Isabelle then pointed toward the kitchen, nodding at Maeve. 'Missy in there?'

The women nodded, polite and dumb, stunned to hear the crude basic English tumbling from the girl's full mouth. Her sooty eyes flashed over them with guarded curiosity. She beamed an innocent smile then shambled away, the child silently watchful trailing close behind.

As Ginny and the boy disappeared, Maeve leaned closer to Isabelle and whispered, 'Wouldn't be surprised if that Duke isn't a white man's child.'

Isabelle raised scandalised eyebrows.

'Well, he's paler skinned. Any man around here could be the father.' She kept her voice low.

Isabelle was shocked to hear of such goings on. A half caste child?

'Well, Mr. Penross did warn us about the men, didn't he?' Maeve grinned, giving Isabelle a gentle nudge.

She asked Irish tentatively, 'Do you think it would be all right now to go and explore the house?'

He gave a half nod. 'Boss has ridden out.'

Given the freedom to explore, Maeve enthusiastically wandered off through the cottage with its freshly painted walls and fine furniture. Isabelle hesitated. On unfamiliar ground, she felt like a trespasser but cautiously followed her friend. All eight rooms opened off the wide central hall, each with cedar doors and deep window sills jutting out before latched square paned windows similar to their own rooms at the back.

'The dining table near fills the room,' Maeve whispered as though someone might be listening, reverent in such a pleasant setting. 'Wonder who he invites to dinner to fill up them ten chairs?'

Isabelle admired an ornate carved sideboard along a side wall and a yawning fireplace at the far end. They'd certainly landed on their feet and would be living in agreeable surroundings. With no regrets, she remembered her family's rented terrace house in Blackburn with its poky rooms and the ginnels behind which people dumped waste and ash from the fire grates.

Across the hall in the sitting room, a thick central carpet square cushioned their boots but a polished timber floor extended around its outer edges. Two deep comfortable sofas and matching single chairs were grouped around the fireplace. On a small side table a half empty whisky decanter and crystal glasses were laid out on a tray.

'Likes a fine drop, then,' Maeve grinned, at ease with investigating her new surroundings.

Isabelle took the liberty to peek under the great hulking shape hidden beneath a dust sheet to discover a piano in the corner. 'Its so shiny, looks like its never been used.'

Beside their own small servant bedrooms at the back of the house, five spacious bedrooms were located at the front half of the house, some opening through French doors directly onto the front veranda. All featured carved timber and tasteful covers with an ample wardrobe, washstand table and bedside lamps.

Maeve bounced up and down on one, giggling, 'Softer than ours,' until Isabelle urged her off.

'Don't make more work for me tidying it up,' she chided kindly.

A massive cedar desk sat proudly beneath a window against one wall in their master's office. The smell of tobacco lingered in the room from his wooden pipes and a stack of station account books and a leather bound diary littered its surface. A number of guns and rifles hung above the fireplace.

Isabelle frowned, feeling a lonely air about the rooms. Not

surprising with just one man living here.

In their first days on the Penross run, Isabelle was satisfied to see that Irish, despite his aged shuffling manner, always managed to keep supplies of firewood stacked and she ensured the logs blazed in the huge fireplaces pushing out warmth into the few occupied rooms.

Ginny appeared erratically in the kitchen, fascinated only it seemed by the two female newcomers, then melting away so that they hardly noticed her missing. When she did help, Maeve constantly grumbled in exasperation. 'The girl knows nothing. I'm quicker doin' the work meself.'

Through hand signals and gabbled communication that took much patience, they soon realised Ginny was more suited to simple tasks but foolishly fond and doting of her son, Duke.

As for Isabelle and her housekeeping, she soon set a routine of daily chores, retrieving a duster, broom, mop and bucket from the laundry to scrub the polished wooden floors. She tidied the master's room and made his large bed, feeling it strange at first to fossick in the cupboards in this private domain seeking out and checking clothes that needed mending, and buttons replaced, appalled at the scruffy basic contents.

It also troubled her that she daily needed to refill the contents of the whisky decanter in the sitting room. Each evening, Mr. Penross used it until late after dinner and work in his office, draining it of a good portion.

Her duties were more or less what she'd done in her father's house back home but at least she was getting paid for the work. She carried it out efficiently with attention to detail. It wasn't long before her pride and dedication in the work drew appreciative grunts from the boss.

Each morning as he left the cottage, Mr. Penross paused to tap and scowl over the barometer hanging on a nail under the back veranda. Truth to tell, she was both relieved and regretful when he departed. His chummy relaxed behaviour toward her seemed too familiar between master and servant, despite her flattery at his interest. With females scarce out here in the bush, she judged his attention understandable, if not forgivable. Her gentle father had bequeathed her a longing for a kind hearted man above all whom she could respect, even if she was not high born. She hoped one day to meet a humble gentleman, most certainly not one like Mr. Penross.

During her master's absence each day, Isabelle easily managed the house. With her tasks complete and Maeve and Irish capably managing the kitchen, Isabelle often set off across the nearest paddock seeking wildflowers, scarce now in approaching winter, or unusual grasses. Early frosts made the ground crisp beneath her boots and the wind stung her cheeks. At a distance from the house, young trees were planted everywhere in rows. After the first winter rains, clumps of willows, poplars and acacias were thick with grass growing about their roots.

Isabelle displayed her floral discoveries in jars and vases about the cottage on tables and sideboards with always a featured display on the grand polished dining table, although she noticed the blooms tended to shrivel almost overnight and needed constant replenishment. She didn't mind for she loved wandering outdoors in the acreage around the house to seek out and collect them.

For all the pleasure she took in her work, Isabelle's mind filled with questions for Mr. Penross had so far given her no rules or instructions. Concerned over the lack, when her master returned one night, she asked him about keeping the Sabbath.

'Ah don't.'

Isabelle swallowed back her dismay. 'Then I trust you have no objection to Maeve and me recognising the day ourselves with a small service.'

She assumed his grunt was approval.

Next Sunday, Mr. Penross blundered into the sitting room after breakfast, intruding on the small assembled knot of servants singing hymns with Isabelle capably playing the piano. She noted he stayed, perhaps ashamed to leave, apparently muddled by such civilisation in his home. Isabelle's sweet voice rose above the others, Maeve's loud and tuneless beside her. Irish, Isabelle suspected, had complied merely to escape work, his practise now that hard working Maeve had capably claimed the kitchen.

Isabelle flickered a swift side glance at her master's shabby appearance for a Sunday service, following which he attended to accounts in his office. Indignant to think he worked on the Lord's Day, she had gathered a willing Maeve and reluctant Irish together regardless. She determined to uphold her faith despite her heathen employer, supported by his lack of supervision over the men cohorting with the native women, a situation that niggled her deep sense of dignity.

It didn't help when she learned from Irish that he deserted the property each Sunday afternoon to visit his neighbouring squatter friends.

'Lookin' for a rich daughter.'

Isabelle's stomach clenched at the news of another woman becoming her mistress and invading what she already regarded as her own small domain. To her surprise, she had quickly become attached and easily settled into her new life.

That evening, Mr. Penross materialised at the dining table as usual in his work clothes. Isabelle, appalled, bit her tongue to staunch a reproach that he had made no special effort with his dress on this special day of the week at least. Bubbling with dismay, Isabelle lost her struggle to remain silent.

'Are you ready for dinner, Mr. Penross?' she asked crisply.

'Aye. Ye can plainly see. Why do y'ask?'

'It's Sunday.' He looked blank. 'Your clothes.'

She wondered a man of his standing didn't take more pride in his appearance. Clearly a lack of polish in his upbringing. Such negligence would lower the standard of his house. Disappointed, Isabelle decided this lovely cottage deserved a more worthy owner. At this rate, looking like he did, he would never secure a quality wife.

Next evening, however, Isabelle noticed that Mr. Penross returned from his day's work out on the run and retreated into his room for longer than normal before reappearing wearing a clean shirt and jacket, his wavy hair brushed but ineffectually flattened in an attempt to control it. Seems he had struggled with a brush and comb to get it in order. Pleased that he had heeded her suggestion, she smiled to herself. The man was still scruffy but at least he had made an effort.

The following week, Isabelle was tidying up as usual in her master's office, always approached reverently as if she was entering a church. Her gaze was drawn to his diary. Tempted by what he recorded and what it might contain, aghast that she should even consider breaching his privacy, Isabelle gingerly opened its pages and leafed through. In a surprisingly readable if looped handwriting, he faithfully chronicled weather, barometer, wind direction, movement of clouds, livestock control and plantings in the garden. A methodical habit at odds with the forthright untidy man she knew.

Filled with shame, Isabelle quickly closed the large leather bound book but not before hesitating over what lay beneath. Absorbed in reading, Isabelle had missed half hidden plans for a house. It was certainly not the cottage for this design was grand and contained an upper storey. Maybe he planned to extend the cottage one day.

As spring arrived and the flats below the cottage grew lush with grasses, fresh leaves unfurled on the willows and bush flowers bloomed wild en masse across the landscape, Isabelle slowly registered that her master held an interest in her beyond being his housekeeper. He lapsed and called her Isabelle, to which she retorted with alarm.

'Miss Waring,' she reminded him tightly, embarrassed by his liberty and overstepping proper master and servant propriety.

As housekeeper, Isabelle happily picked up after the careless man. Dignity and self-respect kept her vigilant and attentive to his every need. Duncan Penross was an exasperating man, inconsiderate and gruff, yet aside from her duty to him, Isabelle also found him a strong magnetic personality. It niggled when he teased her and filled her with alarm to be attracted to such a rough individual so she kept her distance as much as possible when he was present in the house.

She sometimes caught him casting her long stares. Then he stopped visiting his squatter neighbours on Sundays. Instead, he restlessly prowled the cottage veranda and homestead paddock. To avoid him, Isabelle took herself off to her room reading or sewing. Mr. Penross had kindly arranged purchase of bolts of material. Now, she and Maeve carefully hand stitched seams, pintucked the bodice, and added touches of lace to the white or cream cotton shirt waists essential now in the milder weather of spring.

On certain days, bursts of strong sun drenched through clothes, far warmer already than even the balmiest English summer. After a few days, thankfully, the heat was always relieved by a cool change and refreshing breeze. Maeve marvelled that her washing dried within hours where, in winter, back in Ireland it had hung up damp on the laundry rail for days.

Restless to be confined too long in the house, Isabelle set off walking. She shaded her eyes and squinted in the distance to glimpse Duncan on horseback, his spirited black beauty prancing beneath him. Perhaps sensing her presence, he turned in the saddle and looked back. Before she could control the impulse, she half raised an arm, awed by the man's physical power.

Turning away in embarrassment at her lapse, Isabelle strode on through the bush. In her haste and inattention, she almost trod on a snake basking in a streak of sunlight behind a fallen log as she stepped over. The first time she had encountered one of the reptiles, she had frozen on the spot in terror until it mercifully slithered away. Now she carried a long stick. Irish assured her that, unless cornered or threatened, snakes would flee rather than strike.

Isabelle had seen Ginny once boldly approach and kill one. Grinning, the native girl had beckoned to Isabelle. In horrified fascination, she had followed as she dragged the reptile to her camp.

'Big one, missus. Plenty tucker,' she said, tossing the whole animal onto her camp fire.

Not wanting to be part of her barbaric ways and offered a share in the meal, Isabelle scurried back to the cottage. Ginny's happy laughter had carried to her as she fled.

That night, Isabelle kept her head down when serving Mr. Penross his dinner. Later, he called her into the sitting room and she had trouble meeting his gaze, his soft blue eyes at odds with his character.

He studied her a long time before turning to stare into the dying fire.

Duncan grew uncomfortable to be so aware of his housekeeper as a woman. Out on the run all day, he occupied body and mind. But in the lonely confines of the cottage, the sight of gentle efficient Isabelle and the sound of her soft swishing skirts as she moved about, made his longings peak. He cursed that Portia was so far away.

In times past, he held his drink. Now he didn't bother, frustrated and wired, he sank into liquid oblivion to blank out the annoying images cramming his mind of the very woman standing in front of him now, hovering, judgemental. She was so bloody respectable. He longed to take advantage.

He wanted a woman. Needed one. To satisfy the torment to sire sons to inherit his growing empire. A greater dream than the indifference he felt for this woman who could perform the task he had in mind. The idea had been brewing for some time.

These days he rarely took comfort in Ginny's body. She was black and unacceptable now with his rising social status.

He grew hot at the thoughts of his first ruttings with the girl in his randy isolation. And heaven help him, Portia was too old to bear children and so far away. He'd begged her to move closer to Geelong. Tempted her with the promise of setting her up in a house but she refused.

Now, of all women to trap his fancy, he'd never have wagered it would be his prim housekeeper, Miss High and Mighty Waring. But she understood him, seemed to accept him. Even tried to help him improve. And, curse him, he was trying to please her because, although she would never know it, she held all the cards. As she bustled about the cottage, he heard her soft humming. Her hair was usually piled up, wispy bits soft around her face. Lord help him, he was beginning to find her appealing.

It annoyed him to be liking her but he needed to break her down. Tease one of those rare sweet smiles onto her face. He'd caught it once or twice and stood still, watching, because it lit her up and made her softer. But blast it, she was so nice and proper it was sickening. Pity they seemed of a like mind and caught each other staring against their will.

She maybe felt a spark of something, too, and seemed to be thriving in the bush. With his bairns to keep her busy, she'd not be lonely. It would be a challenge to try and rouse her body up but she dodged him and he was stumped how he should go about it. He'd have to take it slow, he decided. Isabelle Waring was a woman for courtin' just when he couldn't spare the time. He'd even put up with bringing religion into his house. It seemed to be important and please her.

Yes, with Isabelle Waring by his side, he'd be even more respectable and with that fertile young body, she'd bear his longed-for heirs. Sons to ride out and manage the property with him. He'd teach them all he'd learned about culling and breeding the best stud merinos in the colony.

Duncan pushed out an impatient sigh and stole a glance at Isabelle, sitting waiting for him to speak. What he felt for her was lust not love. He shifted uncomfortably just thinking of getting inside her and filling her up with his seed for sons. If he could just convince this angel of goodness he was a decent enough man, she might be won over. Sooner rather than later for he was anxious to start and secure the future of his runs. He could never love such a stiff and proper woman. He preferred the likes of the exciting Mrs. Herrington.

But he could tolerate his housekeeper well enough. She was easy on the eye, amenable enough and seemed to fancy him. He rubbed his chin. By God, if it meant sons, he'd force himself to lift her skirts, get between her legs and bed this puritan soul.

Isabelle waited impatiently, hands clenched tight at her waist. She thought Mr. Penross had fallen into a trance or dozed off but he stirred and rallied.

'Did you wish to speak to me about something, Sir?'

'Ye will take care out there, Isabelle,' he said eventually.

'Miss Waring,' she corrected him automatically, unsmiling, dismayed at his slurred words. She presumed he meant walking. 'Yes, Sir.'

She darted a glance at the whisky decanter holding a mere splash of amber liquid in the bottom this early in the night.

'No need to be so formal.'

'There most certainly is, Sir.' Duncan mumbled something obscure. 'Sounds to me like you've had a bit much to drink, Sir.' Not the first time she had voiced her disapproval of his heavy consumption.

'Well, what do ye expect, women, with your skirts flutterin' in ma face about the house all day?'

Affronted, Isabelle straightened her spine, glaring. 'I've done no such thing. I'm here to do a job and nothing more. How dare you blame me for your own fanciful thoughts.'

She left in such a rustle of haughty skirts, it caused a draught. Exasperation fuelled her angry stitches as Isabelle sewed in her room later, pricking herself with a needle more than once and suffering drops of blood on the crisp white cotton for her frustrated inattention.

Regardless, her ears strained for her master's usual blundering as he took himself off to bed. When she didn't hear it, she tiptoed along the hall on her rounds of checking candles and fires were out to discover him slumped and dozing in his chair in the sitting room. Looking vulnerable, sandy hair drooped across his forehead, he was still a vibrant man, even in sleep. Isabelle grew breathless as she leaned closer to check he was still breathing. She jumped when he stirred and opened his bleary eyes to be caught watching him.

'Are you all right, Sir?'

She swiftly pretended her presence was out of concern and not fascination for a man who was likely not worth the trouble. Isabelle took the empty glass from his loose fingers before it slid onto the floor.

When he grunted his objection, she held it up before his rheumy gaze. 'It's empty.'

'I want it refilled.'

'At this hour of the night, I think not.'

'Don't tell me what to do, you churchy prissy woman.'

Isabelle drew back, wounded. She knew perfectly well she and the master were of two different natures and this caused their friction but he'd never been so unkind before. She hoped it was the drink talking and he didn't mean it.

'I'm only trying to help. Against my good judgement,' she muttered under her breath. 'Can you stand?'

'I don't know.'

Hands on hips, she glowered. 'Try.'

'I'll be giving the orders, Miss Housekeeper Waring. I'm the boss, not you,' he growled.

'Then act like one. Do you want help or don't you?'

Duncan struggled to stand and failed. Shaking her head impatiently, Isabelle helped lift him from his chair, avoiding the furniture as he wove a trail across the door. When Duncan lurched sideways, eyes glazed, breath foul with whisky, she draped one of his muscled arms around her shoulder for better balance as they hobbled to his bedroom and gasped under his heavy weight.

Pressed up against her, she felt his warmth through his rough clothes. She had never handled a man this close before. Mr. Penross plunged heavily onto the edge of the bed nearly missing it and sliding onto the floor. Isabelle heaved him further back. She lit candles then bent to remove his boots and socks.

'Can you get undressed by yourself?'

'Ma arms don't seem to be workin'.'

'I'm not surprised the amount of liquor you've swallowed tonight.'

Duncan's eyes glazed over, wavy sandy hair mussed over his forehead. Isabelle eased the coat off his shoulders and pulled out each arm, frustrated that such a powerful man could be so weak from drink.

'Why do you do it?' she said softly, frowning, despising herself for feeling compassion for such a coarse man.

'It's not working.'

She unbuttoned his shirt and tried not to gape at his hair-dusted chest. She turned away. Even by candlelight, his powerful manliness was fascinating.

She frowned, trying to understand. 'Do you mean your arms?'

'No!' He growled. 'Lookin' fer a wife.'

'Oh. I'm sorry to hear it.'

He tilted back his head and trained his unfocused gaze on her. 'I'm thinkin' mebbe I've just been lookin' in the wrong place.'

'Indeed.' Curious to hear why, Isabelle stepped back and listened as he rambled, purging his mind of his troubles.

'Charles, the youngest von Stieglitz at Durdiwarrah on the Werribee River is already married to Sophia.' He frowned and paused, trying to think. 'Charles Griffiths over on Glenmore returned to Dublin last year and is looking to wed Jane Magee.

John Stevens that leases Ingleby has just up and married Frances Cox over in Van Dieman's Land, and George Armytage Junior has taken over the run but he's only young and without sisters old enough. Ma fellow Scot, Gid Lang from Narmbool is always away overlanding and not settled down yet. Ah heard he's just crossed the desert south east of Lake Alexandrina.'

'Interesting.' She had no idea what she was meant to gather from all this information.

'And Atkinson on Beremboke has long been married to Elizabeth. Do ye see? Ah've no hope.'

Isabelle was too slow when Duncan reached out and grasped her waist.

'Mr. Penross!' She gripped his hands to remove them and felt their rough warmth beneath her palms. He was too strong and held her firm.

'Call me Duncan,' he grinned.

'I most certainly will not. You're my employer.'

'And you couldn't be doin' anything that wasn't right and proper, now, could ye?'

His bitter tone left her feeling starchy and deficient. She might have had a poor upbringing but she knew right from wrong and owned sound morals.

Suddenly his voice softened. 'Do ye ever think of me as a man, like?'

Isabelle stilled. She most certainly had but what was he implying? Disturbed by his endearing change of tone and trapped in the risk of not wanting to lie, she paused.

'Isabelle?' he prompted.

His hands briefly tightened at her waist, his thumbs sitting just beneath her heaving breasts. It was a wonder he couldn't hear her heart pounding, it was galloping that fast.

'Ye haven't taken off all ma clothes,' he teased.

'I should think not. You can sleep half dressed.'

'You could be taking off your clothes, too,' he suggested with a leery grin.

Isabelle was shocked by his scandalous proposition, enticing her to consider improper behaviour. Then she realised it was the whisky talking and clouding his brain.

Hiding her surprise and embarrassment, Isabelle smiled self-consciously. 'You're intoxicated, Mr. Penross. You have no idea what you're saying.'

Their eyes met and held before he lay back against the pillows and he closed his eyes. 'Ma mind's not that blurry.' He yawned. 'Ah know exactly what ah said.'

Monday, as with every day on the run, began early. It was barely daylight when Maeve and Isabelle each stirred in their rooms to the sound of cocks crowing from the fowl yard and barking dogs further out. Cows bellowed, heavy with milk, reminding Irish to rouse himself. They soon heard the clang of his buckets and whistling that faded as he wandered away.

While Maeve scuttled about the kitchen preparing breakfast, Isabelle set up the dining room. After last evening's encounter and the master's familiar behaviour, her mind was in a muddle. She could be worrying for nothing if he didn't remember a thing.

Isabelle bustled in and out of the dining room delivering food, relieved to see Mr. Penross not yet at the table, lifting the domed lids on the sideboard dishes to check his oatmeal porridge was still fresh and hot. That there were plenty of his favourite baked eggs, grilled ham, fresh bread and butter and jams, with always a large pot of tea.

These days, with the approach of shearing, Duncan was usually out from morning until dark with his men, mustering sheep in from the outer paddocks all over the run. Then the flocks were plunged into the river to wash the wool.

When Isabelle returned to the dining room a short while later, unable any avoid Duncan any longer, he was spooning up his porridge with purpose.

'Is all to your liking, sir?'

'Aye.'

'Will you be needing anything else, sir?'

'No.'

As she hastened to leave, Mr. Penross said, 'Isabelle.'

Because she had no choice, she slowly turned to face him. 'It really should be Miss Waring,' she reminded him lightly, unable to hold any resentment when she saw the roguish humour on his face.

'I think we're gettin' past first names, don't you?'

'If you insist,' she said stiffly, cautious, confused. Was Mr. Penross expressing a genuine interest in her as he had indicated last weekend?

'I thought we could take a walk together.'

She stared at him, speechless, thinking it sounded a mighty personal suggestion.

'Would ye step out with me, Isabelle?' he prompted.

'Did you have a purpose in mind?'

'None in particular.'

'If you're meaning now, after breakfast, I must refuse. Mondays I help Maeve with the laundry.'

'Will Sunday afternoon suit ye?'

She hesitated then nodded stiffly. 'I suppose I can manage the time.' She didn't want to sound too eager.

All week, Isabelle's mind blurred. It didn't help that Duncan acted as though the close encounter the previous Sunday never happened and treated her, as always, like a servant. Isabelle felt confused and discouraged. The following Sunday morning she misplayed keys on the piano during the small service. Later, she deliberately lingered as long as possible on exactly how she should dress. She changed from her dark work clothes and wondered if he would notice she had taken trouble with her hair?

When she finally ventured from her small room at the back of the house, Mr. Penross waited, smoking his pipe under the veranda. He had tidied himself up, his hair damp and combed, groomed into some order. His clothes now reflected her handiwork. Tears mended, missing buttons replaced. At least outwardly more of a gentleman.

His eyes danced over her hair and the neat white pin tucked blouse and dark skirt, newly sewn.

'Nice day for it,' he said by way of greeting.

'Most certainly.'

He continued smoking his pipe as they fell into step together. From the kitchen window, Isabelle saw Maeve watching them as they left. Catching her eye, Isabelle shrugged. She silently followed his lead as they headed downhill toward the river.

'You're doin' a fine job in the house.'

'Thank you.'

'You're a good housekeeper. Everything's runnin' smooth, like.' He paused. 'Do you like it here? Feel like you're settlin' in?'

'The working conditions are very acceptable. Maeve and I enjoy our work.'

'I was askin' mainly after you.'

'Oh. I see.'

There was a long pause as they strode together through the long grass away from the cottage.

Eventually, he said, 'As I said last Sunday, I know ye don't approve of all ma ways.' Isabelle opened her mouth to object but he quietly silenced her with a raised hand. 'I'll not pretend to be anything other than who I am, ye understand?'

'Of course.'

'I'm asking ye to accept what you see, Isabelle. So we get on better.'

For such a big blustering man to use her name so softly when he was more comfortable on horseback among animals and men, she was disarmed.

He scowled. 'Can ye do that?'

'I shall try.'

She wasn't sure what he was offering but it sounded like he had in mind a more personal friendship between them. She reluctantly acknowledged her fascination for him but filled with frustration that she should be attracted to such an unruly rogue and not more of a gentleman.

'I'm sure most people wish they were a better person,' Isabelle hedged, remaining cautious until she was more certain of his intentions.

'You're a mite stiff for yer own good.' He followed his blunt observation with a chuckle. 'But it's clear you were raised different to me. I come from a lowland sheep farm and I am who I am. But you've brought a touch of class to ma home, Isabelle.'

Flattered but wary she asked, 'What exactly are you trying to say, Mr. Penross?'

'Just askin' that we try to get on with each other, like.'

'I don't dislike you if that's what you're asking,' she said tactfully.

Despite their tendency to bicker, the pull between them seemed mutual and strong. Where it might lead, Isabelle was too terrified to contemplate. One Sunday afternoon walk at a time, she decided.

'Could you ever see yourself having an interest in me, then?' he asked cautiously, stepping closer. 'Or will ye make me suffer and keep lookin' over squatters' daughters.'

By now they had reached the sparse shade of a eucalypt, Isabelle grateful for its shelter to cool her rising heat at his words.

'I may give it some consideration.'

'Could you call me Duncan?'

'As your housekeeper, that would place me in an awkward situation. Everyone will notice-'

'I don't give a damn what others think.' He threw an arm in the air and paced.

Alarmed by his outburst, she said, 'It's highly improper, of course, but … all right. Duncan.'

Her brave glance up at him as she tested the sound of his name happened at the exact moment he looked down on her. Suddenly, he bent down and planted a warm kiss on her mouth. The touch shattered all thoughts from her mind and her whole body tingled with the soft moist pleasure of it.

'I'm away to the sheds, then.'

She was about to protest, 'On a Sunday?' but he was already striding off, dry bark and leaves crunching under his booted feet.

He had kissed her and left her just like that. She raised a trembling hand to her mouth. Duncan Penross was courting her! Shaken and excited, she needed to confide in Maeve.

'What did Mr. Penross want then?' Maeve asked a short while later in the kitchen as she poured tea from the large pot and sliced a piece of her famous tea cake.

'He suggested we use our Christian names.'

'What on earth does that mean?'

'He seems to have an interest in me. He offered friendship.'

'It's gettin' rather personal, then?' She hesitated. 'And how do you feel about him?'

'Heaven help me but I like the man. I know he's rough but he's making an effort.'

'To do what?'

'Be nicer. But it doesn't feel right, me being a servant.'

'Well he's hardly high born either, is he?' Maeve said with her usual blunt honesty. She shrugged. 'You could do worse.'

Isabelle half smiled. 'Out here in the colony, a man succeeds by his own efforts it seems. But squatters do seem to be the gentry here.'

'You're more of a lady than me,' Maeve admitted. 'You'd suit him.'

'Perhaps, but he's disappointed he hasn't found a squatter's daughter.'

'That a fact?'

'Do you think I'm only second choice?'

'Till you find out the answer to that question and you're more certain of him, I'd be takin' it slow.'

CHAPTER 4

One evening during the week when Isabelle brought a platter into the dining room, Duncan said, 'Ah noticed ye like going for walks. Would ye be interested in learning how to ride?'

Isabelle clattered the tray onto the sideboard. 'On a horse?'

He nodded and grinned, his blue eyes twinkling. He was certainly taking an interest. Isabelle was flattered but worried it was improper for any master to be favouring a servant. And Maeve had suggested caution.

'I've never thought about it.'

'Ah've a docile mare would suit ye. Tell Maeve to pack a picnic lunch next Sunday. For after your service, of course,' he added liberally, clearly having given the offer and excursion some prior thought.

Isabelle fretted for the rest of the week. What was she supposed to wear for riding a horse? Next Sunday morning, she barely concentrated on serving Duncan his breakfast and during the small staff worship service grew even more distracted from the Lord's word.

After lunch when she drew aside a front room curtain to see Duncan lead and tether two horses to the cottage railing, she gingerly stepped outside to greet him. From the mounting block, the brown horse loomed large and frightening but stood docile as Duncan helped her into the side saddle and settled her long skirts to cover her boots. Uncomfortable for her first time on a horse, Isabelle sat rigidly gripping the pommel.

'Relax,' Duncan chuckled, unlooping the reins and handing them to her. 'Find yer balance and let yourself go with the sway of the horse. Lucy'll follow yer lead.'

'I'm sure I'll get used to it,' Isabelle said grimly with more confidence than she felt.

'Practise'll do it. Ye've just to stay on.' He grinned.

In comparison, he easily swung up astride his black gelding, his strong legs in black polished boots up to his knees. With the wide hat he always wore outdoors half shading his handsome sun browned face, Duncan Penross certainly made a fine figure of a man.

Maeve appeared and handed small wrapped parcels which Duncan packed into his saddle bags. He clicked to the horses and they moved off. With a nervous smile and a wave, Isabelle gasped as she swayed with the mare's motion.

At first, they walked. The breeze brushed her face beneath her bonnet and she began to relax.

'Ye're doin' fine, Isabelle,' Duncan murmured with a wink. Too soon, he challenged her to press the mare into a trot.

'I'm not sure.' She tensed, breathless.

'Ye'll be fine but keep your wits about ye and watch out for overhanging branches. Don't want ye being knocked out of the saddle.'

Isabelle gasped, looking down to the ground. It was a long way to fall so she held on tighter. Duncan's impressive muscular horse jogged ahead as he paced his mount faster.

'Give her a nudge,' he dared, glancing over his shoulder.

Isabelle cautiously urged her mare forward, working to keep her balance with the jolting rhythm.

'Did you have horses on your farm back in Scotland?' she asked when she caught up to him.

Duncan pulled a wry grin. 'No, but I always admired the purebred horses strutting about on the laird's property.' He grew serious and their horses slowed to a walk again. 'Breeding fine horseflesh out here is as important as breeding fine-woolled sheep. A colt can sell for three hundred pounds and a three year old stallion for over five hundred guineas. The best horses are of Arab descent. Well-muscled, good temperament and don't tire easily. Every landowner hereabouts needs a thoroughbred stallion for breeding.'

Isabelle's mind flashed with images of what took place all over the property. Bulls covering cows, Duncan's prize rams paddocked with his top merino ewes. She took a deep gulp of fresh air against the fluster of embarrassment filling her chest at the thought.

When they reached the river, Duncan caught up the reins of Isabelle's mare and led their horses to stand up to their fetlocks in the clear running water. The animals dropped their heads to drink.

'We should rest awhile. Don't want ye too stiff to be doin' your housework tomorrow, eh Isabelle?' he chuckled.

He was incorrigible but she couldn't stem a smile.

'If ye like, ye can go out ridin' whenever ye want. Just tell Irish or one of the man to saddle Lucy for ye.'

'I'm not sure I'm confident enough to ride alone,' Isabelle said.

Duncan scowled. 'Ye never set out alone unless ye've experience in the bush. Always take Irish or Duke out with ye.'

'Duke?' Isabelle repeated in amazement. 'But he's just a boy.'

'Aye but the natives have a natural instinct for riding. Good trackers, too.'

Duncan dismounted first and tethered his reins over the limb of a gum tree with filtered shade to rest. He reached up for Isabelle as she unhooked her leg from around the saddle, her foot from the stirrup and slid down into his arms. When his hands settled about her tiny waist, she caught her breath.

'All in one piece, then?' he murmured.

For a confident, brash man, Isabelle was surprised to see Duncan hesitate where they stood, aligned together. His bravado deserted him for the moment and she thrilled to a small sense of her own power yet still felt awed by him.

With a grunt, Duncan released her and retrieved the food parcels from his saddle bag. As they settled on the grass together, she nibbled on one of Maeve's beef sandwiches and, for a time, they ate in mutual silence, letting the peace of the bush surround them.

The warm day and unaccustomed exercise of the ride induced a laziness that drugged Isabelle's limbs. She watched, captivated, as Duncan drank from his water flask. Droplets trickled down his chin and spread a wet stain across his shirt. Barely aware it was taking place, Isabelle's eyes lifted to catch Duncan studying her intently.

'Isabelle…'

'Yes?' Breath caught in her throat.

He leaned closer and kissed her mouth. Instinctively, Isabelle closed her eyes to savour the sudden gesture. She grew hot, as if running a fever. Mercy, his hands were straying all over her, sliding around her waist and rising higher until he cupped his hands beneath her breasts. Then he started rubbing his thumbs back and forth across them until her nipples hardened. Such liberties. And she enjoyed it. Was she supposed to? Shocked but curious, she let him have his way a while longer to see what happened next.

Another kiss, harder and deeper than the first, swamped her with pleasure and left her breathless.

'I think that's enough for today,' she gasped when it ended, quietly firm, knowing she had overstepped decorum.

A blazing passion lit Duncan's gaze, his breathing ragged, too. 'I can assure ye it gets better.'

Isabelle dabbed at her hot cheek and his blunt honesty. 'Well, I must take your word for that.'

'It's a warm day. I could loosen your clothes.' He ran a hand roughly through his hair.

Although scandalised by his suggestion, Isabelle wondered what that next step involved and how it might feel. What she should do.

'Duncan...?'

He stood, cursed and turned his back to her. When she realised he was adjusting the front of his trousers, Isabelle hurriedly swivelled away to re-button her shirt waist and fussed about packing up their picnic.

Duncan's head roared with resentment and frustration. He needed release but he wasn't going to get it today. He might need Ginny tonight after all. Anger rose in him because of her self-control and irritation boiled that he was unable to change her mind. But she'd be ready soon. He'd guarantee it. One time with her was all he needed.

She'd proved not such a weakling and grudgingly admired her stance and wanting to please her. Damn the woman but he needed her in every way including her approval and acceptance. It was vital to his plan.

This prudent snippet of a woman who had swept into the Melbourne hotel with such humble grace was intelligent but naïve. Winter had delayed any chance to visit Portia in Melbourne. Ginny only appealed these days when he was desperate. He needed someone regular and available and socially favourable for him. Sadly, Miss Isabelle Waring fitted his dreams.

He scowled. No time to dwell on it now because shearing was near, the most important time of year. But he wanted to act soon.

Over the coming weeks, Duncan treated Isabelle less like a servant and more like a companion. He took her aside in the dark for a kiss of an evening on the veranda. And it became easy to use his Christian name. Her thoughts and hopes steered toward a possible future with him.

Thousands of sheep in heaving flocks moved through waves of floating dust, their distant smell and bleating heavy in the air as they passed between paddocks, each day closer to the shed after being washed down in the river. Sheep dogs barked in excitement and leapt across their backs. According to Duncan, wise men aimed to finish shearing by November's end so their wool was free from grass seeds.

Unable to stifle her attraction toward him, Isabelle knew

she must bide her time until he was done.

The first shearers started arriving, straggling in pairs carrying a swag and wearing a battered hat, either on foot or riding a horse and leading another pack animal.

With the frantic weeks of shearing done and the wool finally got up, the men trailed away from the property and life returned to its peaceful idyll.

By spring's end, the heat of advancing summer seeped into the air and the pace on the run slowed. Maeve slaved in the kitchen, red faced and diligent. Irish felt the heat like everyone else and the cook complained when he didn't chop enough wood or fetch water. Tempers frayed and all work needed more effort.

Doors and windows were flung wide open at night and shut up all day, the thick house walls keeping it cool.

One evening before Christmas, Isabelle sat on the front veranda with Duncan as usual, dressed in a light cotton shirt waist and skirt, fanning herself. He discarded his jacket, shirt open at the neck and sleeves rolled to the elbows. With all the lamps snuffed in the house to deter insects, they were plunged in utter darkness, her senses heightened by only smell and touch. The fragrance of blooms and perfumed lavender drifted in from the garden.

When it grew late and their conversation ebbed, she stood to leave. Duncan stepped closer for his usual kiss, each one more demanding than the last. Isabelle panicked with pleasure. He explored the bare skin of her neck and arms, possessively sliding his work worn hands inside her partly unbuttoned shirt, kneading her breasts to a pitch of excitement.

Tonight, for the first time, Duncan also pressed hot kisses along her neck and drew her toward the French door that led into his room.

'Duncan, I don't think-'

'It's no longer time for thinkin', Isabelle,' his deep voice gravelled persuasively, edged with impatience. 'Make up your mind woman. It's embarrassing for a man to be led on and rejected.'

'Leading *you* on.' She pushed her hands against his chest. 'It's *you* that does the leading.'

'Only because you're so prim and slow,' he growled. 'For the Lord's sake, woman, ye know I want ye for mine.'

He ground out the words as if he despised himself for liking her. No whispers, just demand. He pressed her tighter against him and silenced her with another ravaging kiss. Her mind protested but her body yielded. She sank into the feel and taste of him, so familiar now. For all his roughness, he was skilled and persuasive so she let him take control.

Still struggling with thoughts of right and wrong, she surrendered, afraid of losing the man she loved if she refused him. Although he offered nothing as he led her into his shadowed bedroom, he only murmured about sons and heirs. No mention of marriage. Just for a moment, she fretted over becoming an immoral woman, against all her religious principles but became so overwhelmed by the passion he wrought in her, she passed the point of no return.

Wrapped in his arms, tasting his whisky breath, breathing in the familiar tang of his tobacco, Isabelle was defenceless, his murmurs reassuring. She admired his muscled sun browned body, new and fascinating in the gloom as he undressed.

'Take off your clothes, Isabelle,' he urged.

Scared witless by the unknown, she slowly did as he asked, one button and one garment at a time until only her under things remained.

'Everything!' he panted, struggling with his flannels.

Finally standing naked before him, Isabelle shivered, embarrassed. Duncan drew her onto the bed, then his hands invaded her, thrilling her, his mouth sucked her breasts and a strange sharp sensation built so fast she caught her breath and gasped as her body peaked with an unfamiliar painful pleasure.

Like a dark ghostly phantom, Duncan slid on top of her

and stretched out skin to skin. Isabelle knew a man and woman joined but not how. When he pierced her hard and fast, she soon learned. A cry of surprise escaped her and she clutched his shoulders. Moving in her, slow at first, then faster, his breath coming in sharp bursts on her neck and face, he continued until his whole body tightened and stopped.

'You're mine now,' he grated before he rolled away and soon began to snore.

Isabelle pulled the sheet up to her chin, although it was too late to be feeling modest. Amazed at what they had just done, she relived every moment and sensation until she, too, slept. She woke first before daylight, filled with embarrassment and slipped from Duncan's room back to her own to thoroughly wash the heat and betraying smell of him from her body ready for another hot and busy day.

Isabelle became doubly aware of Duncan, now eagerly awaiting his return each night. It gave her a deep pleasure to see him clean up. After dinner, they talked on the veranda in the dark. Duncan smoking his pipe, Isabelle sitting companionably nearby as he talked about the day's work. All candles and lamps were extinguished against ferocious mosquitoes. Before venturing outside, Isabelle rubbed oil of lavender, peppermint or vinegar on her skin. She found that bruised catmint leaves from the herb garden helped red lumps and itching. And then he led her to his room and pleasured her body before taking his own.

Over the coming weeks, the cottage hummed with preparations for Isabelle and Maeve's first Christmas in Australia. Whereas back home they celebrated in the depth of winter, here the heat descended with baking force. No clouds marred the fierce blue sky as the sun burned down on the browning landscape.

In the heat of the day, magpies sat in the trees and sang in a sweet low voice. When it stirred, an evening breeze brought whiffs of dry grass and, nearer the house, the scent of honeysuckle.

On the hottest days, butter melted and Maeve wrapped up the blocks in a wet cloth on a plate and kept them on the cool bricks of the dining room fireplace. Everyone withdrew into the shade.

Learning to push through the heat, Isabelle scrubbed floors and polished furniture until every surface shone, arranged bunches of wild and garden flowers. All window coverings were taken down and laundered so all was nearly in readiness for a grand Christmas day the following Thursday.

Maeve toiled before the fire in the kitchen, flushed but dogged to produce a feast from whatever was locally available. Kangaroo tail soup, a roasted turkey well stuffed that had, until recently, strutted and gobbled freely in the yard, its red wattles aquiver but which now took pride of place on the table for Duncan to carve. As well, boiled leg of mutton, potatoes and green peas filled platters before them.

The master and all his household staff assembled at the long table in the dining room two hours after noon, eating from his best china, seated royally together, drinking liberally of the first wines from Swiss winemaker Pettavel's first vintage in sparkling glassware Isabelle had diligently found and shone.

Maeve had steamed a huge plum pudding for hours and found enough fruit to fill a gooseberry tart served with plenty of cream. Later, with the dining room cleared and dishes done, Irish disappeared for a nap and Duncan receded out on the veranda to glower over the unlandscaped garden that had naturally evolved around itself and the long vistas beyond while he smoked his pipe.

That morning, a brief bible service had been held in the sitting room with a small eucalypt cut down and brought in to adorn the corner, decorated with paper chains Maeve and Isabelle had pasted together over many evenings out in the cool away from the kitchen's warmth.

As heat settled over everything like a heavy pall in late afternoon, everyone gathered again in the sitting room to exchange simple presents. From Duncan for each employee including Isabelle, a small handful of gold sovereigns.

Maeve's greatest treasure of late was a longed for and welcome letter from Ireland. Unlettered, she begged Isabelle to read it for her, prompting Isabelle of an evening or Sunday afternoon to teach Maeve her letters and numbers.

By summer's end, despite Isabelle regularly and willingly yielding to Duncan's lovemaking, it was still a shock when she realised her monthly bleeding had stopped. The indignity of it hit her first, then the wonderful reality. She was going to have Duncan's child. A son if he had his way, and the knowledge filled her with joy. She must tell him. Surely he would be pleased. She stilled in horror. Unless, unmarried, she now became a burden. She would be at his mercy.

Uncomfortable but not repentant for what she had done, Isabelle realised her condition would be revealed soon enough for all to see. She shook her head to scatter any negative thoughts until she spoke to him. And then she must confide in Maeve, for her best friend knew Isabelle shared his bed. Ironically, Maeve's words of warning months before now rang in her ears.

'Take care or you'll have a babe.'

Isabelle had glowed. 'I should like that. Give Duncan a son.'

'Unmarried?'

'I know,' she had replied indignantly.

That evening, Isabelle waited for Duncan to invite her out onto the veranda after supper. For three nights he had retired to his study or the sitting room alone and had recently spent a week in Melbourne during which Isabelle felt abandoned and unsure. Since his return, Duncan had remained distant, their relationship master and housekeeper again, as if strangers. Isabelle panicked that he no longer cared for her just when she discovered she was having his baby.

So when Duncan finally rose from the dining table as usual and fate allowed them to collide as he left the room and

Isabelle entered to tidy up, he frowned at her and muttered almost resentfully, 'I'll be takin' a pipe outside if ye'd care to join me.'

She was so elated to finally have the opportunity to divulge her news that all doubts fled.

She smoothed her skirts, clenched her hands together and walked outside to join him. He never rose when she approached. Sometimes, the stubborn romantic part of her longed for more respect but she hesitated to nag in fear of rejection.

'Irish tells me ye've not been riding while I was away,' he said before she had barely seated herself opposite in another carved wooden chair.

'No.' Isabelle drew in a long steadying breath at the perfect opening and plunged ahead. 'I wasn't sure if I should now I'm with child.'

Duncan sat upright and whirled about to face her. He hesitated then barked, 'Are ye sure?'

She nodded, devastated by his abrupt response.

'Ye've done well,' was all he grunted. 'Let's hope it's a son.' He managed a disarming grin to temper his calculated reply.

Isabelle beamed proudly, knowing a son was his dearest wish. She waited but he did not mention marriage.

'What if it's a girl?' she ventured lightly, fearing he might disown them both if it was.

'It won't be. And ye'll take yer meals with me in the dining room from now on.'

Glowing with warmth at her rise in the household, Isabelle's next thought was for Maeve, that it might offend her when she no longer ate in the kitchen.

Duncan eyed her hesitation. 'We've started a family Isabelle. It's only proper.'

'Of course,' she agreed. But in the eyes of the Lord, no matter how much she loved him, she still fretted over their shameless relationship.

'And ye'd better take the other double bedroom at the front of the house.'

Isabelle sighed with pleasure. That lovely room? She flooded with delight and relief that she was at least to remain in his household.

'I'm responsible for ye now, Isabelle,' Duncan said dutifully. 'I'll take care of ye.'

For now, if that was all he was offering, she would accept it. All the same, Isabelle felt like one of his prize ewes, only valuable for breeding champion offspring but smothered her disappointment with an uncertain smile.

One evening weeks later, Isabelle's mood lightened when, with great ceremony, Duncan ushered her into the sitting room and presented her with a parcel that a rider had delivered from Geelong that very day. A gift! She held her breath, secretly praying for a ring. With trembling eager fingers, she untied the string and unwrapped the brown paper to discover a beautiful gleaming gold locket on a long chain in its own special dark blue box. Isabelle fingered the pendant with awe, for she had never owned such a treasure, but her private expectations were dashed.

'Thank you, Duncan. I shall wear it always,' she breathed, silently offering up a plea for a son.

He beamed and grunted, pleased yet awkward over his offering.

When she proudly showed her precious gift to Maeve in the privacy of her room later, she asked her friend tentatively, 'It won't bother you, me eating with Duncan in the dining room in future. You won't mind serving me?'

'Lord in Heaven, why would I? You're my friend.' Maeve firmly clasped her hand. 'You've done well and good luck to you.'

'It wasn't planned,' Isabelle hastily explained.

'Isabelle Waring, I know that. We don't choose who steals our heart. If we're lucky.'

She frowned and fondled the gleaming necklace, its chain

slithering between her fingers like liquid gold. 'Duncan and I are so different. I'm not so sure but that he wants me only for giving him sons.'

'Deep down, Mr. Penross is a good man. He's not a criminal. As far as we know,' Maeve chuckled. 'And he doesn't beat us. Many's a time our mam took a stick to us kids. More out of despair with life I'm thinkin' than us misbehavin'. If the master ever mistreats you, you come to me, then. Promise?' Maeve said staunchly.

Speechless at her vehement plea, Isabelle hugged her with gratitude and nodded. The tiny young girl, the only other white female on the run and for miles around, who had become her dearest friend, was no more than a slip of a thing. Yet she was such an industrious cook and faithful friend. Isabelle treasured her companion more than she could say.

In the coming months, Isabelle felt the first quickening flutters in her gently rounding stomach. From early on, she was amazed at how rapidly and large she grew, making her slender body look incongruous with her burden. She prayed it meant a big healthy boy for his father but also hesitantly expressed her concern about their isolation to Duncan.

'When your time's getting closer, we'll arrange for a midwife or I can take you down to Geelong to Dr. Thomson's care. He's a fine Scotsman.'

Summer mercifully lost its grip and autumn grew busy for Maeve making preserves. The first soft rains quenched the soil, fog clung in wisps over the distant ranges and shortened visibility in the bush.

Isabelle took advantage of the cooler months to sew baby clothes. Duncan had allowed the purchase of yards of material, buttons, ribbons and lace from Melbourne, even making the journey to fetch them himself. Although he hadn't invited her along on the journey, Isabelle treasured her new position in his life.

One morning, when Ginny ambled up to the cottage, Isabelle caught the native woman watching her. 'Piccaninny close up few days'.

This prediction filled her with alarm because it seemed too early and weeks before her time and Duncan was away in Melbourne again. It was difficult travelling in winter with tracks often impassable but he had ridden a horse to Geelong and taken the regular steamer to Melbourne. Isabelle's protruding stomach and weight made her slow as she waddled about the house.

Next day, cleaning the dining room, a fierce pain gripped her stomach. She dropped her duster and clutched the back of a chair as a warm wetness trickled between her legs. For a moment, her mind blanked, ignoring the truth. She had not expected any sign yet until the end of the first month of spring, many weeks away. When the pain subsided, she rested a while on her bed but the clenching cramps returned. Eventually, needing reassurance, she tottered out to the kitchen.

Maeve's red face blanched. 'We should get word to the master.'

'It will take too long. He'll be home in a few days anyway.' Isabelle smiled, trying to be braver than she felt.

Maeve ignored her protests and summoned Ginny up to the house. 'She's had a baby. She should know what to do.'

'Picaninny come along. Go little camp dere.' Ginny's outstretched arm indicated the direction of a different track leading into the bush that Isabelle had noticed she took regularly of late.

Confused by her meaning and what was happening to her body, Isabelle obeyed as Ginny led her away from house. Perhaps she meant a walk would help her. Maeve followed.

'Go camp one little time,' she repeated.

A bleak sun shone and Isabelle wrapped a thick warm shawl about her shoulders before they left. When they reached a small clearing in the bush, Ginny quietly worked, scraping a carefully shaped hole in the sand lined with a bed of tiny acacia and eucalyptus leaves. When lit, it gave off a soothing scented smoke. For relaxation, Isabelle wondered?

Nearby, the native woman scooped out another larger hole and beckoned to Isabelle. 'All about here sit down.'

By gestures, Ginny indicated Isabelle should squat above it. She realised Ginny was helping prepare for her birth out here in the open. When she objected, the native woman gently and silently urged her down.

As the short daylight hours and labour progressed, Ginny soothed with words and sometimes chanted softly in flat tones. Maeve sat helplessly to the side, eyes wide, absorbed.

As the pains grew more and more intense like someone was slashing her stomach with a knife, Ginny remained calm and watchful. 'You plenty tired. Piccaninny come quick close up.'

Exhausted and moaning through the pain, soon Isabelle responded to her body's natural urges and pushed her baby out into the world. Still crazy with agony which she thought would stop now with the birth, Isabelle turned aside to see the black woman cutting the cord with a little stone knife but no sound yet from the newborn child.

'Ginny?' The woman was silent. Shouldn't her baby cry? 'Ginny?' she demanded again in growing fear.

The black woman shook her head. 'Picaninny all finish up.' She cuddled the infant, rocking and softly singing.

Isabelle watched in horror. Her heart clenched and she cried out, 'No!'

The woman reverently swaddled the stillborn baby. Isabelle saw Maeve take the child into her arms and her face crumple with distress. Isabelle didn't have time to fully mourn the significance as another pain ripped through her and she gasped with the power of it.

'My baby, Ginny. What was it?' She stared dumbly. 'Boy or girl, Ginny?' Isabelle prompted, panting.

Then the native woman's eyes brightened in understanding. 'Picaninny boy, Missus.'

Isabelle cried out in agony. Duncan would be destroyed. She had failed him.

'More piccaninny close up now.'

'What?' Isabelle puffed.

'More piccaninny come, missus.' She beamed.

Isabelle shook her head, incredulous, believing she had misunderstood. 'Another baby?' She clenched her teeth. 'Twins?'

Ginny nodded and grinned, white teeth gleaming in her shiny brown face. Isabelle struggled against the pain then gave up and let it swamp her, to rip mercilessly through her body. She heard a deep wail from her own throat and, from a haze of semi consciousness, knew the blessing that there was still a chance of another son. Within half an hour, her second baby slid into the world, caught in Ginny's gentle black hands.

'This one piccaninny balya.'

Since the woman was all smiles, Isabelle took it as a positive signal. Her second child lived. She sent up a silent prayer of thanks to God. Again, Ginny swiftly cut the cord with her knife and rubbed warm ash on the end of it.

'What you call 'em this one?'

Isabelle gave a nervous laugh. 'Depends what it is. Girl or boy?' she held her breath.

'Girl piccaninny, Missus.'

She exchanged a glance with Maeve. Tears of regret and relief mingled on her lashes and drizzled down her cheeks to know happiness and anguish in the same moment.

Ginny rubbed the healthy baby girl with soft warm ash and a layer of goanna fat, gently kneading Isabelle's stomach until the afterbirth passed. Then she gave the new mother and child time together while she lit a fire in the other hole she had made in the ground. Isabelle gazed with instant love and adoration at her beautiful round faced daughter with a damp crop of golden hair.

When aromatic smoke drifted across to them, Ginny helped her over to the warm scented bed where she crouched over it while the native woman placed soft paperbark under and around her to prevent the smoke escaping. She lay on the warm ash and Ginny packed it over her stomach and legs, covering it with warm sand.

Content after her ordeal, Isabelle dozed, to wake some time later and see her daughter being cradled and gently crooned by Ginny. Feeling rested, she moved from her warm outdoor bed and greedily embraced the baby in her arms. She nudged the tiny baby toward her breasts but after only some brief suckling from the infant, exhausted mother and child fell asleep.

Isabelle woke to gentle shaking, roused also by the sound of Maeve's voice and urging. Stirred and wakened, she slowly struggled to her feet. With Ginny holding two swaddled bundles, and Maeve's arms about her for support, they slowly walked back to the house. Isabelle focused all her strength and will onto her surviving child, as though denying the loss of her son enabled her to carry on.

Two days later, Duncan returned. Emerging from a doze, safely ensconced in the big comfortable bed with her daughter sleeping in a crib alongside, Isabelle heard his thumping footsteps carry down the hall.

'Is Isabelle all right, then?'

She couldn't decipher Maeve's murmured response but she plainly heard him ask, 'Did she have a son?'

There was a further muffled conversation. Isabelle squeezed her eyes shut tight but soon heard him move toward her room. Because she knew she must brave this first encounter, she opened her eyes to see him standing in the doorway, glowering. One glance between them at the deep despair on Duncan's face and Isabelle's tears flowed, rolling in rivers down her wan cheeks.

'I'm sorry, Duncan,' she whispered. 'But we have a beautiful daughter.' She turned her head toward the crib.

He ignored it and glared at her, barking out hoarsely, 'Where's ma son?' sparing not even the briefest glance for his surviving child nearby or a kind word for its mother.

'Maeve laid him in the small bedroom.' As Duncan

swivelled on his boots, Isabelle called out weakly, 'We must name them.'

He hesitated, his back turned against her. 'Ma son will be called Duncan,' he ground out. 'Ye can call the girl what ye like.'

Isabelle turned her face into the pillow and sobbed. Later, when she had recovered a little, she defiantly decided to name her daughter Nichola after her older brother, Nicholas. Although she and her siblings were never close, Nicholas was kindly like her father and Isabelle hoped the naming proved a good omen.

Ginny, drawn to children, became Isabelle's regular help in the house. One day, when Nichola was only weeks old and they revelled in spring warmth, the black woman pointed between the baby as Isabelle fed her from the breast and Duke playing contentedly nearby.

'Duke boss child, too.'

The comment was dropped so casually, at first Isabelle failed to comprehend. Then, assessing the lighter skinned boy and recalling Maeve's words, her mouth went dry and her charmed innocent world stood still.

She glanced in horror from Duke to Nichola, trying to grasp the truth and the fact that the children were half brother and sister. It seemed there was not one, but two, bastard children on Kooringal run. Black or white, Isabelle suddenly fathomed she was just another woman in Duncan's bed and felt cheap.

Devastated that his son had died, Duncan ignored Isabelle and spared no interest in his living child. Estranged through his grinding anger, Isabelle slept with Nichola in her bedroom. Duncan did not care. At least his daughter's squawking did not disturb his sleep.

Oddly, he missed Isabelle in his bed. She was a passive partner but as soon as she healed, he needed to try again for another son. This need alone kept his interest in her.

When he reconciled the worst bitterness of his son's death and two month old Nichola's survival, he confronted Isabelle. Her weeping each night across the hall annoyed him. It cast her as weak when he thought she had more backbone. He grieved over his son, too but he didn't approve of the way she doted on her daughter.

A stranger to it, he stepped into the nursery and forced himself to view his squirming child, gold curls framing her soft pale face. He didn't expect to be moved and wasn't. Why had she lived when his wee son Duncan had died?

'A word with ye, Isabelle.'

Folding clothes into a cedar chest of drawers, she swung around at his unexpected appearance, cool contempt on her pale face. Motherhood favoured her and his loins stirred at their closeness. Her sweetness was enhanced now by full breasts and a new aura of self-assurance. He longed to plant his seed again but was canny enough to realise he had to win back her trust.

Submissive Ginny was exotic and exciting Portia fully experienced and chained his heart but Isabelle Waring was the key to the heirs of his future wealth.

Silent and calm, she brushed past him to move into the sitting room. Duncan followed and closed the door.

'Do you want my daughter and I to leave?' She stood with her back to him, arms folded across her waist gazing out of the window, her voice without fear and tight with resentment.

'Of course not. Don't speak rubbish, woman.'

She whirled on him. 'I never speak rubbish. You don't want Nichola and ignore her as if she doesn't exist. What else am I to think? And my question is sound.'

She was sharp. He'd have to be careful. 'Ye ken that I need sons to inherit but the girl will still have ma name and a rich future.'

The girl! With a bitter smile, Isabelle looked helplessly at Duncan, frustrated that, more than physically, she was bound to him simply because she loved him. And hated herself for it. Who would have thought love could be such a burden? What woman, smitten, would not love such a charming rogue? Love and passion were persuasive forces. A heavy sadness settled in her breast for she'd had time to absorb Ginny's innocent revelation about Duke.

Isabelle settled her gaze on him. 'If I give you a son, will you marry me?'

She needed security for herself and her daughter. The hesitation after the surprise of her audacity was slight. Was that a gleam of respect twinkling behind those blue eyes?

'Ah promise.'

'I'll expect you to keep your word.'

He nodded. 'Ye have it.'

She had gained his agreement, so why did she not feel any elation from the victory? At least he would do right by her and give their children his name. Should she press for another condition to lessen her humiliation? No harm in trying.

'And can you also swear to give up Ginny?' she asked with deadly softness.

Duncan's sharp glance taught him that Isabelle knew Duke was his son.

He stared at her in silence before growling, 'You're ma woman now.'

'Promise!'

'Aye.'

His pause crushed her hope and his discomfort exposed his lie.

He ran a hand over his strained face. 'Ginny was offered to me in hard times,' he explained gruffly. 'Her tribe traded her for food.'

Isabelle raised her eyebrows in surprise.

'A man has needs,' he continued, harsh and unapologetic. 'Course I took her. The first years on the run were lonely for every man. When Ginny's son was born, she stole away from her tribe and brought him to me for protection to save him. It's their custom that half caste children are killed at birth.' He turned and strode from the room.

Isabelle gaped after him. She felt something in her heart soften and change. Ginny did what any mother would have done to save her child. Knowing the deep tug of love for Nichola and faced with the same situation, Isabelle knew she would have, too. But as time passed, Ginny and Duke continued to be a thorn in Isabelle's life. She almost envied the woman's happy innocent nature, conceding she was both a product and victim of her tribal culture.

When Duncan's attentions increased again, Isabelle accepted them with reservation and caution. They resumed dining together and their conversations out on the veranda. He discussed recent developments in the colony; the new land acts and regulations that finally allowed squatters wealthy enough to buy up their property.

'Ah've employed a surveyor,' he said, obsessed with securing his land, 'and contractors to fence ma paddocks now we have the fourteen year leases.'

He made regular business journeys to Melbourne. Upon his return from his most recent trip, Duncan encouraged Isabelle into his bed again. But his lovemaking seemed mechanical, determined on a single purpose only. To give her a son.

The following year, his longed for heir was born. Blair Penross was named without consulting the new babe's mother.

'Has a good Scottish ring to it,' Duncan pronounced.

Isabelle didn't care. The children had become her life. Nichola was an adorable and charming girl, if temperamental at times. Isabelle knew it was wrong but, for the sake of peace and to ease her conscience over losing her twin, she yielded to the child's needs. And adored baby Blair, so ravenous at the breast, the image of his father with sandy curly hair.

Duncan, of course, immediately favoured the boy. He questioned whether his son was getting enough milk, suggested solids long before he was ready, and invariably criticised Isabelle for spoiling their toddler daughter. He only ever scowled at the girl, never touched or spoke to her. In his eyes, she was unimportant. Isabelle tactfully begged Duncan to take some interest in her, hoping the enchanting child would dissolve his antipathy, but he refused. So Isabelle ceased trying, defending Nichola from her father instead. He scolded the slightest tantrum and Isabelle inevitably scooped up the wailing child into her protective arms, ever the peacemaker.

Duke, eight now and often bare back on his pony, was rarely seen. Piqued by Duncan's patriarchal dominance, Isabelle obstinately banished the boy from the cottage. Only Ginny was permitted entry for work, although she was mainly in the kitchen with Maeve.

Ironically, Ginny proved an endlessly patient nanny with the children when required. Although once Maeve found Nichola wandering unsupervised in the courtyard near the kitchen.

True to his word, soon after Blair's birth, Duncan wrote to the itinerant circuit minister to arrange their marriage. Isabelle privately scoffed at his duplicity in consenting to a church ceremony when he refused to attend the small Sunday services in the sitting room, so she couldn't resist rebuking his sculling of much whisky each night.

'We should be setting a good example for the children,' she lectured, still unable to fully forgive him over Nichola's neglect.

'They're not old enough yet to know or care,' he snapped.

Isabelle dressed them up and taught them to sit still during worship, determined they should be raised as Christian ladies and gentlemen. Sunday mornings, Duncan was off in the saddle while his family and servants reverently sang and prayed in the house.

Within weeks, the itinerant minister, who did the rounds of squatting homesteads in the district, arrived at Kooringal. A rare guest and dour individual, he slept in the house and dined at Duncan's table.

The service would be held outdoors under a eucalypt beyond the cottage fence. Irish carried out chairs from the house. Since it was the first such auspicious occasion ever held on the property, not only the household staff but all workers on both runs as well as some neighbouring squatters were invited to the ceremony and banquet afterwards. Wagons and horses rumbled and trotted in to the property for days beforehand. In the kitchen, Maeve was frantic but coped and most visitors contributed supplies.

On the day and standing at the front, Ginny grinned, holding baby Blair, and Duke stood beside his mother taking charge of Nichola, prettily dressed in pink with a big Holland pinafore, white stockings and thick laced boots. Bessie, an orphaned native girl recently employed in the kitchen now shared a gunyah down by the river with Ginny and Duke who called her a *wild blackfella* because she belonged to another tribe.

Isabelle had altered her best stiff silk dress in mother of pearl with a pointed bodice and tiny sleeves, adorning it with extra lace. A long rope of pearls, Duncan's gift on Blair's birth, was draped in a lustrous cascade to her trim waist where she clutched a trembling bouquet of fresh wildflowers. Maeve caught up her thick long hair beneath a grey bonnet with pink rosebuds under the brim and covered by a lace veil.

Duncan grudgingly accepted Isabelle's advice to wear his best suit with a gold fob chain draped across his waistcoat.

As she walked along the short track from the house toward him and the large gathering of guests clustered beneath the trees, serene yet nervous, Isabelle could not help but admire him. He was a grand figure of a man, handsome, slim and muscled from hard work. Cautious and shrewd, he lived only for his land and sons and an anxious part of her wished she held a higher place in his heart. He did not care for her as she loved him but, despite his hard nature, she was confident he would always protect and provide for his family.

Wife. Isabelle contemplated her new position and status with this marriage. A higher social standing in the district, the comfort and security it promised. She had come a long way from the sooty terraces of Blackburn. She privately vowed to be a loyal wife and mother to his children who had brought such joyful rewards.

And then her hands were in his. The minister's words of ceremony drifted across the gathering carried by a soft breeze as they repeated their vows. With a pleasure that warmed her heart, if only briefly and for this moment, Duncan's blue eyes danced at the sight of her as she stood resolute beside him.

When he slid a wide laced wedding band onto her finger and the stern minister pronounced husband and wife, Duncan bent and kissed her. Holding her hands, smiling. For now, Isabelle's reservations slid away. The day was filled with happiness and sunshine, and her children would rightfully take their father's name.

The wedding feast at long tables on the grass in the garden continued all day. Duncan swilled an alarming quantity of drink and sent her covetous glances. Isabelle knew exactly what they meant and blushed.

As evening drew in, shadows stretched longer, lamps and candles lit, the celebrations eased. House guests faded to beds and floors of spare bedrooms in the house and workmen returned to their huts. Single men rolled out swags to sleep under verandas, wagons or beneath the stars.

When they finally retired to bed, Duncan impatiently undressed his wife. In demure shock at his haste when he stripped his own clothes, she found herself roughly pulled against him in the dark. With his greater strength, despite intoxication, she could do no more than yield as he dropped onto the edge of the bed, pulling her astride him. She gasped as he plunged into her, his big hands cupped over her bottom, grunting and thrusting with hungry speed until he was done.

Duncan had acted like an animal and Isabelle felt ashamed

as she crept beneath the covers, trying to forget the episode. During the night, he woke her again, heaving himself on top, urgently taking his own pleasure. Isabelle turned her head away from the whisky breath blowing in her face.

Afterward, he rolled away and snored. Feeling used, with the prospect of the years stretching ahead, she questioned what she had done.

Blair was barely walking when Isabelle bore Duncan another son. As always during her pregnancies, he left her alone but made regular business trips on one of the three daily paddle streamers that plied between Geelong and Melbourne. He returned as always, bearing gifts. This time diamonds no doubt in his pride at having a second son to consolidate his holdings.

Duncan named him Alexander. From his early easy smiles and mischievous chuckles, it was clear this new baby would be a happier and more adventurous son than his older brother. Blair was always watchful and alert, aware of his father's stern voice and attention, staring at the giant man in silent awe. At times, that same childish gaze also held resilient defiance, remarkable for his age.

Duncan gloated over the successful purchase of all his lands. 'Through ma sons, ma properties will continue in the Penross name.'

He managed Kooringal himself but employed an overseer on Lakeham, regularly riding across to stay overnight checking account books and stock. His culled breeding merinos and prize rams were eagerly sought by private buyers and at sale. Because of his zealous selection to quality, his stock commanded high prices as both breeding stock and for wool.

The following winter was dry and the spring hot with cloudless days and searing north winds that parched the grass and wailed through the young pines Duncan had planted as a protective shelter a short distance from the house.

In November, an Act of Separation of Port Phillip from

New South Wales created the new colony of Victoria, named after the Queen. The news that the Bill had passed through the British House of Commons was received by the ship Lysander and quickly transmitted across the country districts by beacon fires.

The wealthy and powerful colonists and squatters in particular had long petitioned for this independence because it gave them control of their lands. All colonies could now create their own constitution for self-government and the new Victoria would have its own Legislative Council like New South Wales.

The colonists had known by imperial decree since the year before that the district would become a colony in its own right so four days of celebrations and general rejoicing followed. When the news became official, bonfires and fireworks were lit for this festivity which marked the beginning of a new era. On Kooringal, the cottage and every hut was deserted in the evening as workers and staff drank toasts in commemoration.

Isabelle was excited but restrained. Duncan joined the gathering and arrived back later as good as drunk. Even dedicated Maeve abandoned the kitchen and stole away to join in the revelry around the fire lit in the homestead paddock. Standing outside the cottage with Nichola in her arms to share in the sight as sparks leapt into the night sky, loud singing and shouting drifted across to them.

Isabelle squinted across the dark distance. Was that Maeve on the arm of a tall dark haired man? She did not recognise him but that was not surprising since Duncan employed many men. With the man's arm around her, heads close together, talking and laughing, Isabelle was both envious and happy for her friend. The girl rarely received any male attention nor had time for it. Although the tiny Irish cook was now twenty-three, Isabelle felt protective of her friend and ally since their arrival together on the run five years before. Then chastised her concern. Wasn't hard working Maeve entitled to celebrate on this special night?

By the year's end, Alex was growing and crawling into everything in the house, unafraid to explore, which meant he sometimes escaped Ginny's attention. Like spring, the summer continued hot. To keep the children cool, Ginny often took them down to the billabongs in the river. Ginny fully clothed in the water with them, splashing and playing with fussy Nichola and reckless Blair. Duke, never far away, joined in, ten now and growing taller every year. Since he enjoyed the Penross children's company, Isabelle had gradually eased her ban on his socialising with them. Being a native and some years older, he watched out for them and taught them his bush ways.

Isabelle sat on the riverbank under her sun umbrella with Alex dozing in her arms, waving away pestering flies as she watched the happy summer scene. When Ginny had first seen Isabelle's parasol, she had pointed to it in glee, calling it a gunty and running in and out of its shade like a child. The native woman's amusement and natural cheerfulness made it hard for Isabelle to feel continued resentment. And yet the sight of them in the water together, Duke's gleaming wet brown body in stark contrast beside her own children's white skin always reminded her of the lad's paternity.

At dinner one evening only days later, Duncan raised the matter of stolen property on the run.

'Guns, rifles and ammunition,' he scowled. 'Some sheep had their throats cut and coins were taken from men's quarters.'

'When did all this go missing?' Isabelle grew concerned. Although the men were a rough breed, they respected bush law to watch out for your mate so it seemed odd to have such thievery.

'Men can't say. No one's owning up to it, of course, and we have no proof. They were all in high spirits after the November celebrations and Christmas. Been rumours of bushrangers lately. We'll all need to be careful,' he warned.

Always a time of fire danger, this summer burned

particularly hot and nasty, creating an increased threat. Every day brought the same rituals. Duncan and every workman constantly circled the property on alert. They rode out to the best vantage points to scan for any sign of rising smoke.

At night, Duncan sat uneasily on his front veranda, eyes vigilant, his pipe smoke mingling with the perfume from honeysuckle thickly abundant and heavily in bloom as it wrapped itself around the veranda posts. Watchers were posted day and night and horses saddled ready to bolt. Isabelle often heard Duncan wake in the night and leap from bed to pace outside in the dark.

The first Thursday in early February was a sultry oppressive day. The sun rose livid and red and the hot wind increased with the heat. Dust and gravel whirled outdoors, pushed by fierce northerlies. At breakfast, the butter slithered into its dish and Maeve's freshly baked bread was already dry before it reached the table. As Isabelle patiently encouraged her listless children to eat, a workman thumped on the back door. Duncan's chair hurled backwards and tumbled to the floor as he jumped to his feet.

As he strode into the hallway, Isabelle heard the disastrous words, 'Fire, Boss.'

By the time she rose from the table to follow, Duncan and his man had already disappeared. Filled with alarm, Isabelle's thoughts were only for the safety of the children, her anxiety high on such a foul and merciless day.

Late morning, Irish told Isabelle, 'Thermometer outside says 115 degrees, Missus. Me poultry's all drooped their wings and they're gaspin' fer breath.'

She had been furiously fanning Alex all morning and stripped the two older children's clothing to their lightest cotton undergarments. Sapped of energy in the heat, everyone moped about, lethargic.

When Isabelle paced to the window and drew aside the curtains, even the panes were warm to the touch. Her horrified gaze dwelt on the murky landscape outside, dirty with smoke and fine sand. The barely visible sun glowed red and the sky was a fearful mahogany.

'Let the fire go out in the kitchen, Maeve,' she instructed as an extra precaution.

Around midday, Duncan briefly returned to the house. Covered in black ash from the ominous day, he barked, 'It's bad. The whole Moorabool valley's ablaze.'

Such tales of distress and horror followed, Isabelle scarcely believed. Mobs of horses had broken loose, galloping in terror with the wind into the hills.

She clutched her throat, speechless, terrified for her children. 'What can we do?'

'Little enough. It's nought but a sea of fire out there sweeping along like a racehorse.' He shook his head and related visions of flames leaping over creeks, springing up into the trees, curling around them and flying from one to the other. 'Get ma sons into the cellar,' he ordered and disappeared again.

Isabelle smarted that his request did not include his daughter but heeded his words and gathered the children together in the nursery under Ginny's care. She prowled between the house and kitchen block outside keeping watch on the fire's alarming progress closer.

When it threatened the house, Isabelle joined Maeve, Irish and Bessie in fight the racing flames with buckets of water filled from the courtyard pump. They tied wet handkerchiefs over their face against the wind and smoke, working frantically against the heat and wind and grit being flung into their eyes.

In the nursery, Ginny dozed.

'Daddy gone.' Blair watched his father ride away through the howling wind and dust, standing on tiptoe to see out of the window.

When he toddled out into the hall, Nichola followed. 'Blair, come back.'

But her little brother, always stubborn, ignored her. He grappled with the front door knob and it opened.

'No, Blair, we can't play outside today.'

But his swift chubby legs took him across the veranda, down the path, through the open gate furiously banging in the wind, further and further away from the house.

Nichola judged his distance and wavered in fear. He was heading downhill for the river. Afraid of being seen outdoors without proper clothes, Nichola cringed on the veranda. It was scary outside today. The wind whipped her curls into her face, stung her eyes and tugged at her drawers. The heat on her bare arms felt the same as when she stood near the fire in the nursery in winter. If she went too close, mother scolded.

'Blair!' she yelled but her tiny voice was torn away by the wind.

He disappeared into a dusty cloud. Frightened for her brother, for he was father's favourite and she knew she must fetch him back, Nichola left the safe veranda and struggled after him. Grit filled her eyes so she covered them with her hands, dipping her head against it and running blind. When she opened them again, she glanced back at the cottage now far behind. Ahead, Blair had paused, laughing.

'You're a naughty boy,' she yelled at him, sprinting to catch up.

She reached out and grabbed his arm but he squirmed and pulled free, toddling on.

'Blair!' she screamed, as much in anger as terror.

The ground was black everywhere and burned her feet. In the distance off to one side, fire licked and raced through the grass among the trees. Pushing through her fear and determined to catch her brother, she followed. Then Blair stumbled and fell and cried. Reaching him, unmoved by the tears streaking his miserable black face, she hauled him to his feet.

'Come back now or father will be cross.'

She gripped his arm tight, hoping it hurt but when she

turned to take him back to the house, the fire was racing closer all around them. The only place to hide was behind a big fallen tree trunk. Nichola pulled Blair down beside her, pushed him hard up against the log and cuddled him close. Whimpering, Blair gave up struggling and lay still. His baby sobbing upset her and as it grew hotter, she started crying too. She wanted to be safe with mother. And father would be angry with them when they got back to the house.

She heard the rush of crackling flames and felt her skin hurt from the heat.

She stiffened and yelped in fear.

CHAPTER 5

Isabelle, Maeve, Irish and Bessie toiled for what felt like an eternity until they mercifully contained the blaze near the house, watching it sweep on further away, fed by the wind, blackening everything in its path. Isabelle had no idea of the time in the afternoon when Duncan emerged through the dark haze and rode wearily up to the house. Her heartbeat altered in relief just to see him alive.

He brought heartening news. 'The wind's changed. The fires are burning down and the men are trying to get some of 'em out. Is everyone all right?' He scanned them all and glanced toward the house, his face, clothes and hair completely black.

Isabelle assumed he meant the boys and nodded. 'They're inside with Ginny.'

'Why's that gate open?' He scowled at it banging loose in the wind in the home paddock fence.

'It must have come unlatched,' Isabelle said wearily, moving across the yard to bolt it again.

At that moment, Ginny rushed from the cottage carrying baby Alex. Unusual, for she never hurried. 'Picaninny all gone, Missus.'

Isabelle frowned, her mind and body heavy with exhaustion. What were the children up to now? 'Can't you find them?' she flared irritably.

'No, Missus. Door bin open one long time.'

Ginny's distress finally alarmed her. Her head slowly began to clear and function. 'What do you mean?' she demanded, even as she found a new burst of energy through fear and picked up her skirts.

'Where are they?' Duncan bellowed.

Ginny shook her head and gabbled in her native tongue. Everyone swarmed into the house, scouring every corner of every room when they realised the two older children were missing, calling out their names with no response. The silence was eerie.

After five precious heartbreaking minutes, Isabelle said 'We're wasting time. They're out there.' She cast a frantic glance toward the window and the menacing outdoors, petrified of the implications.

Duncan roared at Duke, the first time Isabelle had ever seen him angry with the boy. 'Go get your pony and plenty blackfella.'

The lad nodded and fled as if pursued. Isabelle's mind screamed *Why?* before she snatched Alex from Ginny's arms. Thrusting him at Maeve, she snapped, 'Don't let him out of your sight.'

'Come with me,' Duncan ordered Ginny.

Isabelle knew the more blacks for tracking, the better. Their sense for hunting and finding quarry was mystical but a gift no one on the run ever questioned.

Surprisingly fast, Duke returned, leading his pony and another native man. Immediately all three blacks had their heads down looking for footprints or any signs for which way the children had wandered. The man raised his head as if sniffing the air and took off at a lope toward the charred bush at the front of the house.

Duke followed. They wove this way and that, paused, continued on. Everyone followed but Isabelle silently screamed inside with heartache and frustration. Duncan dogged Duke's heels, the boy oblivious to the hot ashes under his bare feet. Isabelle felt it through her boots and worried for him.

As they tracked nearer the river, Isabelle froze. The children could not swim. What if they had fallen into the water and drowned? She tore herself up inside with blame, cursing Ginny's neglect but needing the woman to help find them.

'Stop one little time,' Duke murmured, slightly ahead.

His comment caught her attention again. Her heart filled with expectation and she prayed *Please Lord let my babies be safe.* When Duke, Ginny and the man slowly edged on, Isabelle gasped with impatience.

Leading, Duke paused again. 'Close up soon.'

He glanced at her and his boyish face lit up in a smile. His sure brown feet broke into a trot. Isabelle dashed after him, Duncan alongside now.

'Nichola? Blair?' she cried out.

Duke halted and raised his short arm for silence. Then a curly blonde head peeped from above a burnt out fallen log.

Isabelle's throat went dry and she rasped out, 'Nichola!' She raced towards her daughter, tripping over charred timber and stiff burnt animal corpses.

'Where's Blair?' Duncan bellowed at her side.

'Picaninny here, Missus.' Duke beamed, pulling the boy out from underneath a pile of debris and brushing it away as Nichola staggered to stand.

Isabelle sobbed and dropped to her knees on the hot black ground. Relieved her precious babies were alive, Isabelle scooped them both into her arms in a crushing hug, Ginny standing quietly at her side. Nichola was bedraggled, her soft face and hands black and scratched, her pantaloons torn and singed from where, at some stage, they must have caught alight. Blair was in a similar miserable condition.

'What were you thinking?' Isabelle appealed to Nichola.

'Blair was looking for father. I told him to come back,' her daughter sniffled, eyes large in terror.

'You followed him?' Nichola nodded. Isabelle marvelled that her temperamental daughter had been so unselfish and resourceful in the face of danger showing hidden courage.

'A likely story,' Duncan growled, looming behind Isabelle, wrenching Blair from her arms and into his own. 'The girl probably led ma son astray. She shall be punished for putting Blair in danger.'

'It wasn't my fault, father.' Nichola wailed, tears rolling down her sooty face, her tiny frame buckling with exhaustion. 'He ran away.'

'Silence!'

Blair sucked his thumb, staring at his father, silenced by his booming voice. As the three natives headed back toward the house, Isabelle laid a hand on Ginny's arm but addressed them all.

'Thank you.'

Irish offered to carry Nichola but Isabelle clutched her protectively. 'Thank you. I can manage.' She lifted the grimy trembling girl whose thin arms crept around her neck.

'I didn't do anything wrong, Mother. I followed Blair to get him back. Tell father,' she whispered, a distraught look on her begrimed angelic face.

'Of course, darling.' Isabelle crooned. 'Everything will be all right.'

Isabelle withheld her fury at Duncan's harsh lecture to Nichola in front of everyone, ashamed of her husband's biased behaviour and disregard for his daughter.

Once reassured that his son was safe in the house, Duncan immediately prepared to leave again. Before he did, he warned Isabelle, 'Keep the children indoors. Sights out there are not to be seen.'

'And do you count Nichola among your children?' she asked bitterly.

Duncan glared. 'Do as ah say.'

'Nichola has no reason to lie. You give Duke more respect than your daughter.' Isabelle muttered an insolent challenge in a low voice, then turned her back on him and whirled from the room to tend her children's wounds.

With Maeve's help, Isabelle carefully stripped the children's clothes from their sooty bodies, gently bathed them in precious cool water and smeared treacle and turkey fat over their burns. Nichola whimpered, lips trembling but drawn into a thin line that Isabelle perceived as anger more than shock. A surprising show of resilience in the wake of her father's wrath and wrongful accusation for Isabelle had no doubt of her daughter's innocence.

Nichola had long ago learned to beguile for attention, the forsaken child of her father's brood, but she usually told the truth. Whereas, although Blair behaved in his father's presence, he tended to be disobedient, shrewdly sensing the difference. She could well imagine the boy had deliberately stolen away in childish mischief, far too young yet to understand the consequences on such a dangerous day.

Isabelle and Ginny put the exhausted children to bed. With the dramas of the afternoon, they were soon all asleep.

During the night a cool breeze swept through bringing a light refreshing rain, greedily absorbed by the parched earth. The following morning, as if to mock them and disregard the horror of the day before, the sun rose in unclouded brightness.

Within days, the Geelong Advertiser and Melbourne Argus reported detailed particulars of the horrific destruction and tragedies across the district. While all on Kooringal had been engrossed coping with the devastation on their own property, horrible revelations emerged for all.

When Isabelle scanned the articles in the newspapers, brought by riders up from town the following week, she was horrified by the accounts she read. *Extensive fires on the Moorabool… Country in a complete blaze... As far as the eye could reach, scene looked as though swept by wings of a destroying angel.*

And stories of personal tragedy and loss. *House burnt to the ground… A few cinders and charred rafter all that marked the spot… Roasted carcases burnt black... All furniture and apparel gone except one pair of boots and a shirt... Plunged into the creek for safely... Cripple was carried out on his wife's back.*

One evening, Duncan flung a newly-arrived newspaper down in disgust and splashed more whisky into his glass.

'Read the cause.' His mouth curled in disgust, knocking

back a swig of whiskey. 'I'd drag the culprits by the collar out to see ma best stud ewes and rams black and stiff on the ground. I'd push their faces into the dirt of thousands of acres of ma wasted pasture before I took to 'em with ma rifle.'

He strode from the room. Isabelle had never seen him shake with such fury nor heard him threaten such violence. She picked up the scattered pages from the rug to learn that timber splitters camped in the ranges on the other side of Melbourne had possibly and ignorantly caused the widespread devastation by neglecting to extinguish a campfire. Isabelle placed a hand over her mouth that an unmindful act had wrought such catastrophe.

All summer and autumn, Duncan and his men buried dead animals and rebuilt sheds. With no rain and drought spreading its dry tentacles across the countryside, Isabelle watched her husband tormented by the mammoth challenge and heavy losses. Lack of grass frustrated his efforts to begin the long and expensive process of rebuilding his flocks.

Although the heaviest stock losses fell upon the squatters, at least they were able to bear them. Isabelle heard of many smaller settlers, destitute, forced to desert their properties.

Isabelle's world was further shaken when she found Maeve one early autumn morning quietly weeping in a corner of the kitchen when she went to check why breakfast was delayed. Usually positive and cheerful but now red hair unkempt, her good friend had recently seemed irritable and easily upset. Seeing the cook in such distress, Isabelle quickly despatched Bessie to take breakfast into the dining room and not keep Duncan waiting any longer.

When Isabelle approached Maeve, the girl's green eyes red from rubbing, she crumpled a wet kerchief in her hands and collapsed into a fresh flood of tears. When she recovered, her story and troubles tumbled out in a verbal rush.

'I met this handsome man at the bonfire. You know, on the night of the Separation? Seemed nice enough. I supposed he worked here, too, but I'd never seen him before with the master employing so many men. When I asked him where he worked, he was vague. Then he asked me where I worked and was right interested when he knew it was up here at the house in the kitchen. On that very first night, he took the liberty of a kiss which, of course, I enjoyed,' she admitted ruefully. 'After that when he got word to me, I stole away as often as I could and we met from time to time.'

Isabelle remembered once or twice seeking her out and finding her missing. Now it all made sense. Another time Isabelle had queried Maeve's intention to go for a Sunday walk.

'In this heat? Alone?'

'I won't be going far.'

'Well,' Isabelle remained dubious, 'don't forget to take a stick for snakes.'

At the time, Isabelle thought Maeve flushed from the heat but now realised it might have been embarrassment instead.

'He was so nice.' Maeve continued, 'but he asked for money and I'd precious little of that. Said his name was Charlie Turner. Course that's probably not his name. Likely fibbin' but I don't know where to find him. Irish asked around for me and he's not employed on the property.' She scowled. 'Now I think on it, he never said he did. Well, of course, none of the men had ever heard of him either. Not here on Kooringal or even over on Lakeham. So who knows where he's gone.'

Maeve looked down at her hands, still wringing the wet kerchief on her lap. 'But that's not the worst of it. We got friendly, like, and he was so romantic and…'

'Oh, Maeve.' Isabelle's shoulders drooped. 'You didn't.'

'I did.'

'You're not-?'

She nodded, looking miserable. 'I am. I'll lose me job when the master hears, won't I?' Maeve grew distraught.

'I run the household,' Isabelle declared, back straightening. 'All the staff, including you, are my responsibility. You're not going anywhere and you won't lose your job. We'll manage. Everything will be all right.'

'But the babe?'

'We'll work around it. All will be well. Don't you worry yourself. I've travelled that road myself, remember?' She squeezed Maeve's hand in reassurance and gave her a kindly smile. Difficult while witnessing the continual flow of tears dripping down the girl's cheeks.

'Did he tell you anything at all about himself?'

Maeve shook her head, freckles invisible beneath her flushed face. 'No, but he asked me all kinds of questions about the master of the house.'

'What kinds of questions?'

Maeve shrugged. 'Where he kept the guns and how a rich man like Mr. Penross would be needin' to protect his valuables.'

Isabelle frowned, Maeve's words tugging at her memory. 'So you've not seen him recently?'

Maeve looked miserable and embarrassed. 'He's not been in touch for over a month.

Isabelle rose to pace the kitchen, her nagging thoughts raising a suspicion. 'You first met him at the November bonfire?' Maeve nodded. 'And you've no idea where to find him now?' She nodded again.

Isabelle was reluctant to suggest it but, if nothing else, as friends they had always been open and honest with each other. She paused and laid a hand on Maeve's shoulder. 'Maybe he doesn't want to be found,' she said gently.

Understanding blanched Maeve's face. 'I was beginning to wonder,' she admitted in a small voice, 'but he was a handsome devil and he told me he fancied me. And he had such a smile.' She moaned with tearful regret.

'Well, we'll wait and see if he turns up again.' Isabelle reached out for Maeve's hands. 'But I think you should be prepared for a broken heart and to be raising your child on your own.'

'I'm such an eejit,' Maeve growled. 'What am I going to be tellin' my brothers and me Mam?'

'Its early days. Wait awhile. See if this Mr. Turner ever makes contact again. If he does, don't you dare meet him alone. You come and tell me. We'll deal with him together.'

When Isabelle finally left a less troubled Maeve and returned to the dining room she repeated her conversation and voiced her suspicions to Duncan. He had a right to know and it was better she told him herself.

'A bushranger, ye think?'

'She met him a month or two before you mentioned the guns and ammunition that went missing early last summer. It all adds up based on what Maeve told me. I didn't say anything to her for she'd be even more devastated that she innocently breached our trust.' Isabelle sighed and poured another cup of welcome tea. 'Sounds like this Charlie Turner was quite a charmer.' Many men were, Isabelle reflected. Hadn't she fallen for one herself?

For months, Maeve pined and cast longing glances out of her kitchen window or stared vacantly into the distant bush but her rogue of a man never reappeared. It was clear he had deliberately exploited the girl and seduced her for his own criminal ends and financial gain.

In May, the Geelong Advertiser reported gold discovered in New South Wales colony. By winter, Port Phillip erupted into a fever of news over the astounding discoveries of the precious metal in June at Clunes, not fifty miles distant and in August at Buninyong, even closer, less than twenty miles and a day's horse ride away. The latter found close to a road by the village blacksmith less than a mile from his forge.

In the midst, almost overshadowed by the excitement of gold, Port Phillip colony officially became Victoria on the first of July with Charles La Trobe appointed the first Lieutenant Governor.

Far from being elated, Duncan grew furious. 'Ma workers have all deserted me to seek their fortunes and the masses are trampling ma paddocks and camping on ma land. Did ye see what they did yesterday?' he roared to Isabelle one morning at breakfast. 'They've picked all our vegetables and stolen poultry and livestock.'

The tracks became rivers of men flowing in an endless tide of humanity toward the diggings. So Duncan posted armed guards from the few men who remained day and night in protection. He constantly squinted through his telescope from the front veranda checking the movements of the pedestrian hordes along the tracks. Worse, the signboard warning intruders of his private property was ignored, knocked down and used for firewood.

Ginny, Bessie and the other local natives stayed contentedly on the run. In fact, when labour grew scarce, Duncan employed as many as could be found. A wise move to his benefit since they were blind to the payment of wages and innocently only worked for food and keep.

Until the weather improved, the depth of winter forced some Ballarat diggers to return to pastoral runs because conditions were so unfavourable on the goldfields. To his annoyance, Duncan was forced to hire any man available. In return, they promptly demanded higher wages which doubled within weeks.

The newcomers brought tales of both success and failure. Some men made hundreds of pounds within weeks, others lost all their money. Even the bush workers found mining harder work than shearing for little or no profit.

But food prices rose with the demand of the increased hungry population. Tens of thousands arrived by ship and trudged inland to the diggings. Because of its proximity, the port of Geelong became the gateway for the rush.

Coupled with the disruption of life and the influx of newcomers, Duncan's valuable stud flocks were now at the mercy of dingoes. Like other district pastoralists, he took the initiative and began fencing his land into paddocks to contain and better manage his sheep. At first with shepherds missing, he hastily erected brush fences by felling trees and piling them along his boundaries. As a result, he also soon discovered shepherds were no longer needed and could be replaced by boundary riders.

Although Duncan growled at the expense, his outlay became unimportant because his runs were so close to the diggings, he made a quiet fortune selling meat to goldfields butchers.

In August, with Ginny's help and tempestuous weather blustering outside, Maeve gave birth to a daughter, Mackenzie.

'It's me mam's maiden name,' she said. With chubby cheeks, auburn hair and dimples, the babe was a sunny laughing child. 'She's a hint of mischief from her father, that's for sure. How can I tell her he was a thief?'

Maeve swaddled her sweet natured newborn in a basket in the kitchen.

The following month, news leaked throughout the colony that the Ballarat diggings were the richest and a valuable gold shipment had been escorted to Geelong.

Maeve said sharply to Isabelle when they heard, 'Be a temptation for a bushranger. Maybe Charlie Turner's keeping a watch out to rob it.'

Meanwhile, Duncan continued selling all his surplus meat, hay and dairy produce by sending Irish with cartloads up to Buninyong and Ballarat.

When the sun warmed and musky wattle bloomed again, diggers gradually abandoned their jobs on the runs to return to the goldfields. But September brought heavy rains and floods, breaking the long winter drought.

'It's the wettest season in all ma years of living in the colony,' Duncan declared.

When a flu epidemic ravaged among them taking the vulnerable and weak, Isabelle nervously coddled the children. It took everyone by surprise when Ginny, young and healthy, caught the virus. When she didn't appear at the house for days, Duke appeared one morning under the veranda at the cottage, hovering.

Bessie called Duncan at breakfast and he went out to investigate. Concerned, Isabelle followed.

'Blackfella all sad, boss. Ginny all finish up.'

The revealing words took Isabelle sharply back to her first born twins and Ginny's similar declaration. They all knew what the phrase meant. The woman had become a trusted member of their household. Originally, Isabelle had resented her son, but looking at the terrified child standing lost before them, understood the pain and loss of his mother by an eleven year old boy.

Bessie quietly moved forward, softly wailing and placed a protective arm around his shoulder, as if marking her right. In death, natives openly showed the pain of their loss.

'Tell the boss when Ginny is buried, eh Bessie?'

The young girl nodded and led her charge away. To her shame, at such a time of grief, Isabelle's only thought was that Duncan might want to bring Duke to live in the house but Bessie's possession indicated he would remain among his mother's people.

'Is Ginny getting better?' Nichola asked. The boys were too young to understand.

'No,' Isabelle said gently, drawing her daughter onto her knee in the nursery. 'Ginny has died. Her spirit has gone to the Dreaming place that she believed in.'

'Where is that?'

'I don't know, darling, but I'm sure she's close by watching over us.' Nichola frowned but accepted her mother's explanation.

That night, Duncan complained to Isabelle at dinner. 'After Ginny's burial, the whole tribe will disappear.'

Although there were less natives about these days since white men had encroached on their land, Isabelle knew he needed any spare man to work on his runs. Those who remained demanded higher wages.

Next day, out of respect for the still-young Ginny taken from life too soon and because she had been there for Isabelle right from her first twin births, working in the cottage ever since, she joined the natives when Bessie sent work with Duke of his mother's funeral. Together with Maeve carrying baby Mackenzie on her hip, she held his hand as they walked to the burial site in the bush. Isabelle stood reverently apart at the rear of the gathering. As the women wailed, she gingerly forced her gaze to watch the proceedings.

Ginny's body was rolled up in an opossum rug with her knees drawn up to her neck with string. The corpse was placed in a sitting position in a sand hill grave a few feet deep. A sheet of bark was placed over her and the sand filled in. A pile of logs was raised above. The men cleared a path around the simple tomb and a spear with a plume of emu feathers lodged at the head of the mound, marking the spot.

Maeve and Isabelle walked in solemn silence back to the cottage.

'Won't seem the same without her smiles, will it?' Maeve paused in the courtyard outside the kitchen.

'She was really Duncan's first wife,' Isabelle replied absently, turning to stare back along the path in the direction of the native camp and burial. 'She was exasperating and lazy but I could not have borne the twins without her all those years ago.' She sighed. 'And she loved my children as much as Duke.'

'He'll be fine with Bessie.'

'Duncan said they'll disappear now for a while.'

'We both know what that means.' Maeve darted a wry glance.

They nodded and chorused together, 'More work,' breaking into mutual laughter.

As they clung together, Isabelle felt tears roll down her cheeks and swiped at them. 'No time to be grieving. Let's get back to it.'

Mackenzie grizzled. 'Time for a feed,' Maeve said. 'I'll miss

Bessie's help,' she reflected as she moved indoors.

Rain delayed shearing and, when it began, rates and costs of rations increased and bullockies trebled their charge for carting wool.

Working from Alexander's first wake time until long after dark and the children were in bed, Isabelle somehow managed the household and her small brood. Little conversation passed between she and Duncan at the dinner table each night after a hard day over at the shed. Although weary from her extra workload, Isabelle still managed to admire her handsome and energetic husband of five and thirty years. And resignedly bore his desires in their bed if only because it proved he still needed her. So it was not unexpected by the year's end when she learned she was with child again. Her fourth.

Privately, deep in her heart, she longed for another daughter for her sons belonged to their father and Nichola continued to be ignored. How she would love another little girl to spoil who would be her own and undoubtedly of no interest to Duncan. Maeve's sweet gurgling Mackenzie was a surrogate joy but she yearned for another.

Knowing she would more easily tire as this pregnancy progressed, as she had done with each one, Isabelle advertised in the Geelong paper for a governess to replace Ginny. She had begun educating Nichola herself but as the boys grew, they would need more formal teaching. Letters of application began arriving with the mail man on horseback.

In rare visits or correspondence with other squatters' wives in the district, Isabelle rather sceptically learned that there should be a definite preference for an Englishwoman or a female of French or foreign background. The least favoured, it seemed, was anyone colonial born even if they came from a good background. If she was an accomplished musician, she was most prized.

Isabelle took the suggestions on board but disregarded them all on first sight of Miss Audrey Bailey. In her mind, Isabelle had employed her even before the interview was complete. The woman arrived by wagon with Red returning from Geelong with supplies.

Some years older than herself with abundant brown hair stylishly upswept and pinned, she possessed a soft English complexion and refined demeanour but most important of all declared her love of children. Not unlike Ginny in nature, Isabelle reflected, and the sudden twinge of thought for the black woman tugged at her heart. She missed her happy innocent company.

'Miss Bailey, do come in.' Isabelle met her on the veranda and ushered her into the sitting room.

'Mrs. Penross, I'm most grateful you have agreed to receive me.'

'Please, call me Isabelle.'

From that moment, reflected in a mutual smile, their friendship was sealed. Isabelle knew she had found a genteel employee and companion who would be an excellent example for the children. After Maeve brought in tea, they sipped and chatted as easily as if they had known each other many years.

'What brought you to the colony, Miss Bailey?'

'Audrey.' Isabelle caught her hesitation. 'The chance for a new life,' was all she offered.

Isabelle noticed her reticence. Perhaps she had been forsaken in love? The past held regrets and secrets for everyone. 'Like most of us. Originally I was Duncan's housekeeper and it has been my good fortune that he chose to marry me.'

'Indeed.'

'I'm from Blackburn in Lancashire.' Isabelle left her comment open. Audrey smiled but paused, as if wondering whether to confide.

Eventually, she said, 'I'm from Norfolk.'

Isabelle sensed more remained unsaid but Audrey's exemplary character shone through and she engaged her on the spot, her bags were sent for and brought out to the run from Geelong, and the new governess settled in.

In her calm and measured way, she and the children immediately bonded. She treated Nichola like the little lady she was to become, in response to which the girl responded, eager to please, the improvement in her behaviour marked.

With another baby coming, extra staff needed and Audrey sleeping in the house now, the cottage accommodations were growing cramped. Comfortable and roomy enough, the little house was becoming inadequate. Isabelle broached the subject with Duncan of building additional rooms.

To her amazement, he replied at once, amenably. 'Aye, ah've been thinkin' the same thing. Ah've plans underway.'

Isabelle straightened in surprise. Her rare suggestions were often challenged but she always stood her ground when confronting him, no longer daunted by his gruff dominating manner.

So his animated response to her proposal led them into his office where he rolled out the huge sheets of plans Isabelle recognised as those she had stealthily uncovered some years before. Paying more attention, she realised the scale of this grander dwelling Duncan planned. Indoors and out, it promised magnificence with wide verandas on all sides on both the lower and upper storeys. She saw a grand curved staircase, enormous rooms and huge fireplaces.

'We need a bigger house. Not a mansion. This is so grand!' she breathed in astonishment, awed by the imposing proportions suggested by the drawings.

Duncan excitedly relayed his vision. 'Once the homestead is built, the whole paddock down to the river will be landscaped to create views from the house.'

Removing another sheet from underneath, Duncan spread out what was clearly a full garden design for acres around the dwelling. 'We'll have swans on the lake and peacocks strutting on the lawn. We need a mansion more fitting for our place in society now. And to accommodate a large family.'

Awed by the scope of her husband's ambition, Isabelle grinned. 'Our family is considerable already. How many more?'

'Aye,' he replied, 'but with this plan we've enough room to hold a dynasty.'

Although spoken lightly and with passion, Isabelle realised he was serious and how broad her husband's goals and aspirations had probably always been. This design had lain patiently dormant for years, the dream of a proud and ambitious man.

'When work starts,' Duncan squinted out through the window as if already seeing the vision in his mind, 'we'll have a grand ceremony for laying the foundation stone. Blair and I together.'

On that significant late spring day, Isabelle walked with him in the lengthening golden twilight up the rise to the level area above the cottage. For the first time in a long while, Isabelle truly felt a part of Duncan's life and plans. Her heart filled with a deep joy in the pleasure of his companionship and wished it could always be so but her concerns overshadowed what should be a promising time in their lives.

She grew troubled by Duncan's hunger for such a visible show of his wealth. Sheep and gold had thrust his fortunes high to become one of the colony's leading men, and she marvelled that they could afford such luxury. But the house, no, homestead, he had said, would pronounce their prominence in society.

'We'll use the furniture importers and warehouses in Swanston Street in Melbourne. We'll save customs duty if we buy all their furniture in the colony.'

For all of Duncan's success, Isabelle felt isolated on Kooringal, rarely leaving the property, her life filled with managing the household and raising her children. She was not lonely but her interest was enticed when she heard from occasional travellers and read in the newspapers of the changes and growth in the colony and towns. Duncan made regular business trips away and she found herself growing resentful that she was never invited.

'I would love to visit Geelong or Melbourne. Even for a short time,' she hinted.

Duncan's head jerked sharply in a side glance. 'Next summer when the baby is bigger, we'll take a house for a few weeks down by the sea at Shortland's Bluff,' he promised.

Isabelle sighed. It seemed she must wait but her spirits lifted. 'That will be wonderful.'

When they returned to the cottage, Duncan produced catalogues for Isabelle to browse and furnish the house.

Duncan strode up to the house along the sea front away from the main part of Geelong. He had discreetly rented it for Portia on the few occasions she agreed to take the steamer down the bay to meet him here. For a number of years now, she had belonged to him alone. A situation only achieved when accompanied by his indulgent gifts of money and jewellery.

Their passion above all bound them together but Mrs. Herrington's tendency to caution and reserve in public contrasted with her private fire when alone with her benefactor and lover.

Duncan halted before the small brick cottage, circumspect behind a painted wooden fence and small garden. Its cost was immaterial to him. He would lavish any attention on this woman and only this woman with whom he shared a mutual unrestrained excitement each time they met. Their spark had never dimmed and on both their accounts had grown into a love they breathlessly declared to each other.

He smoothed down his hair, tugged his coat straighter and in silent irony thanked Isabelle for ordering the latest tailored suits especially for him, keeping him respectable for business and his mistress.

Less than a handful of his male associates guessed of his paramour but the knowledge was safe among his fellow men. It was his constant fear that Isabelle should ever find out about the other woman in his life. It had been tricky enough explaining Ginny.

It amused him how easily his wife could be distracted with furnishing the new homestead and the promise of a seaside holiday in the summer. Such simple pleasures, coupled with the responsibility for raising their children, guaranteed to keep her occupied and staying up country on the run.

But she was growing restless and the purpose of summoning Portia to Geelong. He needed her in permanent residence to lessen the chance of detection or their letters being mistakenly opened or intercepted.

Duncan stepped up to the door, wielded the knocker and, within minutes, expected, was ushered inside.

'Duncan.'

'Portia.'

He swept his luscious vision of beauty into his arms, barely able to keep his hands from the body he knew was his. Their kiss was deep and moist, promising more. Her thick hair was still neatly upswept but it would tumble soon enough. She pulled him down onto the sofa beside her.

'I have been mad with impatience since I received your letter. I am always overjoyed to receive them but it is becoming longer between each of your visits,' she complained.

'I'm surprised you agreed. You keep me waiting. You refuse to come to Geelong and it's not always easy for me to get across to Melbourne too often.'

'Are you testing me?' she breathed, leaning closer into him, her full soft breasts pressing against his coat, half exposed and enticing, threatening to spill from beneath the rich lavender silk and lace gown.

Duncan raised a hand to cup her and slid the other around her slender waist, crushing her tighter. 'No. I trust and want ye.'

The world stopped for another deep kiss. For him, each time was as the first. He adored her and still could not believe such a lush woman was all his. If she ever rejected him, he would shrivel and die inside. Isabelle's routine coupling was no comparison. He bedded her for sons alone. This woman drove him wild with lust, thrilling him in new ways and arousals every time. He was her slave and he dreaded her loss. A foolish unfounded terror since they exploded together when they met, reassuring him.

The urges of their desire always overcame them first so she soon sank beneath him on the sofa. He lifted her rustling skirt and explored beneath its folds as they both gasped with impatience. When she cried out his name, as always at her peak of pleasure, he knelt over her and guided himself inside her warm familiar flesh, surrounded by her redolent floral perfume.

Sated after the first time of what would be many matings this visit, they lounged together, partly clad, entwined, drinking whisky.

'Ah'll be startin' building work on the homestead soon. Ah'll be in Geelong and Melbourne often with builders and the architect. There'll be more opportunity to meet.' He raised the issue dear to his heart again. 'Are ye sure I cannot buy ye a house here in Geelong?'

'Duncan, my love, I could not ask it of you and I've already told you, I'm not sure it's wise this close to your home. Melbourne is more distant and seems safer.'

'Ah'm known in town as much as here,' he growled, displeased. 'A brick cottage such as this is only around two hundred Pounds and a weatherboard even less. Ah've seen a two storey stone house for five hundred. Any one of them could be yours. Would ye not reconsider?'

Portia shook her loose hair, its long tresses trailing over his bare chest. 'If I'm here and always available, you might tire of me,' she pouted, teasing, running her thumb over his mouth and following it with her lips.

'You're seein' trouble where there's none. You're makin' me hard again, woman,' he chuckled as she massaged him.

He pulled her onto his lap and they began their lovemaking all over again.

Later, needing food, they partially dressed and dined from

a cold platter at the table that a morning maid had prepared earlier before she left.

'The family will be takin' a seaside holiday next summer for about a month. If you were lodged here in Geelong, we could meet once or twice a week. Ah've no trouble gettin' away on the excuse of seein' to the homestead now.'

'Do you mean it, Duncan? You would want me over here for so long? I won't bore you?' she queried, genuinely concerned.

'I'll never lose my appetite for you, Mrs. Herrington. Ah'll arrange a house for ye.'

'It's a greater risk,' she whispered between his kisses.

'We'll take it. I can't be without ye.'

Heavy intermittent rain for weeks in May, an unusual heavy fall of wet so early in the season, quagmired roads into a fearful state. The Barwon river banks overflowed.

Isabelle noticed Duncan strangely content since returning from his last visit to Geelong. His meetings about the new homestead must be going well. As he sat opposite, staring into the fire and drew on his pipe, a glass of whisky by his side, she read from the Geelong Advertiser, relating some of the horrid events and damage caused by the deluge.

'A father, mother and daughter in the Hedge family were washed away in the floods with their house,' Isabelle said, shaking her head sadly and frowning. The whole district suffered and mourned.

It is our painful duty to announce the death of Mr. and Mrs. Wedge of the Ex River and one of their younger daughters by the flood on Friday evening last. Towards eight o'clock, so suddenly had their habitation become surrounded by deep water, that they were driven to the necessity of taking refuse on the roof.

And another extract. *Every hour brings tidings of fresh disaster...at Bates Ford, the Moorabool swept over the bridge and flooded the valley on either side of its banks to the base of the hills...Mr. Varey rode into Geelong to procure a boat to succour the insulated inhabitants...the occupants of Mr. Varey's house made their escape by breaking down the ceiling over the bar, crawling through the aperture to the loft above, and this instance will suffice to show the suspense and agony of others in the neighbourhood when overtaken by this unforeseen disaster...on the roof there were clustered together at least twenty women and children crying for help.*

'The water's risen up the hill here as well,' Duncan said, 'the reason ah'm buildin' the new homestead high.'

Isabelle continued to read.

Communication with Melbourne by water is also cut off. No steamer has arrived since Friday owing to the floods in the Yarra rendering it dangerous for steamers to leave the wharf.

She scanned more paragraphs and read on.

A rush of water flooded the plains and country...continuous heavy full of rain soon gave impulse to the river's course and the Barwon bridge stood well until about two o'clock on Sunday morning when it yielded with a crash before the force of the water. Piles and logs have gone, nothing is left but a post and a few rails to mark where the bridge was.

Duncan nodded sagely. 'They'll have to make the town accessible again. It's going to take a time to recover.'

Isabelle noticed Duncan seemed unduly bothered by the road to Geelong when it didn't immediately affect them. She would have assumed the flooding on the lower reaches of Kooringal, his stock losses and the movement of flocks to high paddocks was of greater importance. Perhaps he was concerned that the building would be delayed.

More newspapers, when they eventually arrived, revealed further dreadful catastrophes.

Property of all descriptions has been washed ashore on both sides of the Barwon River...boxes, broken chairs, tables and drawers, and others parts of furniture were stewed about in all directions...a large body of police were busily employed throughout Saturday in rescuing what property they could.

Winter made it difficult enough travelling on the roads.

Any kind of conveyance found it impossible to get through. Wagons and carts had been known to sink in the mud up to the axles and marooned for days or weeks at a time until the track dried out enough to move on. All this didn't deter the streams of optimistic men doggedly heading for the diggings when gold was discovered in the nearby Anakie hills near Fred Griffin's run.

When Maeve appeared in the sitting room one morning after breakfast looking serious, Isabelle glanced up from her desk and the housekeeping accounts in surprise.

'Can I be having a word with you, Isabelle?'

'Of course, Maeve,' she said gently, curious about what her best friend might have to say. 'Sit down. Is little Mackenzie all right?'

Maeve beamed. 'Oh yes. Bessie's in the kitchen watching out for her.'

After a brief stiff pause while the ticking mantel clock and the children's voices drifted in to them from the nursery, Maeve suddenly blurted out, 'I'm leaving.'

When she recovered from the outburst and the impact of its meaning, Isabelle's shoulders sank with dismay. 'You're quite serious?'

Maeve nodded, brows wrinkled and eyes silently appealing as if begging her friend and mistress not to convince her to change her mind.

'Why?' Isabelle managed to whisper after a while, her heart tugging against the recent upheavals in the household. First Ginny's death, now Maeve's talk of leaving. She began to feel unsettled and lonely. Those first familiar faces and friends she'd made were gradually all disappearing.

'You're settled here on Kooringal. This is your home now. I'm still a servant. Since having Mackenzie, I have a need in me to provide a better life for her. I want to make my own way. I can't stay here in your kitchen forever. I need to move on and try to improve myself. Don't take my meaning wrong, Isabelle,' she leaned forward and clasped her hands. 'You've been my good friend here right from the start. We've laughed and shared our troubles together. And you kept me on here when I had my daughter. But there's big opportunities on the gold fields.' Her eyes lit up. 'Irish tells me what the men are saying that pass through.'

'But how can you dig for gold, Maeve? You wouldn't have the strength, surely?'

She chuckled. 'You eejit. I'll not be using a shovel. I'm a cook, right? And thousands of men need to be fed. The money being made on Ballarat is from supplying the diggers' needs, not panning for gold.'

'Oh!' Light suddenly dawned for Isabelle and relief passed across her face.

'I love my job here,' Maeve enthused. 'I have a big kitchen with everything I need and a free hand but I know it means you've to find someone else to replace me.'

'Oh Maeve, no one else will ever fill your shoes. You work so hard, especially at Christmas. You're the best cook. How will we ever manage without you?'

'I don't want to leave but I have to. Do you understand?'

Isabelle sighed. 'Sadly, I believe I do.'

'I know with everyone heading for the diggings servants are scarce. I'll stay for a few months until spring when the roads are passable again. Would that be enough time?' she ventured hopefully.

Isabelle clenched her hands together, disheartened to see since Maeve had made the decision she was clearly eager to go. But she was right. Life shifted for everyone. There came a time when it turned or offered a new opportunity and choices had to be made.

Knowing Maeve all these years, she would have given her future much thought. Although misled and wronged by Mackenzie's father, she had coped, stayed strong and positive, and was planning ahead.

'I'll advertise right away,' Isabelle said generously, hiding the pining she already felt inside. 'I'll miss you, and seeing

Mackenzie grow,' she admitted softly. 'You've been like a sister to me.'

'Oh, stop right there.' Maeve lurched to her feet, lifting a corner of her apron to wipe away her tears. 'You're making me feel guilty. I've lost many a night's sleep over this.'

'I know you would have.' Isabelle rose and moved forward to hug her friend. 'We'll manage but Kooringal will never be the same without you. At least for me,' she muttered, stepping back, her hands on Maeve's shoulders. 'But promise me, if you ever want or need a job,' she emphasised, 'it's yours.'

'Thank you,' Maeve whispered, her eyes as red as her hair. She raised an arm aimlessly, looking lost. 'I should get back to Mackenzie and Bessie. Wretched girl can't do a thing on her own,' she mumbled, then turned and fled.

Isabelle stood for some time staring at the door where she had just left. She plumped back down onto her chair, gaping at the floor, feeling empty and alone, wondering how that could be amid her noisy family.

CHAPTER 6

Callum Penross arrived, a good quiet child in contrast to his mischievous older brother Blair and adventurous sibling Alexander. A blessing for Isabelle because she had new staff appointments to arrange but his birth drained her energy and her milk dried up. Unable to feed him, Audrey gave him a night bottle so Isabelle gained a good night's rest to help her recovery. It had been emotional losing Ginny, and soon Maeve and Mackenzie would be off to the diggings.

After the birth of yet another son, Isabelle had hoped Duncan would ignore her for a while but his passion for building the homestead kept him in a fever of excitement and he took to her in bed with renewed interest. Preoccupied with plans and building, his enthusiasm high, he often needed to travel down to Geelong. She envied him these escapes but was also thankful for the respite of his absence. To his credit, he always bought back whatever she asked. Packages of dress material, so well-chosen and beyond Duncan's expertise, a shop girl must surely have given him advice.

As her strength improved, Isabelle accepted she must begin the tedious chore of engaging another cook and general maid. This time not just a girl to help in the kitchen but who could also share the work in the house. She placed an advertisement then unenthusiastically waited for mail. Isabelle had decided to engage the two new employees together to become acquainted from the start. She was also aware she must try and match personalities to reduce any conflict.

Meanwhile, Audrey Bailey in her capable unflustered way, had become her support and companion. She entertained them on the piano of an evening. Isabelle doggedly insisted over Duncan's queried objection, that their governess be included in the family, unlike the hierarchy that existed back in England where she would be banished, a virtual prisoner in the nursery.

Audrey dined at table with Duncan, Isabelle and the older children, their mother insisting Nichola and Blair join them in order for them to learn proper table manners and etiquette among their elders. Audrey was proving a cultured and respectable Christian woman with whom Isabelle shared an immediate trusting friendship. Their conversations, when time and duties allowed in the sitting room and at meals, were therapeutic for them both.

Miss Bailey was no one's fool, deeply sensible, occasionally spirited and proved a kindred ally on Sunday mornings when they dressed the children for service, Duncan grudgingly agreeing to join them.

Isabelle poured over the servant applications as they arrived on her small writing desk in a corner of the sitting room beside the front window, grateful for their number. Females seemed slightly easier to secure. She knew Duncan's frequent turnover of workmen was a constant headache and complaint.

She penned replies to the most likely candidates and, once again, sent Irish down to Geelong to fetch them to Kooringal for an interview. Although Isabelle had a reasonable sense of judging good character, she dreaded hiring staff for Duncan always insisted they be *up to standard*, insisting that the expense of household servants was an important necessity. She filled with annoyance at his snobbery for their own beginnings were humble.

But Victoria, especially now gold had been discovered, was a colony of possibilities and dreams for all, no matter their station in life. Borne out by the influx of immigrants teeming to the diggings up country, seeking easy fortune or those like Duncan himself who emigrated in the early days of Port

Phillip and worked hard to build their fortune.

The two servant prospects duly arrived. Isabelle tugged aside the lace curtains in the sitting room window, watching Mrs. Reed and Lily Watson alight from the cart. The former was a buxom woman whose booming voice carried indoors with a battered flat black hat squashed down on her greying hair. Despite her size, she managed to keep up with spry Irish, although she wondered if their ageing handyman put on an extra burst of energy just to impress. Lily Watson trailed behind in their wake looking rather timid and weedy.

Isabelle greeted them at the front door. 'Ladies, do come in. Irish, ask Maeve to bring in a pot of tea and refreshments for our guests.' A tactic for her cook and dear friend to separately scrutinise the new pair and later share their opinions.

As Irish shuffled away, Isabelle turned and smiled at the women. 'Miss Watson, if you would kindly wait in the sitting room, I shall interview Mrs. Reed in the dining room.'

'Yes, Ma'am.'

To Isabelle's surprise, Lily dropped a small curtsy before she disappeared. She smiled to herself, noting the girl's small gesture of respect, unnecessary out here but an action in her favour. A maid could be moulded and trained if she was respectable. This lass had either worked for gentry before or been well raised. Isabelle's hopes rose. Perhaps the process would not prove quite so tedious after all.

For now, she turned her attention back to Mrs. Reed seated across the polished dining table. Her gaze had tactfully slid around the room assessing its degree of comfort. Isabelle was proud of their graciously understated cottage that quietly proclaimed the Penross prosperity. Mrs. Reed, on the other hand, had yet to establish her credentials, not only for the present kitchen but in a much larger domain when the new homestead was complete. Isabelle was also interested to hear the older woman's opinion of Lily Watson.

'Mrs. Reed,' she began, explaining their expanding

situation regarding the family and new house, and seeking her professional expectations and capabilities.

The woman's eyes gleamed at the distinction such an elevated position would convey.

'No need for you to be concerned about me skills, Mrs. Penross. I been cookin' all me life. Had four kids meself but they're all older now and I'm only lookin' for a job cos me Frederick's gone orf to the diggings. Don't blame him, mind. We can all do with a bit of gold, eh?' she chuckled and her fleshy jowls wobbled. 'But he ain't much with words, so he don't write and I have no idea when he's likely to return. Can't sit around waitin' till he sends money, can I?'

'I imagine not,' Isabelle kindly agreed. Frederick was like many men, it seemed, lured by gold and leaving his wife to fend for herself. The woman lacked polish but her letter of experience compensated. 'And if your husband does return, Mrs. Reed?'

Her optimism plunged. If the husband returned, would she leave?

'Oh, I'd never desert me job, Mrs. Penross.' She paused, shuffling in discomfort. 'Me and Fred.' She paused. 'Well, I don't reckon he's comin' home, like,' she admitted.

'I'm sorry to hear that, Mrs. Reed, but does that mean you would be available long term for the foreseeable future?'

'Oh, my word, yes,' she reassured loudly.

'Good. My present cook, Miss Dempsey, will supervise your training here.'

'I won't need much of that.' She puffed out her chest.

'Perhaps not. But we all have preferences and you will need to be informed. I am prepared to employ you forthwith on one month's trial.'

Mrs. Reed flourished with gratitude, realising she was hired. 'Thank you, Mrs. Penross. I shall prove meself equal to the task, I'm sure.'

Isabelle prayed she was. 'Before you go, may I ask your impression of Miss Watson on the journey from Geelong?'

'Well, she ain't got much between the ears, that's for sure.'

Isabelle was about to disagree, believing on first impressions that young Lily might prove to be a gem, when Mrs. Reed continued, 'But a good clout around the earhole now and again should whip her into shape.'

Isabelle bit back a gasp of disappointment. Mrs. Reed seemed competent but if her personality proved a problem, she was unable to bear the thought of going through all this again if she had to sack her.

'I must make it quite clear, Mrs. Reed,' Isabelle said firmly so there would be no doubt over who was mistress and who was servant. 'I will not tolerate any bullying in my household. Understood?'

Taken aback, the new cook's bluster faded. Disciplined, she straightened in surprised respect for this assured young woman. If only she knew that, being the housekeeper once herself, at six and twenty years of age, Isabelle felt anything but.

'Absolutely not, Ma'am.'

Isabelle grinned to herself at the new cook's reversal. 'Wonderful. I'm pleased we understand each other. And you realise that, assuming Miss Watson proves suitable, she will be a general maid, working not only in the kitchen with you but also in the house as needed by me?'

'Yes, Ma'am.'

'In time, as I see what is needed, I shall draw up a roster by which you shall both abide.' Isabelle rose slowly. 'If you would kindly send in Miss Watson now, please?'

'Yes, Ma'am.'

Mrs. Reed bustled out, suitably chastened, to be shortly replaced by timid Lily.

'Miss Watson.' Isabelle deliberately greeted her warmly and clasped her hands. 'My apologies for keeping you waiting. Did Maeve bring you some tea?'

The girl nodded vigorously. 'Yes, thank you, Ma'am.'

'Good. Good.' How to begin? Already she sensed great

potential in this girl. Lily dropped a curtsy again and moved further along the dining table. 'No need for that, Lily.' Isabelle flashed a wide reassuring smile and indicated she take a seat. This time she chose a chair alongside her at the table, a little closer to help put the maid at ease. 'I would hope we can all be a family here.' Intrigued to discover more of the girl's background for her application was vague, Isabelle asked, 'Did you need to curtsy in your previous employment?'

'Oh yes, Ma'am.'

'And where was that again?' Isabelle shuffled the two sparse pages of her letter, pretending she couldn't find it. 'I know you have written it here somewhere.' She glanced up at Lily with her most becoming smile.

'I worked for Mr. Williams right from when he first built Como House. Been with him five years and watched their four children grow. Young Hartley's being sent off to school in England and only nine years old.'

Isabelle raised her eyebrows, impressed. Edward Williams was an eminent barrister. He and his wife Jessie were well known among colonial society's elite.

'But I left. I quit,' Lily said softly.

'Are you able to tell me why?' Isabelle prompted kindly, sensing misery in the girl's voice.

Lily's lovely brown eyes widened in appeal. 'One of the other servants below stairs thought himself most superior. He tried to take liberties.' She paused, clenching her hands in her lap. 'I'm a respectable girl, Ma'am, and I didn't want no trouble.'

'Absolutely not.' Isabelle reached over and patted her hand, filled with admiration that Lily felt able to stand up for herself with such dignity. To leave such prestigious and secure employment on principle. 'You were very brave. That step would have taken a great deal of courage.'

'They didn't believe me when I complained. I don't lie, Mrs. Penross. You have my word,' Lily announced staunchly. 'I walked out of that house with my head held high and didn't look back. I was so upset I couldn't bear to stay in Melbourne so I took the first steamer ferry to Geelong three weeks ago and I've been seeking another placement ever since.'

'Clearly our good fortune, Lily. You are a girl of exactly the exemplary character we need here at Kooringal. Most of the staff have been my friends. I hope we can be the same.'

'Yes, Ma'am. I'd be honoured, Ma'am.'

'If you can start immediately, it would be a great relief to me.'

A wide smile and sparkling eyes of excitement revealed her delight at the news.

The following weeks proved a test of Maeve's patience with Mrs. Reed now sharing her kitchen.

'She's all mouth,' Maeve declared. 'But she sure knows her job. Just needs some training on presentation. Arranging the food better, that sort of thing. But she's not complaining over hard work.'

Isabelle sighed with relief. 'And Lily?'

'Can't praise the girl highly enough. She's had an education that one. She deserves a higher position if you don't mind me sayin'.'

'My thoughts exactly. I'll keep an eye on her in the coming year. I have promotion in mind when we move into the big house.'

With the current staff matters resolved, Isabelle assumed she could take some ease but, within weeks, Maeve gave her final notice and date of departure. The news threw her into a quandary of emotion to be losing her best friend and ally of the past seven years.

When the day of leaving arrived, between tears and hugs, Irish waited with the cart to take his fellow countrywoman and her child the few miles west to join the main road to Ballarat. Carrying only her daughter and a small valise of belongings, Isabelle's heart wrenched to think of her friend trudging on foot for two days to her destination.

'Plenty of others doin' it.' Maeve had made light of it,

adding, 'It's something I have to do.'

Isabelle said, 'You can write now so no excuses. I'll expect regular letters.'

'I'll do me best,' Maeve promised, 'but startin' out in me own business might not leave me much time.'

'When you can,' Isabelle said sadly, taking Mackenzie from her arms and enjoying one last cuddle of the sunny child she considered like one of her own. 'If you need *anything*,' she hinted tactfully, 'Just write and ask. You know I would do anything for you.'

'I know.' Maeve swiped aside tears with her sleeve.

Mrs. Reed slipped her an envelope. 'For me Fred. I expect you can leave it at some sort of post office place.'

Isabelle wondered how on earth the letter was supposed to find him among tens of thousands of men and was surprised her new cook should bother when, by her own words, she admitted they were estranged.

In public, with everyone lined up in front of the cottage waving and smiling as the cart rattled away with Irish, Maeve and little Mackenzie, Isabelle held herself together. But immediately Duncan and the household servants returned to their work, and Audrey took the children back to the nursery, she wilted in her bedroom and broke down into sobs. Feeling foolish and weak for already missing her dearest friend when she had barely left, Isabelle knew you didn't replace old friends, you simply acquired new ones.

She was further shattered to discover within months of Callum's birth she had fallen pregnant again and was expecting her fifth child. Devastated that it should happen so soon, from the start she felt thoroughly ill.

Isabelle kept up her spirits with the anticipation of their forthcoming family summer holiday on the coast at Shortland's Bluff. It proved a mammoth undertaking moving the whole family down to the seaside for a month. The wagon was cleaned, harness oiled and polished, two pairs of horses groomed before being brought around from the stables and harnessed. Then the wagon was run up to the front gate, everyone piled in and settled in a bustle of skirts, veils tied firmly against the sun and wind; carpet bags, boxes, toys tucked in around their feet.

Isabelle silently checked over her children. Nichola happy to learn, a model student but still avoided any eye contact with her father. They rarely spoke, Duncan's attentions as usual only focused on his sons. Blair needed the enticement of treats to keep his attention so Audrey, in her wisdom, made learning a game. Alexander, always a chuckling bundle of energy, had long since given up a daytime nap so was proving a mischievous handful. Placid Callum on her lap was still an undemanding babe and she was grateful for his contentment.

Duncan, up front with Isabelle and Audrey, took the whip and reins, the team jumped into the traces and pulled hard before settling into their stride.

At first they crossed the green level plains with a few she-oaks and timber until they reached the river. Then they followed the Moorabool as it flowed and wound through the centre of its lovely valley, fringed with large vigorous red gums until they reached the Geelong road where a constant line of people walked north in the opposite direction, heading for the gold rush, bent beneath the weight of the few possessions they carried. Isabelle's thoughts easily strayed to Maeve and Mackenzie, gone for months now without a word.

The children grew impatient and restless but the women shared their entertainment. At times, the younger ones slept but Nichola and Blair stayed awake, excited by their first journey away from home. Toward evening, to Isabelle's eyes as they neared town, the long dark stretches of shadow between soft fading sunlight across the track looked magical.

In Geelong, dozens of vessels were anchored in Corio bay which came right up to the front of town now, much larger with many newly built houses of wood or brick and stone.

At last they pulled up before Mack's hotel. Duncan jumped down to see to the horses while a weary Isabelle and

Audrey mustered the children inside. When they had eaten and retired to their rooms, Isabelle sought Duncan to find out what time they must leave in the morning, only to learn from their landlord that he had left on business. She frowned, wondering what was so important on the first night of their holiday that he should abandon his family. She had hoped by spending more time with his children, especially Nichola, they might understand each other better.

Duncan strode out eagerly to the comfortable freestone cottage further around the waterfront. His only concern was how often he could reasonably make his excuses from the family and get away to visit Portia. He had already sent a note on ahead.

She greeted him, breathless and shameless in a low cut light blue silk gown most suitable for the summer weather. She immediately drew him inside to her bedroom.

'Duncan, is this not exquisite? And with such a view! You have thought of everything.

He chuckled as she whirled about youthfully, then turned serious. 'Ah only ever want to please you, my dearest.'

Long familiar with the décor of her Melbourne house for which he had paid all expenses now for many years, he also knew her tastes in other ways. Including the grand four poster bed with the best and deepest mattress he could buy, draped with curtains and lace.

'Shall we christen it?' She slipped the dress from her shoulders.

After they made love, Portia nestled against Duncan's muscled sun browned chest. 'Is your wife beautiful?'

'Mrs. Herrington,' he growled, 'we've an agreement. She's only the mother of ma bairns.'

She pouted. 'Tell me the truth. I must know.'

'She's a mite plain.'

Turning apologetic and pleased with his assessment, she leant across to kiss him. When her naked body, lush and trim, rubbed against him, he took her again, selfishly and without thought for her pleasure, angered that visions of his wife should intrude.

With each passing year, Portia grew more insecure, needing constant reassurance, the reason he had cajoled and insisted she move here for the summer. He wanted her close, not only to demonstrate and prove his love. He needed her. She was his goddess. He adored and worshipped her as he never would another, and knew his slavery would last all of his days.

When he was with Portia, he was never troubled with thoughts of Isabelle, except to fleetingly regret he couldn't love her at all. She was a fertile mother, although he knew she had been unwell for some time and unhappy with her latest pregnancy so soon. He had three sons and would not begrudge her another daughter. Isabelle's efforts to civilise him had served him well with Portia.

He looked down on her now, her breasts exposed above the bed linen, gently rising and falling in her languor after he redeemed himself by bringing her to her own ecstasy. Stirred at the irresistible sight of her, he bent to take a nipple into his mouth. Portia moaned, only half awake but soon roused to welcome his lips and tongue with hers. She writhed beneath him, opened her legs and they loved urgently again.

Next day, Duncan announced to Isabelle, 'Ah thought you and the children might like a turn around Geelong before we head down to the sea.'

Such consideration, Isabelle pulled a tight smile. 'I'm sure they'll love it.'

Duncan eyed her warily. 'And you wouldn't?'

'Of course I will. I've never been invited to accompany you before,' she hinted a touch sharply. 'From what I briefly saw last evening upon arrival, Geelong is much changed.'

When Duncan left her room, Isabelle washed and dressed before proceeding to the nearby children's room to find

Audrey organised, the older children dressed and baby Callum in a crib patiently awaiting his turn for attention.

They all took breakfast together in the small dining room, the two older boys plying their father with questions about the sea which he dutifully answered. Isabelle and Audrey sat at the other end of the table with Nichola and Callum between them.

Lively after a night's rest, the children impatiently awaited their wagon's arrival in front of the hotel and clamoured outdoors. Isabelle marvelled over the growth and bustle of the town. The market square, public garden, the sandstone Christ Church in Moorabool Street and the Wesleyan Chapel. Perhaps there would be a suitable place of workshop down at the Bluff.

She voiced her eagerness to stay longer and explore its shops as they passed Bright and Hitchcock's store.

'Ye'll be here for a month,' Duncan said gruffly, displeased at her suggestion, apparently anxious to leave. 'Time enough for more visits then.'

Isabelle grew disheartened for, in her growing condition, she found travelling a jolting burden but she silently accepted they still had a distance to travel today and should not delay the final twenty mile leg of their journey in order to arrive before dark.

How rustic and less civilised Geelong had been only seven years ago. All due to gold, of course, and the influx of hopefuls. How her life had progressed too since then in a direction she could never have foreseen.

Duncan finally turned the wagon for the coast. The day grew warm but a fresh breeze boosted them, bringing drifts of the ocean's salty smell building among them all as they neared their destination.

With the longer daylight hours of summer, it was well before dark when Blair whooped, 'Is that the sea?' pointing to the sparkling blue water appearing on the horizon.

'Of course it is, silly,' Nichola snapped, her back straight and her nose loftily raised.

'How do you know?'

'I've seen pictures.'

'Children!' Isabelle shook her head and sighed. Nichola had remained bitter toward her brother since the bush fire two years ago. She hoped the bad memories would fade and their bickering pass with age.

As the small fishing village of Shortland Bluff opened up before them, its beautiful sandy beach broadened into their vision, spread wide to either side.

Duncan conducted them to a substantial stone cottage rented for the month, one of only a few since the seaside settlement was yet small. Isabelle was impressed at first sight of the house. Duncan had chosen comfortably and well by writing to acquaintances in the district seeking recommendations. It was refreshing to feel the salty cool breeze caress her upturned face as she stepped down.

The boys had already jumped from the wagon before their father reined the horses. The masts and rigging of ships anchored off shore jutted starkly against the cloudless sky.

A small staff emerged from indoors and immediately began unloading the wagon. In her usual efficient manner, Audrey mustered the children inside. Although they had brought dried supplies with them, fresh meat and produce would be provided daily by arrangement with the locals.

'Fish will be on the menu, no doubt,' Duncan had hinted weeks before.

Since she often lacked an appetite these days, Isabelle was unconcerned what they ate. Maybe the change of scenery and sight of all that water, unseen since she sailed from England, would lift her spirits.

Blair begged his father to be allowed down onto the beach.

'You're never to go off alone or into the water,' he warned.

'Yes, father,' Blair said, frowning, clearly confused. 'But Alex is too small to come with me.'

'What about me?' Nichola glowered.

'Girls don't go on the beach, do they father?' Blair's lip curled with derision.

'How would you know?' she retorted and turned to Isabelle. 'Mother?'

'Not now, Nichola. It's been a long journey. We all need a meal and a good night's rest.'

'But-'

'We shall see tomorrow,' she said firmly, holding her daughter's belligerent challenging gaze.

'Why did we come to the beach if we can't play on it?' she muttered.

'Mind your manners, girl,' Duncan bellowed unnecessarily.

Isabelle flung him a black glare for interfering with her discipline when he usually did not. She would soon learn, his meddling was to be a regular occurrence during long idle hours. Duncan prowled about like a chained animal so that Isabelle guiltily welcomed his frequent absences in Geelong that kept them apart the rest of the time.

The irony was, once comfortably settled by the sea, Isabelle had no desire or energy to waste on driving a whole day in the wagon back to Geelong. So that she came to regard Duncan's absence overnight on his regular weekly business trips as a blessing. Especially since he always returned bringing news, sketches and drawings of the homestead, details of trimmings and samples of materials for her consideration which fortunately took no effort as her body grew heavier. Duncan no longer came to her bed but, incredibly, knowing his needs, he seemed unaffected by his abstinence.

On those days when the weather was kind, they all traipsed down to the beach. Duncan occasionally hired a boat and took the boys sailing, leaving Nichola sitting grimly on the sand to play alone.

Isabelle took pity on her abandoned daughter and cheerfully suggested a walk on the cliff tops to watch the ships. They sauntered, taking their time, Nichola understanding her mother's constraint and easing her pace to match. Isabelle thought the girl less resentful at times and even caught a guarded smile now and then.

A number of vessels arrived every day and the pilot cutter was always stationed outside the Heads to be available for them at all times. They watched as the pilot boat neared the new arrival and lowered a pilot and crew aboard to row alongside the incoming ship. A rope ladder was lowered and the pilot leapt onto it from his boat. Nichola always gasped at that moment, fearing the man might fall into the often swirling sea.

Other days found the women sitting with Callum on a rug under a sun umbrella with a packed hamper or reading books brought from home. They had all entered a whole new world and routine of simple tranquil days. Clad only in petticoat and drawers or underclothes, the children paddled in the shallows, squealing and running back up the beach chased by waves. Sometimes it rained and they were forced to play indoor games, their noses pressed to the small windows waiting for it to stop.

As the weeks passed, although they avoided the sun in the heat of the day, everyone's skin turned golden. A mood of ease and companionship spread among the family. Isabelle almost believed Duncan enjoyed their company. Nichola avoided or ignored Blair, usually trailed by Alexander. Isabelle was relieved to see her daughter quietly sink into her own world of reading or hover in the kitchen with the servants and chatting to them like the lady of the manor.

Isabelle and Audrey shared responsibility for Callum. They lazed on chairs in the shade, dozed or took gentle morning or evening strolls to escape the hottest hours, always tempered by a lovely zephyr that sprang up late in the day, reviving their lethargic souls.

The staff proved unobtrusive, anticipating the family's needs, remaining considerate of their privacy and miraculously appearing when required. Everyone began to grow thoughtful and complain as their last seaside days fast disappeared.

'Can we come back next summer?' Nichola asked plaintively, one of the few times she had whined for weeks.

'I don't see why not,' Isabelle smiled and squeezed her hand on one of their last walks, cherishing the rare moment of attachment, afraid their new bond would crumble when they returned home.

A few months later, Christie Penross was born. Immediately her oldest sister grew jealous and her mother frustrated.

Then word came through that Anne Drysdale, one of a pair of lady squatters in the district, had died. Isabelle had always marvelled at how much stronger and more determined a woman must be to manage such an undertaking.

When they read that forty acres had been set aside for a new university north of Melbourne, Duncan declared it as the future place of education for his sons. No mention of educating his daughters, Isabelle noted.

In spring, while Christie was still tiny, Isabelle and Audrey took the children on painting and plant excursions, and picnics. All learning to ride, Duncan provided ponies for each, even Alexander who readily scrambled to be lifted up by Irish, steady in the saddle from his first ride. Even Nichola cautiously took the reins, usually helped by Duke. Perhaps each an outcast in their own way, the two older children developed a connection, kindred souls seeking friendship between themselves. The brown skinned native lad quietly ignored but encouraged the domineering boss's daughter.

Callum was toddling now and Isabelle filled with a new contentment since her second daughter's birth, despite Christie's tendency to wake and demand. She grew stronger and in the cool spring evenings, the older children and womenfolk, minus Duncan in his study, might gather around while Audrey played the piano.

'Do you think it sounds off key?' Isabelle asked, listening intently.

'It may need a tune.'

'I'll arrange one. Maybe he knows a teacher for Nichola.'

Within weeks, the musical matter was resolved when a middle aged German gentleman arrived, as arranged, from Geelong.

'Mr. Kruger.' Isabelle welcome him into the sitting room. Lily helped him remove his damp coat. 'Come closer to the fire,' she beckoned, glad of its blazing heat for the weather had turned cool with a tendency to rain. 'This is our governess, Miss Bailey.'

His gaze lingered as they were introduced and he held her hand for perhaps longer than polite or necessary.

Mesmerised, Audrey blushed. 'Shall I arrange tea?' She rose abruptly.

Isabelle hid her amusement at the woman's unease. 'No, no, Audrey. Please stay. Lily?' She addressed the maid, still hovering. 'Tea for everyone.'

'Yes Ma'am.'

While Mr. Kruger, or Walter as he insisted, backed up to the hearth, chatting comfortably in his thick German accent, Isabelle noticed Audrey looked everywhere but directly at him, leaving her to carry the conversation.

'I visit ozer homes in ze area zo I can call here for lessons mit your daughter, Mrs. Penross,' he suggested when Isabelle enquired.

When Lily brought in the tea, Isabelle asked, 'Would you ask Nichola to join us?'

'Yes Ma'am.'

As her daughter entered, Isabelle beamed. 'Nichola I have someone I would like you to meet.'

Captivated as they all were by this quiet charismatic foreigner, she responded positively to his impeccable manners. Isabelle watched her daughter politely stifle giggles at his accent and patterns of speech but she uttered no snide quips today. Rapt in his endearing charm. Audrey also remained virtually silent in awe. Few men generated such veneration from women but Walter Kruger was certainly one of them.

'So, it's all arranged then.' Isabelle beamed at him, now dry and seated opposite in a deep chair near Audrey, nervously clasping and unclasping her hands. 'You shall visit every fortnight for lessons and tend our piano as needed. I look forward to visiting your music shop in Geelong.'

With a newborn and a bevy of children, she had no idea when that might be. Mischievously, she wondered if she should send Audrey instead.

Hours later when the social tea party had disbanded and everyone had returned to their duties, Walter's discordant plunking could be heard throughout the cottage. Suddenly it stopped and the strains of beautiful classical music drifted in.

Isabelle crept toward the sitting room where Audrey already eavesdropped from the door, fascinated too. Clearly a skilled musician, Walter's long slender fingers caressed the keys with emotion and grace.

Too soon, Lily was handing him his coat in the hall. As he shrugged it on, Isabelle and Audrey bade him farewell, impressed by the gentleman's immaculate suited appearance. The streaks of grey in his hair only added to his appeal and he held his tall frame proudly erect, making him a fine figure of a man.

Isabelle thought she heard Audrey heave a gentle sigh as he rode away but said nothing.

For Walter Kruger's subsequent visits, Isabelle noticed Audrey fussed with her appearance before he arrived, flustered and edgy. Isabelle knew she would hate to lose her since she had been with them such a short while, but it was only fair what was surely a budding romance be given every chance to blossom.

To her surprise, Isabelle heard Audrey actually agree to take a stroll with him across the paddocks and down to the river before he left. But as the months and years progressed, it saddened her to see a devoted Walter remain loyal but kept at arm's length by Audrey so that their companionship survived but never developed. It angered Isabelle that Walter lacked backbone. She wished he would give the obtuse woman an ultimatum to force her hand but it never happened.

Homestead excavations began on the cellar and a foundation stone laid by Duncan and Blair with much ceremony.

When the small timber schoolroom was built, Isabelle offered Audrey the permanent position of teacher since her relationship with Walter was clearly stagnant.

The significant bluestone Penross homestead with outer walls many feet thick slowly rose from the ground on the crest of the hill behind the cottage. According to the plans, it would contain over twenty large rooms, high ceilings and long spacious corridors as big as the rooms themselves. The main living areas were downstairs with double the number of present bedrooms upstairs. Although the kitchen was still at the back of the house, it would be part of it along one side of the rear courtyard. Mrs. Reed preened over the prospect of her new domain.

When German craftsmen arrived by bullock dray, specially sourced by Duncan, Walter chattered away to them in their native tongue on his regular tuition visits for Nichola. Suitable trees were sought for the sawyers, clay for the brick makers, and bullock wagons constantly hauled in special timbers ordered for the rafters and posts.

More cheerful and positive now since recovering from her two close pregnancies, Isabelle often walked up the hill to admire the massive new construction under way and set to dominate the landscape. The cottage halfway down the hill was dwarfed by the emerging stately residence that would enjoy the sweeping views of the property and river from the wide front veranda and terrace with broad steps down to the garden.

Isabelle could not help but compare the cottage, her home

for eight years. Would this impressive house be home, too? Alone but not lonely, Isabelle was gripped by a fleeting pang for Maeve and their early simple days.

Duncan was busy supervising the building and taking frequent trips to Geelong. They did not so much grow apart as Isabelle felt she was being left behind and only hoped she wasn't losing her husband. For all his gruff bluster, he still held a fond place in her heart. They ate together mechanically each evening in the dining room, the children long in bed by the time he returned. Later, he burnt candles until late at night in his study.

Isabelle sighed and turned her attention back to the background of trees already planted years before and growing ready for the house to nestle in its own proper setting. As well as all his other commitments, Duncan also insisted on overseeing the establishment of the extended garden. With labourers, he planted an avenue of von Mueller's Monterey pine seedlings along the driveway track leading in off the main road and passing to the western side of the present cottage.

Frowning over the extent of her husband's empire, Isabelle let her gaze roam over the huge underground water storage tanks and the simpler wooden buildings of a school and chapel further away. Excavations were being dug for new brick quarters for Duncan's growing stable of thoroughbred horses. Sometimes, the scope of his ambitions frightened her and she worried over the driven man he had become.

With fat wool cheques every year and handsome profits from selling meat to the gold fields, a healthy annual income was now assured. But still he seemed to need more and push himself harder.

Late the following year, with majestic new Kooringal imposing itself on the landscape and interior decoration begun, the new village of Meredith sprang up along the Geelong to Ballarat road. It boasted an official post office so mail and newspapers were much closer to collect. Only ten miles into town, it was a pleasant buggy ride for half a day.

The following month in early December, news seeped through from Ballarat of troubles and unrest. There had been an uprising when police troopers and diggers clashed at Eureka lead. Miners had grown discontent over the high licence fees and refused to pay.

Isabelle furiously penned a letter to Maeve on the gold fields in care of the post office as usual where her friend collected her mail, enquiring after her safety. To her relief and delight, a spirited response came within weeks.

Dear Isabelle,

It was right nice to hear from you and receive your Christmas greetings. They are returned. Mackenzie and me are just fine but we've had our share of troubles here at Bullarat. My restaurant is not near Eureka and all the shooting and fighting. I know it were terrible what the diggers did, disobeying the law and all, burning their licences and protesting but I seen the troopers treat them rough and it don't seem fair them paying so much money and being chased for it and beat up. Everyone said it was too high and the miners can't afford it especially since many don't find no gold.

Isabelle smiled at Maeve's turn of phrase and could almost hear her speaking.

The miners want the licence stopped. They held a big meeting on Bakery Hill at the end of November and flew their own flag. Blue with a white cross and five stars. Someone said it meant the Southern Cross and the night sky. Seems strange to me. I don't know what the stars have got to do with mining.

Then they got serious and built a round wooden fort. I heard there was a thousand rebels inside who swore an oath to fight but most of them left. The soldiers and police attacked them at four o'clock on the Sunday morning. I know it was clever but all the diggers were asleep so it stands to reason, don't it, that they soon

Duncan predicted this would be the family's last Christmas in the cottage before they moved into the big house. Isabelle walked daily with the children and Audrey to inspect it up on the hill and try to explain to them it was their new home.

As they slowly climbed the slope, the impressive house gradually revealed its impact. She tried, but failed, to find some sense of excitement over it as they passed through the double entrance gates with stone pillars recently erected at the bottom of the long driveway.

The kitchen and servants wings at the back were finished first, extending out both sides of a beautiful rear inner courtyard. A trap for sunlight with plants in large pots and a splashing fountain.

Isabelle looked up at the broad verandas and balconies right around on both storeys decorated with iron lace work and rows of windows.

As they climbed the half circle of steps to the front cedar panelled door, Nichola asked, 'Who will live in the cottage now?' always wide eyed and impressed.

Isabelle wished she could answer. The boys ran and lost

themselves in its room, getting under the workmen's feet.

Early in the New Year with the homestead build moving rapidly beneath Duncan's bellowed orders to achieve as much work as possible during the summer and autumn before another winter, Isabelle found herself pregnant. She still admired her husband but the manner in which her children were always conceived remained the same. He came to her fiercely, taking the body she gave to him.

A deep fragment inside her remained hopeful that as long as he continued making love to her, she was still useful to him. For all his tenacity, she still needed him. She never doubted her importance in his life as the bearer of his children. The glue that held the household together and made it run smoothly in order that his important work and management on stations continued uninterrupted with all his needs provided and met.

But over the years, a dull ache had begun to settle inside her because their marriage, never strong, had grown hollow. Duncan no longer sought her company as often yet she craved more from him, knowing she would never receive it. She was not unhappy, merely unfulfilled.

She had been a dutiful and loyal wife and loved her babies dearly, each and every one special to her in their own way. But Duncan was so busy creating his dynasty, breeding heirs, stud flocks and swift thoroughbreds, she only ever existed on the edge of his life.

His office was his domain where he handled accounts, paid his men and kept his guns. With its oil cloth on the desk, tobacco cutter and row upon row of pigeon holes on the walls behind his desk for papers, stock returns, shearing figures, land details and endless letters.

In her turn, Isabelle took refuge in her corner of the sitting room down the hall where she, too, wrote letters back home to vaguely remembered siblings in Blackburn who never replied. She sighed, wondering why she bothered. Maeve, on the other hand, probably exhausted, always answered promptly with her latest news on whatever scrap of paper was to hand.

With the advent of their gracious homestead and servants to tend their every need, Isabelle forced herself, especially during her pregnancies, to take up the embroidery needle to craft beautiful linen for her home. She admitted Mrs. Reed to discuss meals and pantry stocks, and took tea with Audrey when her duties permitted after school. There was always the indulgence of the latest magazines from England and visits at times by the older children, usually only Nichola, for the vast outdoors beckoned to her healthy boys where, to Audrey's complaints, they disappeared for hours with Duke, often on their ponies.

If she grew confined and restless, Isabelle drifted upstairs to hold her babies or play with them as her need arose.

Throughout the construction of Duncan's dream mansion, Isabelle's physical strength was challenged to the limit, obeying his commands to view furnishing catalogues. Amid supervising her family and running the household, her thirtieth birthday suddenly arrived to swamp her with panic at growing old, not helped by her expanding ungainly body. She easily fell pregnant and bore healthy children, except for her very first, and always revelled in the feel of another life moving inside her, regardless of the way they were conceived by a dominant father. Duncan, nearing forty, was as handsome and tireless as ever, lines from weather, not age, crinkling his permanently tanned face.

Soon, tradesmen moved indoors to complete panelling and woodwork, water closets in the bathrooms upstairs and even for the servants in the downstairs wing. White marble fireplaces with iron grates were installed, and painters and glaziers congested the rooms, alive with activity. The cedar staircase, polished to gleaming, curved around an oval well from the hall to the bedrooms above.

Duncan's list of furniture to be purchased left Isabelle speechless. Dray loads arrived daily. Beautiful pieces, far grander than anything she could ever have imagined appeared to grace the rooms. Grandfather clocks, impressive corner cupboards, magnificent wall mirrors, wardrobes and tallboys for the bedrooms. Duncan spared no expense and personally scrutinised every article.

Aspidistras in brass bowls magically appeared, framed gilt and cedar pictures, flowered wallpaper, coloured stained glass for feature windows. Kerosene lamps replaced candles. Finally, one of the last dray loads brought crockery and provisions, fine flour and a case of port wine.

A bevy of gardeners began the foundation work for the basic landscape design Duncan was determined to create. On separate plans, Isabelle had seen outdoor walks and pergola covered pathways. Eventually, a summer pavilion would be constructed halfway down the slope but winter set in and much outdoor work was halted.

A withered Irish resentfully accepted the engagement of a Chinese gardener, a skilled fugitive from the gold fields, to help with the increased need for produce from the new walled kitchen garden to feed the growing family and entourage of servants. Over many weeks, Isabelle sought Audrey's help and guidance in choosing them.

Then, on one exhilarating day, the official move from cottage to homestead took place. For days, all hands had been busy transferring the family's personal effects, and leaving only now inadequate skeleton furnishings behind. For a time, everyone was overwhelmed by the magnitude and splendour of the new homestead and, occasionally, lost. Audrey closely watched the children around the stairs but even little Christie, now almost two, managed them in her bold and independent way. Nichola took them slowly and with grace, for effect, whereas the boys hurtled down resulting in trips, tumbles and bruises.

The children's voices echoed through the large rooms and wide hallways, and a grander life was launched although Isabelle often gazed nostalgically from upstairs windows back toward the cottage contemplating humbler times.

Duncan's small flock of peacocks now strutted their

magnificence on the grassy expanses around the house, flaunting themselves at will, spreading their magnificent tails against a background of bluestone.

Audrey had now become the teacher in the new school house for their own children and workmen's families. To Lily Watson's great delight, she was promoted to head housemaid supervising all the under servants, with Mrs. Reed in the kitchen training two new girls.

The English oak Duncan had planted soon after his arrival was now robust with a thick trunk and housed a rope swing for the children, especially Nichola, who often retreated to its sanctuary. Surprising, since she far preferred the indoors and hated getting dirty. Now nine, Isabelle noticed her daughter emerging from childhood into more refined behaviour. She had grown quiet and feminine, graciously charming all she met as though many years older than her age, particular over every aspect of her appearance.

The humble old piano no longer sufficed and was left in the cottage. Isabelle protested at the extravagance of the new grand piano delivered to the downstairs music room. Nichola shone beneath Walter Kruger's regular tuition, her slender fingers gliding across the keys with delicate ability.

Isabelle quietly watched her, proud of her oldest daughter but concerned that she still nurtured an unnecessary jealousy of toddler Christie, hardly rival competition. Although difficult by nature and testing even tolerant Audrey's patience, Nichola still vainly struggled to please her father. With every passing year, Isabelle's heart ached for the child excluded from Duncan's love or attention. Although he watched his oldest offspring, drawn like everyone else to her engaging pale beauty.

Blair was proving wild and reckless, challenging his father's attention and discipline. Disruptive and inattentive in the schoolroom. The indulged heir forcing his limits. Clearly because of Duncan's favouritism the boy sensed his importance in the family hierarchy.

Alexander, five now and fearless, possessed a compassionate heart. A combination of his parents, he often dragged home stray or injured animals. He fed an orphaned joey each morning and kept a pet parrot.

Although barely three, already revealing his obedience and desire to please, easily persuaded Callum was the model son. Duncan's bellowing or angry voice was often heard to echo through the house to Blair, *Why can't you be more like Callum?* This slur niggled the boy and he taunted his brother, always fair game to bait. Alexander became the peacemaker in his brothers' clashes.

A determined Christie, bubbling with joy and energy, only beginning to talk, more often than not was heard to utter, *No!* the word usually accompanied with a frown.

Late in Isabelle's pregnancy, as the children played on the grass between the homestead and the lake, supervised by Audrey when the older children had finished their lessons for the day, she mulled over their idyllic life.

For Duncan alone, it was clear that social standing and a displaying his wealth was important. He obsessed over breeding the finest racing horses, attended sheep breeding shows entering the best specimens from his merino stud winning trophies and ribbons he kept displayed in his study, and expanded plans for their vast acreage garden. He commissioned an Austrian artist, Eugene von Guerard, who painted country properties for wealthy owners, to produce a landscape of Kooringal homestead.

And he was always away in Geelong or Melbourne on business or some crisis because of the more recent dissent being heard from failed miners who demanded their share of the squatters' monopoly on pastoral land.

In late spring, when the ground was dry enough to work again and structural works resumed in the garden, Isabelle's sixth baby was quietly and easily born into the world.

Being another girl, and evening the numbers in their family now with three sons and three daughters, it fell happily to Isabelle to name her. Maira proved a contented child, sleeping long between feeds so that her mother constantly looked down with love and astonishment upon the placid dark haired child, marvelling at how simply she had entered their lives.

Flushed with his own prominence and to Isabelle's dismay, Duncan now regularly flung open the doors of the substantial Penross homestead, insisting they entertain. Flung into the district's eminent and landed society, Isabelle panicked, lamenting her plain deficient appearance.

It was Audrey who quietly suggested a personal maid.

'It might give you more confidence?' she said tactfully as they chatted over tea in the morning room.

Isabelle loved sitting before its paned windows admiring the aspect across the lake and sloping paddock down to the cottage.

'Only if you are in agreement, of course,' Audrey added quickly.

'My own maid? You will think me vain to consider such a thing,' Isabelle laughed.

'Indeed not. I've heard many prominent squatter's wives engage them.'

'Are you quite sure?'

'Absolutely. She would advise on dress and keep your hair in the latest style.'

'Really?'

'You could always employ her for a trial period.'

'Of course. That makes perfect sense.' Isabelle sighed. 'I wish Duncan did not want to lead such a public life now. Our colony is moving on apace it seems,' she added wistfully.

'The roads are greatly improved since gold was discovered and the countryside is well travelled. With Cobb & Co. running regular coach routes, distance is becoming quite nothing at all.'

'Duncan says we shall have the telegraph coming through before long. At least, that's his prediction. He was quite excited.'

Isabelle smiled, still able to reflect on her husband fondly enough but knowing they slipped further apart with each passing year. She stood beside him in public but, at home, they led virtually separate lives.

Choosing to distract her apprehension, she turned brightly to Audrey. 'And how is Walter these days? I've not heard you mention him lately.'

Her friend flashed her an uneasy quick smile but Isabelle was not deceived. It was tinged with sadness.

'He is quite well.' She clattered her teacup back onto its saucer.

Isabelle frowned, wondering how to continue, for the friendship between the couple never seemed to develop. It was obvious they cared for each other so she did not understand why.

'If you ever need a few days in Geelong for shopping or...visiting,' she offered, 'That would be perfectly acceptable.'

'Oh, I couldn't leave you with the responsibility for all children,' Audrey hastily brushed aside the gesture.

'Nonsense. Lily or one of the maids can help. Do keep it in mind,' she urged gently.

Audrey's face shadowed and Isabelle longed to press for the governess to confide but resisted out of respect for her privacy. Clearly there was a problem but it frustrated her to see such a devoted twosome waver when she could see no good reason for them to hesitate. Given another chance for true love herself, Isabelle wondered how she might respond. Unlikely, of course, that any such circumstances would arise. She was bound to Duncan for life.

Still pondering over Audrey's situation, Isabelle set her mind to composing an advertisement for a personal maid. Her choice must be careful for she would be a close companion.

Situation Wanted: Lady's maid wanted at once for a lady. Must be thorough and accomplished in all respects. Must not object to the country.

Replies were slow and scarce. Only one applicant appealed.

'Your father is a Geelong storekeeper?' Isabelle admired the lively and gracious Miss Katarina Perini during her interview in the morning room. Having established the young lady was of Italian descent, it explained the delightful accent to her animated speech.

'Si Signora. We emigrated for my mother's health. With her illness, papa finds her medical expenses and the employment of a nurse...considerable. I wish to help him, if you understand?'

Isabelle admired the girl's honesty in readily revealing her family's financial need. 'Perfectly. And your qualifications?' Isabelle prompted, enchanted by the girl's feminine appearance and natural friendliness.

'I am of age, now, and was educated privately in Italy in dressmaking, needlework, millinery and music. I also speak French.'

Isabelle decided she must ask if the girl would teach the children other languages. She was impressed by this beautiful olive skinned young woman, mature and composed yet still young.

'Miss Perini, you understand you will live out here in the country, away from your family?'

'Si Signora.'

'Do you foresee any problems? With your mother being so unwell?'

'I would only hope, Signora, that perhaps occasionally I might be permitted to visit Geelong. I am sorry, this is so forward of me to assume-' Miss Perini stumbled, frowning above a hesitant smile.

'Miss Perini, before you go on, you should know that I have decided to engage you. However,' she cautioned, 'my concern is that your mother's health might affect your employment.'

'Oh, no Signora. I can assure you of my complete devotion at all times.'

'Wonderful but, in any case, perhaps a trial of two or three months to ensure you...adjust.'

'That is most generous, Signora. Grazie. This will be of much relief to papa.'

'You are quite close to him?' Isabelle envied the way Katarina's eyes lit up each time she mentioned him. If only Duncan and his daughters, especially Nichola, shared such a happy connection.

'Oh, si Signora.' She gently withdrew a gold locket and chain from around her neck and clipped it open. 'I keep his photograph with me always.'

Isabelle wondered why not also her mother. She leaned forward to view Mr. Perini. A handsome dark haired man indeed with swarthy European features. She could see the resemblance.

Having established that Katarina would visit her parents for a weekend each month, she returned to Geelong before commencing employment the following week.

CHAPTER 7

A summer of blue and golden days continued with never a cloud in the sky, a season that Isabelle only endured. When the purple shadowed evenings cooled enough, she and Audrey with Katarina and the older children, sometimes accompanied by Duncan, sat on the front veranda looking out over their domain.

The buggy drive at the front of the house circled the lake, the homestead gradually settling into its beautiful pastoral surroundings with the future expanding garden slowly taking shape and edging closer to the river in one long scenic sweep. Bandicoots and small marsupials hid in burrows or hopped about, the bane of the gardeners. Wallabies peered out from the undergrowth. The dazzling brilliance of red rosellas flashed between the trees. Peacocks strutted grandly about as breezes carried the scent of the season's dry grass.

This year, the first Christmas dinner in the new homestead was set with a new dinner service, lace and embroidered table cloths. Geraniums and young roses picked from the garden, greenery and lavish decorations throughout the house.

Dinner began with a large tureen of soup filled to the brim and Mrs. Reed's large hind quarter of roast pork, all achieved on the new cooking stove from America. Another piece of cooked beef, potatoes, peas and greens, was served on the table. Duncan carved the immense roast, the maids served mountains of vegetables, followed by plum puddings, orange tart and peach pies.

Isabelle fixed a cheerful smile on her face, thinking how much their number of servants and family had grown. She marvelled that Duncan had accumulated all this. But what for? It had stolen him from her in small pieces over many years so that they had become strangers. She well remembered those first heady days of awareness, Duncan's persuasive approaches, her flattered innocent responses. From his first touch, she was lost and still could not help admiring him from afar.

She would be foolish and ungrateful to regret her comfort and position in life, and she loved each of her children in their own special way, but a tug of discontent wrenched her heart more often with every season, every beat of summer sun, every fluttering of another crisp red leaf to the ground and every child borne of her body.

Her reflections dulled her enjoyment of the festive day. Later, with the meal consumed, Isabelle allowed Nichola to pour the tea in the morning room. Her flowering daughter still tended to sullen moods, an effect she feared of her father's relentless persecution.

For once, conversation did not centre on wool, fleeces and stock. The children chattered and played games, the ladies contentedly watching. Christie and Maira were upstairs in the nursery. Katarina had taken the coach to Geelong until New Year. Isabelle missed her bright and charming disposition, already thinking of her as a younger sister, cherishing her company.

Another autumn crept across the countryside. The leaves of English trees turned yellow and crimson, brown grass softened to green with the first rains and bullock teams worked from dawn till dusk hauling hay and grain from paddocks to be stored in barns.

Penross family life assumed a genteel leisured routine. The household servants stirred by five to serve breakfast at six for Duncan so that he could be outdoors by seven. He still rose and worked with his men from sunrise until sunset, riding over his properties, supervising, dressed in finely cut clothes even on horseback. Isabelle remembered when she had done his mending and sewing, replacing lost buttons, now servants did everything. But her housekeeping management and bookwork increased accordingly, too.

Duncan proudly boasted that he doubled his capital every two years. Isabelle privately thought him vain because his success and their social elevation to become squatting gentry was quite plain to see by their homestead and lifestyle. Rather than embracing it, she felt unworthy.

As a result of the Ballarat uprising the year before, thirteen miners were charged with treason.

I heard that all the diggers' demands were met, Maeve wrote, *and those with a licence can vote. Now they only have to pay one pound instead of eight. And do you know, Isabelle, the miners are going to be represented in the government down in Melbourne? Quite a turnabout, isn't it?*

One of many changes taking place in the colony, Isabelle reflected, folding up Maeve's latest letter. A new telegraph line had opened between Geelong and Ballarat, just a single line on a wooden pole. You could send ten words for two and sixpence. Irish, too frail now for horseback hunched in the buggy and took messages between the homestead and Meredith telegraph station.

Travel became easier for everyone. Isabelle occasionally rode to Geelong on the coach with Katarina, a rough but convenient journey, when the maid visited her ailing mother. Once, Isabelle met her father, Luca Perini, instantly disposed toward him for his warmth and cordiality in the face of the family sadness. He was a most charming, polite and handsome man. Isabelle did not take tea with them but stayed only briefly before going shopping but she was impressed and fascinated by the quiet gentleman, moved by the sorrow he concealed in her company.

There were so many new communications now. With the

Geelong to Melbourne railway, Duncan often took the buggy into Meredith, then caught a coach to Geelong to meet the train, saving the vagaries of weather always risked on the bay ferry.

Life was becoming more mobile for everyone.

As he walked to Portia's residence, Duncan noticed Melbourne rapidly changing with every visit. On the highways leading into town, long trains of loaded drays, smart equipages and people on horseback or foot trailed along.

The Criterion in Collins Street, a hotel with a long and elegant frontage, had rooms and a saloon fitted out in splendour. A stone town hall now stood on the corner of Collins and Swanston Streets. Shops had plate glass windows and tasteful displays. Half a dozen banks, four newspapers and countless national and church schools supported its growing commerce.

Duncan stepped past hundreds of men employed in paving the roads and flagging the causeways from stone they carted up from the banks of the Yarra. Water pipes and kerb stones were laid. And such a throng of people abroad in carriages, omnibuses and cabs. Morning and evening, as now, clerks and businessmen streamed in and out of town from dwellings for miles around.

Sandhurst and Emerald Hill were now populous towns with houses, inns and stores, as were Prahran, Windsor, St. Kilda and Brighton, miles and miles of houses springing up in each locality. North of Melbourne, Collingwood and Richmond were becoming populated, too.

Ships lay at anchor in the bay and a crowded forest of small craft blocked up the river for miles, with all the accompanying bustle of loading and unloading at the quay, piled with goods, the clamour and stir of porters and wharf labourers.

Duncan sighed as he produced his key and unlocked the front door of Portia's comfortable neat cottage, much renovated and improved for her. Ten years older, she still loved him deeply and constantly emphasised that she could not live without him. Ageing made her vulnerable and he spent much time in reassurance. Her greatest insecurity was an illogical envy of Isabelle.

'You are still having children with her!' she often complained. 'Does she please you in bed as I do?'

'Of course not, woman. Never.'

'You are so far away,' she protested.

Duncan's impatience and frustration, always thin, but rarely with his mistress, was tested to all limits. 'My family has nothing to do with us,' he would try to explain. 'My life with you is quite separate. I can be with you at any time. Isabelle never questions my absences.'

'Oh Duncan, dearest,' Portia would gush, and her face crumple with joyous relief.

'There, there, my love. What can ah do to make ye feel better?'

'Oh Duncan,' she would dab at her tears. 'You have no need to ask.'

When Maira was two, Isabelle was delivered of a fourth son. Duncan named him Owen, a pale sandy haired baby, smaller than the others, as good-natured as Maira but without her strong appetite. It was the first son in whom Duncan took little interest.

The following year, a huge nugget of gold was found at Bakery Hill on the Ballarat diggings.

And a year later still, Beatrice was born. Their newest daughter was a curly golden haired beauty, a miniature image of her oldest sister. Sweet and chubby, a healthy baby. Her name chosen after Queen Victoria and Prince Albert's daughter born two years earlier.

Exhausted and already in her thirties after bearing eight children, Isabelle grew melancholy. Beatrice was so sweet, she could never regret her precious little life, but Isabelle no longer wanted any more children. This conclusion filled her with guilt because her comfort and troubles seemed small when compared to Katarina coping with her mother's failing health.

White fleeces of mist drifted across the top of the surrounding hills and frosts made the ground crisp as winter descended with all its miserable force. Wind brought colour to cheeks and the unchecked keen wind stung the face.

Isabelle's appetite waned and she could not be tempted to indulge in much of the plentiful food served each morning. Shredded wheat, baked eggs, grilled ham. Nothing appealed. She managed only some toast, butter and marmalade with her tea.

Logs blazed in all the huge fireplaces throughout the house. The morning room on the north caught a little of the sun but even its lovely warmth and snugness could not raise her spirits.

With rumblings and dissatisfaction from all sides, all Duncan's energies and time were now devoted to stabilising his land holdings, and they saw even less of each other. They also disagreed about the boys' schooling. Duncan wanted to send them away. Isabelle did not. She needed to keep her children around her but conceded that Blair, at least, as heir must be released the following year to boarding school at Scotch College in Melbourne.

'But he's only twelve,' Isabelle objected.

'Ah want my sons to have the best education money can buy.'

'And you have plenty of that.'

'They need more than tutoring now from Audrey. She'll do for the girls but the boys need more.'

'It won't help them run your properties. How can more book learning possibly help them?' she argued vainly, seeing Duncan's thin mouth and determined scowl. 'It seems an unnecessary expense shipping them off to boarding school. Surely you can teach them all you know.'

She turned her back on him, anguished, ashamed to show

her tears, anxious that as her children grew she would have no sense of purpose for her life.

'Money will never be a problem.'

'But it is not always the answer.' She voiced the distance between them but he only glared at her and did not respond.

Blair disliked the regimen and discipline of school. He would rebel. If not now while still under his father's hand, then certainly in the future.

'It's all right, mother,' he told her airily, for one so young. 'I shall be happy to leave the country. Melbourne will be far more interesting.'

Isabelle stilled in shock at his blunt statement. Duncan's heir had no love of the land. And such cold logic. Speechless, she could not reply.

Two years later, with great pomp, the Penross family, on Duncan's insistence, attended the opening of Meredith railway station, their nearest town, the line having been extended between Geelong and Ballarat. Jolting along in their new buggy with its buttoned leather seats and drawn by two magnificent horses, this new service even further reduced the isolation that had once been a major factor of pastoral life. A new era dawned.

The shrill tone of a steam whistle announced its arrival. The new trains filled the older pioneers with wonder. In a stiff backed line, they sat on the platform in suits and hats, reminiscing, Isabelle overheard, at how they had been the first to ride through this country. Instead of lumbering wagons, rail now took their wool to market. Journeys anywhere in the colony could be taken within hours, not days.

With a nostalgic sigh not long after, Isabelle accepted Lily Watson's resignation to marry Ronald Smith. *Her Ron,* as she called him, a railway worker based in Geelong. She was sad to see her leave and constantly endured the replacement of changing staff.

With the introduction of the Duffy Land Act to open up Crown land at present on long term leases by squatters, the mood was ripe for property selection by all. Upheaval loomed on the horizon. The new law only asked for erection of a dwelling. At nine pounds an acre and more, prices were far too high for most buyers. Only entrenched wealthy squatters could afford it.

Outraged, Duncan frantically bought up the freehold of the homestead block and most of his land at auction.

'It's downright tyranny and interference with our rights,' he bellowed.

He had no qualms in lobbying or bribing unsalaried politicians and contributed to their election campaigns to get what he wanted. He would stop at nothing now that his land, held under lease for so long, was under threat. The land war was, in fact, a class war between rich and poor. Old money and new.

Tenacious and shrewd, Duncan possessed the contacts, enterprise and resources to fight. He also held a healthy contempt for the newcomers. When he heard diggers talk of small farms and agriculture, he sneered. With gold petering out across the colony, all pioneer squatters clashed with aggressive democrats who wanted to unlock the land and break the pastoralists' monopoly.

He held secret meetings and planned strategies, Isabelle ignorant of the extent of his unprincipled dealings and bribery to district surveyors to ensure he won. Men could not resist squatters' cash. Duncan and others swamped the land offices with hirelings and acquired the land they wanted. The crux of the situation was water. Without it farmers could not exist. So Duncan bought up the choicest land near waterholes, creeks and rivers. Cashed up with money to burn, he easily outbid his competitors.

'Ah've done ma sums on selectors' costs,' he boasted. 'A man'll need fifteen hundred pounds before the land's his own without adding interest. Any man without backing can't afford it. It would take a year's labouring wages to buy eighty acres and pay the first year's rent. Few of those upstart dissenters would have that. The Government's trying to break our power. Well,' he snapped, 'ah'm not bidding against farmers for land I already lease. I was the pioneer of this land. Ah've no affection for new selectors pushing their way in. Ah'll not see all my endeavours snatched from my sons and passed on to strangers who've no right to it.'

But as Duncan greedily shuffled his new bundle of land certificates, he also gnawed with resentment that the era of run-holding was ending.

In time, Alexander too was bundled off to Scotch College, grumbling at the waste of time and money for him when he wanted to be out seeing what was in the world.

'I don't want to live in Melbourne. It doesn't bear consideration.'

Isabelle smiled to herself overhearing yet another clash between father and son's raised voices across the hall. Alexander never shied from a confrontation and Duncan even seemed to enjoy it.

'Ye'll do as I say.' In defence of the college, he explained, 'It was established by the Reverend James Forbes of the Free Presbyterian church. Your mother should have no argument with that!'

Isabelle cringed as she heard Alexander reply, 'Learning Latin and Greek are no good to me.'

'You get to play cricket, lad. The Tait Cup's been played for years now between Scotch College and Geelong Grammar. Besides, ye'll be home for your four week Christmas vacation in no time.'

'I'll try it for one year. No more,' Alexander said between gritted teeth, a surprisingly firm ultimatum from her warm hearted son.

'We'll discuss that later.' She doubted Duncan would be persuaded. 'Meanwhile, ah'll expect ye to shape up and do me proud before Dr. Morrison.'

Bored after lessons finished for the day, Nichola wandered outdoors. The mirror daily confirmed that she had become a beautiful young woman and she had begun to realise her persuasion over people in general and men in particular. She learned to refine her control with subtle teasing to see how far she could go. She enjoyed others doing her bidding.

Not her brothers, of course. Alexander understood and ignored her with a smile. Blair she found exasperating and unkind. Once when they had gone hunting with Duke, he caught and cooked a goanna. On a reckless dare, Blair ate some then laughed at a repulsed Nichola when she refused to touch it. Then taunted her with *baby* and *coward*. At those times, she hated him and wished she had never gone after him in the bushfire when they were small.

Seeing Duke in the distance down by the river, his dark skin gleaming in the sunshine, she strolled toward him. Working for her father these days, they rarely saw him anymore. As children, when they had received their mother's permission and been allowed to play together, she had learned much from him. While the boys joked around, she sat and listened. He fascinated her and she remembered her relief when his was the first face she saw after getting lost in the fire. Duke was always kind and could find his way anywhere. Deft with a spear, he stole among the trees, inched his way forward, and pierced his quarry whether kangaroo in the bush or fish from the river.

She didn't particularly like the blacks and their lives were filled with tales of spirits and legends. They believed the Dreaming created all things.

When Nichola first heard Duke declare this, she argued pompously, 'God created everything, silly.'

Duke had scowled, gabbling and walked away, unseen for days. The natives sometimes did that but usually returned. She had always puzzled why her father had taken an interest in him. From childhood, he's always had his own pony whereas other natives rode station horses. She knew Bessie mothered him since Ginny's death.

His weather predictions were reliable. He would tilt back his head, go still and sniff the air. If he said *Come up great storm* it eventually arrived. Along with the koala, he believed wombats were sacred animals and not to be skinned. As if they would do that or eat one, her lip curled at the barbaric thought. He was so fleet footed, none of the Penross children ever caught him. He was different enough to be exciting.

As she walked closer, Nichola admired his bare chest. He often stripped off his shirt in warm weather and just wore trousers.

'Are you fishing?' she asked.

She never surprised him and he did not turn around. He would have sensed her approach for some time. She perched on a fallen tree trunk at the water's edge. He already had a line of fish strung together.

'Might be.' He smiled. 'How is Sun Woman today?'

For years he had given her his own special name because of her golden hair and she always felt safe with him. He knew the bush and had grown into a handsome brown skinned man, although lighter in colour than other natives, with abundant hair falling in waves almost to his strong shoulders and gleaming white teeth when he smiled. Like every young woman her age, she fantasised and sometimes wondered if she dare touch him.

Restless, she found a stick in the grass and began churning up the water.

'Quiet dere. Fish go away,' Duke scowled.

Having caught his attention, she flicked water at him, careful not to get her dress wet. He frowned and ignored her. Frustrated, she tried again.

'Hey, Missy, don't do that to blackfella.'

She laughed, stepped closer and tried to push him into the river. Swift and agile on his feet, he balanced himself by reaching out to grip her shoulders. Nichola felt his wet hands through her shirtwaist.

It was the moment Duke placed his hands on Nichola's shoulders that Isabelle caught sight of them from the house. She had glanced out in passing one of the upstairs windows. Even at this distance, their familiarity looked alarming. They were both of an age now when it might not be interpreted as childish play. Her daughter was taunting Duke. Reading the signals and knowing their mutual paternity sent her into a panic. Then Duke threw his arms into the air, they both stumbled and fell into the river.

'What were you thinking?' Isabelle hissed, furious, when a bedraggled Nichola returned to the house. 'Why weren't you in the schoolroom?'

'Mr. Kruger is here and they've taken a walk before he leaves.'

Isabelle knew she referred to Audrey. 'Go and change. Those are not the actions of a young lady,' Isabelle scolded.

'Duke didn't mind,' Nichola retorted.

'You are no longer a child.' Her mother pointed out. 'Duke is not for you. He is not one of us.'

'I know that.' Nichola frowned at her mother in disbelief.

'Then I am surprised you did not remember.' Isabelle glared at her belligerent daughter in cold fury at her own lapse of supervision of her daughter's provocative behaviour. 'Go and do as I ask.'

What she saw in Nichola's sapphire gaze was an equally icy disdain. At all costs, she must be chaperoned and watched.

Isabelle paced until Duncan returned for dinner. She swept out into the hall and requested an interview in his study the moment she heard his boots on the tiles. Weary from a day in the saddle but as commandingly handsome as ever, Duncan scowled. Barely hesitating mid stride, he turned and led her into his cedar panelled sanctuary. He poured whisky while she stood in front of his desk, hands twisting at her waist.

'I know you have resisted it in the past but it is time Nichola furthers her education in Melbourne at an appropriate ladies' school.'

'Why now?' He drained his glass and poured another.

Isabelle relayed this afternoon's episode. 'It was bound to happen at some point. She is growing quite...aware,' Isabelle informed him tactfully. 'I know your daughters are not as favoured as your sons but Nichola needs distance from Kooringal and exposure to suitable young ladies and gentlemen of her own age and influence.'

He grunted. 'She'll need to find a husband soon anyway.'

'Not at fourteen!' Isabelle objected, appalled. 'There are respected ladies' colleges in Melbourne where she will be under tuition and supervision for at least a year. I shall make enquiries.'

Duncan held her cool glare that challenged disagreement. She was about to make a further suggestion but stopped.

A few days later, Nichola and Audrey were out on the grass under the trees where they spent two hours one afternoon each week sketching. The young developing garden offered unlimited vistas for watercolours. Today, a peacock, its turquoise head proudly erect, dragged its emerald-eyed tail in a long sweep across the view. Isabelle strolled down to join them, holding Beatrice before her nap. She had given this moment and timing careful thought. She stood at her daughter's side, Nichola displaying a latent artistic gift.

'That's quite lovely, dear.' She noted Nichola's use of the glorious bird in a corner of her painting.

When a maid brought out a table and set it for tea, the ladies took a break. Beatrice soon grew tired and restless.

'Audrey, would you mind?' Isabelle appealed with a smile, feeling guilty for using her friend, but there was a sound reason for her request.

'Not at all.' Audrey rose. 'Come here, pet.' She scooped up the beautiful curly haired child into her arms and walked back to the house.

After a while, Isabelle began, 'Your father and I agree it might be nice for you to attend a ladies' finishing college in Melbourne.'

'Are you sending me away because of Duke?'

Isabelle stilled. Nichola could have no idea of the double meaning to her question. 'It was a silly error of judgement on your part. The actions of a child. We shall expect more ladylike behaviour of you in future.'

'When do I go?' Nichola looked down at her hands calmly folded in her lap but did not seem upset.

'In the first term of the new year I should think. It will be a wonderful opportunity to broaden your cultural education.'

Isabelle noted the glint of apprehension in her gaze as she glanced across at her mother. 'I've never left home before except with family.'

'You're not being cast out, Nichola dear.' She paused, watching the hem of her daughter's pale blue floral dress ripple in the breeze and her bonnet ribbons lift and flutter. Her hat had been removed while they sat in the shade and hung behind her neck. 'You'll make new friends your own age outside the family. We're so isolated out here.' She hesitated again. 'Seeing you with Duke made me realise how quickly you are growing up and how much more you have yet to learn of life before making a home of your own.'

Isabelle inhaled a deep steadying breath to prepare herself for what she was about to divulge to her daughter and the secret she would betray. Slowly rising, she held a hand out to Nichola.

'Walk with me, dear.' Frowning, the girl obeyed. As they moved out into the sun, Isabelle reminded her, 'Bonnet, dear.'

She set her own broad sun hat in place as Nichola tied her ribbons, then linked their arms and headed past the lake down the slope away from the house.

'Is there something wrong, mother?' Nichola asked when the silence lengthened between them.

'Yes,' she sighed, 'but I don't know how to begin. What I

am about to tell you, although you may still occasionally act like a child,' she gave her daughter a teasing smile, 'Is because you are on the verge of womanhood. I believe you are ready to learn something that you must swear will remain in the strictest confidence between us.' Isabelle brought them to a stop, turned to her daughter and gripped her arm. 'Promise me, Nichola.'

Her daughter's troubled wide gaze pleaded. 'How can I promise when I don't know what you are about to tell me?'

'It's about Duke and your father.'

'Is it bad?' Nichola whispered.

'It is a delicate matter but I believe when you know, it may help you understand your father better.'

'I doubt that. What about Duke and father?' She frowned.

'Keep walking, dear, with your back to the house.' They slowly moved on. 'You remember Ginny?'

Nichola nodded. 'Duke's mother. She died many years ago. She helped find Blair and I with Duke and the other native man in the bushfire.'

'Your father is Duke's father.'

Nichola halted and stared at her mother. 'Father and Ginny were together?' She nodded. 'Did he make her?'

Isabelle had her reasons for forcing her daughter to grow up quickly with this declaration. 'He said not. She was given to him by her tribe when she was quite young in exchange for food. A man's...urges,' she continued awkwardly, 'can be quite strong. Your father promised to be faithful to me once we were together and married. He has had to be a hard man to survive.'

'He's kind to the boys.' She pouted. 'Except Owen. He doesn't bother with him much yet.'

'No. When he's older perhaps.'

Isabelle knew she lied. Her youngest son was a timid child and his father not instinctively drawn to him. It should not have surprised her that Nichola should notice. Seven year old Christie was as boisterous as Maira was gentle. And little Beatrice, the golden image of Nichola, trying to walk but still anchored to the nursery, was yet far too small to be of any interest to him. But then Duncan had only ever paid scant attention to his daughters. Sadly, for the very reason they were discussing, Nichola least of all.

'So,' Nichola's brow drew into a frown beneath her bonnet. 'Duke is a half-brother to all of us?'

Isabelle swallowed. She had always struggled against the knowledge of this tie. 'Yes.'

'So that's why he's not as black as the other natives. Did father tell you?'

Isabelle managed a faint smile. 'No. Just after your birth, Ginny innocently told me.' Isabelle's gaze travelled across the paddock into the distance, her thoughts in the past. 'She helped at your birth. There were few women on Kooringal then. Only Maeve and I. And there's something else you should know.' Her throat went dry yet her eyes welled with tears. She had never cried in front of Nichola before. Once, she and Maeve had shared all their private moments but Isabelle always decided she would portray a happy face to her family.

'You're upset! Why?' Nichola was staring at her and waiting.

'You were a twin. Your brother, little Duncan, was stillborn.' Isabelle pressed the edge of a lace handkerchief to her lips to staunch their trembling. 'Your father only ever wanted sons,' she said bleakly.

Nichola absorbed all this information holding her mother's gaze with a cool detachment quite mature for her age. 'That is so unfair.'

'Yes. And sad and unfortunate but I hope it has helped to explain your father's attitude. It is entirely his own personal perspective and neither your fault nor mine. You understand that, don't you?' Nichola nodded. 'But still hurtful,' she admitted for the first time aloud to another person.

'Who else knows?' Nichola insisted.

'Your father and I. And Maeve. I'm not even sure Duke was ever told. Ginny raised him as one of her own people.'

Isabelle glanced across at her daughter, alert to the narrowed steely gaze beneath her bonnet brim. 'You will remember your promise?'

'I shall always do right by you, mother.' She squeezed her hand.

Isabelle found her loyalty touching and, in the moment, did not analyse Nichola's choice of words. For now, she just needed her to be told, take strength and confidence in the truth. Her persecution had gone on long enough. Her daughter would soon be a woman and she resolved that, approaching adulthood, she deserved the right to no longer be kept ignorant.

Isabelle had long planned this move when the time was right. That time had come. Being the oldest, Nichola would produce the next generation soon enough. She discreetly regarded her, praying she found a husband to love and respect where she had not. Nichola deserved a spouse who would restore her faith in men. Isabelle also knew her sons needed to be raised with every due regard for the woman they one day chose.

Nichola Penross adored and thrived in Melbourne society. She soon ignored the self-righteous prudes and attached herself to the bolder and more adventurous among her fellow boarders. Even chaperoned she enjoyed a measure of freedom. Most of the other young ladies at the school were boring and obedient but, flourishing in the legacy of her mother's confidence and their secret knowledge, she began to build a reputation for defiance and challenge to authority.

To be the oldest child of wealthy pastoralist Duncan Penross, proved of great benefit. Safely settled in Melbourne and guardedly exposed to more young men within her correct social circle, she discovered most, with subtle persuasion, weak and pliable. They parted where she walked and, from the beginning, her influence was absolute.

With access to her father's accounts at certain favoured

Melbourne stores, she soon acquired a delight in fine clothes at Alston and Brown's brick building filled with elegant dresses, bonnets and mantles. If her father ever dared challenge her spending, she would confront him with his own shameful flaws.

She had promised her mother to keep the confidence, it was true and she felt bad because she had no issue with her but the news was too valuable to be ignored. Thoughts of retribution burned slowly inside her and one day she would have her revenge.

East Leigh girls, like those of other ladies' schools, were prepared for the role of ornamental wives. They learnt English, Italian - of which she knew a little already from Katarina - and Parisian French taught by Mademoiselle, although they never knew her name. Languages they were assured were essential on the assumption many of them would make an overseas tour. With Nichola already accomplished on the piano, music and singing proved familiar and undemanding. As did drawing and painting which came naturally to her. All skills considered desirable feminine accomplishments. Dancing, often partnered with another girl and raising giggles, although tutored by a debonair middle aged gentleman, had the added benefit they were told of improving carriage and bearing.

Besides attending church, the girls were taken to concerts and exhibitions at The Museum of Art funded by works from wealthy citizens and occupying a small exhibition space at the Victorian State Library.

Invitations to parties and dances of fellow squatters' daughters and friends filled most weekends. In her social flurry, Nichola gave her mother's latest regular letter no more than her usual cursory attention especially since it only mentioned her father was in town and to expect his visit. Nichola deliberated on how she could avoid him so it surprised her one day while out walking in town with her chosen group of girlfriends after a sanctioned matinee visit to the Haymarket Theatre in Bourke Street that she thought she recognised her father from a distance.

She was about to raise her hand and politely wave out of courtesy but not desire should he notice her, when she realised it could not be him. This man had a lady companion and mother was at home in Kooringal for she never accompanied him on his business trips.

As the open carriage rolled closer, Nichola positively identified him with another woman some years older but shapely and attractive, her dark hair piled up beneath a broad jaunty hat.

Nichola stood transfixed on the unpaved footpath. Against the regulations of staying together with the other girls, she detached herself from her companions, forgotten and moving ahead in a crowd of pedestrians, to stride out briskly alone to try and follow them. She lifted her skirts and carefully navigated a foot bridge over the gutter, dashed across the busy street avoiding orderly boys sweeping, clattering wheels and horsemen.

Mercifully, their carriage turned after only two blocks at the end of the street and travelled a further short distance along William Street, halting before a brick cottage opposite new public gardens. Her father took the woman's elbow when his companion stepped down, his arm in a personal gesture around her waist.

Nichola gasped. This was more than a casual acquaintance or friendship. The shock and disgust of it curled her lips.

'Poor mother,' she whispered, repulsed.

The following weekend on Sunday, after an exchange of mail during the week, Nichola had grudgingly arranged to meet Blair and Alex, treating them to tea at the Cafe de Paris in Bourke Street. She hired a handsome cab and bowled along St. Kilda Road, joining the throng of horse omnibuses and traffic all heading the short distance into town. She waited outside the boys' College in Eastern Hill where her brothers soon emerged.

Although not unhappy in Melbourne or being separated

from her mother, Nichola's heart warmed to see the two oldest of her growing brothers. It would be four years yet before obedient Callum and little Owen, still in the nursery with Beatrice, would attend school here.

After they had all shuffled into the seat and before they moved off again, Nichola said, 'Mother wrote that father is in town. Should we send a message to his Club in Collins Street to meet us?'

The boys looked guiltily between them. 'Girls aren't allowed in. Besides, he's already taken us out for lunch.'

Nichola despised herself for feeling so deeply wounded. 'No doubt since women are excluded, his lady friend was not with him,' she retorted in an angry fit of stinging pique.

Seated opposite, both boys gaped at her shocking outburst.

'That's a dangerous charge,' Blair scowled though his eyes sharpened with interest.

'Only if it is untrue.' She revelled in her advantage. 'I saw them together. They were quite familiar with each other. I would say they have been acquainted for some time.'

Blair smirked with adolescent amusement but Alexander stared in silence. It pleased her that the man they regarded with awe and whom she hated since her mother's disclosure, was now demoted in their eyes. Nichola determined to ask Lydia from school to try and find out the woman's identity. She came from a working class family whose father had done well in business from the gold rush. She had contacts.

'We should tell mother,' she said grandly which met with a lengthy silence.

Finally, soft-hearted Alexander spoke up. 'I don't think you should.'

'Why not?' Nichola pouted. 'She has a right to know.'

'Because I think she loves father and you'll break her heart,' he said, sounding far older than his schoolboy years.

'Well, he certainly mustn't love her and does not deserve her.'

'Perhaps not,' Blair said. 'It must be hard living with a person all your life and still trying to like them.'

'If this woman is his mistress, then father is being unfaithful,' Nichola disagreed importantly.

'Well, I'm not staying on Kooringal forever,' Alex declared.

'What does that have to do with this?' Nichola asked.

'I won't be around but I think you should leave things as they are. For mother's sake.'

'You can't leave. You're only twelve.'

'When I'm older. In geography they have this big globe of the world.' His eyes grew bright and wide. 'There's all kinds of places out there to be explored. Far more than Miss Bailey ever taught.'

'Father expects both of you to stay and take over his properties.'

'I don't care. I intend to explore. I want to have adventures. Blair can have it all,' he announced.

'I don't want it either. I know it's big and Father's been buying up land before the selectors get it, but I'd only put in a manager anyway and live here in Melbourne. I'm not spending my life in the bush in a saddle.'

Nichola glowed from within. Her brothers would desert their father. None of them wanted Kooringal or Lakeham. 'Father will be furious,' she crowed.

'There's still Callum and Owen,' Alex pointed out.

'Good idea.' Blair laughed. 'Callum does whatever Father asks. He'd probably stay out of duty even if he doesn't want to.'

Nichola pulled a wide smile of pleasure. 'Father is assuming you'll take over, Blair. He has your future planned, you know.'

Blair slouched in the carriage and squinted out at the passing scenery. 'I don't care. I'll do what I want. He's talking about Oxford after I finish at Scotch. I'll be glad to get away.'

'I'm not doing any book learning at university,' Alex said darkly. 'I'm wasting enough time down here already.' He brightened. 'But science and geography are exciting.'

Armed with the triple ammunition of Duke, his mistress and the boys' rejection of their inheritance, which bolstered her growing confidence, Nichola dutifully penned a note to her father, as mother would expect, knowing he would never initiate an approach himself. She did not resist the temptation to plant a subtle comment within its few formal lines that she hoped her invitation did not impose on his social obligations. If he felt any guilt, which she doubted, he may read into the words what he may.

She felt no desire to see him but, amid the excitement of so many recent discoveries that bubbled in her mind, her rebellion craved release. The time for her father to be called to account. A change of power was at hand.

Out of obligation alone, Nichola assumed her father would reply. Although the encounter promised to be strained, Nichola approached the Wednesday afternoon with wicked delight. The outing, excusing her from music lessons in which she was already proficient, was approved because her father was so wealthy and influential.

Waiting in the school hall on the appointed day, Nichola straightened the skirt of her latest and smartest deep blue dress, suitably modest for her age and bringing out the colour of her eyes, a female replica of the man who sired her. The older boys had inherited their mother's attractive darker colouring. How it must sicken her father that she so visibly reminded him she was the child who had wrongly survived. A double thorn in his side.

When a private hired carriage drew up at the East Leigh entrance and her father stepped out, it was impossible not to admire his handsome turnout. The tailored suit, a gold watch and chain glinting in the afternoon sunlight, giving the impression of the successful man and devoted father instead of the disloyal tyrant she knew him to be.

'Father,' she greeted him as he entered, unsmiling and as

composed as she could be on this momentous day in her life.

He frowned at her, staring. 'Nichola.'

She sensed a hidden wariness. She knew she presented a transformation from the sheltered innocent girl at Kooringal to a young woman attired to fit her station in life. She had applied herself diligently to achieve it. Especially for today.

Mrs. Tripp stood patiently at Nichola's elbow and nodded a greeting. 'Mr. Penross. We're most honoured.'

'Likewise, Madam.'

So polite in public, Nichola marvelled, withholding a sigh. Where was the brash unloving father she knew? To her surprise, he extended his arm and she was forced to accept it.

'It's such a pleasant day for autumn, I thought we might take a drive,' he suggested helping her into the carriage.

Settled opposite in her comfortable seat, Nichola beamed. 'Perfect.' He would not wish to be in public when she exposed him.

The conveyance rattled through the three acres of gardens around the school, turned out onto Commercial Road then south toward St. Kilda and the sea. Ensconced inside, their driver could not hear their conversation. Nichola wondered if her father's lady had occupied this very seat.

'Mrs. Tripp's schools seems to suit ye,' he ventured.

'A compliment, father?' She arched her brows. 'It is proving educational living in town. I realise I am privileged and shall appreciate everything I learn. It was mother's suggestion I should contact you, of course, not mine.'

She glanced from the small open window letting him know their presence together was tedious for both of them.

'How long are you in town?' She injected enough indifference to let him know she asked only from courtesy and to stimulate their stiff conversation.

'A week or two yet.'

'Not long enough, I expect, since Melbourne surely contains many pleasures for you.'

Her father flashed her a strange shrewd glance. 'I'm here

on business.'

'And what *business*,' she sneered over the word, 'Might you have with Mrs. Herrington?' Lydia's contacts had proved invaluable.

Tanned from a life lived outdoors, Duncan's complexion visibly blanched. When he recovered, he growled, 'Ma private life is none of your concern. I expect your silence and common sense.'

'You may expect it, father, but you will not receive it. You have a family and a wife who has only ever been loyal to you.'

His steely gaze settled upon her. 'If you tell her, I'll disinherit ye.'

'No matter. I plan to marry well for my own comfort so that I shall no longer be a burden to you. But if you should be tempted to carry out your threat, I shall expose you. Without regret.'

In the following silence, Duncan's glare narrowed and he looked as if he might lunge forward and wrap his large brown hands around her throat.

'Whether you like it or not, I am your daughter. Now you know how it feels to be on the wrong side of injustice. I always wondered why you never invited mother to town.'

Nichola briefly knew a moment of apprehension and her emotions hung by a thread but what exhilaration from power. She missed her mother and the familiarity of Kooringal but had grown to embrace Melbourne and all it offered. Living up country she had now discovered was boring by comparison and she would not willingly or happily return. Cherishing her new lifestyle and partial independence, Nichola prepared to do battle with her father.

'Ye'll not mention Mrs. Herrington's name to anyone, d'y'understand?'

'A threat, father?' Nichola briefly frowned. 'You are in no position.'

He swallowed, gripping the seat beside him, his eyes filled with fear, looking ill. Nichola suddenly realised that her father was unconcerned that she knew about his mistress but that the woman might be exposed. He must care very much for her. More than mother.

Unmoved by her squirming father, Nichola continued, 'Mother told me about Duke and now the boys know, too.'

Clearly accustomed to negotiating, he anticipated her, pulled himself together and snapped in a low voice, 'What do ye want?'

'Our family to take a villa in Melbourne for the summer season and all that such a life entails. I do not wish to return to Kooringal at the end of the year. I will continue at East Leigh.' They glared at each other.

'Done.'

The hostility between them meant their drive was short. As the carriage rolled back into East Leigh grounds and Nichola prepared to alight, she said, 'Please do not come in. I could not bear your false show of affection.'

She stepped down and did not look back.

CHAPTER 8

'Nichola wants to stay in Melbourne for another year and you agreed?'

Duncan nodded grimly. How pliable her husband had become, the change enough for her to be inquisitive as to the reasons why but because Isabelle welcomed the idea, she set her questions aside.

'She has made friends and enjoys town,' he said grudgingly. 'Might help her start lookin' for a husband.'

Always ignored before, Isabelle could not hide her surprise that he showed interest in his daughter. Perhaps he was considering his reputation in society and would no doubt use their residency in town to advantage. She dared not hope that he might be mellowing with age because he seemed unsettled since his return. Isabelle longed to know how his meeting with Nichola went in Melbourne but dared not ask. Although it must have been satisfactory enough since a summer season in town was the result.

'Then I am sure Nichola will love it.' From her few letters, she sounded to be blossoming.

'Ah'll arrange it then. I want to be in Melbourne for the thoroughbred horse races at the Victoria Turf Club in the first week of November.'

'So soon?'

'Can ye be ready by then?'

It was unlike Duncan to be so considerate. 'Of course.'

She would move heaven and earth to make it happen. The whole family would be together and she might see Duncan more often. She never lost hope that their troubled marriage might improve.

Preparations for the November transition and upheaval from country to town took place with much fuss and angst and organisation on Isabelle's part with Audrey and Katarina her two devoted helpers and a body of maids. Kooringal was to be left with a skeleton staff and the best servants would travel with them.

Wagons conveyed them into Meredith then the train to Geelong where they changed for another into Melbourne. Since it was her first ride, Isabelle's excitement was high. To undertake an entire journey the same day and in such comfort!

Their carriage rumbled out over Princes Bridge and along St. Kilda Road, a broad unmade thoroughfare. Dust rose from the constant flow of traffic so the ladies pulled down their veils. They branched off into Gardiners Creek Road toward their house. Until school finished, the three older children would only visit for weekends.

Preferring the rural life as she did, Isabelle gaped when she first glimpsed the grandeur of Kew House. But, as Duncan had said, although Nichola was still young, she was approaching marriageable age and once her schooling was complete, it would be necessary to introduce her into the limelight of society.

Their leased residence was as grand as Kooringal, two storeys and graceful. Everyone alighted and the children tumbled over each other, eager to explore. Callum and Maira stayed close but Christie disappeared.

'Don't go out near the road,' Isabelle called out a warning after her. Probably to no avail. The girl was inquisitive, as spirited as Alex and utterly fearless on a horse. If it was happening outdoors, she begged to participate.

Owen and Beatrice toddled in with Audrey while the servants struggled to unload valises, trunks and boxes. Besides the select staff who had travelled with them, the house apparently came with a few basic servants; a coachman, maid and boy. She left them to find their way to the kitchen at the back of the house.

Inside, Isabelle sauntered and absorbed the comfort of the fully furnished lofty downstairs reception rooms.

'It's more than adequate, Duncan,' she turned to him, standing in the doorway. 'But do we need so much space?'

'It's appropriate to our place in society. We'll need to entertain.'

Isabelle hoped she managed to impress. She flashed a nervous smile past her husband's shoulder to Katarina hovering in the hall, knowing she would rely on the girl's attendance to help make her socially presentable. She was not sure she would feel entirely at ease here but, for Nichola's sake and future happiness, she would try.

'Are ye not pleased?' Duncan growled.

Isabelle puzzled over his concern. Although he had announced this move, he had not seemed entirely happy about it. 'Of course. How could I not? The idea is to impress and you have succeeded,' she murmured moving past him to ascend the stairs to the first floor.

The upper rooms looked out over the treetops of the gardens and orchard. Lawns spread out beneath trees, water splashed in fountains.

'Apparently ye can see Port Phillip from the tower. No doubt the boys will discover it at the weekend.'

Unaware Duncan was behind her, Isabelle jumped. His small attentions lately were welcome and she desperately prayed this summer sojourn might bring them closer again.

The bedrooms were all frothy with lace and rich curtains, the bathrooms complete with round white baths raised off the floor on claw feet.

The first days of town life assumed a routine. Isabelle soon discovered it more artificial than at home. Here, hospitality and a woman's life were tyrannised by petty social doings and she became assailed on all sides from calling cards and gossip.

Breakfast was taken later than in the country and, first thing, Isabelle issued orders for the day, managed matters, attended to shopping personally or sent Audrey, who appeared content enough to be apart from Walter for some months. The younger children continued their daily lessons and her babies played in the nursery.

Duncan adopted the role of landed aristocrat and spent mornings attending to business or at the Melbourne Club. For luncheon, he was often at Scotts or Menzies hotels and might not return or sent a note that rarely explained in any detail the reason for his non appearance or delayed absence. So he was never as available or present as she had hoped.

Later morning and early afternoon, Isabelle attended functions related to church work and appeals. Contacts were important so she endured the sewing circles to give the poor warmth and comfort, and occasional hospital visiting with Christie and Maira.

Afternoons were set aside for morning call. Isabelle announced she was at home on certain afternoons between two and four. This involved many callers, cups of tea, a twenty minute visit then a dash off to the next home. Sundays Isabelle kept sacred for church and the family attended the large fashionable congregation in Scots Church in Collins Street.

The first weekend, Nichola, Blair and Alex arrived to join them.

'Mother.' Nichola greeted her profusely with a hug as she swept indoors, glancing pointedly at the house décor. Judging by the flicker of eyebrows she approved of every detail.

Her endearment and show of affection seemed unusual and forced. Isabelle noted a strange fragility about her. Although she was growing into a proper young lady, her new awareness seemed strained. She sighed, worrying unnecessarily for her children. She could not shield them forever.

'Father.' She managed a respectful nod and quick weak smile. They seemed to have reached some kind of impasse. Warmth was too much to expect.

'A new dress?' Isabelle admired her daughter's stylish

understated taste in pale blue with a fitted bodice and tailored skirt that raised the colour of her eyes. She was much changed with an assured air non-existent six months ago.

'Yes. From Alstons.'

'We must go shopping.' They shared a smile.

So with all the family present and dining together the first night, it became a noisy reunion. The boys gushed with high spirits but, to their mother's frustration, spoke with their mouths full.

'Have you learnt nothing? I thought Scotch would surely have reinforced the good manners I've taught you,' she gently chastised them.

Alex grinned. 'Sorry, mother. They did. We forgot.'

Blair, she noted, made no such apology. He had become much withdrawn. It was more common for Nichola to be sullen and difficult than Blair. She trusted that with maturity and a clearer notion of himself, he might rally and brighten. At his age she had expected him to be full of life like the others.

Duncan remained mostly silent, watchful of the proceedings. While Callum and Christie were wide eyed and enthralled by the tales from their older siblings, Maira remained a passive yet serene observer.

During dinner, it disgusted Nichola to see her father being more attentive to her mother. Playing the devoted husband. Such a front. He had never bothered before. It turned her stomach to observe such false affection when his feelings lay elsewhere. Worse, her mother glowed like a lantern beside him. Flushed, smiling. Glancing in his direction. It was so sad to see that she still cared for him. She had suffered so much over the years, her hopes falsely raised that her neglectful tyrant husband would change.

Appalled, and unable to take another bite even if it was Mrs. Reed's usual superb cooking, Nichola let her cutlery clatter onto her plate. Usually a model of etiquette, both parents glanced across at her, her father sharply so. His oldest daughter sent him a vicious glare. Her mother caught the silent charged exchange and frowned in query, her eyes questioning. Nichola longed to stand up and tell her the truth, save her mother heartache in the future, for it would surely come. How could mother not see it?

'Sorry.' She pretended the noise had been an accident and smiled to cover her blunder. Her mother relaxed but her father was not deceived and she revelled in his discomfort.

In the flurry of preparations for race day the following week, the incident was not mentioned again. Duncan's anticipated day at Flemington had arrived. A logical obsession given his love of horses. Maira was disinterested and not even enticed at the chance to dress up so she happily stayed behind in the nursery with a maid to entertain Owen and Beatrice.

The ladies paid extra attention to fashion for this was an auspicious event. Nichola wore the palest blue silk, Isabelle rich ivory with pearls, her thick dark hair upswept beneath a picture hat trembling with flowers. Her daughter chose a tiny hat with a delicate trail of chiffon and at the last moment, they gathered up gloves and shawls.

Because the city was packed with visitors, it was decided the family should take the train out to the racecourse to avoid the dusty roads. For the children, babbling and impatient, it was their second rail excursion in weeks. With so much activity and excitement, Isabelle feared they might find it dull when they all eventually returned home at summer's end.

Nichola felt herself observed equally by both parents for her silence and composure in stark contrast to her boisterous siblings.

The Penross family were among hundreds of elite who proceeded to the grand stand, a mass of flowers and green leaves, crowded with fellow squatters, millionaires, merchants, professional men, statesmen and politicians. For a one shilling admission, the public enclosure on the hill permitted lesser folk to picnic. The favourable weather drew thousands of spectators. Early in the afternoon, the Governor, His

Excellency Sir Henry Barkly arrived.

The first race was the Maiden Plate with winnings of fifty sovereigns. Nichola thought the six horses cut a wretched pace. She hardly called it racing and the result was never in doubt from start to finish. A horse named Falcon won.

Her father, puffed with delight to spend an entire day around horses, gambled extravagantly. Wearily ignoring his boasting, she was only vaguely interested to learn that the winner of the second race for two year olds claimed one hundred sovereigns and turned out to be Regina, a brown filly apparently owned by a neighbouring pastoralist, Thomas Chirnside. At least the finish home was close and exciting although, until the numbers were put up, they did not know who won. Her father strode off to collect his prize.

Soon after he returned later after having placed yet more bets, they encountered the Morgans. A middle aged man and woman, three young ladies and a man in their wake. Duncan rose and firmly shook the man's hand.

'Stewart,' he greeted him heartily. 'Mrs. Morgan,' he acknowledged the woman. He then turned to her mother. 'Mr. Morgan, may I present my wife, Mrs. Isabelle Penross.'

They both smiled and murmured, 'A pleasure.' Mr. Morgan dipped his top hat.

Nichola caught an air of arrogance and condescension from them all. She marvelled that her father should befriend such snobs but recognised them as landowners of extensive holdings in the Western District on Castle Hill run not too far distant from Kooringal. Their acquaintance was no doubt through wealth.

The girls, attractive and expensively clothed, were individually introduced with pretty creamy smiles from beneath wide ostentatious hats. She forgot their silly names the moment she heard them. Not so the young man, more auspiciously introduced.

'Our only son, Elliott,' Mr. Morgan announced with pride.

Unsmiling, Nichola nodded as they all did but was not

impressed. The black wavy hair, impeccably groomed, face alive with a knowing grin, fully aware he was most handsome. Both father and son wore a rose buttonhole in their lapel. Sophisticated and vain, Nichola decided. Elliott looked older than his sisters. Well into his twenties, she guessed, but such a smug bore that she ignored him. Although in a rare side glance from beneath her stunning hat, she caught him staring.

Nichola was grateful when the men decided to visit the saddling paddock before the Melbourne Cup race to study the character and condition of the competitors as they paced up and down, stripped for saddling. When they left, the Morgan ladies made polite excuses, too, and withdrew.

Betting on the main race was confined to four or five leading favourites. The Sydney horse, Archer, looked superb, the perfection of health and power, Nichola agreed, when her mother leaned closer to comment, serenely absorbed in everything. Christie of course was delirious with enthusiasm. Horses were her speciality and she had studied them all. Two hundred sovereigns had been added by the Turf Club to this event but only seventeen of the twenty-two acceptances came to the post. At twenty-five minutes to four, the flag fell.

'Good start,' Duncan said having re-joined them and watching through binoculars.

As the horses rounded the turn coming into the straight, there was a terrible accident. Rows of people rose to their feet and great gasps of horror issued from the crowd. Nichola saw her mother put a gloved hand to her mouth.

'Children, don't look,' she warned, but the race continued with a depleted field of fourteen.

At the river side, the two Sydney horses led but Archer was never closely approached and came in easily the winner by several lengths. Later they learned that three horses fell, two mares fatally with severe injuries to the riders. The catastrophe during the race was not easily forgotten and cast a gloom over the remainder of the day.

As Christmas approached, the weather warmed. More

eminent families moved to town from up country to the milder climate by the sea for the summer. Social life in Melbourne escalated and flourished. Even more calling cards piled daily on the hall tray at Kew House.

School finished and the boys took to boating excursions on the Yarra or were allowed to stay up late for routs held at home. Nichola entertained on the piano. To her irritation, the Morgan boy was often invited and sat close, staring, either while she played music or during games of whist.

When forced to talk to him, she said airily, 'I shall remain in town next year. I do love Melbourne. Does your family have a house?'

'No, we rent a villa as your father has done. We're pastoralists, after all. The country is our home and Melbourne only a diversion.'

'Do you have a young lady?' she asked pointedly.

He cleared his throat. 'No.'

'I trust you will find someone who will be happy to live in the country for I am not.'

She turned her shoulder to him and strolled away, soon claimed by a knot of young people in whose company she was always in demand. Although these men were less demanding and eager to please, charming in their naivety, she was irritated to discover herself more drawn to Elliott Morgan's confidence.

Yes, he was a wealthy squatter's son and heir and her parents would approve. If a girl played her cards right, he was a good catch. But he would need to demonstrate he could be controlled. And could she abide him?

A week later, they met again in a glittering mansion ballroom. Carriages arrived to sweep through iron gates and up to the door for the wealthy to step out and glide indoors to become a glittering addition to the grand scene. The house was alight and lamps glittered among the trees.

A German band played and, early in the evening, there was much traffic among tasselled programmes. Elliott Morgan, to Nichola's delight and dismay, pressed her for almost every second one of the galops, quadrilles and her favourite waltz, all the rage, danced fast and close.

'Take care or I may misread your interest,' Nichola teased.

'There can be no risk of that for an intelligent lady as yourself.'

'You are most sure of yourself, Mr. Morgan. I insist you pursue others lest you make a mistake.'

They danced again before supper. He had deliberately claimed her so he would be her escort into the lavishly supplied dining room. He held her firmly in his usual proprietary manner. Nichola repressed the peak of her fascination for he was already too sure of her by far.

Breathless, the dancing over, he drew her gloved hand through his arm and led her from the ballroom. They nibbled on fragments of food and eyed each other over glasses of punch, all else forgotten. Nichola knew she was entranced but hardly in love. This was excitement. Surely love was a far headier experience? In any event, she must choose a man with her head not her heart.

Toward the evening's end, she deliberately stole away from her prince and the ball without the courtesy of a goodbye to share a carriage home with friends.

Some days later, Nichola and Isabelle were out shopping, being fitted for yet another evening gown. They emerged from the store out onto Collins Street where all things were calm, quiet and ceremonious. Ladies moved between shops and did not venture into other streets, hopeful to meet friends and encounter admirers.

But it was now after four o'clock and the Block pavements were crowded, skirts and elbows jostled, pretty parasols were raised. To her annoyance, Nichola noticed Elliott Morgan approach and turned aside, engaging her mother in conversation to ignore him.

'Mrs. Penross.' He stopped before them. 'Miss Penross.'

Nichola pulled a guarded smile and watched him

monopolise and flatter her mother, charming and urbane, ignoring her as if she was invisible. She smiled to herself. He was playing the game too so she waited her chance, welcoming the sport and danger.

'Perhaps we shall meet again some time. By chance,' he grinned, addressing Nichola with his clever remark.

She immediately understood. 'It is quite possible, Mr. Morgan. We are often about town and stroll the gardens most days.'

'Which one is your favourite, Miss Penross?'

'That shall be your challenge to discover, Mr. Morgan.'

It pleased her that a shadow of annoyance clouded his face. If he wanted her, he must show enterprise and be patient.

'Nichola!' her mother whispered as they parted. 'That was most unreasonable.'

'If he wants to find me, he shall.'

'You wish to discourage him?'

'Men have enough control. What is wrong with a little fun to make them fret?'

'Careful lest you lose him,' her mother warned.

'I'm not certain I should care.'

Her mother arched her brows in mild surprise. 'No one would guess. You suit so well together.'

For the next few days, instead of her regular garden visits, Nichola took tea with friends or accompanied her mother on morning call, to be admired, hoping gossip reached the Morgan household that she was happily socialising elsewhere.

It bored her as they were ushered into yet another ornately furnished drawing room. The hostess pulled a bell rope and summoned a maid in her best starched apron and cap to bring tea and refreshments, vast quantities of lavish delicacies were produced which Nichola daintily nibbled. Christie, when she accompanied them under sufferance, ate like a horse and gobbled the food. She didn't even seem to mind sitting on a low stool and occasionally having her head patted.

When she eventually invited Christie to join her on a ride one afternoon almost a week later, Nichola chose the Royal Botanic gardens because it was just over one hundred acres and the largest in town. More difficult for Elliott to find her. She was excited at the thought of a romantic chase. Would he appear?

They left their carriage and walked by its flower beds and lawns, its immense aviary and around its handsome ornamental lake. Nichola wondered if Elliott had tried the other town gardens such as Flagstaff in the west or Royal Park at the north end of the city. She had almost given up hope when she spied him approaching in full stride.

'Miss Penross.' He was breathless, his appearance unusually dishevelled.

Nichola laughed at his boyish delight. He rarely smiled and it transformed his face making him even more difficult to resist.

'You have led me astray, Miss Penross and I confess I dislike it,' he said with light humour but an underlying threat.

Impressed by his persistence, she sobered. 'But you found me,' she teased sweetly, trying to soothe him. 'You are an accomplished hunter, Mr. Morgan.' Her niggling sense of mischief would not rest. 'What a pity we did not encounter you earlier. We have been here quite some time and must leave. Come, Christie,' she urged her sister, darkly disapproving throughout the exchange.

'You cannot stay?' Elliott challenged, clearly disappointed.

He was a strong man but not without feelings for her which weakened his power. Nichola privately glowed. 'You have my apologies, Mr. Morgan. Not today.'

'Perhaps I should seek an appointment with you, Miss Penross?' he called out hopefully as the two young women moved away along the path back to their carriage.

Nichola turned and radiated her most charming smile. 'A splendid suggestion, Mr. Morgan.'

Elliott bowed dutifully as the women left, glowering, but

did not speak.

'That was unkind, Nichola,' Christie said.

'It is a game,' she replied airily. 'Mr. Morgan knows I do not mean it.'

Discussing their daughter at home after yet another evening out, Duncan said, 'The Morgan boy looks suitable for Nichola.'

"I don't believe she is fully decided yet. She's barely sixteen.'

'Still, ah'm in favour. I hope she knows it and does as she's told.'

He would not look at her. It bothered her that Duncan should suddenly take an interest in a daughter he had always neglected and push for an early marriage.

'It might be wise if they waited for a year or two,' Isabelle tactfully hinted.

She still suspected her daughter was trifling with Elliott for her own amusement. She had certainly changed into a determined young lady but conducted herself admirably in public and reflected well on the Penross name. Duncan should be pleased enough with that and not be so eager to see her leave home. By the time the boys finished at Oxford, they would be much older when they married. Isabelle would not like to see Nichola wed before she was ready.

'Ah expect your help in making the girl see sense,' Duncan growled. 'A Morgan marriage would see her set. The family's highly esteemed throughout the District and ah'm told Castle Hill homestead is grand.'

She won't be marrying the house, Isabelle filled with resentment, but she could see trouble within. 'I wonder how harmonious a household with Elliott's mother and three younger sisters. It could be years before the daughters marry and he inherits.' She paused. 'I don't want Nichola forced but, whatever her decision, I should hope all of my children marry. For love,' she added pointedly, knowing Duncan had not.

His expression closed and he flashed her a challenging

glare. 'If he asks ma permission, he'll have it.' His words were as sharp as lightning.

At Duncan's cold unfeeling words that suggested he would not be considering his wife's opinion, Isabelle felt as though a piece of her heart had been ripped from her chest. Her expectations for Nichola wavered and she suddenly felt lost and powerless, her heart aching for her daughter's controlled future. Perhaps the girl's new-found strength would help guide her impossible choice. Then she rallied. No. Enough. Her opinion would be heard.

'I will not see any of my daughters forced into a marriage they do not want,' she said in a low voice between clenched teeth.

Duncan only glared vacantly at her challenge. If not for the blessing of her eight children, Isabelle anguished, she might have counted the last two decades of her life with Duncan Penross squandered.

Nichola crept upstairs in Kew House in the early hours of a Sunday morning following a rather fun evening rout with her friends at the Morgan house in Toorak. She had enjoyed ignoring Elliott and fostering interest among the other young men present.

Mrs. Morgan constantly reminded everyone that the Governor, Sir Henry Barkly lived nearby at his residence, Toorak House. Nichola despised the affected patronising woman, comparing her with her own mother. Unfavourably. For all the Morgans professed higher status, Isabelle Penross was by far the finer person. Not as stunningly beautiful but with a warm personality that easily drew her friends. It hadn't passed Nichola's notice that their hall tray daily overflowed with cards and invitations, knowing they were genuinely sent. Although mother did not fully enjoy socialising, she had accepted it with grace and endured her father's false attention in public. She did not support her mother's quiet endurance.

And Elliott's three nasty gossiping sisters were sadly cast

from the same mould and no better than their mother. The claws were always unsheathed during spiteful conversations. Tonight, Verity Morgan in particular had been a bitch making it clear Nichola was not their choice for Elliott but, as the daughter of Duncan Penross, only wealth made her acceptable.

Still feeling livid over a deliberately mean whispered comment as she departed, Nichola inconsiderately woke Katarina to help her undress. It was unnecessary, of course, but her mother's maid politely obeyed, trotting along to Nichola's room in a robe over her nightgown.

She enjoyed ordering servants about, especially this one, some years older and never destined to advance in life. Although she was quite attractive in a foreign sort of way. Pity about the girl's mother though. Apparently she was dying. There always seemed to be letters or telegraph messages flying back and forth between Kew House and Mr. Perini in Geelong to keep mother informed of the woman's declining health.

Next morning, Nichola groaned when Katarina woke her far too early for church. She grumbled all through breakfast, still barely awake, and remained silent during the ride to Scots Church in Collins Street. The whole family attended, including her father, who thankfully rode in a separate carriage with the boys. She, her mother and sisters including dear little Beatrice, now toddling and beginning to talk, a quite beautiful child, travelled together. Mother seemed subdued this morning but concealed her reflective mood with quiet smiles as Christie chattered and Maira listened with Beatrice on her lap.

When the carriage stopped and they alighted, Nichola tilted her head back to admire the Gothic spire at the front of the church. The family had just seated themselves all along one pew when the Morgan family pompously marched to the front for all to see, the womenfolk resplendent in their fashionable costumes and showy hats. Nichola loved to dress up but, for church, most people chose more modest attire.

Elliott glanced aside at her as they sat within sight. As always Nichola found the sermon tedious. After a late evening, her head bent in a doze. The sound of the organ woke her again and she opened her eyes to see Elliott grinning directly at her. His gaze said *caught* and she squirmed in her seat.

Outside after the service, lingering among the fashionable and distinguished congregation, Elliott edged from his family group to her side.

'I shan't say a word, Nichola, if you agree I may call on you this afternoon.'

'How noble of you, Elliott, but you know I do not care what others think.'

She had finally agreed to his suggestion of using their Christian names although Nichola only cautiously allowed herself the privilege because she could no longer deny her growing attraction to him. Her feelings should have caused elation but, instead, the lack of control frightened her.

As promised, or so Nichola heard from Christie who called him her beau, Elliott arrived at Kew House in the early afternoon. She waited in her room for ages but no maid called to inform her of his visit. Annoyed because he was probably detained by her father, Nichola's impatience grew. Then everything happened at once. She was called downstairs.

Mother hovered in the hall. 'I'm sorry, dear. I must go out on a call. An obligation,' she explained, slightly ruffled. 'I shall be back later. I'm sure you can entertain Mr. Morgan. Ring for tea.'

Everyone had deserted the house apparently for one of the maids informed her that father had already left for the Club. Or so he said, Nichola thought. She suspected many such outings were in fact visits to his widowed mistress.

Nichola anticipated Elliott's call with delight. They were rarely left alone together although any number of her siblings would probably bound into the drawing room and intrude at any moment. Especially Blair, who always pestered him about Oxford and Alex who excitedly discussed the recent tragic Burke and Wills expedition to the far north of the colony or any other adventure reported in the newspapers.

As she entered, Elliott stood before the fireplace, hands clasped behind him. His wide possessive smile let her know the trouble she had taken with her appearance was worthwhile. But she refused to let him escape without reference to the delay.

'You kept me waiting.'

'With good reason,' he countered assuredly.

'I should hope so.'

Still piqued, she stubbornly refused to ask why. She settled her dress around her on the deeply comfortable sofa, knowing she presented a picture because she had checked herself in the mirror upstairs before leaving her room. Katarina had deftly transformed her hair since church and she deliberately chose her outfit of palest topaz silk because any shade of blue brought out the colour in her eyes.

'I was in an important discussion with your father.'

As she suspected. Father deliberately provoking her. 'Indeed?'

He paused, pacing before the mantel. 'You have no notion why?'

She cast him a cool blank stare. 'Only if you wish to tell me. Do sit down,' she scolded, annoyed for once by his restless energy. She never knew what he might do. Nichola sighed. She did thrive on the unexpected with him though.

Elliott moved across the thick tapestry rug and towered before her. 'Would you be so kind as to stand?'

'Are we going to dance?' Nichola chuckled, but noting his serious expression, she obliged.

He took both her hands in his. 'You know that I adore you greatly.'

'Do I?' she teased, grinning.

'Nichola, please.'

Honestly, at times he could be so conservative. 'Yes, it seems you do,' she agreed.

'And I believe you share my affections.'

'Perhaps,' she fenced. 'It is not usually a subject a lady discusses.'

He gripped her hands tighter and she felt their dewy moisture. 'I know we have never discussed the future,' he hesitated and swallowed, looking quite uncomfortable.

She began to recognise the earnest direction of their conversation. Surely not? Her heart set up a pounding in her ears. No!

'I have spoken to your father and he has given his consent.'

Wide eyed and appalled, Nichola croaked in a whisper, 'Yes?'

'Is that your answer?' he beamed, flushed with relief.

'No! I await your explanation. Consent for what?' she retorted impatiently, pretending ignorance.

'Nichola, would you please do me the honour of becoming my wife?'

'Oh. Elliott.'

Her despair emerged as a breathless whisper but the way his eyes and tense posture begged for her positive reply made her panic and sicken with desperation.

'I am extremely flattered.'

With difficulty, she pulled her hands from his to unlock their touch and avoid looking directly at him until she gathered her poise.

'But I am just sixteen. I have another year at East Leigh.'

'I know but I had hoped you might agree to an ... understanding or, if you prefer, a secret betrothal.'

She preferred neither. He had not listened properly and completely misread her hesitation, assuming her agreement. Nichola grew cross and strode slowly toward the unlit fireplace to create distance since his presence stirred her body and clouded her judgement.

'We've only known each other this past summer,' she pointed out, turning back to face him, trying to sound reasonable. 'Do you believe that is a long enough time?'

'For us, yes. We know our hearts, Nichola.' He grew irritated at her uncertainty and delay. 'You know I am offering even more than the life to which you are accustomed. Remember, I am my father's heir.'

So like her own father, he used his wealth and its implied security to boast and persuade her. She watched a look of guarded puzzlement shadow his face.

'I must apologise and thank you for the offer, Elliott, but I cannot accept you. At this time,' she added to soften the words he surely had not expected to hear.

He stepped forward, contrite and misunderstanding. 'Of course, how thoughtless of me. You will need a short interval to consider.'

Nichola had not the heart nor voice to explain her uncertainty and did not correct his error. She had stalled him but, knowing Elliott, he would persist and her indecision came not from doubt of good sense on a few months acquaintance and to stem any haste, although he excited her heart. She was simply not sure if what she felt was love. How did one tell? She adored him. He made her heart race but she did not feel overwhelmed or obsessed by him as she had always dreamed. He greatly attracted her but did not sweep her away with longing.

Besides, Elliott's life was up country. She would be expected to live at Castle Hill, a great mausoleum of a house buried in the depths of the Western District. Worse still, she would be forced to endure his family. How would she suffer his mother and sisters? How influential could she be in his home against them?

She had grown to love Melbourne so much but Elliott was no man's fool, proving a stronger personality and not as easily compliant as she expected. She admired him so. He was quite the dashing gentleman and in demand. It would be quite a triumph to snare him. His emotional tug for her was so strong it ruled everything but she must keep her head and manoeuvre this situation to her advantage.

The marriage proposal and her deferral left an awkward barrier between them. Nichola smiled politely and invited him to stay for tea. They pretended all was well but she was distracted and vague throughout his attempts at conversation. She had much to think about. When her parents returned, she must speak privately to both.

Elliott plastered a brave face on their little scene of cordiality but remained restless. Ironically, neither Blair nor Alex appeared to come to her rescue for once so she hardly protested barely thirty minutes later when he made excuses and left, frustrated yet hopeful.

Nichola agonised until Isabelle returned.

'You refused him!' Her mother dropped onto the drawing room sofa, appalled. 'Duncan will be livid.' She spoke as if to herself.

'I'm not afraid of father,' Nichola announced, hands clenched, pacing.

Isabelle regarded her with speculation. 'You have certainly matured this past year.'

'What is love, mother?' She sank beside her, eyes pleading. 'What should I feel?'

Isabelle released a long slow sigh. 'I have been so afraid you would ask me this very question.' She gazed distantly across the room to where a stretch of afternoon sunlight threw lacy patterns onto the rug. 'An overwhelming obsession with everything he does. Your heart is so full of love it floods your entire body. You become his in every way and really are quite mindless to resist him.'

Nichola stiffened in confirmation, recognising her lack of feelings for Elliott. 'Do you love father?'

Isabelle met the challenge in her daughter's eyes. 'I did,' she said softly. 'Once.'

Nichola edged forward. 'No more?'

'Nichola-'

'You have my word.'

After the slightest hesitation, her mother shook her head.

When she could have felt so sad for her, Nichola knew only elation. The admission made it easier for the next step in her plan.

'Thank you for confiding in me, mother. I will never break your trust.'

'I would expect no less of you.'

'Nichola.'

A guarded Duncan Penross acknowledged his daughter as she strode determinedly into the same room where she had spoken with her mother not thirty minutes before, and closed the door.

'You know why I am here,' she began, preparing her words and building composure.

'You have done well.' He pushed back his shoulders smugly and dared to look pleased.

'In your eyes it would be the first time,' she snapped then delivered the news that would destroy his arrogance. 'I have refused his offer.'

His clear blue eyes, so like her own, turned to ice. 'You cannot,' he growled. 'His pedigree is impeccable. Elliott Morgan is a wealthy man.'

'You cannot force me.'

'Ah'm your father.'

'In name only.'

'I insist.'

'By what right?' she challenged, furious for a lifetime's abuse, trembling with unleashed fury. 'You forget you no longer have any power over me,' she reminded him. 'Mrs. Herrington?'

'I told ye never to mention her name again,' he warned.

'Afraid Mother will overhear?' Her voice dripped with spite. He glared and waited. 'However, I might be persuaded to marry Elliott Morgan.'

'Ah'm listenin'.'

'I have terms.'

'Ah'm sure you do. You're my daughter after all. Name them,' he ground out harshly.

'I want my own residence here in Melbourne. In my name alone. Fully furnished. You may consider it part of my marriage dowry,' she suggested wryly.

'Is that all?' His lips curled.

'And a generous annuity.' When he paused, she added, 'Remember what I know. And you can well afford it.'

When he moved forward, she feared he might strike her, so thunderous was the look on his face.

'Done.'

He brushed roughly past her, flung the door wide and left.

Nichola stood elated by her father's easy agreement and stunned by the extent of his concession to blackmail to protect his mistress.

Later, when Isabelle had returned and heard the confident knock on her upstairs sitting room door, she knew it was Duncan. She took a deep breath, rose to her feet and braced herself for his wrath over Nichola's defiance.

'Come in.'

He stood in the doorway, still half open, with his hand on the knob. They stared at each other. 'Nichola has agreed to marry Elliott Morgan.'

Isabelle gasped, astonished to hear it. 'What changed her mind?' she asked, filled with suspicion.

'You knew she intended to refuse?'

Isabelle thought quickly and gave a swift shake of her head. 'Only that she intended to give the offer more thought.'

He eyed her strangely at length. 'She understands the importance of a valuable alliance.' He cleared his throat and shuffled, his gaze sliding away. 'And ah promised her a generous settlement.'

Money! With Duncan it always came back to that. Repulsed by his manipulation and that her daughter had probably succumbed to bribery, Isabelle felt herself slowly die a little from within.

'Then since it is plain she will not marry for love I can only hope she will be happy.'

Somehow Isabelle doubted it but perhaps contentment was not out of her daughter's reach. Her own marriage, she admitted resignedly, almost beyond redemption and it seemed the next generation was already on a path to repeat the mistake.

To Nichola's amazement, within weeks the property title deed was in her hands, delivered impersonally by a servant. Presumably father could not face her himself.

She went to see it, a delightful terraced townhouse in Emerald Hill, comfortably furnished, exactly what she might have chosen for herself. In such a short time, he must have bought it fully appointed. Her joy weakened because she suspected in the years to come it may prove her sanctuary.

With the arrangements for her future now securely in place, Nichola felt able to confidently approach her mother and sought her out for a private meeting. She knew Isabelle disapproved of her change of heart over Elliott's proposal but did not believe she guessed it had been contrived.

Nichola entered her mother's pretty light filled sitting room where she waited expectantly and joined her on the sofa. 'I have a confidence I wish to share.'

Isabelle's forehead dipped into a frown. 'Oh dear. It sounds serious. Is it about Elliott?'

Nichola sighed. 'It is a sensible marriage, mother. I am comfortable with my decision.'

'But not happy,' she ventured softly.

How her marriage evolved, she would deal with as it happened. 'Elliott is a handsome confident man. I have another year while I continue at East Leigh when we can become better acquainted. I am genuinely attracted to him.'

'Then what is it you wish to speak with me about?'

'Father.'

Isabelle raised surprised eyebrows but remained silent.

'Knowing your lack of feelings for him, perhaps what I have to say may not hurt too much.'

Her mother frowned and stiffened. Nichola paused to compose herself, knowing she was about to break a promise but seeking revenge for a lifetime's mistreatment.

'Since living in Melbourne this past year I see how others live. Father has travelled here and to Geelong on *business*,' she emphasised the word, 'for many years.'

'He has had a great deal to manage,' her mother said warily.

'Yet never invited you to join him?'

Isabelle smiled softly. 'I had a household to run and a family to raise. I have always been content in the country.'

Nichola detected a slight fissure in her composure, revealed in the hint of a frown. She swallowed and whispered, 'What I tell you now is only out of loyalty to you.' She paused. 'Father has a mistress.'

Isabelle blanched and jumped to her feet, her face rife with anger at the bearer of the news and clearly disbelieving its substance. Nichola's heart went out to her for, even now, although she had claimed otherwise, she could see a part of her mother's heart must still belong to her father.

Isabelle pressed a hand to her waist. 'Are you absolutely certain of this accusation?'

Nichola nodded furiously, astonished at the extent of her mother's shock. She never intended to hurt her but she should not have her continue to live in ignorance.

'A Mrs. Herrington,' Nichola added nervously over the tension while her mother paced and processed the startling news. 'A widow.' Her voice quavered. 'I am so sorry ... when you said you no longer loved father, I thought-'

'I would feel no pain?' she snapped.

'You have a right to know of his betrayal.'

'And what of yours?'

Nichola frowned. 'Mine?'

'Are you quite sure this is not a lie and you are making mischief?'

Nichola suffered a stab of hurt at her mother's charge. 'Because I hate father? No! I have seen them together. They entered a private house. I understand they have been long acquainted.'

Isabelle glared at her daughter in horrified challenge then her body sagged and she released a soft moan. 'Then my humiliation is complete.' She sank into a chair.

Nichola reached out to comfort her mother but Isabelle shook her head and withdrew. 'You've done your duty,' she said bitterly. 'Please go.'

'Mother, please don't hate me. I did it for you.'

'I said, please go.' She rose and turned her back on her daughter, shutting her out.

'Mother, he has done nothing but hurt you.'

Isabelle whirled about, white faced and trembling. 'We both know about hurt but do not presume to know the depth of mine.'

She gaped at Nichola, perhaps not yet fully realising the truth herself. Unable to bear her mother's daze of devastation, Nichola did her bidding and left the room in a rustle of skirts. She felt no satisfaction, only distress for her mother, and it was far too late for regret.

Isabelle's head pounded with the onset of a headache after Nichola's revelation. She fled upstairs to the nursery where her darling little Beatrice slept, angelic, golden curls tumbling about her sweet round face. How soon would that innocence be destroyed? Even in the depths of her own misery, Isabelle sought only happiness for her children. As the offspring of Duncan Penross, their wealth and comfort would never be in question.

Crushed and heartbroken to have her husband's cheating exposed, she also knew deep down that she should not be so surprised. Over the years, he had been absent so much. In her naivety, she had remained blindly ignorant. In the early days, there had been Ginny. Who else? She wilted. What other women had he known over the years while she bore his children and secured the dynasty he craved?

Indecisive for days and burning with humiliation that she still cared for him, Isabelle finally accepted she would have no emotional peace until she confirmed Nichola's claim about Duncan's unfaithfulness.

Accordingly, she contrived a meeting on one of their rare free evenings at home. Duncan eyed her with surprise and frowning disapproval for the interruption as he read The Argus through a fog of pipe smoke when she quietly appeared in the downstairs drawing room and carefully closed the door behind her.

She endured his glare. 'This won't take long.' She moved toward him but remained standing some feet away. 'I have learned of an issue that greatly disturbs me.'

He lowered the newspaper. 'Aye.'

'I need you to be honest.'

Before she had even begun, his beautiful clear blue eyes sharpened and she despised herself for still feeling any affection for him. Isabelle's heart sank to see his defences so swiftly in place. Without either of them saying a word, she felt sure he knew the purpose of her mission. She felt wronged and cheap, blind and willing to have produced his heirs, unloved. They glared at each other in silence for a long time, all artifice crumbled.

She clenched her hands together until they hurt and, barely above a whisper, asked, 'Is it true?'

To his shame, he blustered, 'I have no idea what you're talking about.'

'Don't, Duncan. I've stood beside you for almost twenty years and borne you nine children which is all you ever wanted of me. Little Duncan's loss was equally as heartbreaking for me as it was for you.' Indignation flared within her like a wildfire. 'I deserve your respect and demand your honesty. Is it true?' she repeated.

'Nichola,' was all he hissed in fury, oblivious of the courage it took her to confront him and caring more for the betrayal than his wife.

So, Isabelle realised, they all knew. After that, his confession was irrelevant.

'Aye', he said defiantly, unrepentant.

The indignity of it. All these years, she had been such a fool. She had lied to Nichola when she said she no longer loved him to save her humiliation and pride when it was clear to everyone Duncan did not return her feelings.

She spun around and clasped her arms across the pain in her chest then swept across the carpet and slammed the door shut behind her, shaking. In a trance, she ascended the stairs, sank onto her bed and cupped her face in her hands. Tears would not flow but her heartbreak was complete.

Within days, Katarina was summoned home to Geelong. Maria Perini's condition had grown critical. As Isabelle farewelled her personal maid at the station, although nothing was said, she read in the girl's eyes that this was likely her last visit to her mother.

Treasuring her friend and employee, Isabelle only hoped she might eventually seek to return to Kooringal for she considered her irreplaceable. Bereft of Katarina's calming companionship and presence, and in private turmoil over Duncan's infidelity, Isabelle was impatient to return to the comforting familiarity of Kooringal again.

Without a word to Duncan, she packed up the children and servants. Wrenched from the social life on which she thrived, but knowing the cause, even Nichola did not object and dutifully accompanied her mother home.

At first sight of her beloved homestead, although far grander than she would ever need, and the carriage pulled up the rise, the landscape flecked with the gold and russet of approaching autumn, Isabelle sent up a silent prayer of thanks for this haven of peace in her life.

As the children scrambled out and raced indoors, the stately residence welcomed the family back into its rooms echoing with life again. Isabelle carried Beatrice. Audrey held Owen's hand and smiled with quiet satisfaction as they climbed the front steps together. The servants chattered happily about them at their homecoming.

Sadly, they received word soon after that Katarina's mother died. She and Isabelle exchanged long letters but, as yet, there was no mention of resuming her service. After an acceptable lapse of time, Isabelle would visit and pay her respects.

At some point, Isabelle became aware that Duncan had returned. Why did he bother when his true love was in Melbourne, she thought bitterly? Nichola and the older boys eventually returned to town for another school year, the homestead emptier without them.

Now that Nichola had consented to Elliott's proposal, Isabelle set arrangements in place for a lavish Kooringal wedding the following summer. It kept her occupied and she felt some relief that her daughter chose to wait but worried that she showed no warmth for the future man in her life.

During school breaks when Nichola returned home, Elliott Morgan became a frequent visitor at the homestead. He and Duncan were as close as a tied knot and talked endlessly of nothing but sheep. Occasionally, Nichola was invited to Castle Hill but returned quiet and despondent. Isabelle had tried approaching her, had even suggested she could change he mind, but her daughter adamantly resisted. Set on what her mother considered a potentially destructive path.

The Perini cottage in Geelong was modest brick with a well-tended garden. Although Nichola had accompanied her mother to Geelong, she preferred shopping, so Isabelle walked the narrow pathway alone to rap the shining front door knocker.

Katarina expected her and flung the door wide, beaming. 'Isabelle.' They hugged warmly. 'Please to come in.'

Isabelle had missed her charming accent and vivacious personality. They moved indoors and settled on plump floral sofas before a low burning fire in a small front sitting room. Isabelle immediately felt at home as they busily chattered and laughed together until Katarina glanced over her shoulder and her face brightened.

'Papa!' She rose and drew him close. 'I have the pleasure to introduce Mrs. Penross.'

'Isabelle, please.' She smiled up into a pair of eyes as equally dark as her own and when she stood before him, discovered he was of a similar height with a handsome olive complexion like his daughter. 'Mr. Perini.'

He took her hand and kissed it. 'Luca.'

The deep warm voice only enhanced his first impression as a fine figure of a distinguished middle aged gentleman of moderate means, but the brush of his lips across her skin felt more intimate than she was sure he intended. Eventually, he released her.

When she politely acknowledged his loss, he nodded silently and took a seat. Katarina poured tea. All the while they made easy conversation, Isabelle was conscious of the girl's father, his attentiveness and devotion, and wished Duncan could have been as gentle and caring with their children.

Strangely, she left the small house feeling more alive than she had done for many years. She did not believe she was mistaken to sense Mr. Perini – Luca, she smiled – regarded her kindly as well. Her step was light as she walked back to the hotel to meet Nichola for lunch. But Isabelle's private happiness was brief and soon tinged with regret when she received a letter from Katarina.

Papa feels the need to return home, to Italy, she wrote. *I know it is so far away, across the world and who can say for how long?*

Papa himself does not know. Our family is from Trento so it is there we will travel.

Isabelle let the pages sag in her hand, dispirited to read such news. She had looked upon Katarina as a daughter and would miss her confidante. But it seemed the girl was also nostalgic about their imminent departure. She continued reading.

I do not like to leave but perhaps we shall return one day. It will of course depend on papa. Without mama now, he may wish to remain in Italy forever.

Isabelle wished she had known on the day of her recent visit so she could have said goodbye. Folding up the letter, she pondered on another person lost to her life. There seemed too much sadness and too many partings of late. How many more could she bear?

CHAPTER 9

Isabelle experienced the dawn of Nichola's wedding day with a heavy heart. It only served to remind her of an earlier time and simple ceremony so many years before, her own wedding day to Duncan. Fortuitous in hindsight, or a mistake? It had brought her comfort and the joy of a large family but limited personal happiness.

In bleak irony, her own daughter was not marrying for mutual love. An ideal, of course, and not considered important among the rich where unions like those of the Penross and Morgan families were about merging two considerable estates. Nonetheless, Isabelle prayed that in Nichola's marriage, given time, love might grow.

Today, the bride radiated a glowing contentment. She floated down the front steps of Kooringal with slow grace and stepped the long carpet runner borrowed from the hallway toward the large assembly of seated family, friends and eminent guests on the lawns.

Resplendent in rich ivory silk and lace, upon which no expense had been spared, golden and regal of bearing on this special day, she outshone her father on whose arm she proceeded toward her future spouse. With bitter reluctance and only because it was tradition, not her preference, Nichola allowed her father to escort her into Elliott Morgan's keeping.

Christie and Maira trailed daintily behind in pastel dresses, flowers tucked into their hair; in their innocence, believing as many would that this was a happy day. While the minister murmured in the background, Isabelle heard little of the ceremony as she contemplated each of her family instead and tried to ignore Duncan seated erect and dignified beside her. The months had not dimmed her pain.

Christie was still years away from ladies' college but already restless and a competent, if reckless, horsewoman. The only indoor subject in which she excelled was geography. Not unlike Alex, she held a great passion for learning about other lands.

Maira, her motherly little shadow, had a quiet inner strength and remained unruffled by anyone, even her father. She was a capable pupil and if unable to be found, Isabelle first searched the nursery for Maira loved to spend time with Beatrice.

She smiled across at Audrey seated opposite toward the front, restraining and entertaining her youngest child who Isabelle would always consider her baby no matter how much she grew because she would be the last of her brood. Beatrice was an adorable beautiful child, as fair in colour as her oldest sister being married this day with eyes as blue, but of a sunnier laughing disposition. Nichola had always been more sullen and needy.

Of her boys, looking handsome and almost grown in their stiff formal clothes, hair oiled for the occasion, dashing Blair was expected to assume the reins from his father should Duncan ever release them. With a tendency to be irresponsible, Isabelle could only hope he settled down as he matured to command the future his father had planned for him since birth.

Alexander, she was sure, would only endure his privileged education until released to explore the world. His adventurous streak was not unlike their independent Christie but Alex possessed an unselfish nature.

Dutiful Callum gave no one any trouble or cause for concern and Owen genuinely loved his books and school work. Always watchful of his father, even if unnoticed, he appeared to be an avid listener with a strong sense of loyalty.

Then the marriage ceremony was over and lavish

celebrations commenced, continuing into the night. Despite engaging double the number of servants, Isabelle was still constantly in demand both by staff and guests answering questions, solving problems, ensuring the smooth organisation of the family's auspicious event.

Massive urns of greenery and flowers adorned every corner of every public room. Beds in the homestead and every habitable outbuilding on the property were fully occupied. It wasn't until the early morning hours that Isabelle felt free to retire.

Elliott and Nichola, together with the last straggling guests, had adjourned some time before to a bedroom suite upstairs which Isabelle had personally readied for the night.

Alone in her quiet room in the early morning hours, Isabelle reflected on her daughter and what lay ahead in these changing times for them all.

Nichola felt Elliott slip from the bed beside her but curled up and pulled the covers about her in the soft large bed, luxuriating in being a married woman. Her husband had proved a strong lover, not that she had any experience to compare, but he certainly seemed masterly if a trifle impatient and rough. Oddly, she did not mind and being completely naked, she found a deeply satisfying pleasure.

Aware of Elliott dressing and leaving the room while she pretended to sleep, she reflected on his heavy breathless excitement before they first made love. He was panting for her, his erection huge and hard as he rutted her like an animal. Caught unaware and not knowing what to expect, she quickly learnt from the experience and finally understood that *this* was the reason why men wanted women.

Now enlightened, she sensed where her true power lay. It had nothing to do with wealth or beauty at all. She only felt disappointment at not feeling the same satisfaction as Elliott while he gasped and moaned until it was over. He had laid over her more than once, each time with less fury but equal need.

She heard the door click shut as Elliott finally left, sighed and smiled.

Only months later, Nichola was not quite so smug. Nauseous, wretching and miserable, she discovered the consequences of teasing and playing with her husband, bartering her body to get what she wanted. If she could not fully enjoy being with her husband, she could at least try and gain some benefit.

Initially, she had tried withholding her favours but Elliott, stronger and determined, soon overcame her attempts to escape him. The roughness that first excited her now became a fear. Frustrated by her games, Elliott lost patience and swiftly seethed, becoming more cruel if she resisted.

Married for less than a year, Nichola already felt trapped and dominated. How gullible she had been to believe a woman could ever best a man. In marrying Elliott Morgan she had exchanged one tyrant in her life for another and cursed her ignorant mistake.

She now grasped the extent of Mrs. Herrington's influence over her father.

In due course, Nichola was worshipped when she proudly did her duty and produced a son, Adam. Mrs. Morgan proudly admired her grandson each day in the nursery but her daughters sneered with jealousy. Attended by a monthly nurse who moved in a week before the child was due and stayed for some weeks afterwards, Nichola left baby Adam with her as soon as she felt able to travel, informing Elliott she preferred to convalesce in Melbourne. Although confounded, he did not prevent her and bathed in the glory of a son while his wife escaped to town.

Her misshapen body gradually returned and she went shopping. Men admired her and she glowed in their attention, albeit from afar. When Elliott visited some weeks later, amorous and sweet, bearing tales of their handsome son and heir, she recognised his intent.

But when he caressed and kissed her with a newfound tenderness, presenting her with lavish gifts, she melted. Her fickle body had missed the excitement. Even as he rolled on top of her again, she wondered if another man would please her more.

On the rare occasion when they actually conversed at dinner, Duncan growled about the recent abolition of primogeniture. Isabelle, numb of any emotions for him, did not care. He had placed all emphasis on Blair, seemingly now to no avail, since their first born need not legally inherit.

'Ah've spent my whole life planning this,' he bellowed, sculling more whisky.

'He is not your only son,' Isabelle pointed out quietly mostly now despising the sight of him but forced to endure for where else would she go?

Duncan's brows knit into a furious scowl but he allowed her comment with caution. 'Ah'll need to think on it.'

Isabelle rose from the table without comment. She had given him what he wanted yet still he complained. Any sympathy she might once have carried for her husband had been crushed.

Besides, Beatrice was poorly and she was anxious to return to the nursery. Her children were all usually so robust in health, Isabelle found even a minor illness alarming. But two days ago, her beautiful lively baby had been caught outdoors in an early wintry storm playing with Owen. The maids had swiftly brought them inside, removed their wet clothes and dried them out. But while Owen remained unaffected, Beatrice developed a cold and she severely reprimanded her servant's neglect even knowing her wrath was unreasonable but she equally blamed herself for lack of supervision.

Isabelle hurried upstairs. Nanny sat by her daughter's bedside, the tiny soul watched over day and night. No one slept for Beatrice wasn't improving. A distraught Maira sat silently beside her mother watching every movement made as willing hands tended to her little sister's needs.

Isabelle administered laudanum and caster oil then gave Beatrice a warm bath while Audrey prepared a mustard poultice. She tested the hot application by pressing it to her own face first but the child's chesty cough worsened.

Despite the late hour, Isabelle instructed a maid, 'Send Irish for the doctor.'

During the night, she continued to soak eucalyptus oil on a warm damp cloth and lie it on her daughter's tiny chest. When her symptoms appeared to ease, Isabelle took a few hours rest but by early morning again, the child had relapsed and her congestion turned into pneumonia.

Audrey straightened her covers, fussing, weeping silent tears. Everyone in the room worked with hushed voices and quiet movements. Isabelle sponged Beatrice with vinegar and water to bring down her fever. The child's restlessness subsided and she grew pale and quiet. Even before the doctor arrived, Isabelle began to fear the worst.

Her mind screamed out in objection. Why should her spirited little angel suffer? It broke her heart to see her normally bright child lying pale and still.

'Fight, darling,' she whispered endlessly, to no avail.

Aware of his daughter's alarming condition but as helpless as everyone else, Duncan hovered, disappeared and returned. Christie and Maira tiptoed into the sickroom, Maira's gaze silently appealing to her mother. Isabelle hugged her, unable to speak. Christie stood at the foot of the bed staring at her sister's tiny damp form outlined beneath the covers, masses of blond curls tumbled over the pillow about her face.

The doctor folded up his stethoscope. 'I'm sorry, Mrs. Penross.'

Isabelle wanted to shake the man and yell at him that he was wrong. Surely Beatrice was just sleeping? But looking down at her thin lifeless body, Isabelle was forced to accept the truth.

Duncan, present for the doctor's visit, moved to her side and placed a hand on her shoulder. Furious that he should dare to touch her and that he finally noticed his youngest daughter, Isabelle shook him off, scooped her beloved inert child into her arms and wept. It was impossible to let her go. She caressed her hair and kissed her cooling cheeks.

Duncan left but the girls stayed with her, Maira quietly sobbing, Christie still and white, the nursery servants paralysed and hovering. So far the family had been spared an infant loss although mortality rates were high, so the house and everyone in it fell silent in their grieving.

Finally, Isabelle relinquished her daughter and dropped to her knees at the bedside to pray. The girls followed her example, whispering their own respects.

Isabelle and Audrey prepared Beatrice, wrapped her in a white shroud and, with gentle reverence the following day, placed her in the small coffin lovingly built by one of the estate carpenters.

Duncan took the reins and drove the horse drawn cart to the isolated family graveyard where little Duncan was buried down behind the cottage a short distance from the new homestead. The musky fragrance of geraniums scented the air and the tiny open grave was lined with grass and bracken.

Still incredulous and inconsolable, Isabelle's faith became her comfort. She and the girls clung to each other during the brief simple service, Duncan nearby with his sons. Nichola and the boys had been telegraphed in Melbourne and hurried home for their baby sister's funeral, now standing distant and resolute among them. At Isabelle's request, only family and household servants attended although, of the few remaining natives on the station, a wailing Bessie and staunch Duke appeared.

Devastated, Isabelle beseeched her Lord that she never suffer the loss of another. Although little Duncan had never taken a breath, his brief existence in her body had been no less difficult in its own way at the time for its implications.

***

After a sombre week, Nichola and the boys returned to Melbourne. Isabelle did not have the strength to question her daughter's continued residence in town at the neglect of her husband and baby son. Sunk into a malaise whenever she passed her baby daughter's empty room or looked upon her little clothes, she was gripped by a painless ache, consumed with sorrow.

The following year in a simple ceremony, Duke and one of the native housemaids, Bonny, were married according to their custom. The woman simply went to the hut of the man for whom she was intended and was handed over by tribal males into his keeping. Bonny was a comely girl, always smiling with white teeth and long black hair. It occurred to Isabelle that any children of the union would be Duncan's grandchildren.

What a web of intrigue was their family.

Then a brief moment of joy came in the form of Katarina's first letters from Italy. As Isabelle dreaded, they were to remain in their home country indefinitely but at least she now had an address for correspondence, the distant flimsy link something tangible on which to cling. A measure of comfort when her spirits were lowest for her dormant thoughts still lingered towards not only Katarina but also her father.

'Audrey.' Isabelle welcomed her into the morning room some months later. 'Interesting news.' She paused. 'Duncan has suggested a Grand Tour.'

Her friend's surprise as she seated herself was predictable. 'For such an exciting experience, you don't sound enthusiastic.'

'I know but I have given his suggestion consideration over recent days and I realise it may be a blessing and an opportunity. Besides, the preparations might prove a helpful distraction.'

The school teacher had been the recipient of her most personal confidence and reached out to squeeze her hand.

'You would travel with him?' Audrey asked softly.

Isabelle shrugged. 'What is the alternative? That I remain here alone and wallow? We may travel together but he is nothing to me.'

'When?' Audrey's expression was a combination of wonder and fear.

'Soon. In the autumn. It will be spring in Europe of course. Duncan wants to follow his wool clip to London and visit Blair at Oxford. I suspect to check up on him.'

Even before leaving for England, Blair has shown no direction and had begun to favour alcohol. He forgot appointments or arrived late and generally idled his time. Not the character of the presumed son and heir Duncan had always planned. Isabelle knew he was savagely disappointed but, for herself, she felt only a deep and growing concern.

'I shall write to Katarina and let her know I'm coming.' The possibility of seeing the girl and her father again had lit a spark of life within her and been a strong factor in her decision. The lure to see them again was irresistible.

She grew pensive. 'Audrey, as you know with Nichola expecting her second child, she must remain here at home.' She paused, unsure how to phrase her question. 'Naturally you are expected to join us but we would be away for at least six months.' She hesitated then rushed on, 'Could you leave Mr. Kruger for so long?'

Clearly surprised by the enquiry, Audrey stiffened in her chair opposite and an embarrassed flush stained her cheeks.

'Audrey?' she prompted when there was no response. 'I have no wish to offend you but-'

'It's all right, really. I knew this moment would come one day.' She sighed, slowly set down her floral tea cup onto its saucer and rose to her feet, drifting across to the open French window to pause before the long lace curtains floating gently back and forth in a warm late summer breeze.

'You have guessed corrected and I *am* deeply fond of Walter but no matter how much I pray it could be otherwise, we can never marry.'

'You prefer to remain single?' Isabelle prompted gently, aware of her distress.

Audrey glanced back at her friend and mistress, her face blanched with dread. 'I am already married. Well, I was. Briefly.'

'Married?' Isabelle whispered, astonished.

'Yes.' Audrey sank dejected onto a chair, worrying a kerchief, her gaze remote. 'Bailey is my maiden name. My parents arranged it when I was barely eighteen. He was supposed to be respectable and well placed but within months he deserted me and took all my money, leaving me destitute. My parents were horrified and devastated. I returned to live with them and a much younger sister for some years, a burden and a shame. It was plain he would never return. When my sister married, it was agreed she would live with her husband in the family home to care for our aging parents.

'I had no wish to be a liability and was being crucified by gossip and pity in the village. So I emigrated to get as far away as possible and start a new life for myself.' She smiled weakly. 'I had been alone all those years in England yet I met Walter soon after I arrived. I almost left you know,' she admitted miserably, 'because I knew nothing could come of it. But he had become so dear to me and has been steadfast all these years.'

'Oh Audrey, how dreadful for you. I'm so glad you stayed.'

'I have no idea where my husband Edward went. If I cannot find him, I cannot even try for a divorce. But the scandal-' she broke off, distressed.

'It could be done discreetly.' Isabelle's optimism was genuine. 'You must try and find him,' she urged.

'How?' The plea came with an air of desperation. 'Where do I begin?'

'*We*, Audrey. We shall pursue this together. Let me ask Duncan. If nothing else, he has powerful contacts.'

Audrey rose, distracted, and resumed pacing in a quandary. 'It's impossible,' she said eventually and gripped the back of a chair.

'Shall we try?' Isabelle smiled hopefully, suddenly filled with new life and purpose.

'I cannot pay.'

'You are family,' she scoffed. 'There is no need.'

Audrey pressed a hand against her trembling lips. Always so stoic and composed, rarely given to emotion even in Walter's company, Isabelle finally understand the reason why.

'All right but only if you explain it all to Mr. Penross. I couldn't bear to speak to him on such a private matter. I have misled you all.'

'In the circumstances, understandable and forgivable,' Isabelle brushed aside her concerns. 'Now, write down every single detail you know about your husband and I shall give it to Duncan.'

'And I shall inform Walter we are sailing for Europe.' Audrey's expression was a blend of excitement and dismay.

'You could perhaps explain your ... situation to him,' Isabelle suggested.

'Oh, I couldn't possibly,' Audrey said hastily in alarm.

'Why not? By your own words, you said he is devoted.'

'He will hate me.'

'Never. Walter is too compassionate.'

'He might believe I have taken advantage of him.'

Isabelle shook her head. 'He knows your true character too well. Give him credit and allow him to judge.'

'What if I lost his friendship?' Audrey breathed.

Isabelle shrugged with compassion. 'The decision must be yours, of course, and it will not be easy.'

After a moment, Audrey asked, slightly more hopeful, 'Do you really think I should?'

'It might ease the waiting.' Isabelle suggested and sprang to her feet. 'Now, let's go and tell the children.'

Arm in arm, like two sisters, they climbed upstairs, fresh

hope in each of their hearts.

Duncan hunched over a bureau in his room at the Melbourne Club, keen to finalise Isabelle's unusual request. From fellow members he had gleaned the name and address in Paddington Green of a Private Inquiry Office in London run by a man called Ignatius Pollaky. Hungarian apparently, but experienced.

In scratching out a letter of direction now by lamplight, enclosing Audrey's detailed handwritten information, he hoped to get the process under way and maybe some results by the time they reached England. Audrey Bailey married! He'd never have thought it. He stopped writing and let himself brood.

Everyone deserved love and happiness. He knew that now. He'd found it with his dearest Portia but if he'd married her, he'd not have any sons. He would miss her dearly while he travelled. He'd begged her to accompany him with her own private cabin aboard ship to be discreet but she had still refused. He didn't like her decision but understood. It would be damned awkward yet it was she and not Isabelle whom he loved.

His wife had borne heirs but to what advantage? Blair was proving useless despite giving him the best education.

He swilled the last of yet another whisky and finished writing then took the addressed envelope to an attendant. He summoned his carriage to Williamstown to clear his head and check on his clip. After being dumped at port, he intended following the progress of his wool to London. Every year saw its quality and financial reward increase.

He was annoyed by Isabelle's insistence they sojourn in Italy to visit the Perini family. She'd taken an unnecessary interest in them since the mother's death. If Portia would travel with him, Italy might not seem such a waste of time. He still wrestled with her refusal but she would not be convinced.

He opened his fob watch. He would see her soon and had

one more card to play. But time was running short and their date of departure drawing close.

'It's not too late,' Duncan teased when he saw her later. 'Ah've reserved a cabin for ye, just in case.'

'Duncan, you're making this impossible for me.'

'I don't want to be without ye for so long.'

'Nor do I but you know the difficulty in such an arrangement.'

'Aye, ma dear,' he conceded, 'and there's nought to do about it.'

Portia sighed. 'I want it more than anything. To be with you. But I simply cannot.'

When first told of his travel plans, she had appealed, 'Why must you go?'

His plea still drew rejection. Never troubled at leaving Isabelle, he hungered for Portia and had regularly written to her when they were apart over the past twenty years.

'Then this must be goodbye for a wee while,' he felt an equal sorrow in his chest.

She moved closer and grasped his lapels, pressing herself against him. 'Then we must make this a night to remember,' she whispered, her voice husky with desire, the fire between them still easily kindled, 'to last until we see each other again.'

'Ah remember every moment with ye, woman, and still fancy ye strong.'

Except for weeks, rarely months, they had never been apart this long.

Portia turned to him in the dimness of early evening in her bedroom and smiled. It was their usual custom to make love in the dark.

'Light the lamps, woman. I want to see as well as feel every inch of ye tonight,' he growled, drawing the silky undergarments from her shoulders to release her luscious breasts.

He bent to draw her nipples into his mouth, thrusting his hardness against her.

'Duncan, I want you inside me.' She was always eager for him, a real woman.

Pushing her against the turned bedpost for support, he cupped his hands around her buttocks to raise her higher and obliged.

She gripped his shoulders and panted as he pulsed inside her. 'What shall I ever do without this?'

'Pleasure yourself as ye've always done when I'm not here,' he ground out, barely able to speak just before his release.

Later, lying on top of the bed covers propped against mounds of pillows, he slid his hand over hers between her legs and sucked her breasts, following the rhythm she set for herself. They often shared pleasing her but tonight Portia was high with excitement and intent on indulging her own satisfaction. She was a rare woman and she was his, and he'd have her willingly again tonight.

She gasped and caught her breath and cried out at her peak. High with love and euphoria, she rolled against him. He was hard again from watching her and she steered him inside her.

Afterwards, they dozed. Later, still in bed and naked, they drank wine.

'And will you still be away for six months?'

He chuckled. 'Ah'll need that long to recover.'

'You're muscled and brown and in good condition for a man of fifty.' She ran her hands over him.

'Don't remind me. Ah've aches and pains already.'

'So long as you only ache for me.'

'Ye can clearly see ah'm in pain,' he grinned, his body tight with need again.

'Ye'll not be swayed?' he begged next morning as they dressed.

Portia, arms raised piling up her hair, shook her head. He walked up behind her, filled his hands with her semi clad breasts and kissed her neck.

'Then ah think ah'll be undressin' ye again until you do.'

She turned in his arms and laughed as they fell onto the bed together like new lovers.

For Isabelle, the following weeks grew frantic. Writing letters to family in Blackburn, unsure if they still lived at the same address, feeling guilty for her poor contact over the years. It seemed like a lifetime since she emigrated, would they recognise or even receive her? Her siblings were all older and married so there would be Waring nephews and nieces she had never seen.

More exciting still, she had sent word to Katarina hoping her mail arrived in advance alerting them that they were en route even if the exact date was unknown. The wonder now was that telegraphs could be sent from almost anywhere.

And then there were the clothes. For everyone. When Duncan returned from Melbourne, to her amazement he brought Alex and Callum home having released them from Scotch declaring that travel was an equally useful education. So their arrival threw her into a further frenzy of orders to maids for extra packing.

Alexander and Christie were the most ecstatic of them all, the ramblers of the family who reminded her of Duncan in her first years at Kooringal. He had arranged an overseer to manage both properties while away.

'The man came highly recommended,' Duncan had muttered to her at dinner one evening, since they were rarely together otherwise. 'He better be for ah'm payin' him three hundred pounds. It's a snug gentleman's billet for sure.'

Then, finally, a few days before they were finally to sail in March, with the caretaker installed in the cottage and a skeleton household staff left behind to take care of their lovely homestead until they returned by the year's end, the family, Audrey and the maids climbed into carriages, their baggage piled into wagons behind, headed for Meredith railway station.

The entourage stepped up onto the foot board and occupied two compartments in the train carriage. They had made a booking on the passenger service and were barely loaded when the monster locomotive shuddered and steamed and they were away. The boys were fascinated, even Owen who usually had his head in books. Isabelle spared a thought for Nichola, pregnant again and devastated to be left behind.

The children bubbled with chatter, noses pressed to windows. They slowed to cross a viaduct then the train climbed for most of the remaining journey into Geelong. In the ten minute break while the locomotive was changed, Isabelle purchased a hamper and would hand in the basket at their destination after their three hour expedition.

The Monday of their departure dawned dull and cloudy and particularly hot. They boarded their P and O passenger and mail ship the Ellora and settled themselves into their private first class cabins before steaming from their anchorage in Hobson's Bay about two in the afternoon. Isabelle, Audrey and the girls share two cabins between them with Duncan and the boys sharing two more.

Some of the Chirnside family from nearby district stations were on board. They and a number of other passengers were to disembark in Marseille. As they took to sea for Adelaide and then the predicted turbulence of the Bight, Isabelle's thoughts centred on enjoyment of their travels ahead. The distant intangible reunion with Katarina and Luca Perini. Seeing Duncan's scowl back toward shore from where he stood further along the rails, Isabelle bitterly presumed his thoughts lay on who he had left behind.

A Miss Rye disembarked at King George Sound. Then it was only the blue and immeasurable expanses of the Indian Ocean and sunlit days on deck as they sailed north. At Galle, they opted for lighter clothes as they strolled among the natives beneath coconut palms.

Isabelle constantly restrained an excited Christie and often sent up a prayer for her safety if she remained on board leaving her adventurous daughter in the care of Alexander, equally enthralled. Callum quietly accompanied the menfolk but Owen, like Maira, was often content at his mother's side. Audrey surprised her most of all, eagerly trailing behind the family to participate in as many excursions as possible. At least another responsible female adult accompanied Christie.

She saw Duncan glance at their teacher anew, no doubt in the context that she was a married woman. Isabelle hoped Duncan's private investigator bore fruit and some solution be found for she believed Walter and Audrey belonged together.

At Aden, sleep became impossible in the oppressive heat, far worse than a Victorian summer. Maira wilted but Christie thrived going ashore with Duncan and her brothers, soon all lost to sight among hordes of raucous Africans. Each time, her daughter returned flushed both from the heat and excitement.

'Mother, there is so much to see. Can we stay longer?' she pleaded.

To which she always replied, 'Ask your father.' To Christie's frustration, the reply was always *No*.

The last leg of this stage took them up the lonely length of the Red Sea flanked by flat red desert sands and occasional small trading ports invariably dotted with palms. Although they had all suffered from sea sickness to some degree, those days had long passed but they were still grateful to disembark at Suez.

When Christie would have disappeared, anxious to explore, Isabelle reminded her, 'We must still travel overland. Stay together,' as she and Audrey herded their charges.

Christie grumbled but not for long when both mail and passengers from the ship were whipped off through the desert to Cairo in fast and rather exhilarating carriages with two mules and two horses in the traces. Taken at a full gallop, their hair and hats flung back, laughter and smiles abounded from everyone. The women tied their scarves tighter and hung on for the ride.

Exotic Cairo. Their carriages drew up before the splendid

Shepheard's Hotel having navigated the crowded streets, their occupants overwhelmed by the uproar of hucksters and bazaars as they passed.

'We're staying here?' Maira gaped, content with the simpler things in life.

'Apparently so.'

'Mother, isn't it wonderful?' Even Christie was impressed, a girl who happily slept beneath the stars.

The wide ornately trimmed front portico before the entrance was attended by a bevy of white clothed porters and footmen. The grand and opulent hotel, apparently the centre of British social life, lent them respite from the restricted ship's cabin they had endured for weeks.

'We'll stay a few days for a rest before moving on,' Duncan said.

While Isabelle welcomed the break, she was also aware that every passing mile and every unusual conveyance brought her nearer to Italy.

If Isabelle thought Egypt meant a lull she soon learned otherwise. It was now April and the weather was as pleasant as spring back home enabling them to venture out on many expeditions.

A cruise on the Nile in a small local boat; an excursion by donkey to the pyramids with a hamper of food and drink. Isabelle's reward for returning weary each evening were the rapt faces of her children. Sons and daughters alike all began to fully embrace their adventures.

Duncan was not always with them. He disappeared early one day, returning to announce that he had haggled for carpets and rugs all being sent home. Isabelle silently wondered where they would put them for Kooringal was more than amply furnished already.

As a family, they admired the pageantry of the palace guards and visited mosques. But within a week, with dust in the air blown in off the desert from the west, they headed for Alexandria where Duncan had booked berths on an Italian steamer to cross the Mediterranean.

Isabelle could scarcely believe that she would soon see Katarina but knew her main preoccupation lay with her father. She wondered if her hidden hopes were mistaken but clung to the smallest thread of optimism. After such a long time apart, perhaps his hesitant interest had waned.

'You don't seem your usual self,' Audrey commented with quiet perception as they strolled the deck before reaching the Bay of Naples.

'Don't I? In what way?' Isabelle pretended ignorance but doubted she would fool her friend for long. They had shared the same house for years and knew each other too well.

'You seem anxious and thoughtful since Egypt.'

Isabelle smiled weakly, shrugged her shoulders and chose not to confide her apprehension lest she be humiliated. 'Perhaps I am. There's much to contemplate,' was all she said but did mention her discovery of the telegraph in Cairo that had only added to her torment.

Isabelle recalled her simmering anger at the time when it had been mistakenly delivered to her room. The envelope had been unsealed and simply addressed to Penross. She had opened it to discover the sender was a Mrs. Portia Herrington of Melbourne. Isabelle had frozen, knew it was not for her and tried to forget the words she could not stop herself from reading.

My dearest Duncan, I cherish your telegraphs and feel I am there with you, perhaps even wish a little that I had come with you when you asked...

He had invited his mistress on the trip to flaunt her and humiliate them all? It had given Isabelle the deepest satisfaction to set a match to the message and watch it burn. Why had she been so upset? She knew him. Had he not warned her once to accept him for who he was? Duncan's audacity cut deep and only confirmed the destruction of even the smallest portion of feelings she still felt. Her love for her husband was finally over and her heart and thoughts drawn toward another. Was it foolish to still long for love at her age?

'Can you ever leave him?' Audrey asked, drawing her back to the present, perceptively guessing the direction of her thoughts.

Isabelle shook her head. 'No. But I long for a happiness of my own. The children are growing. Nichola is already married and I am a grandmother. I fear growing old alone,' she confessed.

'You will never be alone. You will always have family around you. You are much loved and they will come back to you.'

'Perhaps.' She turned to Audrey. 'Do you love Walter?'

The teacher hesitated but eventually, glowing, conceded to a brief nod.

Isabelle clutched her arm firmly. 'Then I hope Duncan's private man in London has success. If you were free, would you marry him?'

Again Audrey nodded. 'He has already asked,' she admitted. 'Many times. Even though he knows I would not hold him to our friendship if he found another.'

'He has remained loyal all these years. His love for you is deep and genuine.' She sighed and leaned on the rail. 'To be loved is what we all seek, is it not? Whether we confess it or not. It is our heart's secret dream.'

They fell silent and thoughtful as the steamer ploughed through the sea, the mild night pressing in around them.

Sicily and Capri proved to be all blue waters, sunny skies and enchanting scenery. The islands alive with the vitality of their people and bright colours, although Isabelle willingly sacrificed a visit to Palermo monastery when she heard of its gruesome mummies. Christie and the menfolk returned ecstatic with horror.

Finally, on the Italian mainland after yet another boat trip, they reached their hotel. By day they chartered a vetturino, riding through the countryside in the luxury of the comfortable horse drawn carriage, passing mile after mile of vineyards on the road to Capua inland from Naples. Isabelle soon developed a taste for the wine. The local vino slid easily over her tongue, helping settle her nerves at the approaching visit to the Perini household. She had sent a telegraph ahead and received a delighted response from Katarina. But what of Luca? For it was his approval she craved.

Duncan grumbled they could not stay long declaring the detour an unnecessary delay to their journey overland across Europe and arrival in England. He made no secret that he was bored and restless.

In fury one day, Isabelle almost snapped, *Then you should have brought your mistress to entertain you.*

As the family pushed north, they explored ruins, ate in hillside cafes and, alone early one morning, Isabelle joined in the singing of a village church mass. In Tuscany, Duncan's interest briefly regenerated when they saw flocks of sheep. He held them up for ages while he stopped and talked to the shepherds.

They made Sienna and Florence by train and coach. Glad of freedom again after continuous travel, they walked the Ponte Vecchio and other beautiful bridges across the reflective Arno. The women strolled the Boboli gardens while Duncan and the boys ventured elsewhere.

Because the girls agreed, Isabelle told Duncan, she would travel on to visit the Perinis alone. While the children remembered Katarina fondly, they did not know her father. Fully embracing travel, she had no wish to deprive them of any sights.

Katarina was over thirty now and still unattached. Remaining a spinster to be her papa's companion? Isabelle could not believe Luca would expect his daughter to be so noble. But they had always been close. Katarina would not regard the sacrifice as a burden. Perhaps she was destined to remain single.

So from Florence, she journeyed on alone, pushing deep into the Alps of Trentino province by train while the others remained behind until they met up again in two days. The trip allowed her time for contemplation.

As she steamed into Trento nestled in its beautifully verdant glacial valley, she tried not to dwell on her first reaction at seeing Luca again. Katarina would be easy. Her father was an unknown. She anguished that she might have confused his warm glances. He had a way of holding and absorbing her gaze that left her breathless. And all without saying a word.

Deeply charismatic, an unexpected flare of attraction at this stage of her life had burst into life within her. This visit would be the test. She must let him know her marriage was in name only. So much depended on his response.

Isabelle glimpsed them first through the window. Katarina expectant and smiling, searching for her face in the train. Luca composed and handsome beside her. Sitting on the edge of her seat, she caught her breath and stared at him.

Clutching her valise, she stepped down from the train and caught Katarina's eye.

'Isabelle,' she exclaimed in her lovely accent, waving and rushing forward.

Clasped in a fierce warm hug, Isabelle glanced over her shoulder at Luca, standing back, watching and waiting, and her heart stopped. His eyes revealed all she needed to know. It would be all right. The long separation and interminable wait had not dimmed the magic between them. They stared at each other, Isabelle too relieved to cry.

Katarina finally released her and then Luca's hand clasped her and he was taking her bag. 'Welcome to Italy, Isabelle,' he smiled warmly, planting a kiss on each cheek as was the custom here, his face brushing hers, his breath a warm whisper against her skin. She resisted the temptation to cling to him longer. 'You will stay with us, of course.'

Katarina beamed, linking arms. 'That is understood.'

Against the brisk mountain air, a fire crackled and spread its warmth when Katarina, still chattering, ushered her into their large stone cottage on a hillside on the edge of town. Luca quietly disappeared to take her valise upstairs.

Katarina grasped both her hands again. 'Oh, I cannot believe you are here with us. How long can you stay?'

Isabelle shrugged. 'Only one or two days, I'm afraid.' Katarina's face fell. 'The family is waiting,' she quickly explained. 'There is so much to see in your beautiful country but we must move on.'

Katarina grew serious and drew her onto the sofa before the fire. 'We were so sorry to hear about Beatrice. She was a golden child. It must have been very difficult for you to write and tell us.'

Isabelle nodded, not wishing to dwell on the pain that had eased with the distractions of travel but still settled in her heart like stone. Luca returned to join them and she allowed herself a precious moment to admire him. Perhaps a little more salt at the temples of his dark hair but still the gracious attentive gentleman. These humble cosy surroundings suited him. Katarina, on the other hand, was a flower in full bloom.

'You both look well,' she covered her confusion with chatter and could not resist adding, 'There must be young men who are happy for your presence back in Trento.'

Katarina laughed and smiled shyly at her father.

Luca sagely nodded. 'She has many friends and cousins here.'

Isabelle casually voiced the question on her mind. 'And do you ever plan to visit Australia again?' She held her breath.

Luca answered for them. 'It is possible. We still have our house in Geelong and I can see the attractions of Victoria.' His warm gaze lingered over her.

'So, you might return? One day, perhaps.'

'I think it is a definite prospect.'

She smiled at his subtle meaning. 'I am delighted to hear it. I have missed you both. Let me know should you return and I shall visit.'

'Your family are all well?' Luca asked politely.

Isabelle skimmed over the details. 'The children have had their eyes opened to the wonders of the world beyond Kooringal boundary fences, Melbourne and Geelong. I fear Christie may become a nomad. She is utterly enthralled by everything we have seen.'

And so followed two days, far too short, of independent happiness for Isabelle. Luca's discreet and gentle hand at her waist. Guiding, supporting. All three wandered together for hours about the Trento streets of medieval buildings, the castello, to the romantic Gothic cathedral on one side of the piazza in the heart of town with its fountain of Neptune. All superior to anything Isabelle had seen, and so old.

She felt so light and free. And the food. It began with Katarina cooking her hearty breakfast of speck and eggs on a bed of potatoes. Then there was soups, wild game, sausage and bread dumplings, all accompanied by glasses of crisp white wine grown on the hillside vines trained into overhead frames and forming a fresh green leafy canopy now in late spring. And always finished with the small cups of strong coffee, delicate almond biscuits and pastries baked by Katarina's loving hands.

On Isabelle's second and last evening, although the air was cool they sat out on the small patio sampling another of Katarina's simple wholesome meals accompanied with humour and wine. She had never known such ease.

'So you continue on to London now?' Luca asked softly.

'Yes, Duncan has taken a house for some weeks and we will meet Blair in Oxford. I am also planning a visit to my family in Lancashire.'

'You will see many changes, no? After these many years.'

Isabelle sighed. 'I imagine so and we expect to be back home in Victoria by Christmas.' Isabelle smiled bravely to hide her inner sadness, perceptible in them all at her leaving tomorrow.

'By coincidence,' Luca suddenly announced. 'Katarina urges me to return about the same time.'

Isabelle gaped and caught his daughter's strange questioning glance of surprise.

'And when did we have this conversation, papa?' she teased.

'I am certain we would have discussed it soon.'

The women exchanged happy knowing smiles and no more was said on the subject. But Isabelle hugged the promise in her heart for Katarina, too, looked delighted about the unexpected news.

Their farewells next morning were difficult and poignant.

'How I wish you could stay longer,' Katarina said, squeezing Isabelle's gloved hands.

As the engine steamed and hissed, Luca pulled her close and once again pressed kisses to both her cheeks. 'Ciao, cara mia,' he whispered, far more personal than his greeting of two days before.

But then Italians were effusive in their affections, she had learned, so perhaps she was imagining too much. She longed to reach out and touch his olive skinned face, tell him in words that she felt the same but, for now, she smiled and let him hold her hands a few moments longer.

She was a married woman and not free. What could become of a friendship between them?

After Italy, as the family travelled overland across Europe in various legs by train through Switzerland and into France, Isabelle knew a strange but satisfying serenity. She forgot Duncan but absently smiled and responded to Audrey and the children, aware of them yet detached. For the young ones, it was one long magical holiday experience. Despite her clouded past and uncertain future, Audrey thrived, rising above it all and assuming responsibility when Isabelle lapsed.

When she grew reflective, she might discover intuitive Maira's hand slipped quietly into hers for comfort. Isabelle always acknowledged it with a warm smile and an answering squeeze.

For her this journey was proving cathartic. Slowly, one by one, the links in the chains of her deepest grief began to fall away and she started to believe in a new hope and light ahead in her life. That Luca was responsible for the glow she hardly dared acknowledge. How did a married woman conduct her life, aching for another man?

Once they were settled into the Hotel Dieu de Paris on the Seine, crossed by so many arched bridges, how Isabelle wished Luca and Katarina were here with them to experience the glory of the city, too. Fluent in the language, Katarina could have smoothed their path of communication but Audrey had a rudimentary grasp for basic directions and conversation.

Even in its winding cobbled back streets, Isabelle began to see beauty again. But Napoleon III was modernising his city with new boulevards like the Champs-Elysees running through its heart, creating vast perspectives. Arm in arm with the children, they promenaded in Tuileries Park crowded with people, admired the ornate and magnificent cathedral on the river isle.

And the dresses. Everywhere she looked, Isabelle admired the ladies in their elegant fashion, feeling dowdy. On an inspiration one morning, she suggested to Audrey and the girls, although Christie was typically resistant, that they must all go shopping and be measured for new clothes. In conversation with fellow guests at the hotel, Isabelle learned of the fashion house of Mr. Worth.

'He is not French at all. He was born in Lincolnshire,' Isabelle laughed, 'and his house is patronised by the Empress herself.'

Audrey was stunned when Isabelle insisted she arrange gowns for her, too. 'Who knows?' Isabelle gently tapped her hand, her mischievous smile rare in recent years, 'you may need a special dress one day. And sooner than you think.'

'Only if Duncan's investigation is successful,' Audrey

sighed, blushing.

Isabelle understood the longing in her eyes. She must press Duncan for results when they reached London.

As live models graciously paraded before them in a variety of prepared designs and staff fluttered about them, Audrey and Maira gaped. Christie was almost impressed and Isabelle contemplated her humble roots in Blackburn, marvelling that they could afford such clothes. The new colours of mauve and pink and purple complimented the day dresses with their wide sleeves and high necklines ruffled with lace.

'Skirts seem flatter at the front now.' Isabelle leaned closer and whispered discreetly to Audrey.

She merely nodded, speechless, stunned with awe at the opulent surroundings of the salon.

'I shan't wear a corset or I will die,' Christie announced, yawning. All the same, her gaze settled at length on a white silk gown with a frothy overlay of sheer fabric and draped for extra effect with a floating net shawl.

Isabelle caught her daughter's gaze and raised her eyebrows in query.

'Perhaps,' she admitted, trying to hide her interest.

Knowing her daughter's great love of horses, Isabelle also suggested a smart riding outfit with a short jacket. Her interest sharpened and she agreed. Audrey chose a modest day dress and a beaming Maira contentedly accepted her mother's choice.

Then Isabelle made her own selections plus the indulgence of a bronze evening gown rich with layers of black lace. Heaven knew when she would wear it but they planned outings to the theatre here in Paris and London. Then came an evening gown for each with their lower necklines, short sleeves and lace gloves or crocheted fingerless mitts. For Maira though, a more formal young lady's dress. Isabelle had never before so recklessly shopped.

Next came shawls and capes, bonnets with smaller brims

now that revealed more of the face, in straw and prettily finished for the coming summer; velvet for winter. And elegant stylish hats worn tilted to one side or dipped forward over the forehead, perhaps finished with a quivering plume.

And then they were whisked away to be meticulously measured since apparently Mr. Worth paid much attention to fit. Their selections would be tailor made in his workshop and delivered to their hotel or forwarded on to London.

Afterwards, chattering and exhausted, the women drank strong French coffee and nibbled on pastries.

Too soon, Paris was behind them, even Christie reluctant to leave since she had been allowed to go riding with her father and brothers in the parks. She was only consoled when promised more of the same in London.

They travelled the 140 miles to Le Havre in five hours from Paris through the Normandy countryside by express train. Because the ferry to Southampton only left three days a weeks, they lodged overnight in the grand white painted wooden Hotel Frascati directly on the waterfront.

After the long day's travel, Isabelle soaked in the luxury of a bath in her own room, contemplating Blair in England. He had only left last year but she worried at what they would find. His departure had been apathetic and careless and she disliked the way he was changing. She knew if he applied himself, he could achieve but, in recent years at Scotch, further removed from his father's eagle eyes, his dedication to his studies had slumped.

Almost a man now but, in her opinion, drinking far too much. Already rich, his own ambition seemed hard to find. She must try and encourage him to decide on a course in life if managing the stations was not feasible. Which seemed likely.

The ferry crossing over the English Channel next day proved frightening. The steamer bow rose and fell as it plunged through the rough water. Maira and Audrey grew quite ill but Christie thrilled with the excitement of it and the menfolk also seemed to endure.

To distract a pallid Audrey, Isabelle asked about her family.

'Mother and father have both died. My sister wrote many years ago.'

'Will you visit her?'

Audrey shrugged and pressed a handkerchief over her mouth as the boat rolled again. 'I'm not sure I would be welcome. She hasn't responded to my mail for over a year. But I would like to pay my respects at my parents' graves.'

'Of course. Would you like Christie or I to come with you? I wouldn't see you travel alone.'

Audrey gave a gentle smile. 'I sailed halfway around the world Isabelle, as did you. I expect I shall be fine. Perhaps while you are journeying to Blackburn I shall consider it.' Her gaze turned reflective. 'I do sometimes wonder what my village looks like now after all these years. Shall we be disappointed or regretful do you think?'

'We shall soon find out. I see land ahead.'

'I'm afraid to look,' Audrey admitted, clutching the bench seat tighter, looking grey and miserable but trying with a touch of humour to be brave.

As they steamed past the Isle of Wight and into beautiful Southampton harbour, stability returned. Safely anchored to the quay, everyone shuffled from the vessel, eager to leave. Duncan hired a cart for their baggage but the family, grateful for their land legs again, walked to nearby Radley's Hotel for an overnight stay before continuing the final leg of eighty miles by train to London in the morning.

Being the mail packet town, Southampton and the Royal Victoria pier were brisk with carriages and pedestrians although a sharp wind blew in from the sea.

'I'd forgotten the grey and damp of England,' Isabelle sighed with resignation as they shook the misty rain from their cloaks and entered the hotel.

'Are you glad to be back home?' Maira asked, studying her mother carefully.

'Victoria is my home now,' she answered readily without a second thought.

'It's freezing,' Christie grumbled. 'Egypt and Italy were much warmer.'

Isabelle suspected both countries had fond memories for all of them but in different ways.

CHAPTER 10

The following day, they all bundled themselves and their luggage onto the train for London. As the green and thickly wooded countryside sped by, Isabelle briefly spared Duncan a glance seated at the opposite end of their compartment. She had been his dutiful pawn. Since the death of her darling little Beatrice, she had glimpsed the fragility of life and decided her own life and happiness now were paramount.

Soon they passed through Windsor and Richmond then over viaducts at Lambeth and caught glimpses of the palace residence of the archbishop before the Houses of Parliament came into view across the river.

At the Waterloo Road terminus, the family took an omnibus to their rented house; as in Southampton, swallowed up by the large grey world of the city. Their furnished terrace was comfortable and quiet with bay windows, a tiled entrance and polished timber floors with thick rugs. With Audrey supervising, the children immediately explored, taking over the three story house as if it were their own.

There was a small staff of servants so Isabelle ordered tea to be served in the front sitting room. With her back turned to Duncan, she removed her gloves and hat and spread out her hands toward the leaping flames in the fireplace for the early autumn was bitter. They usually avoided being alone together. She heard him strike a safety match to light his pipe.

'I shall send off a telegraph to Blair,' he muttered. 'Let him know we've arrived and arrange to meet.'

'As you wish.'

And then he was gone. She craved a life without him but

was she brave enough to conduct one? Her worried confusion was interrupted when her bubbly daughters burst into the room and joined her, filling it with their chatter. Although grateful for their company, sometimes, even amid her noisy family, Isabelle felt quite alone. Over tea and cakes, they made plans for exploring London and riding arrangements for Christie.

At dinner, Duncan announced he had already made travel bookings for two days hence to visit Oxford. Isabelle had hoped to rest in London but they packed bags again for an absence of up to a week and all gathered again on Paddington station platform with its many lines of rail and immense covered arched roof. They boarded and the train threaded from the station past green embankments, hedges and avenues of trees, picking up speed through the Thames and Avon valleys.

'It's all so green,' Maira marvelled.

'But so much smaller than home,' Christie said.

On arrival in Oxford, a hired carriage took them to the grand first class Randolph Hotel. They were swiftly transported by an American elevator up to their handsome suite of rooms with charming prospects from every window.

'Electric lights, mother.' Maira always seemed fascinated and appreciative of such small details.

There was scant time for enjoyment. Blair was summoned and Isabelle waited nervously. What changes did she expect?

At first sight of him, her heart dropped. In the prime of life with every advantage, he should have glowed with robust youthful health. Instead, they were confronted with a pale version of the son he should be, nervously smoking a cigarette. Isabelle has noticed their popularity in France. His suntanned complexion had disappeared. Isabelle tried not to feel too critical. Perhaps it was the English climate. She disliked that Duncan offered him a drink.

The reunion did not go well. Blair sat edgy and distracted while Duncan silently studied his oldest son. At first, conversation proved awkward, his siblings awed and overcome by the change in their worldly brother. But slowly the initial tension among them eased and Christie and Alexander in particular regaled him with tales of their travels.

When they finally drew breath, perceptive Maira asked quietly, 'Are you liking England, Blair?'

He drew on his cigarette and squinted at her. 'It's not all bad. Not much sunlight, of course, and life at weekends is dull.'

'Do ye not have study, boy?' his father bluntly interrupted.

Blair's narrowed gaze settled on his father for a moment before he continued as if he had not spoken. 'They don't care that I'm a wealthy squatter's son over here. Means nothing to them.' His lips curled with disdain, clearly affronted by the indifference. 'Sometimes I'm invited to the farm of friends. Tedious, but I accept to be polite. Their acreage is so small compared to home. All very small and bucolic.'

He gave an unkind laugh, finished his drink and extended the glass for more.

His father ignored the silent request. 'Perhaps ye should not be so concerned about your social life but concentrate on your studies.'

'Duncan!' Isabelle reprimanded. 'This is a social visit, not a lecture.'

He frowned at her mettle. 'Few have the opportunity for university. The boy should not be wasting it.'

'Blair is no longer a boy, Duncan,' Isabelle snapped, tired of her husband's constant criticism of his son. 'He is a young man of the world now.'

But not a countryman at heart. Isabelle feared he liked city living too much and she judged his privileged education squandered.

All eyes glanced in her direction that she dared challenge her husband. The visit deteriorated. Blair seemed totally disinterested in everyone and impatient to leave. After more strained conversation, within an hour, his duty done, he was gone, refusing their invitation to remain with them for dinner.

Isabelle paced in her room, furious with Duncan for tearing their son to shreds and fretting where she had gone wrong. She should have supported Blair more against his father. She did not dine with him that night and, instead, asked that a simple meal be brought upstairs, pining for what she could not change.

Duncan and Isabelle continued on separately to the places of their birth, having agreed to meet back in London in a few days. Alexander and Owen elected to travel with their father, the girls with their mother. They had barely been able to appreciate the architectural beauty of Oxford with its spires and domes, and long curved High Street.

The onward first class rail journey to Manchester was exciting as always for the girls but Isabelle was hardly aware of the countryside as they passed. Leamington and Warwick were a blur and she only stirred herself as they steamed into the New Bailey Street station.

They secured rooms at the Queen's Hotel overnight before pressing on by local train up to Blackburn through cotton towns and Ramsbottom where the line followed the course of the river over several bridges. Finally, they reached the town where she was born.

Stepping from the station and walking briskly straight along the blustery windswept High Street toting their bags, Maira said sadly, 'It's very grey, mother.'

'It is indeed. I'd quite forgotten.'

It was also not as comfortable and sweet as she remembered. She'd idealised it in her mind all these years. She flashed her daughters a smile of encouragement, struck by the difference from back home beyond the fences where you could cast your eye far and wide and nothing interrupted your view. Here, her remembered world had shrunk. Tiny and compact after the wide acreage of colonial paddocks.

The streets were poorly paved as they trudged in the bleak air to the Bull Hotel for the night, thankfully at least lit with gas. Isabelle was glad not to endure the icy cold of snow-laden winters any more.

She had forgotten how the town chimneys belched smoke from the mills and hearths of hundreds of terraced houses with their small poky rooms. Compared to their affluence back home, much of the population here lived below the poverty line. Lying in a valley, Blackburn never escaped the pollution of a constant smoke haze.

Later, after warming up with hot drinks and a light meal at the hotel, clutching her daughters' hands, thickly gloved against the cold, Isabelle led them to her old home address. Her parents were long gone, of course, even before she left but she hoped some of the family still lived in the same narrow house. They had done when she last wrote but never received a reply.

How would they be received, unannounced, although she had written to inform them of her visit? She had come all this way on a kind of obligatory pilgrimage. Standing at the front door on the street, all three women exchanged glances.

'I'm sure they'll have a nice warm fire going inside.' It was difficult to be cheerful. 'And you'll meet your aunts and uncles and cousins.'

Isabelle removed her glove and knocked. It took time but eventually the door opened.

'Maria?' She barely recognised her sister.

'Isabelle, my God.' She laid a hand on her chest in shock.

Her sister looked older than her years with lank grey hair, a lean frame and tired face. Hands wrinkled and raw from work. Isabelle quickly explained their travels from Victoria and their temporary lodgings in London, expressing concern that perhaps they had not received her letter.

Maria's expression grew blank and she said bluntly, 'Hope you're not plannin' on stayin' here. We've no spare beds.'

'No. We're staying at the Bull.'

Maria regarded her visitors unfavourably head to toe. 'Expect it's not what you're used to.'

'It's quite comfortable.'

She turned proudly to her gaping daughters and introduced them. Blessing her insistence on manners, they each gave a quick curtsy and shook her hand.

Still standing in the cold on the front doorstep, Isabelle asked, 'Would we be intruding if we came in for a chat? We've already eaten,' she hastily added noticing her sister's alarm.

Maria clutched up a handful of apron. 'Of course. I'll put the kettle on for tea.'

They followed her inside, their smart full skirts dragging against the sides of the narrow hall. In the kitchen, Maria introduced her grown children, two daughters and grandchildren, thin and wide eyed clinging to their mother's skirt.

'All my family are married now,' she said wearily.

Poor and struggling like their parents, Isabelle noted. Clean but ragged. She was appalled to find this struggling despair and think she had once lived in similar sordid conditions not realising it. A tug of pity swept across her heart. This would have been her had she stayed, overworked and coping with need.

'Millie, off round to your Auntie Lena and tell her Izzy's here. Then go get your uncles from the pub.'

While they waited and the kettle sang, Isabelle said, 'We shall still be in London for some weeks. Could any of you possibly come down for a visit?'

Lena laughed. 'Can't afford a third class train ticket, Izzy.'

Isabelle dared not offer to pay lest they be offended that she was flaunting her wealth. 'I'm afraid we're returning down south tomorrow. We can't stay any longer.'

She managed a regretful smile, knowing she had no reason nor did she wish to remain. She had nothing in common with these people any more, her own family, and winced that she no longer felt any connection. Too many years had passed. Distance and time had severed any attachment. They gave the impression that she was above them and therefore not worth their time. Certainly they lived a comfortable life but they were still her family. Isabelle stung from their dismissive attitude. Still, she had done her duty and taken the trouble to visit. They should not fault her on that.

'You're all well?' she asked cheerfully.

'Lancashire's been devastated by the American Civil War and blockade of raw cotton for mills. There's been riots and depression. The industry's ruined but the mills won't recover. The menfolk get work where they can. Nick and Christian are working at the brewery. The girls and I take in washing and do some cleaning for upper folks.'

Then her other sister, Helena arrived, bursting in the front door sending a cold draught all through the tiny house. She strode down the short narrow passageway to the kitchen at the back where they were all huddled, mostly standing because there weren't enough chairs to sit, around the meagre heat coming from the low fire.

'Izzy! We all thought you was mad goin' all that way. Be drowned at sea or murdered in your bed by all them convicts. Look at you now, eh, so grand in your sponny clothes?'

'My husband,' she cringed to use the word, 'has done well.'

Isabelle made light of the obvious differences in their social status but at least she received a hug. Lena always was honest and offended some but at least you knew where you stood. Her older brothers eventually appeared. Good solid working men, aged before their time, care worn and weary by the looks of it and ruddy from a good fill of beer. But warm hearted.

'Izzy, what a grand lady you've become.' Nicholas couldn't take his eyes from all three of his guests. He was her favourite sibling. A caring man, the kind she'd wished she'd married if she'd stayed.

'Annie and the children?'

'All fine. She's away to her folks in Bolton so I'm on me own for a while.'

Christian never said much but Isabelle nudged him into conversation. 'Ellen and your family are well, too?'

He nodded, grinning. 'We'd four children. Two oldest girls are married and young ones of their own. Ellen works in a shop. Be there till late. You could call in, but she'd maybe not recognise you.'

Isabelle noted the name of the shop he gave her but had no intention to follow it up. Ellen was sharp and spiteful and she'd never liked her. It would give her great pleasure knowing Christian would mention their visit but that they did not bother to make an effort to meet and renew their acquaintance.

It was a relief, finally, to escape the crush of kinfolk and emerge back out onto the street. Isabelle even welcomed the nip in the chill afternoon air.

'I need to pay my respects to my parents,' Isabelle announced apologetically.

So Christie and Maira accompanied her, pushing against the stiffening breeze beneath a dull grey sky, to the cemetery. Through the imposing entrance gates, wandering the graves until they found the simple headstones for Thomas and Martha Waring.

Standing solemnly together, Isabelle said, 'These were your grandparents, girls.'

'You've never mentioned them, mother,' Christie said.

'They both died before I left for Victoria over twenty years ago. It was known as Port Phillip back then,' she sighed with reflection. 'Mother died of a wasting illness when she was quite young. Me being the youngest and single, I stayed at home to look after father. The others as you saw today are all married.' She reached for their hands and gripped them tight, a lump catching in her throat. 'I'm so glad I left England for a better life. My brothers and sisters don't know any different but it's a hard life for them. We are so blessed, girls, and never forget it.'

'No, mother,' they chorused in union, sensing her gravity.

Isabelle turned her face into the wind and whispered, 'Goodbye Mother, goodbye Father,' knowing she would never return.

Meanwhile, in Scotland, Duncan Penross and his sons had taken the North British line to Hawick and now rode together on fine hired horses across the arched stone bridge over the Slitrig River and out of town where they had lodged overnight in the Tower Hotel. Before striking out, he'd sent Portia a message from the telegraph station, needing the contact. He'd be looking for one from her when he returned to London.

Beside the bitter weather with strong sharp winds whistling up the valley, having long forgotten how raw it could blow, he was struck by the small holdings. His stud merino sheep with their dense rippling fleeces were far superior to anything he could see grazing in the hills. Heading east for his old family farm, he saw the humble valley houses and bleak living conditions with fresh keen eyes and felt satisfaction in his wealth and achievements.

Greeted warmly by his sister in law, Maggie, his older brother Alistair's wife, and invited indoors, Duncan and the boys now sat around the table, Duncan puffing his pipe with his long legs and shining booted feet stretched out beneath.

While their hostess piled oat cakes and apple scones onto plates and the kettle whistled gently on the fire, Alexander sprang to his feet. 'Can I help you, Aunt Maggie?

She eyed him in amazement and laughed. 'Ye must tek after your mam for Duncan was ne'er one for helping in the house. Ye could set out the cups from the dresser.' She smiled kindly at her nephew then addressed her brother in law. 'So, your Isabelle's in Blackburn visiting her family?'

'Aye.'

'Ye could ha' sent a letter when your own parents died, Duncan,' Maggie chided. 'We wrote ye but ye never replied.'

'Can't be doin' nothing about it now,' he snapped. George and Frances Penross were most likely buried in the plot out back, the stony field at the bottom of the north hill where other generations had been buried, too. 'That brother of mine be much longer?'

'I've sent Mary's boys out for him over on the common. They've cattle and sheep out there. They'll get back when they can. Ye can sleep in the barn if you'd like to stay overnight and most welcome.'

'That's right kind of ye.' His sons raised interested eyebrows, apparently willing. 'I'll think on it.'

For Alex at least, it would be another adventure to be relished. Callum and Owen, amenable, would agree if their father decided. Duncan privately puffed up with importance, knowing he had done far better by leaving than he ever would have staying here.

He was thankful after all for being the second son and restless. Scotland and this green misty country of his birth was only a nostalgic memory now. Victoria was his home. How far he had come and how different his life compared to his brother. Yet they seemed content enough.

'Where's Aislin?' He asked after his favourite sister, afflicted with the same wandering spirit as himself.

'Off tramping the hill pastures as always. Lives up there for days or weeks. Makes the most of it while the weather lasts.'

'And the other girls?'

'Lara's married and went off to Glasgow wi' her man, Mac Cameron. She's three children all attending school. Fiona, Rosie and little Mac. Mary and her Kenney Brown's livin' here o'course wi' us. Their Donnell and Evan are out lookin' for their grandad. As well they've the new bairn here. Maggie-May.' Her grannie smiled down fondly at a curly sandy haired babe in a crib the other side of the kitchen. 'Mary'll be finished soon in the dairy.'

Duncan didn't envy them all living cramped up together in the same draughty stone cottage that would survive for just as many more years to come. He didn't mention his own grand homestead back home for, around the kitchen table that night as they all dug into a meat and potato stew with dumplings, the family talked only of themselves and treated Duncan and his sons as though they were just neighbours joining them for the meal, not interested to ask after his life on the other side of the world.

They stayed and slept in the barn, warm enough, and joined the family again for breakfast of porridge, eggs, wheaten bread and cheese before they left.

Duncan held mixed contemplations as he waved and rode away with his sons, sad to be leaving for he'd likely never see this family again leading their cheerless life here ignorant that anything better existed for them. Probably not bold enough to make the leap. He could pay their fares and see them all set up and comfortable but he'd not even bothered to offer, canny enough to see they accepted their familiar ways. Knowing he could never have settled for the same.

When the family were reunited back in London a few days later, a telegraph from Elliott Morgan in Victoria and a letter addressed to Duncan awaited them on the hall tray. Isabelle quickly opened the message from home.

'We have another grandson,' she informed Duncan with polite restrained excitement, scanning the few lines. 'Darcy. What a lovely name. We must send them a telegraph of congratulations and let them know when we expect to return.'

She glanced at him for confirmation but he was scowling over his letter and his face was thunderous.

'Aye,' he muttered, distracted. 'Is Audrey back yet?'

Isabelle tensed. 'I don't know. I'll ask the staff.' She paused. 'Is it news from the investigator?'

'Aye,' he grunted. 'When she returns, I'd best see ye both in the sitting room.'

Whatever information he had received was either bad or unwelcome for Duncan was rarely this incensed. She hoped Audrey was not going to be too upset over the reason.

She picked up her skirt and hurried upstairs, issuing orders to the maids to be informed the moment Miss Bailey returned. After which she paced anxiously before taking herself in hand and settling down to write a letter of thanks to Katarina for their hospitality in Italy, knowing she would share the contents with Luca. As she wrote, she felt as though she was talking to them, gathered around the fire, sharing her news of their grandson and travels in France. The honest disappointment of her Blackburn visit.

When she heard Audrey and the girls chattering, Isabelle flew downstairs. After a brief welcome and small talk of her Norfolk visit, she drew her aside.

'Audrey, Duncan wants to see us both in the sitting room. Word from his investigator.'

He sat drinking whisky and reading the London Times before a warming fire even though it was summer. When they entered, he rose and poured each of the women a glass of port. To help steady their nerves for the bad news to come, Isabelle wondered, accepting it in surprise? The ladies exchanged worried glances.

Duncan cleared his throat and turned to face them, his back to the fire. 'This,' he scooped up the investigator's letter from a small side table, crumpling it roughly in his hands, his expression bitter, 'is about a man as cowardly as ye could get. Miss Bailey, for you, its all good news. For me, it's been a revelation and needs some serious thinkin'.'

Audrey sat up straighter and took notice, an air of hope about her. Isabelle looked at her husband with amazement. Always a man of firm convictions, she'd never heard him sound so bewildered.

'Your husband was an Edward William Linton is that right?'

Audrey nodded. 'As far as I knew, yes.'

'Is this him?' He handed her a sketch of a male face.

Audrey took the paper and gasped. 'Yes, indeed. Has someone seen him?' she asked in a small voice.

Isabelle saw her expectation fade, knowing if he had been sighted there may be little chance of a new life with Walter. 'Take another sip of port, Audrey,' she whispered.

'Ah knew him as William Lincoln.' Duncan's announcement stunned them both.

Isabelle frowned and raised her eyebrows in silent query. She'd never heard Duncan mention such a man. It must have been before she arrived.

He went on. 'Ah met him on the boat out from England and we chose our runs together. I squatted on Kooringal,' he hesitated, 'and William leased Lakeham.'

The women gaped in astonishment. Duncan had known Audrey's husband? Speechless, they waited for an explanation. Isabelle had assumed Lakeham had always been Duncan's holding for he already owned it when she was first employed as his housekeeper.

He ran a hand wearily through his hair and poured himself another whisky. After the first mouthful, he said, 'William … Edward,' he corrected, 'had plenty of cash to set himself up but he refused to cull his flocks and he was no manager or farmer, so Lakeham declined. In the depression of the early forties, he gave up and sank low.' He tossed a wary glance at Audrey. 'Do ye want the truth?'

She paused then nodded.

Duncan took another swig of whisky. 'He hanged himself.'

'Oh!' Audrey cried out and a hand instinctively raised to cover her mouth, but while it was tragic news, it also meant Audrey's freedom.

'He always was a weak man,' Duncan sneered. 'Must o' lost heart. I cut him down myself and his men helped bury him. Grave's still there over on Lakeham … with the wrong name on it of course. I took over his lease. In those early days, ye grabbed what ye could to get ahead.'

Audrey's eyes widened in disbelief at all this disclosure. Isabelle spread an arm around her shoulder for support.

'So you're a free woman, Miss Bailey. Or should I say, Mrs.

Linton. Your husband's been dead for over twenty years.'

Isabelle never knew whether it was from regret or relief but Audrey broke down into heartbreaking sobs. As she held her friend tight, all Isabelle could think was that at least now she knew. The shock would pass. But most importantly, she could accept Walter when they returned home. Isabelle wondered if that happy possibility had registered yet in the distraught woman's mind. At least her future looked settled.

Isabelle glanced across at Duncan, scowling and furious, clearly still reeling from the news himself, as they all were, and would feel as affronted and duped as Audrey by Edward Linton's deception and injustice.

Turning her attention back to her friend, Isabelle gently urged, 'Take the last of your port, Audrey.'

Her hands shook as she obeyed, dabbed her wet cheeks and looked up at Duncan. 'I can hardly believe all this but ... thank you, Mr. Penross. From the bottom of my heart.'

Duncan looked wretched and embarrassed. 'So, it was all your money he flashed about and used to set himself up?

Audrey nodded. 'Apparently so.'

Isabelle sympathised with her humiliation at being lowered from a lady of even modest means and forced into humble service through her husband's fraud.

'Ah feel bound to repair Linton's theft and your distress with compensation, Miss Bailey.' Duncan shuffled awkwardly.

Audrey frowned. 'I don't understand.'

'When we return home, ah'll write ye a cheque to pay for any house you choose for yourself, and arrange a small annuity.'

Audrey gasped. 'Oh that's not necessary, I'm sure. Mr. Penross.'

'Aye, it is. He cheated you, too.'

Disbelief swirled through Isabelle's mind, stunned by his generosity. She stared at him and allowed herself a small grain of respect for his decency.

Duncan frowned and scratched his head. 'What ah don't

understand is why ye never knew. Ah sent a letter with his personal effects back to a Mrs. A. Linton at an address in Norwich.'

'Was it St. Mary's Cottage, Church Lane?' Audrey put in quietly.

'Aye, that's it. Did ye never receive it?'

'What year was it?'

'Forty two or three.'

Audrey sighed. 'That was about the time I went to care for an elderly aunt for a year but, from when Edward left me until when I emigrated to Port Phillip, I lived with my mother and sister.' She frowned and murmured, 'I wonder ... did my mother or sister receive my mail and-' She faltered and placed a hand on her chest. 'Perhaps for some reason never handed it to me or ... destroyed it.' Then looked up at Duncan again, her expression cross. 'I wish I'd known all this before I went to visit my sister. I would have confronted her. She was always jealous. Why, I don't know. She was always mother's favourite.' Audrey sniffed.

'Oh, Audrey,' Isabelle sighed with compassion.

Audrey took a deep breath and gathered her poise. 'Mr. Penross, thank you again, Sir.' She slowly stood, bewildered, and said almost to herself, 'I must write to Walter,' drifting from the room.

By the year's end, the Penross family were returning to Victoria by the clipper route that took them three weeks and three thousand miles south across the equator, bringing them to Trinidade in the Atlantic Ocean. Following the winds and currents, their next landfall was another rocky volcanic island, Tristan da Cunha, from where they turned east around the cape at the bottom of Africa, in all, seven weeks since leaving London.

For most of the family, it seemed this two month long outward bound journey was only to be endured as their thoughts led them home across the lonesome icy stretches of the southern ocean. The adults for the changes each would encounter; for the children it signalled the end of their adventures.

'Travel suits you, Mother,' Nichola commented grudgingly to Isabelle after she had resettled at Kooringal and journeyed to Castle Hill to visit her daughter and new grandson, Darcy.

Isabelle, of course, knew the real reason why but merely smiled and did not elaborate. When her life was more settled and Nichola happier, she might choose to confide in her own newly discovered joy.

Mrs. Morgan senior had effusively welcomed her into their grand homestead overnight in her graceful superior manner. Although Isabelle would have stayed longer, instead she encouraged Nichola to come for a visit soon with her boys in an effort to get her away from the stifling atmosphere of so many females in the house.

To Isabelle's dismay, her daughter's response was dismissive.

'I will always love to see you and my grandsons,' she added warmly, continuing with news of home. 'Christie is resisting ladies' college but has agreed to attend. With very bad grace,' Isabelle smiled. 'She spends so much time out exploring and riding horses, I fear she will hardly learn anything. The year might help her become more of a lady.'

Nichola hardly responded, lethargic, draped over a sofa in the grand drawing room, too lifeless for one so young. Isabelle anguished for her daughter's obvious sorrow and her disinterest in two beautiful little boys, abandoned to the nursery with maids and scant attention from their mother.

'Alexander is home from Scotch College,' she added brightly, trying to keep her interest, 'and refuses to return or consider university.'

'Good for him. It doesn't do to become too compliant,' Nichola said with soft resentment.

Isabelle let her bitter comment pass, distraught at her

daughter's miserable attitude, feeling more wretched in her unhappy company with each moment that passed. At a loss to raise her spirits.

'So Callum is at Scotch College alone next year. At least he seems content in his schooling. Eager to learn. Maira and Owen will continue to be schooled at home by Miss Bailey, of course. For the time being.' Isabelle had already revealed Audrey's incredible story and her plans for a small wedding with Walter Kruger soon. 'Did I mention I made a brief visit to Katarina Perini and her father while in Italy?' she went on quickly, unable to bear the strain between them. 'I understand they are to return to Victoria.'

Again, Isabelle received only a vague response and feeble hug when she left the following day.

As if in telepathy, within days of returning to Kooringal again after her unrewarding visit to Castle Hill when she had expected to be joyfully received by Nichola, especially after their extended absence overseas, she received mail postmarked Geelong and in Katarina's familiar graceful handwriting. She tore open the envelope in her private room.

They were back and invited her to visit!

Too excited to concentrate properly while she and Audrey packed for a few days visit to Geelong, Isabelle also knew an aching distress. She knew she was close to loving Luca with little control over her passion. They were connected in the most elemental of ways, drawn together by some fine and mysterious thread.

Luca felt it, too. She saw it in the small moments of pleasure he communicated to her with those delightful sparks of life in his warm flashing eyes, the deep smooth notes in his voice as if he spoke only to her. She marvelled in gratitude that he openly conveyed his feelings. Katarina must surely have confided the true situation within Isabelle's marriage.

They were no longer young but she dared not lose even a small chance of happiness. Felt no guilt at pursuing any involvement but, bound in a pointless marriage, she dwelt too long on where it could possibly lead for, unlike Duncan, she could not be unfaithful. She had yet to discuss and resolve with Luca the extent and acceptance in such a chaste relationship.

Katarina met them at the railway station with a buggy to take them for their overnight stay at the Prince of Wales hotel centrally located in Market Square. Audrey to visit with Walter and discuss their future in Geelong, Audrey now able to bring a portion of wealth to their union with Duncan's promised largesse.

Thrilled at the prospect of seeing Luca again, Isabelle's heart beat faster with expectation. She felt as heady as if this was a first youthful love. She had waited too many long months since she saw him last in Italy. When Audrey departed to meet Walter in his music shop, Katarina continued on in the carriage with Isabelle.

'I am sorry Papa works in his store today but he will return for dinner tonight. I do hope you can join us?'

Isabelle's exuberance floundered and she sighed. She must wait even longer.

'Papa speaks of you often,' Katarina smiled broadly with mischief as they shared afternoon tea in the Perini cottage later. 'I believe he greatly enjoyed your company while you were in Trento with us.'

'I am flattered he remembers our time together in Italy fondly, too. I have such wonderful memories of those two precious days we all spent together.'

Katarina tactfully shared her reflections. 'I believe that my parents were content with one another. It was an arranged marriage, you know, between their families? Papa had great respect for Mama but with her poor health, he became her carer more than he could be a husband. So, for him, I believe it was an unsatisfactory marriage.'

'It must have been difficult for you all.'

Katarina nodded. 'Certainly, but Mama did not want more children. She grew unwell soon after I was born, and I felt I was to blame and a burden.'

'Oh you could never be that, Katarina. You must never think so.'

She slowly shook her head. 'It is true. I overheard Mama complaining when I was a child. That night I cried myself to sleep.' She shrugged, adding sadly, 'Mama and I were never close as I would have wished to be with my mother but Papa and I grew to share a special bond. Perhaps because much of the time there was only the two of us together. Mama was often confined to bed. We learned to cook together and he made me laugh.'

Katarina grew serious. 'Papa was bound to Mama and always a dutiful husband.' She paused and continued carefully 'But I don't believe he found true love with her. I intend only to marry for love,' she announced firmly. 'If I never find a grand passion, I will happily remain a spinster.'

Her glorious uninhibited laugh carried around the room, tinged with sadness, yet she was serious. Her declaration made Isabelle wonder if it was not a wise attitude. To wait for your heart's desire. Both her own and Nichola's marriages, although embarked upon with a certain spark between their spouses, lacked deep love and adoration. The optimism of youth soon fell to reality and life's hopes, over time, shattered.

While Katarina prepared dinner, Isabelle wandered their small comfortable cottage feeling as if she belonged. To think that Luca's marriage had not been completely rewarding either. Could such a coincidence be an omen?

And then he arrived. He appeared in the doorway and hesitated.

Isabelle's brief moment of exhilaration at the wonderful sight of him was splintered when Katarina exclaimed, 'Papa!' and brushed past to hug her father.

Of course his daughter would take precedence. She supposed their meal was delicious because her every heartbeat and glance was only for Luca and she remembered nothing of what she ate. They drank and laughed and talked until late.

Finally, Luca rose and extended a hand. 'Isabelle, I will deliver you back to your hotel. Miss Bailey will be anxious.'

Her elation soared. They would be alone together. 'I suspect she has had an equally wonderful evening with her Walter.' She suppressed her excitement.

Jolting along in the buggy, knees and shoulders brushing together, they drove through the cool night, comfortable and serene in their silence. Isabelle noticed Luca did not directly return to the hotel but took a more indirect route along the sea front and past the long railway pier that stretched out into the dark water silvered by faint threads of moonlight.

Taking the opportunity while they were alone, Isabelle said urgently, 'Luca, I must confide in you.'

'Of course.'

'Duncan and I,' she began hesitantly, 'have not had a successful marriage.'

Luca frowned and said reflectively, 'Ah, sometimes this is so.'

'We have been blessed with a large family but he loves another,' Isabelle confessed softly, needing him to know. 'He has a mistress and our marriage is lost.'

His dark eyes widened. 'Ah, cara mia, you know this?'

She nodded. 'For many years.'

Luca sighed. 'Isabelle, for you I am so sad.'

'But I am still a married woman. Do you understand?'

He transferred the reins into one hand and with the other reached out to her. 'Si, cara mia. To know your friendship is all I need.'

'I am sorry there cannot be ... more,' she whispered, close to tears.

'Ah, tesoro mio, to share even a small part of my life with such a beautiful lady as you is my honour.'

'Oh Luca,' she choked back a sob, having no idea what he had called her in Italian but it sounded lovely, 'I have so missed being loved all my life.'

Tears of relief trickled down her cheeks in the dark but

Isabelle did not care. She had needed some kind of assurance or promise and it was given. He reined the buggy to a stop, turned to face her and gently caught her hands between his own.

'Please tell me I will be your one and only dearest friend,' he murmured.

'Oh yes, please,' she enthused, hoping he might seal their pledge with a kiss but, ever the gentleman, he remained discreet. Perhaps in the future he might be encouraged. She must coax it for she craved his deepest affection. 'Might I call on you for counsel from time to time?'

He chuckled. 'But of course.'

For now, they had confided and reached an understanding. When they moved on again, her heart sang as he delivered her back to the hotel.

'Caroline Anderson's parents are happy for her to travel, so long as she has a companion. We could travel together. It's the perfect solution. Please tell me you both agree?'

Christie Penross stood before her parents having returned from her year in Melbourne at ladies' school restless and miserable. Her wavy hair coming unpinned after her usual energetic and long morning ride through the bush, her cheeks whipped to a healthy flush. She had accosted them separately and requested a discussion.

'Why can ye not stay home and settle down?' Duncan scowled.

'I do not wish to,' she stated in her usual forthright manner.

He eyed her. 'You wish to wait?'

'No. It is never my intention to marry.'

'And ye expect me to finance ye?'

'Caroline's parents have agreed to do the same if you approve.'

'Perhaps we should meet her?' Isabelle said.

Christie's face lit up with promise. "Shall I invite her to

stay?"

Duncan grunted. 'Ah've not given ma consent yet.'

'Yes dear. Do invite her.' Isabelle ignored his protests. 'But you are inclined to impatience, Christie. You don't always think before you act. Can you promise us that you will take every care?' Isabelle put in, alarmed at her daughter's impassioned request and the thought of allowing her to go off into the world alone.

'Of course, mother. We shall quite capably take care of ourselves.' She whirled from the room and was gone in a flurry of dusty crumpled skirts.

It was most unusual that a young woman did not wish to meet a young man and settle down, yet her strong impulsive daughter seemed determined to seek adventure in her life without a man, marriage or children. How could they stifle the light of excitement in her eyes? Perhaps she would change her mind in the years to come.

As much as she was afraid for Christie, Isabelle could see their attractive headstrong daughter, always so independent, was mature beyond her years. She prayed Duncan agreed yet felt a resistant maternal tug against the decision.

They had barely recovered from their daughter's begging and pleas, when studious Owen unexpectedly approached them in the sitting room while they still remained. Had he been waiting at the door?

'Instead of attending Scotch College, father, I have decided to continue on to Wesley College for my further education.' He stunned them with his confident statement.

Duncan eyed him with interest. 'Why?'

'According to their prospectus and annual report,' he calmly stated, clearly well informed, 'they aim to provide a classical and general education of the highest order to fit a young gentleman for mercantile life, the public service and matriculation in the university.'

Isabelle silently observed her youngest, often invisible, son with amusement. So assured at twelve. All these years, he had been quietly plotting his career. She beamed at him for encouragement, proud and impressed. He had been born for an office desk and home fires. She was confident he would do well and be content in life on his own merits.

He calmly bore his father's narrowed silent glare and continued, 'After Wesley, I will need to continue on to university to study law. Trinity College in Melbourne is well established with distinguished teachers and has had a law faculty for some years, now.'

'You want to become a lawyer?' Duncan thundered.

'Potentially a most useful profession, Father. I am not interested to manage landholdings but my legal knowledge will be an advantage to any man of property. Now or in the future,' he hinted, stating his case firmly and well, holding his father's scowling attention. 'The law will be a challenging practical career.'

'Indeed.'

By his wry tone of voice, Duncan sounded unconvinced but Isabelle watched him sit up and take notice of his quiet bookish son, contemplating him with something akin to respect.

'Yes, Sir. It is my preference.'

'Then I shall give it due consideration.'

'Thank you, Father.'

And then a satisfied Owen departed as efficiently as he had appeared, leaving his mother amused and his father astounded.

As the following two searing summers conceded to crisp falling leaves of autumn and the years sank into the chill soaking rains and mud of winter, everyone welcomed the reviving warmth and colour of spring. The bustle and movement of shearing as flocks were washed and brought up to the shed. Clouds of dust, barking dogs and lines of men tramping onto the station.

The first golden splashes of wattle through the bush in

August. The fresh green that sprouted along the bare limbs of English trees. Roses and geraniums bursting into bloom, painting the garden in vivid pink, red and white.

Only slow progress was made on Duncan's landscaping plans. He seemed to have lost focus or inspiration. He spent much time endlessly pounding the countryside on horseback and disappeared, often for weeks at a time, to Melbourne. Isabelle had no illusions why nor cared.

Her own heart lay in Geelong with Luca, her saviour and comfort, their love deep and safe in the care of each other. She longed to be with him as his wife but conceded that was unlikely to ever happen. So they stole as much time as possible together. Katarina seemed content for the moment to continue keeping house and assisting Luca in his business when needed.

A glowing Audrey and proud Walter Kruger married in a simple touching ceremony, so longed for after all these years. Isabelle missed her company but living so close, and with the attraction of Luca in Geelong, she made frequent visits.

Nichola mostly resided in her Melbourne townhouse but occasionally wrote to her mother and even less often returned to Castle Hill. Isabelle pined, deprived of her two delightful grandsons, fiercely coveted by the Morgans, fearing they would grow up not knowing their Penross kin. So whenever Nichola returned to the country, she contrived a visit. Four year old Adam was almost ready for schooling and toddler Darcy, a lively chuckling child, both strictly supervised by a household of women. Isabelle hoped that as his sons grew, Elliott stepped in and raised them as sturdy young men.

Of Blair at Oxford, scant was heard. He rarely penned letters or bothered with even a few words in a telegraph. Only Duncan's contact with the university yielded any particulars, none of it encouraging. He continued indifferent, his poor results reflecting his lofty casual attitude.

'Ah've no idea what to do with the boy when he gets back. He has no aptitude or interest in anything,' Duncan grumbled once in a rare moment he and Isabelle were together.

She worried too, sharing his despondency. Although they had nothing else, she and Duncan would always have the children in common.

'When is he due to return?'

'He's booked a saloon cabin on the maiden voyage of the new clipper Hampshire due to sail about the end of May. Be home in August. Ah'll talk to the boy then.'

Duncan remained oblivious to the fact that his *boys*, except for Owen, were now already young men.

Rugged Alexander became increasingly unsettled by the day and talked of pioneering in Western Australia.

'Ye won't sit still long enough for me to train ye,' Duncan complained to his second son. 'You're only interested in what's happening out west. What about Kooringal?' he thundered.

'This and Lakeham are yours, Father. I want to blaze a trail of my own. There are hundreds of thousands of acres for farming. New unexplored lands begging to be settled. Not the Swan River. Further north. I could take a ship from Fremantle up the coast to Shark Bay. Francis Gregory has already explored the Gascoyne River along the coast declaring it suitable for pastoral leases.'

Duncan shook his head and Isabelle sighed at their son's enthusiasm. Soon, another of her brood would be lost to her and she mentally prepared herself for the trickling exodus taking place as each of her children left home.

Callum was finishing at Scotch College and would soon be off to England. Christie ungraciously endured another year of ladies' college with the promise of travel at its end. Her friend, Caroline Anderson, often spent weekends and holidays at Kooringal.

Maira would shortly be boarding in Melbourne. Isabelle thought she might wish to remain at home but quietly and happily accepted her further education, apparently ready to follow her sisters and spend time at East Leigh, too. Isabelle knew she would miss her dearly for she was the child with whom she shared an uncanny perception and close bond.

Finally, however, the wheel of time circled until futures could not be delayed. For Isabelle, it all seemed to happen at once. One event tumbling upon another.

Christie and Caroline had finished school and, like twins with shared identical dreams, their excitement peaked, both girls fearless and determined to explore the world. Two positive souls attuned to one another, animated when discussing plans, well read on their destinations, feverish to leave and begin their experiences. The vast homestead echoed with the excited chatter of loud laughing females, both with a keen sense of humour, seemingly devoid of any maternal instincts.

'America?'

Isabelle suppressed her anxiety and tried to sound enthusiastic for the two travellers surrounded by volumes of books and piles of newspapers on the morning room table. Both girls had taken to wearing their riding trousers inside the house, not bothering to change after their long daily rides. Both disregarded convention, reflected in their manner and dress.

'We'd like to leave soon. We've been patient all year,' Christie groaned.

'Have you asked your father?'

She nodded.

'Mine, too,' Caroline added.

Isabelle sighed with resignation. 'It's all decided then?'

'We shall leave from Sydney and head for New Zealand first,' Christie said, breathless with pleasure. 'From there, we should be able to make for Honolulu and on to San Francisco on the west coast.'

'Do you know, Mrs. Penross, we shall be able to travel much of the way east across America on the transcontinental railroad?'

'Amazing. Quite an adventure ahead of you both. You will take every care?' she pleaded.

'Of course, mother. We shall keep in touch. Just think, we shall end our journey in New York.' Christie's eyes sparkled.

And from there, Isabelle knew, they were so much closer to Europe. And beyond. She might not see Christie again for years and found the thought terrifying.

When the young women were finally waved off at the Sandridge pier, Isabelle managed to stay strong and not cry. Their exuberant youth was impossible to deny. With all their lives ahead and the wealth to indulge it, they were free spirits. Shunning normal female expectations.

Within weeks in August, as expected, Blair was back in Victoria. He only spared them a few days at Kooringal before returning to the city and rented lodgings, ignoring Kooringal, no prospects for his future direction.

Maira had already been settled for some months now into East Leigh, having resolutely kissed her mother goodbye, and regular word was received from Callum at Oxford.

'At least he seems to be applying himself. He's a good son. Solid and dependable,' Duncan said, almost with pride.

So many train journeys down to town delivering or collecting children from schools and ships, Isabelle sighed with resignation.

CHAPTER 11

Elliott crept into Nichola's room when she was almost asleep. Again. His sly method of achieving the least resistance. Their hostile marriage had not improved and neither disguised their lack of love or respect for each other. Nichola had long ago realised that wealth brought you security but not necessarily happiness. She felt Elliott's weight depress the other side of the bed.

In public, they remained cold and polite. In private, they were no more than two wild animals baring their teeth at each other.

He slid into bed beside her. One arm immediately wound tight around her body so she found it difficult to move, the other explored beneath her nightgown.

Unwilling and repulsed, she muttered petulantly, 'I was asleep.'

Still, there was a certain fascination and desire in sleeping with a man if he was kind to her and she gained some benefit. Which she had already done with others beside her husband. To useful account and in a much more pleasurable manner. She now knew her Elliott's selfish and impatient pawing was not the standard by which coupling should be measured.

'You already have two sons.'

'I want you, not more sons.' He rolled her over and pinned her arms above her head.

'You don't desire me, Elliott,' she pouted, 'you only desire a body that will give you release. Can you not find a whore?'

He slapped her face. 'You are my wife and you will do your duty.'

'Let me go. I am not interested.'

He frightened her. Elliott was always insistent but becoming rougher. His face had grown distorted and wild, as though he was in some kind of trance yet she could not smell whisky on his breath.

'You cannot stop me.'

'I can try.' She wrestled beneath him and raised a knee against him.

He gasped in pain and in the fleeting moment while he was distracted, she tried to leave the bed. He reached out and caught the hem of her nightgown. His sharp tug made her stumble. She knocked her head on something and sank to the floor, hazily aware of Elliott looming over her, his brutish hands on her body and turning her head aside in dizzy pain as she felt him thrust inside her.

She grew conscious as Elliott stood over her pulling on his trousers.

Summoning all her depleted energy, she hissed, 'If you ever touch me again, I will kill you.'

His harsh mocking laugh echoed in the hall before he closed her door. She struggled from the floor, dragged herself onto the bed and huddled into a ball. Tears she would never allow to escape.

Next day, in a quiet secretive moment when her other four female adversaries in the homestead rested, she stole into father-in-law Stewart's study, slid open the lower drawer and retrieved the key to unlock the arms cabinet. This sat grandly in a corner of the men's domain, the billiard room. She selected one of the many small hand guns with beautiful scroll work on the silver plated frame, trusting the menfolk did not notice it missing. At least until tomorrow.

That night, Nichola's maid helped her pack and stow her bags in a cupboard in case Elliott appeared. Fortunately, he did not.

Next morning, forsaking breakfast, she dressed long before daylight, hurriedly whisked her bags down the back servants' stairs and drove herself to Kooringal in the buggy she had ordered to be waiting.

'Nichola!' Isabelle exclaimed at her arrival mid-morning. 'You must have left early. The boys are not with you?'

'I should think not,' she sneered. 'I cannot remain in that house a day longer.' She swept past her mother and paced the morning room, ignorant to its lovely comfort and generous vase of wildflowers it was still Isabelle's habit to pick almost daily. 'I have come to tell you I'm leaving Elliott. Forever.'

She indicated for her daughter to sit down but Nichola shook her head. 'I must meet the midday train at Meredith. If Elliott catches me he will force me to stay.'

Isabelle had never seen her so white and determined. 'What has happened?'

Nichola would not meet her eyes and slid a desolate glance through one of two long windows flooding the room with light. 'Elliott ... forced me last night. On the floor.' Her jaw set with fury. 'I am full of shame and I can do nothing about it. This is his right? Violence is acceptable because he is stronger?'

Isabelle glanced concernedly toward the open door, praying no one heard. Although horrified for what Nichola must have suffered she whispered, 'What about Adam and Darcy?'

'They have a nanny.'

'How can you leave them?' she implored, aghast.

'I have no choice.' Nichola erupted. 'Elliott would never release them.' Her eyes blazed with hatred. 'Knowing he sired them, can you blame me?'

Isabelle felt the deepest anguish for Nichola's misery and dared to ask, 'Did you ever love him?'

'Good heavens, no. Father threatened to disinherit me when I learned of his mistress so I blackmailed him for the townhouse and married for wealth.'

Isabelle stilled in shock, horrified to think her daughter had stooped to such heartless depths and finally understanding her reasons, then immediately blamed herself.

She should have opposed Duncan's neglect and abuse of his daughter which had clearly left a harmful legacy. Elliott, she truly believed, regarded his wife as a prized possession, worthy of his social status but little more. And while Nichola's place was legally by her husband, he had no cause to hurt her.

But what could be done? Within the sanctity of marriage, how could she expose him and have anyone believe her?

Fighting back tears and anxiety for her daughter's future, Isabelle watched her leave, Nichola's back straight as she rattled away at speed in the buggy, her attitude determined and brave as she had been all those years ago as a child when she ran after Blair to save him.

This time, she was saving herself.

For the first few days of Nichola's residence in Melbourne, she left instructions with her few servants that she was not to be disturbed, and slept.

For the rest of the year, she refused any contact with Elliott and locked her door against his visits. She became a hermit while her third baby grew inside her and summoned her mother when it was due. Isabelle travelled down to Melbourne by train, amazed to see her daughter so thin, considering the child she bore.

'I have arranged to hire a wet nurse for a month until the baby is old enough to travel.'

'You're returning to Castle Hill?'

'No!' Nichola flared, 'but Elliott's child will be. I want nothing to do with it.'

When her labour began, she ground her teeth and stoically endured the pain until the baby slid from her body and she was free. She heard faint cries but hardened herself to feel nothing.

'You have a son.' The midwife beamed thrusting a shawl-wrapped bundle toward her.

'Take it away. I want nothing to do with it.'

Nichola turned aside but before she closed her eyes, she

saw her mother scoop up her grandson lovingly into her arms.

A few days later with her daughter recovered and propped in her comfortable bed, Isabelle guardedly enquired, 'What will you tell the boys?'

'That I need to live in Melbourne for my health. They may visit without their father. If he lets them.'

'Otherwise?'

'They will never see me.'

'How could you bear to be without your children? Is it worth the sacrifice?'

Nichola's ice blue glare was her answer.

On her way home to Kooringal, Isabelle stopped in Geelong, desperate to confide in Luca, needing to share her burden of Nichola's unhappiness. They had announced their *friendship* to Katarina – of course, she had guessed - and no longer hid their feelings in the Perini home. He held her hands, offered smiles of understanding and compassion but, best joy of all, he kissed her with delicious fondness each time she arrived and departed.

'I am a grandmother again,' Isabelle sighed, devastated and vulnerable after seeing Nichola abandon her newborn son. 'Am I too old for you?'

Luca shrugged. 'I could be a grandfather, too, if Katarina was married.' She had considerately disappeared for the evening with a friend. 'I long to kiss you, bella mia. May I take the liberty?'

'Oh yes, plea-'

Her whispered plea was smothered and Isabelle sighed within it, embraced and held. He would have read the longing on her face. They had kissed much and deeply but it had become his teasing habit to ask and the heady wait only enriched the pleasure. For now, there could be nothing more and she ached when forced to leave him again.

One day, she prayed, their time might come.

***

Blair Penross first saw her at a rout of some old acquaintances and blessed his refusal to be buried up country in Kooringal and return to Melbourne instead. Her fair hair fell in soft ringlets about the sweetest face and she wore ice blue. If she came closer, he wagered her eyes matched the colour.

'Who is that golden haired beauty, George?' he leant closer, enquiring of one of his few friends. Only the most dissolute fellows remained loyal.

'Miss Victoria Grantham. Local doctor's *only* daughter,' he emphasised with a grin. 'First season out, I understand.'

Blair's interest had already sharpened in her direction but settled upon her now, hoping for a return glance. She was poised but very young yet he considered how to devise an introduction. For the next few hours, he contrived to be in her line of sight and continually watched her.

Later, he asked again of George, 'Do you know her?'

'Of course, old man. Our families knew each other back home.'

Unlike Blair, born in the colony, George was from Oxfordshire and they had met at university. Rakish George had been encouraged to visit Australia by Blair, the irresponsible pair equally idle.

Blair cursed, wishing he has asked sooner. 'No interest yourself?'

'Good Lord, no. I'm looking for someone much older. As should you.'

'All the same, introduce me,' he demanded.

George chuckled. 'Not sure you're her type, old man, but I shall do as you ask if only to witness your pathetic failure.'

'Then let's work our way across, shall we? Slowly. Mustn't appear too keen.'

A healthy bolster of drink already quaffed leant him courage as they edged closer, deliberately pausing to chat with other parties of friends along the way. And then he was virtually at her side.

Close, her skin was downy soft, her neck sculpted in a

delicate curve above partly exposed creamy shoulders, held erect with perfect posture. Her youth and loveliness took his breath away. He stared, completely overcome.

George cleared his throat above the chatter to gain her attention. 'Victoria, delighted to see you here.'

She half turned and beamed, catching his hands. 'George. Father was asking after you only last week when he heard you had travelled out.'

Immediately, he turned to his companion. 'Allow me to introduce my good friend, Blair Penross.'

'Delighted to meet you, Miss Grantham.'

Her flicker of interest lingered over him slightly longer than discreet and her head dipped in the slightest of nods. 'Likewise, Mr. Penross.'

He hesitated for effect and lowered his voice to a seductive murmur. 'May I call you Victoria?'

She stood very still, utterly composed and regarded him. 'You are very forward since we have only just met. But, yes, since you're acquainted with George,' she smiled at their mutual friend, already tactfully subsiding, 'I suspect you may.'

He sensed he had passed an important point of acceptance. 'I'm recently returned from Oxford.'

'How extraordinary.' Her attention was captured. As a ploy, he stepped back and she followed, successfully removing her from the circle of friends. 'My father's family are from Chipping Norton. My grandparents still live there. I've always longed to visit.'

'You were born out here?'

'Yes.' She tilted him a coy glance. 'You, too?'

'Guilty, I'm afraid. And back to stay. Returned on the maiden voyage of the new clipper Hampshire.'

'How exciting. I long to travel. The thought of a voyage fascinates me.'

'You have never been?'

She shook her head and her ringlets quivered. Had they been alone and he knew her better he would have taken the liberty to stroke them. They looked thick and lustrous. Caught up so fully, they would no doubt tumble down when released. His thoughts leapt ahead that one day he might have that pleasure.

'Since my mother died some years ago, father promised we should return to England but he is always so busy in his practice.'

'Pity. I have no doubt you would love it. The Hampshire's arrangements for passengers were of the first order and her saloon was a most spacious apartment. Suited forty passengers with ease. Of course, there were more in second and steerage.'

'And did you have fine sailing?'

Her eyes positively sparkled and he had been right. They were of the softest blue green. More promising still, she appeared equally fascinated by him and hung on his every word.

'Mostly, but in the wildest weather she behaved herself beautifully. We had foul weather from the Cape so that we were driven south and struck heavy seas. Only a bit rough again around Otway. Glad to make the heads and be towed up the bay to Sandridge.'

'I should think so. Now I'm not so certain about sailing after all,' she laughed lightly, tilting her glowing face up to him.

He was smitten. For the first time in years, he felt a sense of manly responsibility and a desperate need to care for this fragile creature.

'And what occupation employs you, Mr. Penross?'

'I am the oldest son and heir of my father's estates.'

She smiled sweetly, absorbing the status of his birthright as he intended.

'I may put in a manager on our properties,' he added importantly, having no such intentions, 'If father ever lets me take over,' he chuckled, trying to charm her with humour, 'but I confess I do prefer the town. And since my return,' he showered her with the winning smile, reliably successful with females, 'I see it has many benefits to offer.'

Their gazes held until, to his annoyance, Victoria was reluctantly enticed away by a giggling circle of friends for a hand of whist. He only saw her again briefly in the entrance hall, surrounded by their fellow partygoers, as everyone prepared to leave.

'I wish you goodnight, Miss Grantham,' he called out hastily, forcing his way closer and catching her eye for only the shortest moment.

'And you, Mr. Penross,' she laughed before disappearing into a carriage.

She liked him. He knew it, Blair mused, walking briskly back to his lodgings, George's warning still ringing in his ears. *It won't be easy, old man. Don't favour your chances.*

Blair watched out for her socially but it was some weeks before his eyes alighted on the fair and lovely Miss Grantham again. In a corner filled with their smoke, chatting to chums, he stilled when she entered.

His first thought was of an angel because she wore a creamy froth of silk, strands of pearls at her slender throat, arriving among a throng of friends. Thank God it was a ball. He would sign her card and anxiously contemplated her immunity to him. Surely when he held her close for he intended to monopolise every waltz?

The night became a whirlwind of her light floral perfume as she floated in his arms, the gleam of candlelight gilding her hair, half down and caressing her shoulders; both entranced with each other. He had captured her attention. Could he win her heart? His beat faster at the grace of her. They conversed little and spoke mainly through their eyes.

One of her few remarks out on the crowded terrace had been, 'You smoke?'

Loaded with innuendo and censure, although it was quite the common thing, he wisely replied, 'Not if you do not prefer it.'

"Father does not approve." Her satisfied smile and silence

told him he had chosen the right response. So when he offered to escort her home and she refused, her rejection cut deep.

'Next time,' he murmured bravely.

'We shall see.'

Still smarting from her rebuff that night, he turned to a dose of laudanum which soothed him and helped sleep come more easily since her acquaintance.

Alexander had ridden out to one of the far corners of the property and camped overnight as was his tendency these days, to be alone and think. He strained with unleashed energy to leave for Western Australia and make his mark in the world. Although sheep were productive in the Avon valley of the Swan River colony in the south, farming had spread north as far as the Pilbara region a decade ago but his interest lay on the Gascoyne river district.

He decamped next morning and saddled up, trotting home at a leisurely pace along Kooringal's western boundary adjoining the Ballarat-Meredith road. Knowing that as much as he loved this country, he also had no interest to stay here any longer, he decided to go back to the homestead, swallow his pride and ask his father for wages or a small stake to see him started out west on a property of his own.

He stopped to check the wiring on a fence and heard what sounded like a baby crying. He pushed back his hat and scowled in the direction of the noise. It continued, so he led his horse along the track, finally detecting someone up ahead slumped beneath a tree. Wise in early autumn while the summer heat still lingered.

Coming upon a sorry sight, his heart wrenched. A slip of a girl not much older than Maira lay propped against the peeling bark of a eucalypt trunk, her blood stained dress rolled up to the knees, a baby cradled in its folds. Thick dark hair hung over her shoulders. With her head bent forward, he couldn't see her face but her sobs echoed softly in the still morning air.

She cried out in fright at his appearance.

'It's all right, miss. I won't hurt you.' Alexander calmly stepped closer. She choked back a sob and swiped at her tears with her sleeve. He crouched down before her. 'What are you doing out here on your own?'

She looked up at him, her streaked face wet with tears, brown eyes glinting with more pooled to fall. Alexander's gentle voice and kindly manner could only have reassured her to confide.

'I was travellin' with me bully of a step dad and me step brothers.' Her voice broke and her mouth trembled. 'But they left me when the baby was comin'.'

Alexander cursed, forgetting he was in the presence of a woman. Rich or poor, his mother has always charged him to respect them. 'How long ago?'

'Couple hours.'

'Why would they do that?'

'Because they hate me.'

'That's no cause to be inhuman. I'll go after them and make them wait.'

'Oh, no, you mustn't. They're a bad lot with guns they'll wave at anyone. After me mam died a year ago, I had nowhere's else to go so I stayed with 'em doin' their housekeepin'.'

'My name's Alexander Penross.'

'Sarah Cooper,' she whispered.

He gently tugged aside her dress to reveal the sleeping baby.

'I think she's fine. She slept when I nursed her.'

Alexander smiled. 'Have you named her?'

'Emma.' Her face crumpled afresh.

He leapt up for his saddlebag retrieving a canteen of water and a linen cloth. He poured some liquid into a tin mug and she gulped it down.

'She's named for me mam.' Sarah hiccupped with sobs.

Alexander's instinct was to hold and comfort the girl but it didn't seem proper. And he dare not ask about the child's father although his intuition leant a guess. 'I think it's best if I take you home.'

'Oh no,' she objected. 'But if you could spare me a bit of food and water, I'd be obliged. I should be able to move on tomorrow after a rest.'

'And where are you going?'

She hesitated and shrugged. 'Follow me family to Ballarat, I suppose.'

'You'd seek them out after they treated you so badly? I can't allow it. You need time to recover. Soon as you feel able, I'll get you up on my horse and back to a nice comfortable bed for a few days.'

'I can't impose and I don't know you.'

He grinned. "Yes, you do. We just introduced ourselves.'

Sarah's bleak face broke into a faint smile and Alex saw its potential. Her tawny eyes sparkled and he noticed freckles.

'I've not a coin to me name.'

'No matter,' he chuckled. 'My family's rich.'

Sarah gasped. 'Then I could never-'

Alex raised a hand in objection. 'I'll get my swag so you're more comfortable and you can rest while I build us a fire, boil the billy and cook up lunch.'

She stared at him. 'You're a kind man, Mr. Penross.'

'Alexander. I'm sure you've met others.'

'Not often.' She spoke low as if to herself.

It pleased Alex to see Sarah settled more comfortably, relax and doze, and little Emma snuffle with contentment. He still had a mind to go after the bastard cowards that deserted her and punch them senseless. Lean but muscled, he usually won fights but never incited them.

Some hours later with all three of them rested and fed, Alex packed up, trying not to stare in embarrassed fascination as Sarah suckled Emma again, although discreetly behind her raised skirt. Then he carefully helped the shaky new mother to stand and struggle up into the front of the saddle, hoisting a tightly swaddled Emma into her arms.

Still weak, Sarah swayed, so Alex quickly hurled himself astride behind her and wrapped an arm firmly about the pair of them in support. Halfway home, she dozed again and her dark head dropped back against his shoulder. With the warm sun on them and gentle walking rhythm of the horse beneath, a sense of life's simple peace settled over him.

At the homestead, having ridden his passengers right into the rear courtyard with its splashing fountain and tub trees, Alex called for help. Soon, concerned arms and hands reached out to assist Sarah and Emma down. After issuing tactful instructions, always instantly obeyed for this considerate member of the family, and a quiet command to summon a doctor, Alex strode through the homestead in search of his mother.

She glanced up from her bureau in the morning room. 'Alex, you're back.' Then, seeing his earnest expression, asked, 'What is it?'

He explained Sarah's arrival and circumstances. Hearing the story and compassionate like her son, Isabelle gasped in outrage.

'I'm sure we can find a spare bed in the servants' quarters until she's recovered,' he suggested.

'Of course.' His mother readily agreed.

Daily thereafter, Alex found himself drawn to the kitchen where Sarah had begun to help an aging but still capable Mrs. Reed and her girls. Emma, serenely sleeping in a basket amid the noise, became a magnet for them all, especially in a bustling room filled with females. Chores were interrupted and peeks taken, not the least by cook herself, all unashamedly softened by Sarah's tale and her squirming baby.

Mornings now usually found Alex delaying his daily rounds and responsibilities out on the station until he had checked on his charges. The servants cast knowing grins and glances between themselves at the young master's attention toward Sarah and her responding blushes. And sighed in awe when he scooped up the tiny bundle into his big powerful arms for men rarely took an interest in babes.

So it was no surprise that the guests remained in residence indefinitely in the guise of providing Sarah with employment.

'Until she gets back on her feet, so to speak,' Alex appealed to his mother.

Isabelle agreed with a hidden smile but privately reflected on the outcome, eventually releasing any sense of authority over her son's life. He was old enough to resolve his own future and she could imagine Duncan's explosion when it did.

Each time he left Sarah in the homestead kitchen, Alexander rode out, bothered by his keen ongoing sense of duty and interest toward her and Emma. His mind flashed with images of her dark hair and shy smile, her appearance and manner so vastly different from his first sight of her. The colour in her cheeks, her untroubled and happy nature, no longer nervous, dressed neatly and smelling sweet. Until the situation registered, he sat astride, resting his horse near the river, hands on the pommel, shaking his head and muttering.

'Wildest idea you've ever had, Alexander Penross.'

He would miss Sarah when he left and felt an equal tug of attraction for her as his pull toward adventure.

He scowled anew, burdened by a fresh weight on his mind. He'd need to fathom the answer soon for summer's end signalled his departure. He had already broached his proposition. After his father's inquisition and grumbles, he had agreed, deeply disgruntled that yet another of his sons was deserting the Penross stations.

Alexander clutched baby Emma in one arm and swung Sarah's hand in the other as they stepped through the long dry autumn grasses until they found their favourite place under an old eucalypt beside a billabong on the Moorabool. It had become their custom to go for a stroll after Sunday service and lunch. He no longer hid the fact that he was fascinated with the child and increasingly sweet on her mother.

He had spent many evenings teaching Sarah how to read and write when their conversations often turned to his plans for adventure.

'You are so decided on what you want for your life. I admire you greatly, Alexander.'

'Because I rescued you?' he teased.

'Oh, no. Much more than that. I care greatly for you. As a person. As a man,' she stammered and her voice broke.

'Sarah-?'

She suddenly turned to him, clinging, almost crushing Emma between them. 'Alexander, please don't leave me behind when you go.' Her eyes filled with tears. 'I couldn't bear to be apart from you. Me life would be so empty.'

Alexander wrapped am arm about her in comfort. 'Sarah? You know that would be my dearest wish but ... I can't.'

Large teardrops rolled down Sarah's cheeks and she swallowed firmly against them, as if determined to be composed and strong. Alexander's heartbreak stirred up when Sarah sobbed again, pressing her face into his shoulder.

'Listen to me,' he said firmly. 'Hear me out. I can't ask you both to come along,' he said as gently as possible. 'Life will be hard over there. I shall be pioneering new country. It's not settled like here in Victoria. There'll be few comforts for women and children.'

'No harder than I've already endured.'

'There'll be no medical facilities.'

'And did I have any when Emma was born?'

'Sarah, I would be afraid for you.'

'You mustn't worry about me. Ever.' She paused before adding hurriedly, 'You don't need to marry me, Alexander. Just take us with you.'

'Ah, Sarah.' Alexander's soft smile was matched with a wry grin. 'If only you knew it, that's exactly what I want.'

'To take me with you?' Her face lit up like a moon-filled night. 'Oh, Alexander, I'd go anywhere with you, you know that?'

'No, I couldn't allow you to just tag alone.' Her expression saddened again at his statement. 'Because I'd want to marry you first.'

Sarah gaped and pressed a hand over her mouth. 'You like me enough to do that?' He nodded. 'I wouldn't want you to do something you'd regret later.'

'Oh, my feelings go beyond caring, Sarah. I do believe I've fallen in love with you.'

Baby Emma struggled between them as tall, handsome Alexander Penross swept off his hat and bent to kiss his future wife. Although he had not actually asked nor had she given her answer, that they would spend their lives together was acknowledged.

When their excitement and passion was spent, for the time being, Alexander warned, 'You can back out and I won't think less of you. It won't be easy.'

'Oh but I'll be with you.' She beamed.

'I don't know what we'll find when we get there. Unknown country and lands just waiting to be discovered.'

Sarah wildly shook her head. 'I don't care, Alexander. I just want you.'

'Only problem now is getting past my father. He's frightening as you know but, remember, no matter what happens or what he says, I'll be at your side. Now and forever.'

Back at the homestead, being Sunday afternoon everyone was at their leisure somewhere about the house. Alexander summoned his mother from upstairs to meet in his father's large panelled study.

Duncan sat behind his massive desk surrounded by papers and ledgers, his favoured pipes, his whisky tray of decanter and glasses, the detailed landscape painting by von Guerard of a young newly-built Kooringal on the wall behind. His window overlooked a side garden with an appropriate view across to the stables and wool shed.

He glowered when Alex and Sarah entered. Isabelle quietly appeared in a rustle of fine skirts and smiled at them, standing alongside.

Alex plunged ahead without hesitation. 'I have asked Sarah to be my wife and she has agreed.' He heard a small excited gasp from his mother. 'We would like to marry before we leave for the west.'

'Congratulations, Alex. Sarah.' His mother embraced them both but her delight was soon crushed by Duncan's blast.

'She's nothing but a common stray.' He waved an arm wildly at Sarah who tensed beside him.

Alex saw his mother cringe at his father's tactless words. 'I would stake my life on her character.'

'Ye know nothing about her.'

He turned to Sarah and placed an arm about her shoulder. 'Would you mind?' he asked gently.

Although she trembled in fear, she bravely shook her head. 'I've nothin' to hide. Me mam and dad were respectable folk.'

'What would you like to know?' Alex challenged his father.

'Where were you born?' he barked.

'Ballarat gold fields,' she replied with quiet dignity.

'And yer parents?'

'Thomas and Emma Cooper from Islington in London. My father was a miner but a carpenter by trade. He was killed in an accident when I was twelve. Me mother and I fell on hard times so she remarried but died in childbirth.'

'What of your step-father? Why aren't ye with him?'

'Because he left me on the road to have me baby alone. That's when Alexander found me.'

'And where's the father of yer child then?'

Alex heard Sarah take a deep breath, sensing her dread as she was forced to explain. 'He's the one what left me on the road.'

Silence dropped across the room while Duncan covered them with a black glare and Alex felt his mother's hand grip his arm.

'Satisfied father?' he snapped. Duncan grunted. 'I love Sarah and I will not leave without her. I hardly need your permission to marry but I'm telling you out of respect.'

'She's too young. She'll need permission,' he growled.

Isabelle stepped forward. 'I'll give it.'

'Thank you, Mother.' He cast her a grateful glance then turned back to his father. 'Since you don't appear to approve of my choice, I realise you may wish to withhold the promised funds. But we're still going.'

Duncan shuffled uncomfortably. 'I wouldn't do that, boy.'

'I'm twenty two, father,' Alex pointed out sharply.

A tense and lengthy pause followed. Eventually Duncan addressed Isabelle. 'Ye'll arrange a wedding in the garden, then?'

'Of course.'

'Alexander,' Sarah spoke up hesitantly, 'if you don't mind, could we marry in a church?'

He squeezed her hand and smiled. 'Since we'll only be doing this once, you can have whatever you wish, my love.'

Sarah blushed and Duncan pushed out an impatient sigh. 'Then ah'll send a rider into St. Andrews in Meredith, see when preacher Stoker can wed ye.'

'I'll send a telegraph immediately to Nichola in Melbourne,' Isabelle said as they readily escaped Duncan's study, leaving him to brood. 'She'll contact Owen, Blair and Maira to come home.'

'Oh I don't want no fuss and put you to bother, Mrs. Penross.'

'Isabelle, my dear,' she said warmly. 'You must call me Isabelle from now on. You want a wedding to remember fondly with no regrets. All the family will love to come. We haven't had one since Nichola married nine years ago.' She regarded Sarah for a moment. 'Is there no one you would like to invite?'

She shook her head. 'I only have Alexander and Emma.'

'And now all of us!' Isabelle laughed.

There was also someone else Isabelle had in mind to summon. While she was happy for her son's genuine love, she was also naturally sad that he was leaving and for so far away.

Her oldest children were all grown and, one by one, trickling away to forge their own lives. She sighed. Which was as it should be, of course.

Merely weeks later, all was arranged and the family arrived home from Melbourne together for the appointed day, having travelled by train across to Geelong and taken the country passenger service to Meredith to be met by carriages at the station.

The greatest surprise was the appearance alongside Blair of a Miss Victoria Grantham. At first sight of them, their visitor exclaimed over the gardens and would not move indoors until she had wandered it all at length for an hour. Blair look bored as he trailed after her but his interest in the girl was plain. So the family did not formally greet his attractive female companion until dinner where everyone could not help but be impressed by her poise and style for one so young, indicating fine breeding.

Meanwhile, Isabelle and Nichola chatted in the morning room. 'She is utterly lovely and gracious but too good for him, Mother. Blair's nature was established from childhood when he wandered off into the bushfire. He'll never change. As much as I like her, I do hope Victoria doesn't linger, expecting he will. She deserves better.'

'I worry about him.' Isabelle frowned.

'You mustn't. He's an adult. He needs to pull himself together. Maira seems happy though.'

'Yes. I must talk with her.'

Isabelle covered her daughter's hand with her own. 'I'm sorry you're not happier with Elliott.'

Nichola shrugged. 'I have my own life now even if it is not the one I planned.'

'I have a confession to make.' Isabelle began cautiously.

'Brace yourself, dear, but hear me out. I have invited Elliott to Kooringal for the wedding.'

Nichola sprang to her feet. 'How could you?' She shook with fury.

'I told him what I knew and-'

'That was a private confidence, Mother,' Nichola gasped in horror.

'Listen.' Isabelle caught her arm as she rose and whirled in anger to leave. 'I warned him to stay away from you and that he would be watched. I also insisted he bring the boys so they should meet their new aunt and not be so estranged from our family.'

Nichola stared at her mother and asked, barely above a whisper, 'My sons are coming?'

Isabelle nodded. 'They are already here. Go to your room. I will inform nanny to bring them to you.'

For Nichola, the reunion with her separated sons was bittersweet. On the one hand, Adam and Darcy remembered her but remained understandably distant. On the other, two year old Andrew, whom she hated at birth and had never seen, was now an adorable toddler. And so like herself in appearance with twinkling blue eyes and fine golden hair, Nichola was instantly and irresistibly taken with him. The innocent sight of him brought her to tears.

Of all her sons, he should have been the least likely to engage her attention but the bond caught her by surprise so that she neglected the family in his favour, indulged every possible moment with him during the weekend and was rewarded in full measure.

Because he was too young to understand, Andrew was trusting and somehow sensed her importance to him. He nestled into her when she read stories, stretched out his hands to be picked up and when he cried because he did not want to leave her, she let him sleep with her in the big soft four poster bed each night.

Duncan, who largely disregarded females, took an

immediate interest in Blair's guest, Victoria Grantham. Noticing the attention, Blair strutted about, preening that his prized companion had impressed his father. Still, insecurity lingered, Isabelle noticed, because Blair sought consolation in much alcohol. More than once, he stumbled or presented at dinner already half intoxicated.

Seeing his undisciplined behaviour, Isabelle despaired for him and watched Victoria's anxiety, too, from a distance. Was their early friendship already in jeopardy? Surely such an intelligent cultured young woman would not tolerate her son's indulgent selfish behaviour?

Owen appeared only when expected for meals or family gatherings. Maira – always romantic at heart - glowed with her own inner light all weekend and cheerfully devoted herself tirelessly to tend Sarah's every need before the wedding.

The grateful and excited bride at first protested when Isabelle produced one of her own lustrous light patterned gowns for the maids to alter after a fitting since she and Sarah were of a similar height and build. The perfect complement to her brown hair, glossy from a thorough washing, caught up and waved for her wedding day, her head and shoulders draped with a flourish of fine gathered lace.

When the hour arrived, the homestead emptied, carriages rattled away toward Meredith carrying the ladies while some of the men rode horses.

Elliott, as threatened, avoided Nichola, was charming to everyone else and, as always, cornered Duncan.

An impatient Alex paced outside the small timber church as the Penross family gradually arrived to fill it. Soon, standing before the altar alongside Blair, sober thanks to Victoria's overheard whispered insistence at breakfast and watchful eyes to ensure he remained so, at least during the service, Alex finally stood still. It was clear from the glowing expression on his face that all his anxiety was replaced the moment he turned to see Sarah enter through the tiny porch and walk toward him.

Isabelle had willingly taken charge of her first granddaughter, Emma, barely two months old, marvelling that although she was not yet fifty, she had already acquired four grandchildren, even if this little cherub was acquired by chance. Duncan scowled on one side of her, Nichola sat rigidly on the other with Elliott nearby, torn, Isabelle suspected, at being deprived of Adam and Darcy seated with their father, Andrew at the rear on his nanny's lap.

Maira walked behind the glowing bride as Sarah's maid, Isabelle conscious that it might not be too much longer before her youngest daughter was also wed.

Her own quiet joy had been to invite Luca and Katarina in the guise of family friends boldly insisting they sit in the pew immediately behind. Her awareness of her true love, felt if not seen, was high throughout the ceremony.

And then Alex and Sarah were pronounced husband and wife. Isabelle had gifted her gold and pearl ring to him which he had refitted in Geelong and his bride now wore it proudly on her left hand. Showers of rice were tossed over the newlyweds outside then the entourage returned to Kooringal bathed in warm late afternoon sunlight that stretched golden fingers across the track back to the homestead.

Inside, Mrs. Reed and her kitchen staff had excelled themselves yet again, the long formal table in the grand dining room resplendently set, glittering with crystal and silver, bedecked with greenery and late season blooms spilling from huge urns atop pedestals in each corner of the room. A candelabrum in the centre flickered with lights.

Sarah's awed gaze absorbed the Penross opulence and she stayed close to her new husband.

Although Adam and Darcy were allowed to sit with their father, Andrew and baby Emma were in the nursery. Summoned by a maid later, Sarah slipped away during the feast to feed her daughter. Isabelle watched with a sigh of motherly pride as Alex rose courteously from his chair as she left, leaving her in no doubt of their happy if hard future ahead. She was even a little wistful of their bliss.

She sent a long meaningful gaze across the table to Luca. He smiled and raised his glass to her. In shock, Isabelle realised Duncan had caught the small gesture and prayed he did not guess. She must be careful and guard her secret with care.

For all the merriment and chatter around the table, Duncan appeared not so much lonely as distracted. Always difficult to satisfy, especially as he aged, she had placed Elliott and Victoria Grantham nearby, those with whom he seemed most comfortable.

He visited Geelong and Melbourne less often these days and had grown more bad tempered than usual. Isabelle often wondered why when town had been such an attraction and consolation for him over the years. What of his Mrs. Herrington?

Nichola had dressed to perfection in an extravagant gown of watered blue, its elegant overskirt gathered up into a bustle, the colour soft against her creamy skin. Had she chosen the becoming shade and flattering style to taunt Elliott, for she looked stunning? She and Victoria might almost be sisters, Isabelle thought, as she glanced between them.

Apart from Callum, buried no doubt in what was probably a bitter early English spring at Oxford and Christie in raptures over her travels, detailed in occasional letters, all of her family was about her. Isabelle felt nothing but the deepest sense of fulfilment and pleasure. She loved and worried over them all.

By early Monday morning, they were all packing to leave. Alex, Sarah and a sleepy Emma first, having sent a wagon load of possessions on ahead to be loaded aboard a Henty brothers' ship in Geelong bound for Fremantle.

Isabelle sought one last cuddle of the baby and planted a kiss on her tiny forehead, hugged her son and daughter-in-law at length and tight, and steeled herself not to cry.

'Write Sarah. Of everything and often,' she implored.

A smiling Sarah seemed not in the least distressed to leave. 'I'll do me best,' she promised.

Duncan stood aside, shook his son's hand and wished him well, no gesture offered to Alex's wife and child. And then they were underway, Isabelle like all of them left wondering when they would meet again, sensibly realising because of the distance, it could be years.

Elliott and the boys were next, their farewell restrained and polite. Duncan remained on the porch steps as they departed, everyone else had returned indoors.

Nichola twitched aside the drapes and watched from an upstairs window as her husband took her sons away. Had he not been such an uncaring brute, she might have appealed to him and negotiated some visits with her children. Isabelle made sure she was by her daughter's side for this moment. Normally cool and stoic, Nichola broke down and sobbed.

'How can I bear to part with them?'

'We will make legal enquiries. We will arrange something.' Isabelle murmured in reassurance, having no idea how she might proceed.

'I cannot return to Elliott, mother,' Nichola cried. 'I'm afraid he will hurt me again.'

'I know, my dear.'

She held her daughter tight until she was more composed, determined that now Nichola's maternal instincts had finally arrived, she must not be deprived.

Next day, although Nichola remained subdued and miserable, she declined Isabelle's insistence to stay longer. Maira readily assumed the role of comforter. So the Melbourne group, too, departed.

It was impossible for his mother to offer Blair advice on his problem for she doubted he would listen. She could only wish Miss Grantham well. Since the girl was mature and wise beyond her years, Isabelle trusted she knew best how to cope with Blair's difficult situation. She asked that her greetings be passed on to Dr. Grantham.

Within weeks, a parcel arrived at Kooringal from a photographer in Geelong. It was a picture of Alex, Sarah and Emma. Her son must have had it taken quickly before they left. How typically thoughtful. Isabelle fondly ran her hand over the images of all three as if touching them in person and placed it on the morning room mantelpiece.

It was many months before Sarah wrote of the pastoral lease Alex had acquired on the Gascoyne River inland from Shark Bay, and named Wilgorup Station. Apparently it was a native word meaning red ground. Sarah's handwriting was simple and clear, her command of English good.

Alexander has natives working for him. We live in a tent but he is building us a home of local stone. Drovers pass through on the stock routes but it is very isolated here.

When we first sailed up from Fremantle, the coast was all islands, inlets and tidal mud flats. The rivers are mostly dry with some waterholes. Alexander was told the Gascoyne only flows from about February to August. The country is just red dirt.

We have been told that it is warm all year round with low rainfall, hot summers and a tropical climate but there are south east trade winds most of the year so it's not unbearable like the Pilbara further north. I am so glad Alexander did not want to go up there.

We send you all our love and I will write again when we can.
Love, Sarah, Alexander & family

CHAPTER 12

In Melbourne, determined to outwit Elliott since seeing him at Alex and Sarah's wedding, Nichola kept her eye on the mantel clock, splashed more whisky into another glass and settled herself beside the Morgan family lawyer, Henry King, at her townhouse. Tall, distinguished and therefore not too onerous to persuade. By whatever means. Because of what was at stake, she was prepared to use them all.

'You do understand, Mr. King.' She paused for effect. 'May I call you Henry?'

He blustered and politely sipped his drink. 'Well, I-'

'It will be so much simpler, I agree.' So far he had been patient and responded to her pretence of being a weak flattering female but he was growing apprehensive. She trusted the alcohol to help. 'I appreciate that you are prepared to see me privately. I know you understand my ... situation.'

'Most certainly, Mrs. Morgan but-'

'Oh, Nichola. Please. We have become friends.' She sighed dramatically. 'You know my dilemma. Mr. Morgan still supports me financially as you know since you advance me the funds regularly. On time.' She smiled sweetly. 'I can always rely on you, Henry. But I need to set my mind at rest that this state of affairs remains permanent.' She waved her graceful arm in the air. 'There must be some document that could be drawn up,' she proposed with an edge of challenge in her voice.

'Mrs. Morgan-'

'Nichola,' she reminded him sharply. 'I insist you draft it and my husband sign it. I trust you to convince him of its

325

worth and that I need my finances confirmed.' Her demand was a test to see how far she could stretch Elliott's support although she lived comfortably with her father's annuity.

'It is somewhat unusual,' he hedged.

'Henry, please do it for me. I promise,' she drawled, leaning closer, 'you will be rewarded and you may call on me at any time.'

If it meant security, Nichola was quite prepared to fulfil her offer if he accepted. Nichola welcomed the rumours of his roving eye. In fact, she counted on them. Since she had deliberately brushed against him, his interest had risen. She snatched another glance at the mantel clock.

'And please contact me as soon as it is done. Now, I know you are busy, Henry, and your time is valuable so I will let you go, but before you leave,' she rose and waited while he stood before her, 'I must thank you for safeguarding my welfare.'

She swayed forward and clung to his sleeve, tilting her face up to waft her perfume over him. He responded as she hoped to her artificial instability by reaching out to steady her. At that precise moment the sitting room door opened and she pressed her face against his to suggest an embrace.

The maid, Dolly, with Maira gaping over her shoulder, apologised profusely. 'I'm sorry, Mrs. Morgan but Miss Maira is here and you did-'

'Dolly!' Nichola cut her short and made a show of springing apart from Henry with faked surprise. 'It's quite all right. Is it that time already?'

A lie. She had heard their muted voices in the hall and timed her manoeuvre to perfection. She had deliberately invited her youngest sister at a specific time knowing her punctuality and directed Dolly to announce Maira the moment she arrived.

Nichola laughed nervously. 'Henry was just saying goodbye. Never mind,' she linked an arm through his, 'we shan't tell your wife. I'm sure Maira and Dolly can keep a secret.'

Henry King looked alarmed at the prospect but for Nichola's purposes she needed influence over him so that he did as she asked. Other witnesses were vital to that plan.

'Henry, this is my sister, Maira Penross. My lawyer, Mr. Henry King.' She introduced them.

'Miss Penross.' He nodded.

'A pleasure,' she murmured in reply.

'Dolly, show Mr. King to the door.' She leaned closer and addressed him intimately although all could hear. 'I look forward to good news next time we meet.'

When the sisters were alone, Nichola hugged Maira and rang for tea. 'I should explain Henry,' she confided. 'He's quite known as a ladies' man but I must tolerate him because he is the Morgan family lawyer. I know you will not breathe a word of his little ... indiscretion.'

'Of course not. Why was he here?'

If nothing else, little Maira was frank and Nichola always knew where she stood. She paused while Dolly brought in tea and when she left continued, 'Just some business.'

'Elliott's not divorcing you, is he?'

'Good heavens, no. That would be the ultimate scandal.'

'Are you on good terms with him?'

'No. We communicate only when necessary.'

'And ... you don't mind living alone?'

'All these questions! I am perfectly content,' Nichola smiled as she poured tea.

'Oh.' Maira helped herself to cake. Always her sister's weakness and Nichola indulged it, making sure the larder was well supplied whenever her sister was expected.

'Something wrong?' Nichola prompted gently, sensing distress.

'Actually, no. Everything is quite wonderful.'

Nichola leant back into the comfortable sofa and sipped her China tea, amused. 'Indeed. I'm pleased to hear it. No doubt you're anticipating the end of your final year at East Leigh?'

Maira nodded, beaming. 'Nichola, may I ask you something?'

'Of course dear.'

'Do you no longer love Elliott? Is that why you don't live with him?'

Her young sister was becoming quite grown up with questions to match. 'We simply no longer suit, dear.'

'You must think me quite impertinent but the reason I ask is because I know you can't be as happy as I am which makes it hard for me to tell you but I simply must,' she gushed, her cake forgotten, her tea growing cold. 'I have met the man I shall marry.'

'Indeed.' Nichola grew sick to see the serene glow on Maira's face. Her little sister was barely seventeen but then she had been a similar age when her own heart had been swept away, to a certain degree, and she had misguidedly married. 'And how does *he* feel?' For what was more important?

'The same I believe.'

At twenty six, Nichola suddenly felt old and jaded. Used. And accepted a portion of blame herself. She lived comfortably with an occasional flattering admirer. She encouraged them if they were handsome and generous but the friendships soon died if they grew demanding. But otherwise she had no close friends. To surrender her independence and return to Castle Hill meant living in violence and misery. Too afraid to risk returning, she remained alone.

'Then I envy you,' she replied eventually, 'for no one can conceive the horrors of an unhappy marriage but those who have experienced it.' Maira's expression softened. To cover her discomfort at her compassion, Nichola asked brightly, 'So, who is this young man?'

'One of my teachers. Mr. William Green,' she sighed.

'Take care, dear. It sounds unprofessional.'

'Oh, we are never alone together. William is a most proper gentleman but he returns my long glances,' she grinned with delight.

'Are you sure it isn't just a youthful fancy?'

'Oh, absolutely not,' she enthused. 'My whole body bursts with life when I even think of him. When I see him, I can hardly breathe or speak.'

'Then it does sounds serious and promising.' Not that Nichola knew what true love felt like. Her experience had been more like infatuation and the chance of escape.

'Later in the year, when I am finished school and it is proper, would you chaperon William and I if we walk out?'

Nichola marvelled at humble Maira's scheming and laughed at her earnest plea, as though she might refuse. 'Of course, dear. I am all interest to meet this man.'

'I simply cannot wait.'

In the entrance hall later, as Maira left, Nichola could not resist asking, 'What is it like? To be in love?'

Her sister tossed her a look of horror. 'But what about Elliott?' Nichola shook her head. 'Oh dear.' Recovering from the revelation, Maira thought about it only briefly before responding with unleashed enthusiasm, 'Overwhelming but most rewarding.' She clasped her sister's hands. 'Thank you for listening. I have written to mother but I needed to tell someone.'

Nichola hugged her, this quiet slip of a girl, beautiful dark hair sinfully pulled back strictly into its usual looped knot when it should have been allowed to fall thick and free. What few strands showed lay hidden beneath her bonnet. Envy for her sister's youth and happiness tightened her chest.

All year Blair tried in vain to earn Victoria Grantham's favour but she remained guarded with him. At a recent function he had taken her outside into the privacy of a secluded corner of their host's garden. Even in the dark, her eyes sparkled for him. When he held her hands and drew her closer for an illicit kiss, she sighed and responded to his advance.

'We should not, Blair.'

'We know how we feel,' he murmured, lost in her nearness

and perfume, hinting at their future.

Still drinking heavily and smoking, although he had promised otherwise, Victoria had laughed deeply. 'You are too confident.'

Blair says, 'And you are too prudent but I can wait.'

He adored her, his very happiness depended on her and he dreamed she would eventually accept his offer when he made it. But because of Victoria's hesitation, Blair's worry and despair surged and fell. Her wealth and beauty allowed her to be selective. Despite the strong desire they felt for each other, he genuinely feared that he might not win her hand so he increased the laudanum to help him sleep.

'You feel as much as I do. Admit it,' he had begged.

'Oh, Blair Penross,' she sighed in despair, 'you have quite turned my head, but father would not approve. He is so protective of me since mother died.' She paused to consider her next words. 'Perhaps if you had a position. Presented your future to him?' she suggested eagerly.

Blair groaned. 'Prove I'm respectable? My future wealth is assured.'

'I know. But ... on your own account," she suggested carefully, 'to reassure him.'

She frowned in thought. 'Do you have a sister whom I could befriend for recommendation?'

'Nichola's unhappily married and Christie's off exploring the world.'

Victoria's gaze widened in astonishment. 'Really?'

Blair shrugged. 'Maira's still at school and boring. Victoria, my blonde princess,' he murmured, 'I love you.'

'I know, Blair,' she said desperately, 'and I love you, too, but if there is to be any future for us, you must change. Do you understand?'

'Of course. I'll do anything for you,' Blair wildly promised.

'If you will be a husband and father, I need you to reassure me that you will be more responsible. You must settle to some occupation. Could you not reconsider managing Kooringal one day? I am sure your father would welcome it.'

'Absolutely not. I hate sheep.'

She chuckled. 'Then something here in town? What is your interest?'

'You,' he whispered. 'Only you,' he muttered, almost in agony. He pulled her close and nuzzled her neck, pressing warm kisses all over her skin.

Victoria groaned and sighed. 'Blair,' she breathed, 'you must not take such liberties.

He kissed her again and she drowned in her passion for him. His hands were on her waist drawing her against him. Good Lord in heaven, he was so hard to resist. Blair enchanted her, not only for his handsome face and winning smile but because of her strong greedy feelings for him. She longed for him when they were apart.

As the oldest son of a wealthy squatter, her future comfort in life would be assured but his character was unstable. Should she consider him? Ignore his idle streak for love of him? Then her father's kind face loomed into her mind and she knew with his wisdom he would object. She could never displease or hurt him.

Nonetheless, Victoria clung to Blair desperately in the dark, filled with joy and despair.

When Maira's final term at East Leigh ended, she sought out her former teacher, William Green and approached him. Her heart tripped in anxiety at the familiar sight of him. Tousled head bent, rumpled tweed suit, that perpetual scowl on his dear pale face.

When she had his attention, she nodded in acknowledgement and stepped forward. 'Mr. Green. Or perhaps now I can call you William?' she dared.

He chuckled and fell into step beside her, walking a discreet distance apart in case anyone should be carefully watching the school grounds from the upper windows. 'Your father is my employer, paying my fees.'

'Ah but, as you know, I am now finished school and no longer a student here. So are we not equal?' she challenged.

'We will never be equals, Miss Penross. Our backgrounds make it so.' He seemed more amused than enamoured. Maira despaired. Had she been wrong about him? 'And you are very young.'

'It seems you would prefer an aged spinster. Then I hope I shall age quickly else I shall never catch your attention.'

'Miss Penross,' he struggled for words, 'you have always gained my notice.'

'Maira,' she insisted and beamed. 'Honestly?' He gave a single precise nod. 'Would you mind should I call you William?' He regarded her with such disarming gentleness, Maira resisted standing on tiptoe to kiss him on the cheek. 'I should certainly enjoy it if you called me Maira.'

He stopped to look down at her. 'Maira. It's a very pretty name.'

She smiled. 'I agree. I've always liked it.' Her smile widened and she glanced around the school grounds massed with beds of roses and geraniums. 'Spring is such a lovely time outdoors, I always think it's such a pity to waste it, don't you?'

William revealed a charming grin. 'Absolutely.'

'Perhaps we could enjoy it together, some time? Of a Sunday afternoon.' Seeing his slight hesitation and frown, she wondered if he was just being polite or awaiting her explanation so she continued hurriedly, 'My married sister, Mrs. Nichola Morgan, lives in Emerald Hill and is agreeable to accompany us should we decide to take a walk together.'

'You are most forward, Miss Penross.'

'Oh, William,' Maira's shoulders drooped as she heaved an injured sigh. 'I thought you liked my name.'

'I do but-'

'Then please use it. I had hoped we could be far less formal. I know I am still seventeen but my sister is always available.' She suffered a dreadful thought. 'Unless of course you would rather not?'

'On the contrary.'

'Wonderful. Then we shall meet again?' she suggested. Goodness, he was making this conversation difficult. 'We do seem to enjoy each other's company, don't we?' she pressed on.

William studiously laced his hands behind his back. 'It seems we do. Maira.'

She clasped her hands together and laughed. 'I return home to Kooringal next week but I'm staying with my sister, Mrs. Morgan, and will be free every day until then. Should you wish to call,' she added pointedly.

William shuffled awkwardly but eyed her directly. 'I most certainly would.'

'I'm so relieved you have no prior arrangements.'

'If I had, I should have immediately cancelled them.'

'Mr. Green,' Maira lowered her voice to barely above a breathless whisper and the smile faded from her shining face. 'I do believe we are about to embark on something wonderful.'

'Miss Penross, I completely agree,' he murmured before stepping aside, making a polite bow and walking away.

Maira closed her eyes and could have danced with happiness.

Their courtship over the summer, except for some weeks over Christmas when she returned to Kooringal, was conducted mostly in Melbourne while Maira stayed with Nichola. It was intense, their love instantly deep and abiding, and his proposal mere months later sudden but enthusiastically welcomed.

Maira laughed through her tears, said *Yes* and wrapped her arms about his neck, warm and secure in his embrace, dissolving into his kiss. One of many in which they had indulged, mostly on warm summer nights. Her happiness was boundless.

From her usual discreet distance, Nichola looked on, plagued with envy. She had watched in awe as her little sister's love had flowered into life.

At home again only a matter of days later, for her

exhilaration could not be contained, Maira approached her mother and father alone with a certain amount of excited trepidation but quiet confidence. Nothing would break her devotion to William. When he had offered to accompany her and face her parents together, Maira had sternly objected.

'I will not allow you to be insulted, for that is all father will do. I shall brave him myself.' She had reached out for his hand, which he had squeezed compassionately for she had already explained her father's difficult nature but assured him of her mother's sanction. 'We don't need him in our lives to be happy, William. We only need each other.'

Seated now beside Isabelle and opposite the tyrant who had sired her, with her usual calm frankness, Maira announced, 'I am in love with a teacher, Mr. William Green. He has proposed marriage and I have accepted. I would like your approval and blessing, of course, but will marry without it.'

'A teacher?' Duncan scoffed.

Isabelle gasped and beamed, catching her daughter's nearest hand between her own, already privy to her secret and happiness. Maira returned her smile but they withheld their excitement until later.

'Yes. And most highly regarded.' Maira did not bother to mention his recent promotion for her father would neither be impressed nor change his mind. To him, a teacher was still a teacher, a low professional and therefore unsuitable.

'Could ye not have done better?' Duncan grumbled.

'I appreciate your honesty, Father,' Maira remained unruffled and serene, 'but William *is* the best. He is an admirable man whom I love and respect deeply.'

Such maturity in one so young, Isabelle thought, looking with fondness and pride on her determined daughter.

'Ye're not yet eighteen.'

'Then we shall wait until I am of age. If you prefer,' she added generously with a hint of mischief he appeared to miss.

'I do not prefer him at all. How will you survive on a

teacher's salary?'

'We shall manage I am sure.'

'Well,' Duncan thundered, 'ye'll not have ma permission and I will not support you. Any daughter of mine could marry well but your oldest sister cast us into disgrace by leaving her husband and abandoning her sons. Christie is gallivanting all over the world refusing to settle down. Alex has married an unknown stray and now you want to marriage well below your station.'

'I am in love and perfectly happy. Social status means nothing to me.' Her steady gaze held his and she barely blinked.

'I forbid it.'

'I had no doubt of that.' Maira stood, still poised and calm before him. 'Will you not even agree to meet him? If you do, you will change your mind.'

'I doubt it.'

'Mother?' She appealed to the woman who had always been her closest companion and best friend.

'Naturally I disagree with your father,' she said gently. 'His opinions are not mine.'

'Isabelle!' he roared.

She ignored her husband's explosion, knowing now what it was to be mutually loved and stood to face her most beloved daughter. 'I wish you both every happiness although it clearly shows on your face that you already have it.'

Maira hugged her mother.

'How dare you!'

Isabelle released her daughter and held Duncan's black glare. 'I dare, Duncan, because Maira is a sensible young lady and in love. Which we all hope to find at least once in our life time, do we not?' she pointed out crisply.

She noticed the shock on his face at her words of challenge.

In the moment's silence while he remained speechless, Maira said quietly, 'I am sorry you do not wish to meet my future husband or, presumably, any future grandchildren for I plan to have many. It will be your loss not to know such a good man and I imagine one day you will regret your decision.'

'I'll cut you off!' he threatened.

'As you wish,' Maira said politely. 'William will provide for me and our family.'

'Ye'll starve.' He threw over his shoulder as he strode from the room.

A few months later, on the morning of her wedding day, preparing at Nichola's townhouse for the small church ceremony soon to come, Maira asked her mother, 'Why isn't father happy with any of us? He seems so sad and bitter.'

Isabelle sighed. 'He was an ambitious man in his youth and I believe he expected his children's lives to be as he commanded to reflect what he achieved. Which, in his life time, has been much. But he has discovered he cannot control people. I am so proud of each and every one of you, Maira.' She hesitated and frowned. 'I am concerned only for Blair but I love him as much as the rest.'

She hesitated, wondering how much to share and decided with the sense and maturity of her favoured child, only because they were both motherly home makers that she would confide.

'I married your father for love but he only chose me because I was young and healthy to bear him sons to inherit what he built.' Maira gasped. 'He didn't care for daughters which is why I named you. He would never admit it but his greatest disappointment is that his oldest son has no interest in either Kooringal or Lakeham. I am sure it is the source of Blair's unhappiness. Duncan has made it obvious that he considers him a failure.'

'Did father never love you?' she whispered, distraught.

'No.' She was surprised to find how the confession grieved her still. 'But you must not upset yourself on your wedding day. Nichola will attend you and it is such a grand coincidence that Callum is home from England now and can stand up beside William.'

'I hope Blair behaves himself. He is bringing Miss Grantham.' Maira shook her head. 'I don't know why she endures him.'

'For the same reason you're marrying William, dear,' Isabelle said gently. 'It is clear she adores him but Blair is so ... unsettled. I believe that is the reason for her delay in committing to him. She hopes he will change but I'm afraid she may be disappointed. Such a pity,' she reflected wistfully, 'that sometimes one's happiness is so completely reliant on another.'

'For better or worse, the vows say, and I am prepared to make that pledge,' Maira stated.

'You have a wonderful loving man who will make it easy and for that you must always be thankful.'

'I am.' She smiled.

Isabelle was furious that Duncan did not agree to attend Maira's wedding ceremony. So far he had not met William nor wanted to. There was little fuss and only the most discreetly placed announcements in the papers.

On the day, Maira walked proudly alone down the aisle of the lovely Gothic Scots church in Collins Street, a vision of smiling dark haired beauty, her simple fitted gown adorned with lace and pearl buttons, eyes focused only on her intended standing at the altar ahead.

Victoria rushed in moments before the bride. Blair had not appeared to escort her as arranged. Owen, as usher, rose to the occasion, gallantly took the beautiful young woman's hand and led her to a pew. Callum's gaze settled on her at length as he half turned to investigate the cause of the minor disturbance. When Victoria caught him staring, he quickly turned away. Isabelle observed the personal moment with interest.

The service was well under way when Blair reeled down the aisle and slumped beside Victoria. At his muttered whisperings, she spared him only an injured glare then reverted her attention back to the ceremony. Isabelle smelt a faint waft of something sickly about her son and filled with unease. Especially since, at Maira's request and because she knew it would please her mother, she had suggested Walter and Audrey Kruger and Luca and Katarina be invited. All for moral support as well as the rare pleasure of their company. Blair's misconduct threatened to shame them all.

Because Duncan was absent, Isabelle relaxed, was even a little careless in her company with Luca. A small rebellious part of her wanted to expose the family to her fondness for him.

Victoria rejected Blair outright for the entire evening, the greatest punishment she could have delivered. Her cold dismissal sent him a clear message.

If ever he saw Miss Grantham flounder, Callum appeared nobly at her side in rescue. Victoria seemed grateful for his company and support. Many times, Blair and Callum exchanged sharp words until the undercurrent exploded at the end of the evening at Nichola's townhouse.

Blair said embarrassingly loudly in front of everyone to Victoria, 'I'll take you home now, Princess.'

She politely stalled him, 'Not unless you are sober, Blair, and that will not be until at least the morning.'

'Whadya mean?' he slurred, growing hostile, shaking off Callum's restraining hand on his arm as they all gathered in the hall to leave.

'I mean I shall make my own way home tonight, Blair.'

Callum shielded her from his menacing advance. 'Steady on, brother, you can see her tomorrow.'

Blair lunged forward and pushed Callum. 'You trying to shteel my girl? Keep your hands off her,' he sneered.

Nichola stepped in. 'Blair, I have called a hansom cab for you.'

'He can come home with us,' Isabelle suggested quickly hoping to diffuse the tense situation.

'D'ya think I might get loshed, mother,' he laughed harshly.

Victoria cringed, close to tears, her expression anguished.

'The horse won't get lost, dear, even if you might.' Isabelle made light of the situation to lessen her own personal humiliation in front of her family and dearest friends.

They all hugged and kissed goodnight. Isabelle particularly reluctant to leave Luca but they were to stay in town for a few days and planned to meet again.

'I am sorry,' Isabelle whispered to Maira, annoyed that yet again Blair had ruined a special family event, having disgraced himself a year earlier at Alex and Sarah's wedding.

She no longer knew how to help her wayward son but simply knew that something must be done for him.

'It's not your fault, mother, nor your place to apologise on Blair's behalf,' Maira said kindly.

The new Mr. and Mrs. Green departed for a leisurely evening carriage ride before heading back to a suite in the Menzies Hotel, both arranged by Isabelle as a gift for their enjoyment. Maira and William would leave by the passenger mail train leaving at eleven thirty for Geelong in the morning for a few days together on the coast at Queenscliff, formerly Shortland's Bluff, where the family had once taken a month-long idyllic holiday.

Now, it was a two hour paddle steamer excursion from Melbourne with new hotels and coffee palaces being built in the popular seaside town. The newlyweds would return to Melbourne to live in a small timber cottage in the inner suburb of Collingwood William had proudly bought for them with his savings.

Callum and Victoria lingered after the wedding guests were safely despatched. In the silent hallway, they waited until their hansom cab was hailed by a servant and awkwardly tolerated the journey back to Doctor Grantham's residence in Collins Street.

'It was most obliging of you to see me home, Callum,'

Victoria said as they stopped. She glanced toward an upper window and a faint flicker of light. 'I see father awaits me. Could you spare a moment to meet him?'

'Of course. If you prefer.'

'Thank you. It would please me greatly.'

He assisted her down and a servant admitted them indoors. In the elegant tiled entrance hall introductions were made after Lloyd Grantham came downstairs, brief explanations given why Callum accompanied his daughter and not Blair, and polite conversation ensued.

Callum tactfully refused the offer of port. 'Thank you all the same but it's very late. I won't detain you longer. Miss Grantham.' He acknowledged her with a nod.

'Thank you again for bringing me home.'

'Again I must apologise for my brother's ... indisposition.'

When Callum left, Victoria followed her father upstairs to his study where a warming fire burned low.

'So, it has happened again.' Lloyd Grantham frowned.

Victoria wrung her hands together, torn between her loyalty to Blair but shattered by yet another display of his poor behaviour and the dissolving likelihood her father would approve him.

'Yes,' she reluctantly admitted in a small voice.

'Mr. Callum Penross on the other hand seems a very decent young man. Unlike that brother of his.'

Victoria smarted from her father's criticism and was consumed with misery because she could not disagree. Blair was weak but she loved him. He always kissed away her fears until she relented and forgave him.

'He is still finding his way,' she said defensively, excusing him.

'A man of his age,' her father challenged in disbelief. 'Mid-twenties, is he?'

'Twenty six.'

'Exactly my point. He should know where's he's going by now. Clearly not a sheep man like his father. What *does* he want to do?'

'I don't believe he knows yet father.'

'Well he damn well better decide soon if he ever expects to gain my approval. Victoria, my dear,' he allowed his daughter a sympathetic glance, 'if he can't organise himself as a single independent man, how on earth can he expect to support a wife and family?' He paused. 'Am I correct in believing your affection for him is still strong?'

'Yes, Father.'

He shook his head. 'Unfortunate.' He stepped closer and placed his hands firmly on her slender shoulders. 'Blair Penross comes from a respectable and wealthy family, and is indeed a good catch. But a responsible man-?' The doctor heaved a deep sigh and let his words trail off.

Chastened and unable to argue with his doubts, Victoria hung her head and mumbled, 'I'm being cautious until he's more settled but I simply cannot decide what to do.'

'Any young man who hopes to impress me and claim my daughter must be upstanding and in charge of himself.' His voice softened. 'There will be no shame if you should reconsider your affections for him, my dear. A lady must see clearly to her future.' Touched by the misery on his beautiful daughter's face, he explained, 'I loved your mother, dearly, Victoria. I wish the same for you. It may sound harsh and prove a difficult decision for you to make now but it will affect your whole life. All I ask is that you give the matter further serious thought.'

'Yes, Father.'

He kissed her forehead. 'Good night, my dear.'

'Good night, Father.'

As she turned to leave in a rustle of skirts, Grantham said, 'Decent of Callum Penross to see you home safely. What of his plans now he's home from England, do you know?'

'I gather nothing has been decided but from snatches of family conversation I overheard between Callum and his mother, it seems possible he will help manage the Penross properties under his father's guidance.'

'Admirable. He seems a fine young man,' he murmured sending his daughter away deep in thought.

CHAPTER 13

The following year, Benjamin Green was born to William and Maira, and all went well. Isabelle knew how much her youngest daughter had longed for motherhood and journeyed to Melbourne to meet her sixth grandchild.

As always, she used both directions of travel to pause in Geelong and visit her beloved Luca. Because of their mutual connection, he and Katarina often socialised with Walter and Audrey Kruger. Too old for children of their own, they occasionally fostered wayward children until permanent homes were found. From Audrey's inner glow, it not only seemed that marriage suited her well but that she thrived on the responsibility and challenge of the children who passed through her care.

As it happened, Callum's courtesy to Victoria Grantham fostered an awareness and friendship between them that may not have otherwise developed.

They met socially in Melbourne whenever Callum was in town, which he regularly arranged. He always took the opportunity to casually drop gentle timely hints that Blair's behaviour was set and Victoria should not expect a reversal of character, raising alarm in her big innocent blue eyes.

With the addition of a discreet helping hand, a touch here and there in support as well as comfort at times of difficulty with Blair, Victoria grew to rely on the younger more respectable Penross brother more and more. Victoria could not fail to compare them and Blair did not emerge favourably in her mind.

Yet her desire for him never dimmed and her blood

turned hot at his touch and stolen kisses, lapses she would never reveal to her father who remained unconvinced over his poor character.

She still loved Blair but he was breaking her heart, clearly unsuitable as a potential husband. What to do? Victoria was clever enough to understand that if he always misbehaved so, she would not know a happy or successful marriage. Whereas Callum, although unexciting, was handsome and personable, dependable and well mannered. All she wished Blair to be but without the same longing.

So with reluctant caution, she gradually transferred her interest to Callum since Blair was often absent or ailing. But with her diversion of choice emerged a new dilemma. Giving up Blair, which crushed her heart, for their passion still continued fierce. Just to be in the same room, catch each other's burning gaze, be touched and covertly kissed.

Victoria found herself wishing Callum lived in town or visited more often to occupy her mind against the man she really loved.

Blair's reaction to his brother's interest in his lady love was blind jealousy and resentment if he even caught Victoria and Callum innocently dancing or chatting. Her constant pleas that he improve passed unheeded. More than once, Blair's bitter anger sparked physical violence resulting in scuffles that Callum was forced, with the help of strong male friends, to step in and settle, or his eviction from a party household.

As much as it hurt his family to witness the dissolution of the heir which reflected badly on them all, Callum also hated to see his brother reduced to such a pitiful condition. He lost weight and became a society outcast. At Victoria's prompting, Callum approached his father to take action, force him home and clean up or at least intervene. But Duncan Penross, bleeding with private sorrow over his wayward son, only bellowed his outright refusal.

Blair begged and pleaded for Victoria's continued forgiveness. It tore her heart to abandon him from her life but she could give no more without clear proof of change. The strong happy man she originally knew and with whom she had fallen in love, no longer existed or lay hidden beneath a cover of constant illness.

Blair's dependence on laudanum spiralled the night Victoria officially ended their friendship. Sleep came so much more easily with drugs, it was hard to resist. Its first effects had been soothing but he eventually succumbed completely to its lure and control, until indifference ruled him. He lolled all day on the sofa in his lodging room, sleeping and reading and drinking. He rose late, occasionally took a walk.

When an anxious Maira visited with baby Benjamin in the hope of cheering him up, she grew horrified at his half-dazed state or awareness.

'Why are you doing this to yourself?' she appealed.

Maira had asked Nichola to accompany her, fearing what she might find but Nichola refused with the biting comment, 'I saved him once when he was a child. Now he's old enough to save himself.'

Blair's memory worsened and the few times he ventured out, he was apt to forget people's names. He felt weary and numb. Tossing and turning day and night, finding it impossible to lie in one position or sleep – the reason he'd taken laudanum in the first place.

He grew irritable, tried to stop taking it but failed because his body ached, dripped with sweat and trembled until he was forced to surrender once more to its hold. Since no regulations controlled its use, he easily obtained the brown coloured liquid from pharmacists over the counter.

Seeing him less and less and therefore unaware of the full extent of Blair's decline, Victoria began to savour Callum's pursuit. As her father had pointed out, he was a good man who promised security and prestige for her life, so she tried hard to make their friendship work. But, honestly, at times she wanted to shake him. Always the leader in their relationship, she wished he had a stronger nature and she encouraged him to more boldly confront his father.

Callum's compliant personality frustrated her. He thought she had recovered from her feelings for Blair but she could never extinguish such intense passion. So she returned Callum's courtship with logic, not her heart, for that would always belong to his brother.

Tonight, Callum was to return to Melbourne after an absence of some weeks and Victoria suspected he might propose. The possibility kept her impatient but also curbed her spirit knowing what she had sacrificed to reach this place. When he arrived at her father's house, she greeted him with warmth and resignation, accepting her future was fated to him.

She led him up to the sitting room, discreetly alone while her father attended the last of his patients for the day in his professional rooms downstairs.

'Victoria,' he breathed, pressing a kiss to her inner wrist, redolent as always with the familiar perfume of roses. He was not without his own appeal and at times was quite sweet and endearing. 'I have missed you.'

'You will keep disappearing up country,' she teased, hinting, 'a situation you could easily rectify.'

'Indeed?' He stepped closer, smiling.

'You know you occupy my thoughts.' She was careful not to declare that he had also claimed her heart.

He turned serious. 'Are you sure?'

'Callum Penross,' she tried to be modest and proper, 'you are making me blush to declare myself.'

Victoria just wanted the formality over and the announcement made so that wedding preparations could begin. Maybe then, absorbed in planning, she would not think of Blair so much and how she missed him in her life. She hated his weakness that had destroyed their future together and reflected that perhaps Callum was stronger after all.

'Then I shall save you any further discomfort and make my feelings and intentions known. I have approached your father so I can now tell you how much I love and adore you. I can only hope you share a small fragment of my feelings for I dearly wish to marry you and must ask if you would consider the possibility of becoming my wife.'

While he took a deep breath after his emotional outpouring and hung with innocent rapture on her reply, Victoria both feared and welcomed the moment now that it had arrived. Sensibly, she knew Callum Penross was her future but a wistful corner of her heart briefly resisted the response she knew Callum expected her to give.

'Yes, Callum, I should be pleased to accept you,' she grinned, hiding any regrets, resolving to use every effort to forget what her life may have been with another and make her marriage succeed.

'Oh Victoria.' He clasped her hands tight. 'You have made me the happiest man. I shall arrange an appointment with Gaunt jewellers in the Royal Arcade where you shall choose the ring of your heart's desire.'

'You are so generous and I am so excited and happy.' And at that moment, she believed it to be true, that she could overcome her private sorrow. 'And now you must kiss me or I shall faint away with waiting.'

All the emotion she had suppressed surged to the fore in the knowledge that this was the correct decision. He did as she asked and their path was set. Callum had kissed her before, of course, the sensation warm and comforting, giving great pleasure but, for Victoria, without the fire she had experienced with Blair.

Much joy followed the moment Dr. Grantham finished his consultations for the day. He glowed with pride and goodwill, hugging his only child affectionately and enthusiastically shaking Callum's hand. They drank and toasted the newly betrothed couple.

Callum sent off a telegraph to his parents notifying them of an imminent visit with his fiancé and Nichola arranged a family gathering at her townhouse that included Maira,

William and baby Benjamin, openly adored, and Owen, now quite the budding young man but no less conservative and studious than he had always been.

The happy event took place, however, in the marked absence of the oldest Penross sibling, Blair. Maira had reported his shocking domestic situation. Nichola's reaction was indifference, Isabelle grew alarmed. She suspected Callum and Victoria's engagement could not have happened at a more precarious time for him and feared it would aggravate his addiction.

It was obvious now since Maira's letter detailing her latest visit to him, that the son and heir on whom Duncan had placed such importance, was possessed by laudanum. Maira had revealed that the small glass bottles of alcoholic tincture of opium with their red and brown labels, lay carelessly everywhere unconcealed around his rooms. They had not been in evidence so much on his mother's call some months prior.

Blair heard of Victoria's engagement and knew only devastation at her betrayal. His humiliation and despair was acute. After weeks of oblivion, he rallied enough to send her a note begging her to see him. He received no reply. So he wrote another until his persistence was rewarded when she finally, tersely, relented and agreed to an evening when her father was absent and they could safely meet.

She arrived at his lodgings to find him in such an alarming state, she scarcely recognised him. Even expecting her visit, he had made no effort with his appearance. Dark hair once groomed to perfection was long and untrimmed, his face rough and unshaven, his clothes loose on his gaunt frame. From the jumble of empty alcohol and medicine bottles discarded about, it was clear he lived in complete chaos.

Shocked, she sought reassurance and fingered her gold and diamond ring.

Blair spied her gesture. 'You have forsaken me,' he accused.

'That is unfair. I gave you many chances to improve and change and turn your life around,' Victoria defended, filled with guilt and compassion.

'Can't you forgive me and take me back? It's not too late. You aren't yet married. I swear I will be different.'

Victoria shook her head sadly, close to tears, torn and aching. 'It's too late, Blair. I told you it was over. My life is with Callum now.'

He stumbled forward and began to sob. 'I love you, Victoria. I am nothing without you.'

She hardened her heart against his appeal. 'It seems you are nothing regardless, Blair. My disappointment also matters. I am hurting, too,' she declared harshly since he saw only his own anguish.

He stared at her in silence.

'Take a look at yourself in the mirror, Blair.' She braved a step closer, her voice softer. 'Your appearance. Living in such squalor.' She swept her arm around. 'Your life is slipping away from you. You must take charge and do something about it. I ache to see you like this in such a hopeless situation.'

'I've failed everyone,' he admitted bleakly, crumpled onto a sofa, put his face in his hands and sobbed again.

Deeply moved, Victoria sank beside him and gathered him into her embrace, pressing his head against her chest. His body shook as she stroked his hair and crooned comforting words.

Eventually his weeping eased and he raised his red watery gaze to hers. She produced a white lace handkerchief and tenderly dabbed his wet cheeks.

'There is no hope for us, Blair,' she whispered resolutely, 'you know that, don't you?' He nodded. 'You must take yourself in hand. No one else can do it for you. Promise me you will try,' she pleaded, gripping his shoulders.

He frowned and feebly nodded. 'There can be no us?'

She shook her head, her throat choked with emotion, the pull of him even now still a torment inside against the sad truth that they could never be together. 'This is goodbye, Blair.'

'You will be with my brother,' he groaned. 'I can't bear to think of you with him.'

'When I am, I shall only think of you,' she confessed, cupping his rough face in her hands. 'I will always love only you.'

'Victoria.' A faint fire flared in his gaze. 'May I kiss you goodbye?' She hesitated. 'Please?'

With a helpless weary sigh, she nodded, knowing she equally craved the contact. The kiss was brief and gentle, innocent. At first. But the fire had been lit and he sought another. He caressed her arms and fondled her body as gentlemanly Callum had not yet dared to do.

Victoria responded to the excitement. Visions of her father and Callum raced across her mind even as her heart pounded stronger and Blair loosened her clothes.

'Blair,' she protested weakly, as his hand found and explored her warm skin beneath layers of laced corsets and silk.

'Please,' he begged in a whisper, 'be mine just once.'

Lit with equal desire, Victoria barely hesitated. 'Then make me yours, Blair,' she breathed, ignoring all decency, 'I want to know what it feels like.'

She allowed herself to be overwhelmed by him and gave herself up utterly in careless abandon. Felt the cool night air in the dim unwarmed room as one by one Blair removed her garments. His eyes adored her, naked before him.

He found the strength to lead her to his bed, undressed himself with impatient fumbling and, as he had always dreamed, reverently prepared her for his own. His hands caressed her pale untouched body, his mouth teased lips and breasts until she was ready and gasping.

She cried out in pain then, soon, in wonder. The world dissolved to become only euphoria and sensations between them. She pushed her hands through his long unkempt hair as Blair placed a hand beneath her buttocks and wedged them tighter together.

Almost in a trance, he breathed harder above her, moved faster inside her until the friction released his pleasure and he groaned with release.

When he stilled, their kisses were deep and soft and they nestled together. Blair dozed but Victoria lay awake, tears sliding from her eyes and across her hot cheeks, to marvel at the glory of the sensations they had shared, the powerful and physical exhaustion of it all.

When he roused later, he kissed her tenderly and with sleepy hooded eyes, hauled her body against him again, Victoria languid and willing.

'After you are married, we could still meet,' he suggested wildly, when they had made love again.

Appalled, she said, 'I could never be a mistress.'

'Not even for me?'

She shook her head violently and sat up in bed, pulling the linen about her. 'Never.'

'Then this is all we shall ever have.' He moaned, 'What torture that we shall never know it again.'

'Perhaps once more, then?'

Drugged with love for him, she leaned over and sought his mouth and their lips clung in the barest touch. Blair tasted her breasts and rolled her on top of him. Victoria gasped as his hardness found its place and he drew her mouth down to his again.

Much later, Victoria's deft hands worked swiftly yet with care to restore her dress and hair, and make haste to return home. They clung desperately to each other for a long time until she slowly withdrew from his arms and tore herself away to steal out into the chill and loneliness of the night, elated and appalled at what she had done.

Since Blair had announced he could not attend her marriage to his brother, the cruel reality descended that they might rarely, if ever, see each other again.

After laying with Blair, Victoria realised the possibility

that she could already be with child. So with both families'
blessing, she pressed Callum for an early wedding, claiming
her excitement and impatience to be wed.

Kooringal gardens were chosen once again, a minister
secured, and preparations capably supervised by Isabelle,
backed by the Penross wealth.

The engaged couple received letters and telegraphs from
Alex and Sarah in the west accompanied by their best wishes,
and Christie in New York revealing her continued plans to
take a voyage to Europe.

The good Doctor Grantham handed away his daughter
Victoria Rosabella. Named for her mother, she sailed across
the Kooringal lawns, a beautiful and elegant woman, superbly
dressed for the occasion, a refreshing golden light in the
family, poised to assume her destined role to everyone's
satisfaction but her own. Callum could not conceal his delight
at the union and Duncan remained proud, approving and
captivated.

Owen, now studying law at Melbourne University, was
home for the marriage along with a stylish if solitary Nichola
deprived of her sons in Elliott's absence and the family's
denial in allowing the boys to attend.

Maira, William and baby Ben, the only Penross grandchild
in attendance, appeared with reservations, invited by Isabelle
without consulting Duncan. It was William's first sight and
appearance of Kooringal. Stunned by the extent of their
affluence, he diplomatically hovered in the background, a
contented Maira never leaving his side.

Duncan snubbed them while Isabelle wished he could
look beyond William's profession to see the doting husband
and father instead.

To his credit, obliging Callum with humble competence
had taken up the reins of learning property management
under his father's strict grudging guidance. Isabelle knew he
quietly suffered Duncan's reproaches but took no offence and
diligently paid attention, mindful that Blair had failed him and

he was his father's lesser choice. Showing all necessary interest in his father's prized merinos, thoroughbred horses and properties.

As well as Callum's commitment to Kooringal, Victoria promised to be a valuable asset. She brought class and breeding into their family with the promise of future heirs since Nichola and Maira's children did not qualify, and Alex out west carving his own pastoral estate.

When the wedding celebrations dwindled and an eager Callum led his bride upstairs, Victoria stoically did her duty. Later, she retreated to her side of the bed lamenting her husband's uninspired lovemaking. How she longed for Blair's hands on her body again.

As the year progressed, Maira and William welcomed another son, Joshua, into their home who would eventually prove, like his older brother, Ben, to be an indulged chuckling child, mischievous and unrestrained. Isabelle adored him, amazed how her love expanded to admit another joyous grandchild into her life.

Any arranged time with Luca was irregular and frustrating for them both. She wrote copious letters pouring out every detail of her life and open declarations of her love. Duncan knew she corresponded with Katarina Perini but not that Isabelle's letters to Luca and his in return were concealed inside.

Duncan worried her as he no longer seemed as strong. She remained watchful since he rarely rode his horse out over the property any more, as had been his daily habit for year, but mostly took a buggy or rambled about the homestead block and surrounds.

Thankfully, when Victoria announced her pregnancy within months after their wedding, Isabelle noticed a measure of life return to her husband.

When he presumed the child would be born at Kooringal, Victoria graciously corrected him. 'I have written to my father and arranged that I shall return to Melbourne for the birth.' Adding with her usual charming smile, 'You understand that I should feel perfectly safe and comfortable there, father-in-law? I hope you are not displeased?'

With her hand gently resting on his arm and winning him over, he gruffly agreed. This refined golden princess disarmed him as no other female in the Kooringal household had ever done.

Throughout her confinement, Victoria was thoroughly ill. During her brief bouts of recovery, she and Duncan, if the weather was unkind, sat indoors by the window together overlooking the garden, discussing his vision, pouring over long-delayed landscape plans still incomplete.

As the weather improved in spring and Victoria's girth expanded with child, subtly covered by full flowing dresses, Duncan often suggested with enthusiasm, 'We need to get you out of the house.'

Whereupon she took his arm and they strolled to every corner of the homestead grounds and surrounding fenced paddocks, heads close together, arms gesturing, deep in discussion. Brimming with youth and maternal bloom, Victoria seemed to inspire him.

Isabelle was grateful for the distraction, stimulated by their mutual love of gardening but still troubled that something was amiss with Duncan.

'I have so many volumes of botany and horticulture in my father's library,' Victoria confided to him one day. 'From my reading of European garden design, yours appears comparable and exceptional.' She laughed lightly. 'I am not seeking to flatter you. It is quite the truth. Your vision for Kooringal gardens is equal to any I have seen.'

Dazzled by this vision of beauty and manners, Duncan said, 'Let's not stand on formality, Victoria. Call me Duncan.'

Her blue eyes sparkled with delight. Crusty Duncan Penross was the lynch pin that had created this empire of splendid mansion and vast lands. Wisely, she respected his position at its head but she also genuinely enjoyed his company and their gardening passion. As a girl at her widowed father's knee, she had long ago learned to please.

'Thank you. Duncan.'

He uttered a rare chuckle. 'So, you approve of ma plans.'

'Certainly. But there is always room for advancement, don't you think?'

Only Victoria Penross could have such delightful audacity to challenge the work already done without his protesting bellow.

Instead, he scowled and snapped, 'You believe my designs wanting?'

'Your garden is splendid. But,' she lowered her voice and paused, darting him an appealing smile, giving them time to absorb the stillness, the distant views, the redolent scents of flowers and minty eucalypts and waving grasses drifting on the breezes up from the river, 'it could be spectacular,' she breathed in awe.

The homestead's elevation was like a crown atop a royal head. It proclaimed its eminence without the need for a single spoken word.

'What do ye have in mind?' he muttered.

'Duncan,' she cast a perceptive eye over his horticultural accomplishments, 'all this,' she waved an arm, 'could be even more magnificent.'

'How?' he grunted.

'Small things.' She considered a moment, then added, 'Would you still proceed with the walled garden?

'Absolutely. Do ye not agree?'

She smiled at his prickly edge. 'Of course. It will become the garden's secret feature but do you not think it would shine with a central fountain? Surely an omission on your plans?' she hinted generously.

Victoria had learned to be patient with him, ignore his ill temper and allow him time to ponder her suggestions. So she withdrew her arm from his, moved on ahead and stooped to pick a bouquet of wildflowers to take back to the house, dipping her nose amongst the blooms to inhale their musty perfume. Eventually he would defer, his old blue eyes would sparkle, he would question her ideas in animated discussions, returning to his chair on the veranda, surveying all he had made, imagining what was still to come.

Meanwhile, indoors, Victoria avidly transferred her designs onto paper, drew fresh sketches to place before him and urged the employment of yet more labourers to begin the work, her creative zeal alight. When she learned that native black swans congregated in large numbers on the waters of nearby Lake Connewarre most of the year, through which the Barwon River flowed on its way to the sea, Victoria suggested they snare some for Kooringal's lake.

His gaze glinted with interest and he murmured his approval.

Summer saw groundwork progress and the first layers of brickwork begin to rise for the extensive walled garden. As she rested a hand on her mounded body and looked through the morning room windows to survey and imagine their finished mature garden in the years to come, Victoria knew she could endure this marriage, reflecting on her baby's unsolved paternity, wondering if Blair was the father.

Time was meaningless for Blair. It could have been days, weeks, months that passed. He lethargically endured yet another charity visit from Maira to his disgraceful lodgings. Happily poor it seemed, she arrived with his nephews. He forgot their names. One toddled, the other she carried.

'You look awful. Come home with me,' Maira pleaded.

Blair gave a harsh laugh. 'What would William think?'

'He would wonder how on earth you could let yourself sink into this disgraceful situation. Look at you? You have a beard! When did you last use a razor?' Not awaiting or expecting a reply, she continued, 'And you smell.'

'Leave me alone. Go and do your good works elsewhere.'

He huddled onto his bed, turned his back and ignored her.

'I'd prefer to help *you*, Blair,' she said gently. 'I care about you. We all do. You have no contact with the family.'

'They don't care. I'm a loser. A Penross is expected to succeed.'

Maira sat on the edge of the bed watching Ben play nearby, resting Josh on her knee, feeling frustrated and powerless at the sight of her brother surrendering to this craving, beyond wanting to be healed.

'If you mean father, he's displeased with everyone. No one measures up. The rest of us are all worried for you, Blair. Especially mother.' She paused, adding softly, 'Victoria asks after you.'

He raised his head and turned his clouded gaze upon her. 'Does she?'

It wrenched her heart to see foolish hope flare in his eyes. She sighed. 'Have you not read the Argus?' He frowned. 'She has a son. Christian.' Maira watched as tears filled her brother's eyes. 'He was born last week at her father's house in Collins Street. She is recovering there. Callum has returned to Kooringal but will return in a week or so to fetch her home.'

Blair heard her droning voice speaking of the family, being the Good Samaritan, imparting news, believing he cared. He barely listened and forgot it all. He only heard that Victoria was in Melbourne. Nearby.

Fortunately, Maira didn't stay long because her baby began to grizzle. Blair stirred himself into action the moment she left. He must see her. Clean himself up. Feeling heavy and confused, he mastered his shaky hands enough to shave, only cutting himself twice. He managed a token wash, found his least soiled shirt and a dusty suit he had not worn in ages.

For once, his heart hammered with expectation, not drugs. He panicked when his foggy brain failed him and he couldn't remember her address. So he told the hansom cab driver to travel up and down Collins Street until he recognised Dr. Grantham's residence.

Unsteady on his feet and sick with hunger for he only randomly ate, yet fuelled with the expectation of seeing his lovely Victoria again, he stumbled from the cab. He was admitted by a maid who cast a critical eye over him from head to foot but led him upstairs despite a scowl of disapproval. He probably only passed scrutiny because he announced he was a Penross.

Appearing unexpectedly in the doorway, Blair glimpsed Victoria's serene glowing beauty in the moment before she turned.

She gasped and a hand flew instinctively to her throat. 'Blair. I thought-'

Shocked to see him again, Victoria clutched the back of a chair and motioned for him to sit down.

He refused and moved closer. 'You are well?'

His concern emerged husky and he cleared his throat. The bloom of motherhood made her glow even more radiantly than ever. His heart ached for her. He would never heal. The curse of it almost made him weep.

She nodded and frowned. 'But you are not. What have you done to yourself?'

He waved a dismissive hand. 'Where is he?'

She hesitated. 'Asleep.'

'I must see him?'

Victoria stilled, growing pale, his request clearly unexpected. Without a word, she led him to the nursery next door. The sleeping babe in his wicker crib rimmed with frothy white lace to match the crisp linen, covered by a soft blue rug, was undeniably in the Penross image with downy sandy hair crowning his tiny head.

Tears of misery and wonder filled Blair's eyes. He turned a silent gaze of query to Victoria standing so close beside him, her billowing gown brushing against his trousers, her rose scented perfume a teasing reminder on his faded senses. She held his gaze, read his mind and pressed a finger to her mouth.

She answered only with a briefest rise of her eyebrows.

'There is definitely a family resemblance,' he said.

'Callum is very proud of him.'

'As he should be. Always assuming he is the father,' he retorted.

Victoria's lovely blue eyes glittered with tears and she whispered. 'You must leave before father sees you.'

She spun about and strode into the hall. 'Mary.' She summoned a maid. 'Mr. Penross is leaving.'

He reached out for her but she retreated. He smarted from the rejection and, in his humiliation, did not look back as he descended the stairs.

So he did not see his love bury her face in her hands and weep.

CHAPTER 14

It was only weeks later when the landlady, Mrs. Wilson, found Blair after he did not appear for the second day. Mrs. Green and her lovely elegant mother, Isabelle Penross, paid her an extra sum to check on him. With two small babes and having to travel by horse omnibus from Collingwood, she knew the young sister could not always visit daily and the mother lived up country.

When the telegraph reached Kooringal, as was the custom in the house unless he was absent, it was delivered to Duncan first. When he wordlessly stepped into the morning room, his face stricken and held out the missive for Isabelle, she was instantly alert to his appearance because he rarely interrupted her and when he did, discreetly knocked. She read it in astonishment.

Her heart went cold and she gripped the arm of her chair tighter.

Horrified, the parents stared at each other in silence, unable to speak. How had it come to this, Isabelle anguished? And wondered if Duncan accepted any responsibility or blame at all as she did for this deplorable tragedy.

Her first thought after the initial shock was the difficulty of not only informing Callum of his brother's death and all the family but Victoria whom she suspected still held Blair most dear. Isabelle offered to tell them both.

Duncan seemed relieved and buried himself in his study writing telegraphs and letters to other family members.

Callum was out on the property and a servant sent to fetch him back to the house. Isabelle anxiously paced awaiting

Victoria's appearance downstairs.

Too soon, her daughter in law breezed graciously into the morning room.

'Ah, Victoria.' Isabelle managed a wan smile.

'Mother?' For that is what she had chosen to call her in the absence of her own, and Isabelle had been touched. 'You sent for me?'

'Sit down Victoria. I have sad news so prepare yourself.'

Her frown and stiffened posture told Isabelle she was ready but who was ever prepared to handle news of such a young and sudden death, especially with the chance of deeper affections involved?

Gently, Isabelle told her. Victoria first cried out in shock then gasped as if choking and fainted. Maids were called to help Isabelle revive her. Callum arrived, was swiftly told, thrusting aside his own astonishment and grief to carry his wife upstairs.

The staff were discreetly informed and Isabelle left alone with her sorrow. She wanted to believe Blair's passing was accidental and clung to her conviction.

To keep occupied until the family arrived and because it was to her true love that she always instinctively turned these days, Isabelle wrote to Luca. She expected Blair would have a private family burial but she needed him to know, pouring out her heart and sadness. She wept as she wrote, finding the process cleansing, though her pain and guilt ran deep.

In Melbourne, William Green and their maid stayed with the boys while a weeping Maira rushed around to Nichola, dry eyed and stiff.

Because a distraught Maira was unable and refused and the insensitive landlady insisted she needed Blair's rooms vacated immediately, Nichola and a male servant retrieved his most personal belongings. She silently moaned at the bother until she found a diamond ring nestled in its velvet box. The sharp truth of its meaning and hidden sadness hit her with unexpected anger at the futility of her brother's death.

'Do keep the rest, Mrs. Wilson,' Nichola snapped tartly as the woman hovered.

'Thank you, Ma'am. That'll be most helpful.'

Nichola shook her head in disgust, pushed past her and left. It had been such a shock to see the ring and all it symbolised as well as to finally see Blair's repellent living accommodation, not to mention the landlady's galling greed amid the family's grief.

Soon after receiving the appalling news, Duncan and Isabelle were forced to discuss Blair's burial. Nichola had already dealt with initial formalities for which Isabelle blessed her daughter's strength and foresight cancelling the need for either she or Duncan to travel to Melbourne.

'He will be brought back to Kooringal, of course.' Isabelle quietly assumed.

'He will not!' Duncan bellowed.

'On the contrary,' Isabelle glared, daring him to disagree, trembling with anger. 'he is my son, too. I bore him and he *will* be buried here with his brother and sister. You may or may not choose to attend,' she rasped bitterly before sweeping from the room.

Although the homestead gradually filled with all the family as they journeyed home in pilgrimage for the funeral, the vast rooms of the grand mansion did not echo with noise or laughter. Conversations were muted, tea and meals taken almost in silence with only a vague murmured comment here and there.

Duncan and Victoria rarely appeared but for vastly different reasons so William Green's company passed unremarked, his presence vital for Maira remained deeply distressed. Nichola demanded her sons' attendance of the Morgan's through Elliott. They were sent over immediately from Castle Hill but Elliott's offer to accompany them refused.

Nichola's happiness at seeing Adam, Darcy and Andrew again was a conflict with the sombre mood of the house, difficult to watch but politely sanctioned because the family knew such visitations were rare. To her credit, Nichola took them outdoors where boisterous young boys much preferred to be at their age.

Duncan, mostly locked in his study, made an occasional appearance among his family, his only interest shown for his grandson, Christian.

For Isabelle, a more worrying mood was developing in her husband. Not anger as she might have expected but a sinister melancholy foreign to his dynamic personality.

The funeral of Blair Penross took place, perhaps significantly for the occasion, in light drizzling rain that soaked into everything, trickled off hats and bonnets and down necks, pattered on umbrellas, casting an even deeper gloom over the proceedings.

Blair's mud-slicked open grave gaped wide, mocking, testing emotions and the reality of life. In order to survive and remain controlled, Isabelle averted her gaze, staring instead toward darling Beatrice's headstone, remembering her curly haired daughter loaned to her for such a short time. *Watch out for them, Lord, please,* she silently prayed, including little Duncan in her thoughts and Blair today most of all.

William comforted Maira, shaking with grief. Victoria openly sobbed and Callum sought Owen's help later in supporting her back to the house. Duncan stood apart, hunched in disappointment.

Close to collapse but quietly watched by Owen at her side, Isabelle refused to crumble. Such moments she had already known in private. The black clothes and dismal drenching day only added to the emotional weight of a son and brother's loss for everyone.

Within months, Duncan's thick sandy hair bleached white overnight and he wallowed in solitude in his study. Isabelle tortured herself with personal blame, horrified that their son had been so lost. Her days became a ritual of remorseful questions for which she had no answers. Callum was saved by his work and Victoria pined. But for Christian over whom she doted and fussed, she might have surrendered altogether. Her personal suffering was survived by the rigorous activity of supervising the garden extensions but Isabelle found her weeping on her knees as she planted seedlings for spring and summer one day. In silent understanding, she squeezed her shoulder and moved on.

For a long while, a shadowed air descended over the house.

The following year slowly brought more happiness and new arrivals into the family reminding them all that life was continuing around them. Sarah and Alex wrote from the west of the bittersweet addition of Blair Penross Junior to their family, and William and Maira welcomed Pippa, their dark haired first daughter and third child.

But the joys for Isabelle were tempered by Duncan's unaccountable malaise. It seemed impossible that such a powerful vibrant man who built an empire should show signs of rapid physical decline. The evidence was clear and distressing. He had no purpose and sank into depression. Isabelle panicked. He seemed to have lost all fight and all interest in his lands yet he was not an old man. Barely in his sixties.

She drew aside the morning room curtains to watch him, grieved and frustrated when he just sat out there on the veranda like that, rejecting the cause as Blair's death although the coincidence was undeniable.

Duncan's purpose and drive appeared to have died with his son leading Isabelle to realise that Duncan had probably never given up hope that Blair might one day return.

As was her habit these days, Isabelle wandered out to join him as he watched their muster of peacocks haughtily fanning out their magnificent tails and quivering them high or dragging them behind across the grass. Flaunting their showy beauty. Duncan had once been as proud.

Today in a rare show of inclination, he began to talk. His murmured reminiscences brought a lump to Isabelle's throat, surprised to find herself so touched and upset. So much life lived. Memories of distant yesterdays. What had it all been for?

Duncan squinted against the sharp morning light. 'Thirty thousand acres,' he muttered, 'and as many sheep and lambs to be shorn. Ah expect there'll be a good seventy thousand pounds of washed wool from it.'

And many thousands of pounds profit, Isabelle knew. With Duncan's emotional slump, his involvement in running his stations had decreased. Callum reported to him daily and checked the rain gauge but, for the first time in over thirty years, control of his empire was slowly slipping from his grasp. A circumstance Isabelle had never considered she would see.

Since Duncan no longer worked on the accounts and ledgers, Callum kept his mother informed of business matters and the prosperity of Kooringal and Lakeham. Perhaps wrongly assuming Duncan had always done so. The stations, she learned, were valued at over a quarter of a million pounds. Each.

Tea was summoned and brought for them. Magpies warbled and quarrelled in the trees. Parrots screeched and made havoc with the fruit thick on sagging branches in the orchard following early spring's froth of blossom. The distant sound of bleating sheep and barking dogs drifted to them.

Callum was out there somewhere on horseback, issuing instructions, working with the men as the intense and important ritual of annual shearing was once again under way. The sounds that had once driven Duncan on now lulled him to sleep.

Victoria, bless her, difficult as it was amid her private desolation over Blair's death, took turns to sit with him and relieve Isabelle. It seemed appropriate when they had each separately shared a hope in Blair that never eventuated. Isabelle prayed Victoria's company would help Duncan recover.

Isabelle, often restless, prowled the homestead alone at night sick with worry. The urgency of Duncan's condition over recent months was not yet critical but slow and significant. With an unwelcome intuition, she secretly contacted each of their children believing they deserved to be told. A telegraph to Christie at her last known hotel address in Europe, aware that she always arranged for her mail to be forwarded on, and Alexander in the west.

Sarah responded and wrote a long newsy letter.

I love spring the most for the wildflowers. Wilgorup is all green grass and red dirt then. The Kennedy ranges are purple hills from a distance but are red and rocky up close.

There's always lots of wildlife about. Galahs, emus and red roos mainly. And all the usual ground creatures like snakes, lizards and goannas. The natives think nothing of eating them.

It takes a few days for us to travel in the wagon to the coast but Alexander

Here, Isabelle paused to smile that Sarah always used his full name.

likes us to go each summer with the children for a holiday. He fishes, the boys paddle in the sea and we eat prawns.

Shark Bay is all red sand dunes, cliffs and white beaches. Carnarvon where the Gascoyne River flows out into the sea is the port for shipping livestock and wool. The streets are wide enough for wool wagons and camel teams that they use up here because they survive in the desert.

They also dive for pearls in Shark Bay. Alexander says when we can afford it, he will buy me some one day. I should feel quite like royalty if he ever did that. I don't need riches, as long as I have Alexander and our children.

Emma is seven now, David is four and I am teaching them letters and numbers as best I can.

Baby Blair is a sweet blessing to us and Alexander is so proud. I can hardly believe we are married over five years already. The west

No mention was made of returning although it would only be a week's journey for them by boat down to Fremantle then another coastal steamer east to Geelong.

It was much longer before Isabelle heard from Christie and Caroline, who pointed out the reality of the long three month voyage home. Was it urgent? She telegraphed by return a simple *Yes*.

Within another week she received confirmation that they had booked passage on the clipper Lincolnshire to sail from London in early December. Isabelle could only pray they experienced fine sailing and a speedy passage but knew their voyage was dependant on winds. It might be three months before they arrived. She looked forward to seeing her adventurous daughter again.

Nichola, as Isabelle expected, knowing her history with Duncan, refused to come. 'Keep me informed,' she wrote.

Owen was also notified at school of his father's poor health but within the lines of her usual regular letters to him. Maira, in a long letter of apology and explanation, reserved her decision to return.

Isabelle's private fear was that Duncan would not rally. He rarely wrote to anyone these days so he must have lost touch with his Mrs. Herrington surely? Ironically, when he no doubt preferred her at his side. According to Nichola, the woman still lived at the same address but their contact seemed to have lapsed.

'May I send for a doctor?' Isabelle asked Duncan one day.

'Waste of time,' came the growling predictable reply. 'Ah know ma fate.'

Isabelle stifled her alarm. 'Nonsense. It's been years since you had a check-up. It can't hurt. We're all growing older.'

Isabelle frowned at his gloom, squinting a glance out across the lake and park like gardens that rolled down to the river. When the walled garden was complete, her beloved view of their first cottage would disappear.

'Wasn't a doctor to be seen in the early days,' he reflected. 'Nothing but the blacks, silence and trees. Port Phillip was all grassy plains and solitude. You could ride forever and come to nothing.'

'You've done well with your life, Duncan. You should be proud,' she said generously.

But was he, she wondered?

'It takes effort to leave your home land and all that ye know for a place where no one knows or cares about ye.'

Isabelle nodded. 'I know. I did it, too, remember?'

'Aye,' he murmured then, after a pause, admitted quietly, 'ah'll never believe Blair is gone.'

Isabelle thought she had misheard, amazed that he had finally spoken of him.

'He had every opportunity but no backbone,' he added bitterly. 'Nichola's a disgrace neglecting her family. Maira married without ma permission,' he grumbled.

'It doesn't matter now. Regrets are pointless She has three beautiful children, is immeasurably happy and that is all any of us can hope for.'

'Ah envy Alex his adventures and ah'll likely not see Christie again.' His voice trailed off.

Isabelle decided to tell him. 'Actually, I've just had word she and Caroline may return home. For a while at least I suppose before they're off again.' She held her breath while the news sank in. 'Of course, she didn't say for how long.'

He snapped a sharp knowing glance at her. 'Callum and Owen will manage things together,' Duncan muttered. 'At least Callum has a son.'

There was nothing wrong with daughters, Isabelle bit back an impatient retort. Dear little golden haired Christian was toddling about the nursery already. Duncan's hope for the future. The next generation to come. Sometimes Victoria brought the child downstairs to sit on her knee when she kept

Duncan company, the boy sharply watched by his grandfather.

Spring ended and summer passed.

In the late evening twilight one day, Duncan said simply, 'Ah've not made ye truly happy.'

'I've had a comfortable life with you. More than I ever would have dreamed or expected of my new life out here in Australia.'

He cast her a lingering glance. 'It's not too late for ye to find a man who can give ye what I couldn't.'

Isabelle froze. Did he know? 'At my age?' she scoffed and felt herself blush.

'Duke's provided for,' he said after a while.

She nodded stiffly.

To Isabelle's deepest relief, Christie and Caroline arrived home in the middle of March and Callum accompanied her to Melbourne to meet them when the Lincolnshire docked at Sandridge railway pier to unload her passengers and cargo.

'Mother!'

Isabelle beamed and opened her arms to enfold her thriving energetic daughter. Caroline spared brief greetings before being embraced and spirited away by her own family. She was to remain in town with them for a time but planned a lengthy visit to Kooringal in the near future.

'Callum.' Christie enthusiastically hugged her brother. 'A married man now. I cannot wait to meet your wife and son.'

He laughed with flattery and pride. 'It will be my pleasure to introduce them.'

Isabelle briefly wondered as Christie grew older if she would ever regret her choice to remain single and not seek a spouse.

'We were on the Mediterranean when I received your telegraph, Mother. How is he?'

Isabelle marvelled at her mature confident daughter so full of energy, now twenty five and flourishing.

She shook her head. 'Poorly. He has given up since Blair's

death.' Isabelle frowned. 'Your father was always a strong man. A fighter. I don't understand it.'

They linked arms as they walked back along the pier to their waiting carriage whilst Callum attended to their baggage.

More interested in her surroundings, Christie made no comment about her father. Instead she glanced avidly about as they strode. 'Goodness, so much has changed. The port is so busy.'

Isabelle sighed. Had time and distance caused this casual air in her daughter or had it always existed? In the excitement of youth and travel, naturally she would have much to tell them. Perhaps it was fate that Christie should breeze back into their lives and help them forget their troubles for a while. Until she actually saw Duncan, his drooped shoulders, hollow eyed gaze and shrunken physique, the reality of her father's health would not register.

'Yes, our state of Victoria has grown.'

When they reached the carriage, Callum helped them up. At least he was able to assist his mother. Christie leapt aboard herself. Such vigour and independence. Isabelle noticed she wore a tailored divided skirt. No more the lady now than when she had left years before. She shook her head and grinned to herself. Christie was healthy and home. All that mattered.

They stayed overnight at the Menzies Hotel. Maira, William and the children joined them later to a warm siblings reunion.

Christie enthused over her little sister and her growing brood. 'Maira married, too. My goodness, and such gorgeous children.'

She openly admired and nursed baby Pippa. The squirming Ben and Joshua, although well mannered, were harder to keep still and entertain. She stood back and surveyed William, overwhelmed by the whirlwind Christie, amused by Maira's perfect choice of educated gentleman whose quiet sense of humour always shone through.

The lively party departed the hotel for a grand dinner at Nichola's townhouse. Throughout the sumptuous meal, Isabelle observed her adult children.

All seemed accepting and independent, not judgemental of one another and felt relieved to see no visible rivalry or competition among them. Each appeared comfortable in themselves. She sat contentedly and listened to their chatter. Maira and Callum boasting of their children, Christie regaling them all with her travel tales and moaning about the long voyage back to Australia.

'Can you believe we left London on the tenth of December? From Plymouth to Port Phillip it took almost ninety tedious days and there weren't many cabin passengers either. One was a doctor and there were a couple of other young ladies, sisters travelling together. We had nothing but fickle weather and continuous light winds.'

Even her frustration sounded exciting. 'We didn't make the equator until the middle of January. And the Southern Ocean.' She threw up her hands. 'Well, I will only say calms, fog and constant rain. As if that wasn't bad enough, coming around Otway the weather turned even more thick and dirty so we couldn't anchor until Saturday night. We were both so pleased to be on dry land again. By comparison it only takes about eight days now to sail from New York to Southampton. Everything is so much closer over there,' she enthused. 'Australia is so far away. We're thinking of some time in the Orient next.'

'How long are you home?' Maira innocently asked.

Christie flashed a quick glance toward her mother, concealed the truth and said brightly, 'Oh, I have no idea. We've not made any definite plans. I'm looking forward to just being home for a while.'

Later, when the children were settled to sleep upstairs and supervised by a maid, Christie entertained them further.

'America is wonderful and so huge. The west is pioneer country but the east coast much more civilised although

Caroline and I don't mind a bit of adventure.'

'Where did you go when you left Australia?' Maira asked.

'My goodness, I can scarcely remember.' She reflected for a moment. 'We left from Sydney after taking a coastal steamer then headed to Auckland in New Zealand.' She frowned. 'Then I think we connected with a ship to Honolulu. Now, there's a magical paradise. Very warm but beautiful. So exotic. And reached America at San Francisco.' She waved an arm about. 'Celestials everywhere, of course, after the gold rush. Much like here really.'

She ploughed on, hardly drawing breath while Nichola's maid served tea and cakes, but the captivated faces in the room revealed a fascinated audience. Isabelle looked around but didn't believe any of her other offspring were envious of their sister's freedom and nomadic lifestyle, except perhaps Nichola watching with particular interest. She wondered if, after hearing Christie's stories, her oldest daughter might be tempted to venture beyond Australia herself.

'After San Francisco – goodness that seems so long ago,' she added, 'we travelled right across America by rail. It's connected from coast to coast. Marvellous. So much to see. The Central Pacific Railway through the Sierra Nevada Mountains starts in Sacramento. Hundreds of miles of track built by the Chinese. It connects with the Union Pacific across the Territories. Nebraska, Colorado, Wyoming, Utah and the Missouri River. Of course we stopped along the way for days or weeks at a time. The western railroads join up with the central and eastern states. We loved New York. So civilised. For a while,' she grinned, 'but the less travelled places are far more exciting.'

'Do you never get lonely?' Maira asked, the only one who seemed to be plying her sister with questions.

'My goodness,' Christie laughed, 'not travelling with Caroline. She may seem sedate but don't be fooled. She's enormous fun.'

The evening grew late before they knew it.

'Christie and Callum, we really must go.' Isabelle checked the delicate mantel clock just chiming midnight and rose to leave.

William gathered up the children and a hansom cab took them back to the hotel. 'Let us know if there's any change,' Maira whispered as they left.

Back at Kooringal, Duncan patiently listened to Christie's chatter. If she felt any alarm at her father's worsening health, she did not show it. She possessed an endless supply of tales that held his attention and brought a nostalgic gleam into his eyes.

One evening, the family had all trooped downstairs as usual for dinner at seven, noisy events these days. Isabelle could never have explained why but she urged both her daughters in Melbourne to visit for the weekend. Nichola still refused but Maira, William and the children arrived.

They had scarcely finished dessert when a distressed maid entered and whispered to Isabelle. She vaulted from her chair and fled upstairs to Duncan's room.

'I just brought up his tea tray, Ma'am,' Jane said, trembling, 'and found him.'

Duncan Penross, family elder, bold adventurous Scotsman who had ambitiously carved the empire of his dreams, lay slumped in his bed. Isabelle tentatively stepped forward and felt his pulse but the open staring eyes and stillness were undeniable. She sat on the bed beside him, dazed and empty.

The life of Duncan Penross was over.

'Jane, send for the doctor,' Isabelle instructed gently.

'Yes, Ma'am.' The maid stifled a sob, dropped a quick half curtsy and scurried from the room.

How ironic and regrettable, Isabelle thought, left alone for a few brief private moments with her dead husband that a once vital and powerful man had slipped so quietly from life. She reached out, closed his eyes and held his hands.

Callum, emerging as the family's steady strength, was the first to rush in to join her, an anxious Victoria and Christie close behind. At their silent query, Isabelle shook her head, her eyes pooled with tears finally released in helpless surprise that what she had feared most had actually come to pass.

Victoria openly cried beside him, a kerchief pressed to her mouth to muffle the depths of her distress, Callum's comforting arm about her shoulder. Still incredulous, too, Isabelle shook with soft weeping and combed her fingers gently through Duncan's thick head of white hair, the curls still as strong and springy to the touch as in his youth.

'I don't understand it.' She moaned. 'Why did he give in? He had so much to live for.' She excluded herself.

'Mother.' Christie stepped forward and laid a firm hand on her shoulder.

'It was not like him,' she persisted.

'Mother, it's over. He's gone. This won't help you,' she said sensibly.

Isabelle took a deep breath to compose her disbelief and frustration, and rose from the bed. Maira and William had appeared and stood calm and respectful together.

Isabelle hugged each of her children. 'Go to him if you wish. Say goodbye.'

Maira moved forward and knelt at the bedside, bent her head and closed her eyes in prayer. How odd, Isabelle thought, that despite her own strong faith, that was an act she had not instinctively performed for her husband. Maybe in church.

'Callum,' she murmured, 'send a telegraph to Owen and Nichola. Surely she will come home now. Insist she return as soon as possible and arrange they travel back together. And Alex, of course. He must be told.'

As she passed Victoria, they reached out for each other and embraced. It felt so good to be just held, Isabelle thought. Comforted.

Duncan Penross had been a hard man, not easily given to show compassion but she had once loved him and his family cared, each to a greater or lesser depth for the life lived but now past. Nichola not at all, probably. Victoria much more so.

As the homestead plunged into mourning, Isabelle retreated to her room. Maira and Callum each had their spouses for comfort. It was a composed Christie who tapped on her door and with whom she talked and wept well into the night until candles and lamps burned low. Who learned the unknown secrets and discovered the truths and successes of her father's life that Isabelle finally felt able and compelled to share.

Who patiently listened and rang down for another tea tray to be sent up or the crystal spirit decanter to be refilled while her mother unburdened a lifetime of confidences. Her voice murmured through the still small hours of early morning but time meant nothing. Neither Christie nor Isabelle sought sleep.

'I feel a traitor,' Isabelle finally admitted, 'to have my husband barely gone from this life and all I crave is the arms of another man to hold me.'

'But as you've said, father also loved another, too. How can a person know and guarantee when they fall in love that their affections will last? I've never felt the need for marriage. Not even the mildest inclination.'

Isabelle so admired her attractive and forthright daughter clad always in simple basic clothes, so fit and strong. She reached out and covered her hand with her own.

'If you are happy and that is how you wish your life to be, then it is right. Some of us stumble onto our path through life, some feel compelled or obliged to take a certain direction. For most of us, I believe our course is fated, predestined if you like. Life simply carries us along and we flow with it. Others have strong inclinations and forge their way, setting it on a certain bearing, steering it to their will. Duncan was one of those, of course. A leader. When I fell in love with him I became his follower.' She paused. 'For a while.'

'Father was harsh and ruthless. We all saw that but you've never given the impression that you regret any of it.'

'Oh my dear, how can I? I have all of you, my beautiful

children. And now grandchildren. And this magnificent home.'

A silence of contemplation fell between them for a while broken only by the gentle ticking of the mantel clock or the rustle of settling embers in the fireplace.

'Life will change for us all now with father's passing,' Christie said. 'I don't believe any of us realise yet just how much. He was a strong force. Whether we admit it or not, he will be missed.'

'Very much,' Isabelle whispered, regarding her daughter with fresh admiration. Such an observant young woman. 'We can't begin to imagine. It will be the little things. It's almost the end of an era. So many of Duncan's early squatting chums are gone now, too. The next generation is taking over but life will go on and I'm sure all you young ones will see as many changes in your own lifetime as we did.'

Isabelle suddenly grew weary. 'Callum is arranging an undertaker from Geelong and he suggested a specialist cabinet maker in Meredith to make the coffin.' She stared into the fire, finally drowsy as much from the brandy as lack of sleep. She closed her eyes and murmured, 'Frankly I would be content with a private family burial but Duncan was a district pioneer who acquired a vast circle of friends and he deserves a fitting farewell. The church service in Meredith and public funeral will allow everyone to pay their respects.'

'He'd like that,' Christie agreed.

Afterwards Isabelle remembered little, felt a blanket tucked around her and fell asleep.

The funeral of Duncan Penross was aptly grand. The small church overflowed and afterward a dusty procession of carriages and buggies and riders followed the tall black hearse on its passenger's last journey home.

Two obedient and stately black horses trimmed with plumes stepped out a few paces behind the distinguished undertaker walking in front. Lean and dignified, the tails of his long coat swinging about his knees, a thick head of snow white hair and full beard a contrast to the otherwise sombre colour of the day.

The restrained service in the family graveyard was deeply reverent and subdued, although Duncan had never embraced religion as part of his life, and followed by bountiful Penross hospitality in the homestead.

In the following days, Isabelle remained dispirited. The family stayed on, none of them in a hurry to break up the assembly. Only William was obliged to return to his teaching duties in Melbourne. With all the homestead bedrooms full, the servants were kept busy.

The contents of Duncan's will, imparted by his Melbourne lawyer before them all in the morning room during a brief visit, bore no surprises. Isabelle was maintained for life at Kooringal and also received a generous separate bequest. She blanched at the sum but sent up a prayer of thanks that it would enable her to be independent for life.

His daughters received equal and substantial legacies making them all wealthy women. Maira wept at the announcement. Why could Duncan not have been this generous of himself in life, Isabelle wondered?

His sons inherited his lands. For now, it was decided that Alex should receive an annual income from the two stations but if they were ever sold, he would receive an equal share of the proceeds. Isabelle prayed that day never came. Duncan would writhe in his grave to know the properties had passed out of Penross family hands.

Callum and Owen now jointly took control of managing their birthright on behalf of the family.

Isabelle was content and satisfied that her children, especially her daughters, had inherited fairly. She had given no thought to Duncan's estate beforehand, caught up in her shock and realisation of what was to come, and still found it impossible to believe that he was gone. Such a powerful force of a man would not soon or easily be forgotten.

As she slowly grew more reconciled to her changed

situation without him over the following weeks, Isabelle wrote to his family in Scotland.

Because it raised her spirits in the disrupted aftermath of his passing, she had taken to exercising one or two of his favourite Collies who romped about her or disappeared, always to return if she whistled or called as she strode downhill toward the river or across the paddocks among the sheep or further afield into the bush.

This morning, she paused at the lake's edge to appreciate the beautiful native black swans gliding across the still surface, rippling the clear reflections at its edges as they passed. Her gaze drifted idly beyond, surveying all that Duncan had built, contemplating the native's belief that after death, the spirit returned to nature. She smiled gently. Duncan would like that. Maybe his spirit even now was in the breeze that rustled the crisp autumn leaves changing colour.

A movement in her side vision in the direction of the rise and family graveyard caught her attention. Someone was up there. She frowned and for a moment her instinct was to head that way. As far as she knew since it was yet early, the family was still indoors. If Christie was outdoors she would be riding far away from the house.

From this distance as she squinted and shaded her eyes, Isabelle detected an elderly woman helped down from a small buggy by a thin middle aged man. Her clothes were fine cut and her grey hair piled elegantly on her head. She wore no hat but carried a large bunch of flowers.

Who?

Catching sight of Isabelle staring back, the woman's glance levelled directly at her. Almost in defiance. Then she turned dismissively away and Isabelle knew. Mrs. Herrington. She had not attended nor would have been welcome at Duncan's funeral.

After all these years, she was to set eyes upon the woman Duncan had preferred all his life. She stood paralysed with irritation.

The nerve of the woman! How dare she trespass on private property!

She watched, transfixed and resentful as the woman bent to place flowers on Duncan's fresh grave, the headstone yet to be carved. Isabelle felt like a voyeur imposing on her privacy as the woman sank to her knees and the male companion laid a hand on her shoulder. Annoyingly, Isabelle understood her grief. She tried to imagine losing Luca and was gripped by anguish. So soon after Blair and Duncan's deaths, it did not bear contemplation.

She called to the dogs and set off in the opposite direction. When she returned to the homestead, she glanced across to the family cemetery but their visitor was gone.

Isabelle strode into her morning room and settled at her bureau, delaying breakfast. The long walk had cleared her mind and she no longer remained indecisive. She withdrew a sheet of her own personalised crisp cream parchment and, ignoring any codes of acceptable etiquette about the short time since Duncan's death, wrote

My darling Luca, I am free. Please come for me. I love you.
Your Isabelle.

CHAPTER 15

Katarina had attended Duncan's funeral representing the family, Luca discreetly absent, so she had not seen him for many weeks. Oh how dearly she missed him. Her only fear was that he might be daunted by her social position and wealth but he knew the woman she was at heart and how much she loved him. Surely he would come? She would know no peace until he arrived or replied.

Sarah wrote with their condolences from the west. They were so far away, Isabelle sighed.

Within days, Luca responded to her plea and invitation. When he arrived, to those of the family still in residence, she introduced him as her dearest friend. A year ago, at the time of Blair's death when the family had all gathered at Nichola's townhouse in Melbourne, she had boldly and publicly shown her affection for him.

They dined privately alone in an upstairs sitting room set up for the purpose. Isabelle wore her most feminine dress and Luca proposed as they walked in the shadowed moonlit garden later.

'Your acceptance would be my greatest happiness,' he murmured and kissed her. No longer waiting or asking permission, he swept her heart into his keeping.

'And mine, Luca. I love you. Yes!'

She was going to be properly married woman again and could not wait. They rushed indoors like a young couple half their age, flushed and joyous to announce their news. The children's polite ripple of modest congratulations released some of the sadness from the house but none of them seemed really surprised.

In the weeks before their marriage, Isabelle and Luca travelled to the coast and found a home together. Although entitled, she did not wish to live any longer at Kooringal, Duncan's masterpiece. As Isabelle had hoped and Luca eagerly agreed, they found a large timber home in Queenscliff with a full veranda and far too many bedrooms. Therefore perfect for the family to visit. She dearly hoped it was often, that the thriving seaside resort where grand hotels were being planned and built would encourage them all to come and share their mother's home.

After a small circumspect announcement in the Geelong Advertiser, the widow, Isabelle Penross, and widower, Luca Perini, were quietly married in a private ceremony before family and close friends in the Wesleyan Chapel in Yarra Street. Both felt the need to make their vows before God who had always been an important part of their lives. Neither cared nor heeded any gossip over their hasty nuptials. They were too caught up in their own happiness.

As the blissful older couple held hands and were pronounced man and wife, the groom leant forward and lovingly kissed his bride. Of late, he tended to take any opportunity but this moment in public was his proudest.

Outside the church, the family hugged and kissed them, Katarina beaming with contentment at her father's renewed pleasure in life. Although she tried to hide it, Isabelle worried for her dear friend and step-daughter. Such a beautiful gracious woman did not deserve to be alone. Perhaps one day.

Isabelle and Luca had time only for brief farewells before taking the train to Melbourne to board the vessel Otway for Fremantle then a coastal steamer north to visit Alex, Sarah and the children.

Only days before, leaving Kooringal with Luca beside her in the carriage, their bags taken on ahead by buggy to Meredith station, Isabelle had asked him to detour past the family graveyard. She did not step down but when he reined in the horses, she nodded respectfully toward a headstone.

'Rest peacefully, Duncan,' she murmured with a hand on her heart valiantly struggling with tears despite her renewed happiness.

She said a silent goodbye to her three children. Little Duncan, Beatrice and Blair. She would be back to visit but, for now, she glanced skyward and smiled knowing they were safe and looking down to share in the lives of their mother and brothers and sisters.

Now, nestled comfortably close to her husband, who ably took up the reins again, she turned and waved to all the people most dear to her in the world. She eagerly anticipated seeing Alex and Sarah again, seeing how Emma would have grown, and meeting her grandsons David and little Blair Junior for the first time. And of course her pride when she introduced Luca to them all.

With shining eyes, a blissful Maira had whispered to her mother before she left for the west that she was expecting her fourth child and, in the light of her inheritance, had recklessly engaged a nanny and maid. Isabelle had hidden a smile and warmly hugged her. Eventually she learnt that William and Maira had used a further portion of her legacy to purchase a modest larger home in a more open and greener suburb of Melbourne away from the long rows of workers' cottages in Collingwood.

Months later, a most pregnant Victoria Penross and her sister-in-law, Nichola Morgan, strolled the grounds of Kooringal homestead. They walked through the Gothic arched gateway into the completed walled garden.

Victoria sighed. 'There is nothing more satisfying than plunging one's hands into the soil. I do love colour,' she enthused.

'I can see.' Nichola openly praised all the new border plantings and roses, the tendrils of young wisteria and honeysuckle already groping their way up the warm red brick walls and edging higher to the top from where they would eventually spill their greenery and blooms. 'It's been much work. And in your condition.'

Victoria smiled. 'We have plenty of staff but I gain so much pleasure from it. Each season is its own reward. I find myself constantly sneaking outdoors to see what's new,' she confessed. 'If a bud has opened since yesterday or if there are new shoots on a particular shrub. Perhaps a bulb has pushed its first green shoot through the earth.'

The women ambled further along the neatly gravelled pathways, past the fountain in the centre with its relaxing sound of trickling water gently cascading over the stone urn on its carved pedestal base into the bowl and finally overflowing into a pond beneath. Smooth green swathes of mown grass stretched between the beds with garden seats strategically placed under young trees for the view.

Victoria sighed and turned to her sister in law. 'May I confide in you?'

'Of course.'

'I believe you and I are of the same mind,' she confided. 'I am becoming so weary as my babe grows,' she placed a hand gently on her body, 'and exasperated with all the management of the household and staff. Mother-in-law was so capable but since she has left, I confess I'm growing more frustrated every day.'

'Why is that?'

'I had thought I should be quite proud to run my own home one day, especially one as grand as Kooringal,' she glanced back through the open arch in the direction of the house, 'but I'm finding it tedious. Supplies and accounts and ledgers. I had no idea the amount of bookwork involved. My head quite spins.' She lowered her voice confidentially. 'Father always despaired that I could never master numbers. Mother-in-law gave me guidance before she left, of course, but I fear I am simply useless. I shall disappoint Callum. He expects me to manage but I am a failure.'

'My goodness, don't upset yourself. Can I help in some way? I have handled my own household accounts in Melbourne now for many years.'

Victoria's lovely clear blue eyes widened and she leapt at the offer. 'Oh, would you? It takes so much time.'

Nichola chuckled. 'True. I find I must devote a certain number of hours each week to the task.'

'Perhaps we could share?' Victoria ventured. 'Now that you have sold your townhouse in Melbourne and bought that beautiful home in Geelong and you visit Kooringal so often, I did hope that you might spare me further instruction.'

'I should be flattered.'

Nichola laughed, a rare emotion in times past but, with Adam and Darcy attending Geelong Grammar and her improving relationship with them now they were older, she had seized the opportunity to relocate.

With both women being refined and feminine ladies, Victoria had become a cherished friend and the first woman of a similar age with whom she felt comfortable and not threatened in any way. Strange when her habits were so focused in the country and Nichola still preferred a wide social life.

She had lost none of her mischievous flirtation with men and even embarked, albeit rarely, on an intimate liaison if the particular gentleman met her stringent standards.

Regardless, and sadly only since her father had died, Nichola felt able once more to think of Kooringal as her second home. Callum and Victoria had made her welcome and begged all the family to share the huge homestead with them, insisting it was to remain so for everyone. Perhaps in the years to come, Nichola contemplated, the situation might change but, for now, they all took advantage.

'I'm halfway between Queenscliff and Kooringal so it is ideal and with the new railway line extended down there, it is most convenient,' she agreed. 'The boys stay with me often. My darling Andrew will be at school there within two years.

My older sons are almost young men. I'm hoping when mother returns that she will allow me to visit with them in the holidays over summer. They love the seaside.' She frowned. 'Elliott talks of sending them away to England eventually but I shall resist it strongly.'

'Education is improving here all the time,' Victoria said. 'One wonders if there will always be such a need to send our children so far away. Speaking of education, Maira's William has been promoted I hear. Headmaster now no less.'

'He seems a natural with children, both as a teacher and with his own. Its his warmth, I expect. He is so conscientious and extremely conservative but he suits Maira perfectly and, in his profession, his character will always serve him well.'

'Maira loves the country but is so devoted to William she will always be at his side wherever that leads.'

'She will return often to Kooringal I'm sure. Her spirited brood thrive out here in the country although little Pippa is a quiet sweetie, isn't she? And their number is about to increase again.' Nichola flashed her sister-in-law a knowing look.

'Yes, she is due later in the year with her fourth. I envy her,' Victoria sighed. 'She sails through each confinement. It takes me so long to conceive, Callum and I had almost given up hope that we should be able to have another. And when I am so ill, I wish it was over already. Another reason for my struggles of late. I was beginning to feel quite overwhelmed with all that is expected of me and want only to do my best. So I am most grateful to you for helping out.'

'You have only ever to ask, sister-in-law.'

'I will continue to supervise the garden and grounds of course until the birth and again next year. Callum is most obliging with everything I wish to do to carry out his father's plans. He doesn't have the same degree of interest, of course, but he sees what we have already achieved and is entirely supportive.'

She spoke with true affection and cast a contented gaze about the acres of gardenscape almost complete, surrounding the homestead.

Nichola watched her closely, knowing her original fondness had been for Blair. It seemed she had accepted her substitute marriage and grown feelings for Callum, a companion to him in every way. Nichola was pleased for he had always been the most diligent and attentive of her father's sons and natural prospect to dedicate himself to the huge load of managing the Penross lands.

As if in mutual perception, Victoria continued, 'Father-in-law had such plans for his garden. In his memory, I shall endeavour to carry out his every wish. I shall make it my life's work. After raising a family, of course,' she said quickly, as if guilty she should hold such a preference and passion for anything else.

'We all have things we prefer and love in life.' Nichola heaved a small sigh, knowing she had not yet discovered her own and wondering if she ever would. 'Christie talks of travel again. She and Caroline huddle over maps of the East.'

'Do you know,' Victoria ventured eagerly, 'I believe Owen will miss them. Have you noticed he watches Caroline closely?'

'Owen?' Nichola frowned. 'Caroline is some years younger than Christie and therefore of a similar age to him. I shall observe them with interest.'

'It is not impossible,' Victoria declared. 'Owen is a qualified lawyer now and in his own practice. Together with the Penross name, he's an admirable catch.'

'He still seems so young and I suspect he must grow in confidence before he will approach any lady. I believe his awareness will come slowly and not for some years.'

'Perfect. Meanwhile,' Victoria reasoned, 'Caroline will continue travelling but must surely tire of it one day.'

'Perhaps even Christie might settle down although she is far more adventurous of the pair and at the moment the prospect seems unlikely. She has always been so independent and will happily remain single I believe.'

'And hasn't Katarina been the sly one?' Victoria grinned.

'You mean waiting to show her hand until Luca remarried?'

Victoria nodded vigorously and leant closer, her eyes sparkling with delight. 'Since Isabelle and her father left on their journey to the west, I have heard she now encourages a certain gentleman doctor in Geelong. It seems he politely remained in the background knowing her devotion to her father.'

'Admirable,' Nichola said, 'but such a waste of so many youthful years.'

'Still, it's quite romantic. No one suspected a thing. Mother-in-law certainly never mentioned it. Sometimes,' she reflected softly, 'it is worth waiting for the right one.'

'I imagine so,' Nichola murmured in wistful envy.

Perhaps that was the basis of the friendship she and Victoria shared. In the inexperience of youth, neither had initially married for love yet her sister-in-law seemed content enough now with her second choice. Would Blair have been a different man if Victoria had accepted him? Callum adored her. Not usually given to seeking comfort in religion, she sent up a silent hopeful prayer anyway that one day she might find a special person herself and know the joy of true love, too. Surely it couldn't hurt?

'Mother looked so much younger and glowed on her wedding day, didn't she?' Nichola observed.

'Indeed. Everyone in the family is happy for them. No one would begrudge them companionship in their old age.'

Nichola smiled to herself. Her mother would disagree that, still being so youthful, her fifties could be considered old. And she would guarantee the relationship between the newlywed Mr. and Mrs. Perini would be far warmer than companionable.

They had inspected every corner of the walled garden and strolled across the lawns toward the old tree as it was known that her father had planted when the homestead was first built.

'Shall we rest while I read mother's letter now?' Nichola asked, guiding Victoria to the wooden bench seat beneath its shade. She withdrew an envelope from her skirt pocket.

'Oh yes, do. The last we heard was that brief telegraph from Fremantle that they were safely returned from staying with Alex but no other details.'

'Well, listen to this.' Nichola unfolded the pages of her mother's careful handwriting.

My dearest Nichola,

Although I have addressed this letter to you, I know you will share it with everyone for there is simply not time to write to you all separately. I do hope Maira is keeping well. We should return before her baby, another dear grandchild, is born.

Thank you for so warmly sharing in our wedding day. It is only one month ago but we are most happily and contently settled into our life together as if it has always been so.

After we said our goodbyes to you, the Otway took us across the Southern Ocean to Fremantle. We stayed some nights at the Crown and Thistle hotel in High Street and are temporarily here again before we leave for Mauritius.

'Mauritius!' Victoria gasped.

'Surprising is it not?' Nichola agreed and continued reading.

Camels and their Afghan drivers are a familiar sight through the streets. All shipping berths at the long jetty that extends out into the sea for over a mile. Cargo is offloaded there and taken down Cliff Street into the town.

Fremantle is a very busy port. A railway is presently being constructed between here and Perth but I understand it will not be completed until next year.

We took the schooner Ariel up the coast to Shark Bay. The weather even toward the end of summer was extremely warm and uncomfortable but we gained relief with some lovely sea breezes.

Our farthest stop was at Carnarvon. It is a quite beautiful region but remote and thinly populated. It is the port for the pastoral industry used by settlers for essential supplies and a centre for pearl divers from Japan and China who operate luggers off shore. The coastal steamers regularly transport loads of shells.

I confess I wept at seeing Alex again after eight years. Such a mature strong man now and his son, David, a suntanned outdoor boy, as energetic as his father.

Alex and Luca warmed to each other quickly. I was greatly pleased when he referred to my dear husband as Grandfather Perini to the children.

A long hot wagon ride took us out to his property and such joy in greeting Sarah again, too, and meeting little Blair Junior.

Their home is built of thick local bluestone with broad verandas, many rooms and quite spacious. Tell Maira that she is not the only one in the family to become a mother this year. Sarah is well advanced in her fourth confinement and, of course, hopes for a daughter. Emma is quite a young miss already, a quiet girl and help to her mother. Both Alex out on the property and Sarah in the homestead have mostly native stockmen and servants.

It was difficult after many weeks when we took our farewell from them all again.

Since returning to Fremantle we await the departure of the brig Laughing Wave for Mauritius. Fortunately, Luca speaks French which should prove of much help since that language is widely used on the island.

It is, of course, under British control now although it was originally discovered and visited by the Portuguese, colonised by the Dutch and ruled for the previous century by the French.

The present Governor is Sir George Bowen. You might remember he was previously Governor in Queensland, New Zealand and our own Victoria. Quite a coincidence, don't you think?

My darlings, it is time for dinner. I must close and see this letter onto the mail packet for Melbourne. I will write again when we are due to return.

Our love to you all, Mother and Luca

'Such a wonderful lot of news.'

Nichola smiled. 'Indeed.' She reflected for a moment. 'Life goes on for us all, it seems. Are you tiring?' She turned to Victoria with concern. 'Shall we go up now?'

They rose together and wandered slowly by the lake and back toward the homestead.

'Spring promises to be lovely, as always, but it will be summer soon enough.'

'Speaking of the weather, Callum has become quite obsessed about it. Do you know he taps that barometer every morning under the back courtyard veranda?'

'Like father used to do.'

With the passage of time, Nichola found herself able to spare a few fond memories of him.

'Exactly. Christian asked what he was doing one morning recently so of course Callum told him it was a barometer. Christian can't manage the whole word so he calls it the bomb!' Victoria laughed.

Their voices faded as they headed across the lawn leaving only the sounds of nature and animals. The distant bleating of sheep being driven from station paddocks closer to the sheds after washing carried on the frisky wind that sprang up.

It billowed the women's dresses, ran its unseen fingers through the long grasses between the headstones of the resting souls in the family cemetery on its way downhill, ruffling the peacock feathers of the birds strutting grandly like royalty about their garden domain, and floated further to the Moorabool River and Brisbane Ranges beyond.

As it had done for aeons before and would for those to come.

The playful morning wind gentled under the warm midday sun, heating the earth beneath, bringing new life and growth for another season.

***

As is the life of the leaves so is that of man,
The wind scatters the leaves to the ground; the vigorous
forest puts forth others, and they grow in the spring season.
Soon a new generation of men comes and another ceases.

- Homer 8th Century B.C.